THE REALM OF THE IMPOSSIBLE

Paul Halter books from Locked Room International:

The Lord of Misrule (2010)
The Fourth Door (2011)
The Seven Wonders of Crime (2011)
The Demon of Dartmoor (2012)
The Seventh Hypothesis (2012)
The Tiger's Head (2013)
The Crimson Fog (2013)
(Publisher's Weekly Top Mystery 2013 List)
The Night of the Wolf (2013)*
The Invisible Circle (2014)
The Picture from the Past (2014)
The Phantom Passage (2015)
Death Invites You (2016)
The Vampire Tree (2016)
(Publisher's Weekly Top Mystery 2016 List)
The Madman's Room (2017)
**Original short story collection published by Wildside Press (2006)*

Other impossible crime books from Locked Room International:

The Riddle of Monte Verita (Jean-Paul Torok) 2012
The Killing Needle (Henry Cauvin) 2014
The Derek Smith Omnibus (Derek Smith) 2014
(Washington Post Top Fiction Books 2014)
The House That Kills (Noel Vindry) 2015
The Decagon House Murders (Yukito Ayatsuji) 2015
(Publisher's Weekly Top Mystery 2015 List)
Hard Cheese (Ulf Durling) 2015
(Crime Fiction Lovers Top 10 Nordic Noir 2016 List)
The Moai Island Puzzle (Alice Arisugawa) 2016
(Washington Post Summer Book List 2016)
The Howling Beast (Noel Vindry) 2016
Death in the Dark (Stacey Bishop) 2017
The Ginza Ghost (Keikichi Osaka) 2017

Visit our website at www.mylri.com or
www.lockedroominternational.com

THE REALM OF THE IMPOSSIBLE

An anthology

Edited by John Pugmire and Brian Skupin

Foreword by Otto Penzler

The Realm of the Impossible

This book is partly a work of fiction. The characters, incidents, and dialogue of the fictional works are drawn from the authors' imaginations and are not to be construed as real. Any resemblance to actual events or persons, living or dead, is entirely coincidental.

Cover by Joseph Gérard

For information, contact: pugmire1@yahoo.com

FIRST AMERICAN EDITION
Library of Congress Cataloguing-in-Publication Data
Pugmire, John and Skupin, Brian, editors.
THE REALM OF THE IMPOSSIBLE Anthology

Contents

FOREWORD

Otto Penzler

The years between the two World Wars have frequently been described as the Golden Age of the detective story, and it is an accurate depiction if your ideal tale is of pure, fair-play detection. The era probably debuts with E.C. Bentley's *Trent's Last Case* in 1913 but the less pedantic may be comfortable with ascribing its beginning to the publication of Agatha Christie's first novel, *The Mysterious Affair at Styles*, in 1920, followed quickly by works from such masters as Freeman Wills Crofts, Dorothy L. Sayers, Anthony Berkeley, Ellery Queen, and John Dickson Carr, along with a deluge of others.

It is this form of mystery fiction, concerned mainly with whodunit and howdunit, rather than today's more popular whydunit, which lays hidden or disguised clues throughout the narrative in an effort to fool both the detective and the reader. If the author plays the game fairly, the theory goes, the reader will have a chance of observing and deducing the solution just as well as the detective on the case.

The concept of matching wits with the detective in solving a puzzle reaches its apotheosis in the "impossible crime" story. Not only has a murderer contrived to kill someone, doing all he can to cover his tracks and elude discovery, but the crime has been conceived and executed (if you will pardon the term, under these circumstances) in a way that utterly defies the laws of reason and physics.

A body that has been stabbed or bludgeoned or strangled to death in the middle of a pristine field of snow or carefully raked sand? Impossible! A victim shot to death, as promised, in a room whose windows are nailed shut, with no secret panels, hidden nooks and crannies, and the only door triple-locked from the inside? Impossible! Someone alone in a constantly watched rowboat in the middle of a lake found stabbed to death? Impossible! A suspect, closely observed by the police, disappears from a telephone booth? Impossible!

All of these scenarios have been described by masters of the impossible crime, and so have hundreds of other seemingly supernatural events, all of which have been explained rationally.

No form of the mystery genre is as difficult to create as the locked-room story, which explains the scarcity of examples in the present day. Its greatest practitioner was unequivocally John Dickson Carr, who produced dozens of novels and short stories to tease readers and listeners into believing that the plot he had concocted could not possibly have a rational solution. When Edward D. Hoch died in 2008 and his fertile imagination could no longer add to his more than seventy locked- room stories, the mystery world lost its last prolific English-speaking contributor to this most challenging sub-genre.

Lack of prolificity does not mean that individual examples of the impossible crime story of recent vintage cannot challenge the Golden Age masters for creativity, and this remarkable collection provides ample evidence of the fact. It also belies the general theory that most of the world's best detective fiction has been written by British and American writers. The range of authors collected in this surprising and welcome volume, and the diversity of their backgrounds, is a tribute to the detective skills of the editors, who have somehow unearthed a cornucopia of virtually unknown stories that deserve the attention they will now receive.

It is...well...impossible to applaud loudly enough on behalf of this landmark anthology.

Otto Penzler
New York, 2017

INTRODUCTION

The simplest, and some would say best form of the locked room murder is straightforward. A victim, alone in a room, locked from the inside with no apparent way for any murderer to have got in or out. But this archetypal form is not all that is encompassed by the general term "locked room mystery."

Not all crimes are murders, so we also have the more general idea of the Impossible Crime: a category that includes the locked room murder, but also such happenings as the theft of a jewel from a guarded room or the escape of a man from a locked prison cell.

But then, not all impossible happenings are crimes, so we have an even more general category, proposed by John Dickson Carr, of the Miracle Problem, which includes the locked room murder and the impossible crime as well as things like the disappearance of a man seen to enter a room, or a man seen to have levitated outside a window with no means of support. This expansion of the original problem was natural given the number of devious writers seeking new and innovative plots to intrigue readers.

Another type of expansion has also occurred. The detective story in general, and the locked room mystery in particular, were primarily written by English and American writers for many years. Anthologies tend to reinforce the English language bias since it is simpler to deal with a single language. Even when stories were written in other countries, most were not translated into English. But they were written.

Consequently most English-language reference works tend to focus, quite naturally, on stories originally published in the United Kingdom or America. In particular, of the stories in the nine English-language locked room anthologies published to date, only two authors from outside the U.S. and U.K. are represented, and only a handful more of these stories are set outside those countries. (A tenth anthology, well worth your attention, called *Locked Doors and Open Spaces*, features exclusively Swedish impossible crimes translated into English.)

But the locked room story is alive, well, and beloved all over the world. In recent years the translations of works by Paul Halter, Pierre Very, and Noel Vindry have awakened many to the great treasure trove of impossible crimes and miracle problems waiting to be discovered in France. The renaissance of *honkaku*, or the traditional mystery, in Japan has also led to a surge of locked room mysteries there, led by Soji Shimada, Yukito Ayatsuji, and Rintarō Norizuki.

But France and Japan, although they may be tops in quantity for now, are just the tip of the iceberg. In searching for international stories, we found locked rooms in Lebanon, problems with footprints in Finland, and an impossible poisoning in India.

In *The Realm of the Impossible* we hope to the highlight the international breadth of the locked room mystery. We have stories written in China, Italy, Germany, and Sweden. Lebanon, Italy, and Greece are represented. Ireland, Portugal, Argentina, and Czechoslovakia are all included too. We have a story set in Canada's Far North, and even one set in outer space.

We have also selected for variety in the type of problem. In addition to locked rooms, we have problems of impossible footprints in the snow, the undetected theft of a railway car from a moving train, and the impossible theft of gold from a locked house.

Finally, we turn to one of the long-term criticisms of the locked-room mystery, that of improbability. Some tales of this type require an immense amount of ingenuity to create, and sometimes even more ingenuity in identifying a set of circumstances that would lead to the impossible event.

John Dickson Carr, the master, famously addressed this by saying, "The last thing we should complain about with regard to the murderer is his erratic conduct... Since apparently he has violated the laws of nature for our entertainment, then heaven knows he is permitted to violate the laws of Probable Behavior... If a man offers to stand on his head, we can hardly make the stipulation that he must keep his feet on the ground while he does it."

Readers must not be too disbelieving. Another related complaint about the probability of locked room murders is, "That would never happen in real life." It is certainly up to writers to do their job well enough to allow readers to suspend disbelief, but we feel it is time to point out that, in fact, this sort of thing happens all the time in real life.

So in addition to the twenty-six fictional stories in this anthology, we have included twelve cases of Real Life Impossibilities from all around the world. How can a man locked in his room without alcohol get drunk every night? How can heavy stone coffins in a sealed crypt be moved? How can hundreds of rare French books be stolen from an ancient library? These are some of the unbelievable impossibilities that have really happened.

We hope you enjoy these stories of miracles and murder taken from the four corners of the earth, and the baffling problems from everyday life. Together they show that all of us really are living in The Realm of the Impossible.

John Pugmire and Brian Skupin
New York, 2017

France
Jacob's Ladder
by Paul Halter

Paul Halter has frequently been described as the successor to John Dickson Carr and is undoubtedly one of the top contemporary writers specialising in impossible crime and locked room mysteries. He has written over thirty novels, thirteen of which have been translated into English, and more than a dozen short stories, several of which have been published in *Ellery Queen's Mystery Magazine*. He is a best seller in France and is widely read throughout Europe and Asia.

On May 21, 2012 he appeared on BBC Radio 4's "Miles Jupp in a Locked Room," which attracted nearly 500,000 listeners, and was a featured author in the October 28, 2013 issue of *Publishers Weekly*.

The Crimson Fog was listed in *Publishers Weekly*'s Top Mysteries of 2013 and *The Vampire Tree* in the 2016 list.

In his Jan 19, 2014 article "The Top 10 Locked Room Mysteries," Adrian McGinty listed Halter's *La Septième Hypothèse* (*The Seventh Hypothesis*) in third place, behind John Dickson Carr's *The Hollow Man* and Soji Shimada's *The Tokyo Zodiac Murders*.

The late Edward D. Hoch once described Paul's work as "a combination of baffling mystery and eerie atmosphere not encountered since the glory days of John Dickson Carr."

There is no better example than "Jacob's Ladder," which is pure Halter: a truly baffling problem with a brilliantly simple solution.

"Even so, gentlemen, I believe there are crimes that are so unbelievable they can't be explained even by the presence of the supernatural."

One could have heard a pin drop in the Hades Club after Major Patrick Merle spoke those words. Seated by the fire, Dr. Twist and Superintendent Charles Cullen stared at the newcomer with astonishment. The complicated criminal case they had been discussing seemed to pale into insignificance if the claims of this debonair and forceful visitor were to be believed. The interruption could not be allowed to go unquestioned. Explanations were called for.

The superintendent, himself an energetic sixty-year old of proud bearing, observed somewhat condescendingly that he hadn't had the pleasure of an introduction. The major, obviously embarrassed, passed a hand through his salt-and-pepper hair before extending his hand with a sheepish smile and describing himself as a former police sergeant in the department of the Lot in France who had married an English girl and entered Her Majesty's service.

Older than his friend Cullen, Dr. Twist was notable for his height and his thin frame. But for the mischievous gleam in his eye and his childlike expression, he could have passed for some sort of Don Quixote – one who tilted at murderers rather than windmills. Affably, he invited Merle to explain his remark.

With a thoughtful air, the major turned towards the black marble mantelpiece, on which stood the statue of the Prince of Darkness.

"The facts and nothing but the facts," he announced. "Even though they go back a very long way. I was barely twenty-five years old and had just been made sergeant. I'd been assigned to a station in a village near Cahors in the Midi-Pyrenees. The circumstances of the incident we had been called in to investigate were so baffling we felt as though we were dealing with a divine presence. Or a miracle, if you can use the term for such a sad event. Judge for yourselves: In the middle of a completely isolated area, and in the presence of witnesses, a man was found whose body had been smashed as the result of a precipitous drop, as if he had fallen from the sky."

As the doctor and the superintendent exchanged surprised glances, the only sound to be heard was the crackling of the fire in the grate. The major continued:

"I remember as if it were yesterday. It was a July afternoon in the late 1930s and the postman had just handed me an urgent telegram from my superior, Inspector Letellier, ordering me to drop everything and meet him at 'crows corner,' a spot out in the open country three or four miles from the village. It was about four o'clock in the afternoon and it was stiflingly hot, which was unusual even for that time of year. I hopped on my bicycle and pedalled like the devil to where Inspector Letellier was waiting in his car with both doors opened wide. He was a solid, reliable sort, but with a tendency to lose his temper when things got too complicated, which was obviously the case here. He was rather corpulent and mopped his brow frequently as he explained that one of the Amalric brothers had been found dead in very strange circumstances, which he would explain in more detail on the way there.

"The Amalric brothers were well known in the area. They were rich merchants whose wealth came from their relentless and pitiless negotiating skills. They had destroyed all those who had tried to avoid paying their debts. More than one unfortunate had blown his brains out after tangling with them. The two older brothers, Mathias and Jacob, lived off the profits from the sale of a flourishing fabric business in Paris. They now lived in an isolated farm next to a dried-up lake just below where we were. Henri, the youngest, only visited the region on rare occasions. I don't know whether he was on good terms with his brothers or not, but apparently he had chosen to stay in the capital, where he had a real-estate business. He was polite, discreet, handsome, and, at about thirty years old, the most sociable of the three.

"Mathias, the eldest, was tall and as dry and thin as a beanpole, with a head like a bird of prey. With his cunning, calculating mind, he was the brains of the family. Jacob was a confirmed bachelor of some forty years, plump, and with an unctuous amiability. More cultivated than his brother, he nevertheless lived in his shadow, deferring to him on almost every decision. Both of them were pious, but Jacob had made the study of the Bible his obsession since arriving in the region. The patrons of *Les Trois Lavandieres*, an inn he frequented in the nearby village of Lassac, swore that his studies had begun to addle his brain. It was Jacob who had died earlier in the day.

"At this point, it would perhaps be helpful if I described the lie of the land because it's an important aspect of the affair. It's undoubtedly the most arid part of the region, and has been so for several years. There's very little that's green and it mostly looks like the more desolate parts of the Auvergne with its mineral outcrops. For miles around, the soil is infertile and stony, with the occasional cluster of heather or the rare stunted tree as the only vegetation. The inspector and I found ourselves standing on a small hill, the highest point in the area, from which a gentle slope descended towards the Amalric farm located due south, next to a muddy pond. Normally, people travelled to the farm from Lassac, further to the south. From there the road wound its way north – a journey of fifteen minutes or more because of the bad road surface. The other way was via the path the inspector and I had taken that led down from the hill. It was badly pitted – a veritable ankle-trap – and obviously only traversable on foot, which also took about a quarter of an hour. But from where I had set out, that was quite a time-saver, because otherwise the inspector would have had to go back to Lassac and then follow the winding road up.

"That was why he had arranged to meet me at such an isolated spot, dubbed by the locals as 'crows corner.' There were in fact several crows in the neighbourhood, who had found refuge in an abandoned farm we reached after five minutes of walking. One of them, proudly perched on the edge of a well, might well have been a harbinger of the death that had just recently occurred. It took flight as we approached, vanishing in the blinding sunlight. It was at that point that Inspector Letellier chose to show his hand:

"'I called you, Merle, because – as you've probably realised – this is a very tricky case.'

"'I hope you haven't overestimated me, sir,' I replied with false modesty.

"'I haven't forgotten your last two cases, which you solved like a flash while we old fogies were stumped. So here are the facts. The victim was, as you know, a confirmed bachelor and something of a dreamer, who was quite happy to talk about himself after a few pints at *Les Trois Lavandieres*. In the last few weeks, however, he'd been more of a dreamer than ever. Several times, he claimed to have seen a golden ladder reaching to the sky.'

"'Jacob's ladder!" I exclaimed.

"'Precisely. Just like in the Bible,' confirmed the inspector.

"'So I suppose he'd decided to get married and raise a family?"

"'Well, I'll be blowed, Merle. Are you some sort of a soothsayer?"

"'No, chief. That's what the Bible says about Jacob's dream.'

"'Hmm,' muttered Letellier. 'Of course. My Old Testament is a bit rusty. No matter. It would seem that our Jacob came to the same conclusion. Anyway, he suddenly took it into his head to marry Victorine, the daughter of the innkeeper Maurice Auriol. She's very pretty and, by the way, about half his age. Jacob was so sure this was the right thing to do that he claimed he'd actually seen the golden ladder itself reaching to the sky. Obviously, since he'd been the only one to see it, it was clear to one and all that he was going off his rocker. He'd written to his brother Henri, asking him to come down to discuss some important business: no doubt his marriage plans. Henri arrived late last night and stayed at *Les Trois Lavandieres*. He only got to the farm this morning.'

"'At 9 o'clock, as was his custom, Jacob set out on his morning walk. His brother Mathias noticed nothing unusual. He himself stayed indoors, checking some accounts and quietly finishing his breakfast. At 10 o'clock he heard his brother cry out in a state of great excitement: "Mathias, the ladder is here! It's here, just in front of the house! It must be a sign. This time, I'm going to climb it."'

"'Accustomed to his brother's ravings, Mathias merely went as far as the door to take a quick look outside. He saw no one near the pond. No Jacob. No ladder. He shrugged his shoulders without giving the matter another thought, and resumed his accounting. A few minutes later a long and hideous scream rent the air, followed by a dull muffled noise heavy enough to shake the windows. After a few seconds of stunned silence, Mathias went outside. The first thing he saw was an open sports car pulling up in front of the house. It was driven by the youngest brother Henri, who looked shocked and anxious, for he, too, had heard the dreadful scream. It was at that point they noticed a broken body lying outstretched on the stony bank of the pond. It was Jacob, and it was immediately obvious there was nothing to be done for him. So together they drove back down to Lassac to alert the police.'

"It was nearly five o'clock by the time the inspector and I arrived at the scene of the crime. We were both perspiring profusely and there was no relieving breeze coming from the dirty grey pond. The victim had already been taken away, but there were still several policemen pursuing their investigations around the premises. Turning towards the muddy sheet of water, Letellier observed:

"'Look at the banks of the pond, Merle. You can see a rather peculiar halo, no doubt due to the water level having receded several feet over the last few years. But never mind that, look at the yellow chalk stones scattered on the bank. They're typical of the area and that's where the body was found, at the spot just in front of us. It's a pity they've taken the body away, or you'd have a clearer picture of the terrible damage. Broken bones, severe contusions –'

"'But what the devil happened?" I asked. 'Was he hit with a club, or an iron bar, or something else?"

"'Nothing like that,' replied the inspector, lifting his eyes heavenwards. 'We haven't found traces of any kind of weapon, at least not so far. His wounds are more consistent with a fall from a great height.'

"'But that's not possible,' I blurted out, following his gaze. 'Unless you give some credence to the tale of the golden ladder.'

"There wasn't a cloud in the pure blue sky, and the sun, a deep bronze disc, seemed to be looking down and mocking us.

"'I know, Merle,' said my superior officer. 'But those are the preliminary conclusions of the medical examiner and his assistant. And, I may add, of anyone who's seen the body. But I want to wait for the autopsy report before jumping to any conclusions.'"

Merle stopped and looked at his audience, a mischievous gleam in his eye:

"So, what do you think of it so far, gentlemen? Amazing, is it not?"

"Amazing is an understatement," observed Dr. Twist, as happy as a child being read his favourite bedtime story. "I've never hear anything so extraordinary in my life. But I'm going to follow the example of your old superior officer, and reserve judgment until I've heard the results of the autopsy."

Superintendent Cullen nodded his head in agreement and Merle continued:

"Quite. In that case, I'll jump ahead in the story and tell you what the expert said – or rather the experts, because the medical examiner took the precaution of consulting with a number of eminent colleagues before releasing his verdict. They were unanimous: Death was undoubtedly the result of a fall from a great height – at least sixty feet. Jacob's injuries – disjointed limbs, multiple fractures, and widespread contusions – were like those suffered following defenestration and other fatal falls."

Dr. Twist and the superintendent exchanged surprised glances and the latter, after a brief moment of reflection, suggested:

"Could Jacob have been thrown out of a window somewhere and then been brought back discreetly to the side of the pond?"

"We looked very carefully into that, as you can well imagine," replied Merle with a smile. "After all, it did seem to be the only solution to the puzzle. Unfortunately, that idea was rapidly discredited. For a distance of ten miles in every direction there was not a building or a construction anywhere near the required height, with the exception of the Lassac church steeple, and we were quickly able to rule that out. Nor were there any cliffs, escarpments, or natural formations anywhere. The little hill we started from was in fact the highest point of the region! As for trees, there weren't many of them and only a couple even reached a height of thirty feet. What's more, the experts were categorical about the scene of the crime. The peculiar nature of the soil around the pond, with its yellow chalk and stones, traces of which had been found in the victim's wounds, left no doubt. As for the time of death, that corresponded to the observed facts, plus or minus half an hour. To sum it up: As incredible as it may sound, Jacob Amalric was smashed to pieces on the pond bank as the result of a fall from a great height."

There was a renewed silence, broken by Twist in a tone half ironic and half resigned:

"In that case, we have no choice but to listen to the rest of the story."

Merle stared fixedly at the fire, obviously satisfied with his account so far, then continued:

"The first witness I questioned was Mathias, the bird of prey. Never an easy person in the first place, he was visibly irritated by the interrogations earlier that afternoon. We were in the kitchen, at the very place where he had sat when the incident occurred. His account was as clear and concise as the books he kept and, I have to admit, convincing. From where he had been sitting, he had not had a clear view of the area around the house or the banks of the pond. Lace curtains and the assorted bric-a-brac around the windows had further reduced his field of vision. His brother Jacob had appeared in normal spirits at the time of his customary 9 o'clock walk. And – although he couldn't swear it on oath – he thought he recognised his brother's voice when he had called, around 10 o'clock, to announce that he had seen the golden ladder. There had been the same fervent, high-pitched tone that his brother used when describing matters dear to his heart.

"'I suppose,' he said, 'that it was his incessant Bible reading that eventually addled his brain. Even though I didn't really approve, I became resigned to his matrimonial project. Despite my warnings about the financial complications that would inevitably arise, he treated me and my objections with disdain. The fact that his wife-to-be was young enough to be his daughter and came from a different background was of no importance. The vision of the golden ladder was, for him, a sign from the heavens. He was so inflexible and so determined that I eventually threw in the towel. That's why I didn't take much notice when he shouted out this morning. He'd claimed to have seen the golden ladder several times in the last few days and had even pointed it out to me, but I – need I tell you? – had seen nothing, other than the reflection of the sun on the surface of the pond.'

"'But weren't you surprised not to have seen him when he called out at 10 o'clock?"

"Mathias shrugged his shoulders.

"'He could have been anywhere outside, behind a rock or a bush. I tell you, the whole business was beginning to get on my nerves. I didn't want to get any more involved.'

"'And the scream you heard shortly thereafter? Was it a long cry of distress, like someone falling from a great height?"

"Mathias pursed his lips, but agreed:

"'Yes, that's how I would describe it. At least, I would now. At the time, I must confess I didn't recognise it for what it was.'

"'And the noise of the fall?"

"'Hard to say. Again, it was all happening so quickly. I had a distinct impression that the ground shook. Whatever it was, it wasn't the result of a gentle fall. I went outside and that's when Henri arrived in his car. That was a surprise, too, because I hadn't seen him for quite a while.'

"While I had been listening to Mathias' testimony, I had noticed a large Holy Bible, bound in faded leather, sitting on a side table. Now I picked it up and opened it at the page where it was bookmarked, which not surprisingly turned out to be "The Dream of Jacob" from Genesis 28, illustrated with a luminous staircase reaching to the sky, on which angels wandered up and down. I thumbed through the rest of the pages and noticed one had been dog-eared at John 4. Once again, it was about Jacob, this time under the picture of a reclining Jesus: '*So he came to a town of Samaria which was named Sychar [....] Now Jacob's well was there. Jesus, being tired after his journey, was resting by the well. It was about the sixth hour.*' I also found an illustration of the seductive Delilah, which reminded me of the young woman Victorine that Jacob had been planning to marry. That prompted me to ask the master of the house how she had viewed her forthcoming marriage with the late lamented Jacob.

"'In other words,' replied Mathias with a bitter smile, 'was she as enamoured of him as he was of her? Or was she marrying him because of his beautiful eyes?"

"His cynical regard made me feel uncomfortable.

"'Yes,' I mumbled. 'You could put it that way.'

"'It would be best, I think, if you put the question to her directly.'

"And on that sour note, the interview ended. Next we went outside to interrogate the youngest son, Henri. The first thing I asked him was to describe as accurately as possible the moment of his arrival at the farm. He said he'd been at the wheel of his car, with the top down and about thirty yards from the house, when he had heard the blood-curdling scream. Hence his attention at that point had been directed towards the road and the building, and he hadn't really looked at the pond or its banks. Certainly not at the east bank where the crime had taken place, and which was in any case partially hidden behind some large boulders which lined the road at that point. That was probably why he hadn't witnessed his brother's fall, although he was absolutely certain he hadn't seen a ladder leading up into the heavens. If there had been such a sight, he couldn't possibly have missed it. He had heard the noise of a fall, but not as clearly as his brother, no doubt because of the noise of the motor. He had seen Mathias rush out about ten seconds later. As far as I could determine, his account was consistent with the known facts. I then asked him to show me the letter he had received two days earlier from his brother, asking him to come as soon as possible to discuss a matter of great importance. Even though the letter gave no details, there was little doubt, from its enthusiastic tone, that the matter in question was the forthcoming marriage.

"'I was quite surprised to get the letter,' explained Henri, a good-looking fellow with a charming manner. 'I hadn't had any news from my brother for quite a while – six months or more – and to be frank, our last meeting had been pretty unpleasant. Nothing really serious, just disagreements regarding the management of some assets our father had left us. In any case, once Mathias and Jacob decided to bury themselves in this godforsaken hole, our paths were bound to diverge. I arrived late last night, so I decided to take a room at *Les Trois Lavandieres*. That's where I met the owner Maurice and spent a little time with the barman Julien, who explained the situation to me.

And once I saw the lovely Victorine...well, it became obvious to me that there was something not quite right about the marriage. How can I say this tactfully? Jacob was not exactly a ladies' man and, for her part, Victorine didn't seem to be bursting with joy. I fell asleep with the idea of bringing everything out into the open the next day. I left at 9 o'clock in the morning, but then I found one of my tyres was flat. It took me longer than I expected to change it and so I arrived later than planned. You know the rest.'

"That evening, Inspector Letellier and I dined at *Les Trois Lavandieres*, waited on by Julien, a sturdy young man with a rather sullen manner. Victorine was notable by her absence. Some of the customers suggested, tongue in cheek, that she had locked herself in her room to mourn alone. There were only a few regulars left by the time we got around to questioning Julien. He turned out to be rather shy, although forthright enough and willing to please. He spoke respectfully of the deceased, but his eyes betrayed the resentment he obviously felt towards him.

"'He wasn't a man you could really dislike,' he said, after accepting a glass from the inspector. 'He was well-educated and liked to chat. But – how should I put it? – he seemed to think he was God...and he never once left me a tip! Anyway, I'm not going to speak ill of him now he's dead.'

"'What did you think about his marriage to Victorine?" asked Inspector Letellier, with a studied indifference.

"The young man's eyes flashed angrily.

"'It's none of my business,' he muttered. 'And anyway, I think you're smart enough to have worked it out.'

"'Worked what out?'" asked Letellier.

"'Ask Maurice.'

"It was a stinging reply. Before he went back into his shell, I decided to change the subject and ask him about his conversation the previous night with Henri. He acknowledged having spoken to him. Henri had asked a number of questions, particularly concerning his brother Jacob's projects. But the youngest Amalric brother had failed to charm him.

"'He seemed slightly less greedy than the other two. But don't let that fool you. He's not much better. If you'd seen how he ogled Victorine when she was around – I'm sure he wouldn't have thought twice about taking her from his brother, if he'd had the chance.'

"'I see,' said the inspector, with a knowing look. 'I'd heard they didn't get on well together. Just one more point, Julien. Amalric claimed he left the inn at around 9 o'clock this morning. Can you confirm that?"

"Julien thought for a moment, then shook his head. 'I don't start work until late afternoon. You should ask Maurice or Victorine, if she's in any state to talk. She might not be grief-stricken, but she's had a shock all the same.'

"After locking the doors of the hostelry, Maurice Auriol was next to be questioned.

"'Maybe that Jacob's ladder was a sign from above, after all,' he said. He was a grey-haired fifty-year-old with a sad, owl-like gaze.

"'What do you mean?" asked Inspector Letellier.

"'That the good Lord heard my prayers and found a way to thwart the odious blackmail against my person.'

"'What blackmail?"

"'Sacrificing my daughter in order to pay off my debts to the Amalrics. To Mathias most of all,' he added, with a look that was a mixture of sadness and bitterness. 'I had borrowed a considerable sum of money from him that I was not in a position to repay. He had me in the palm of his hand. I'd been worried for several months that the bailiffs could come at any time. Then, one bright morning about a month ago, up pops Jacob beaming happily, with all my debt notices in his chubby little hand. He said he'd done a deal with his brother, and now it was up to me.'

"'I think I understand,' I muttered, my fists clenching.

"'Yes, gentlemen, I'm sure you do. The condition – the only condition – was that I let him have my daughter's hand in marriage,' said the innkeeper, burying his head in his hands. 'I was so stunned that I dodged the issue and told him it wasn't up to me. And just at that moment, as if she'd anticipated the question, Victorine came in to the room. Jacob repeated his demand without a trace of shame, as complacent as a cat that's swallowed the cream, as if it was just a simple business transaction with the only remaining question being the price. And dear, sweet, brave Victorine said "Yes" as she tore the documents into a thousand pieces.'

"After a second, he added: 'If her poor mother had been alive today, she would never have forgiven me. I should have acted like a man and sent him away with a fist in his face. The really strange part was his utter confidence that his vision would come to pass. After he left, I tried to talk Victorine out of her sacrifice, but she would have none of it. She was betrothed to Jacob and would no longer be a free woman. When Julien learned the news, he flew into a terrible rage. He wanted to go to the farm and break all their heads, and if Victorine had not talked him out of it, I'm sure he would have done so.'

"'I suspect the lad has a soft spot for the girl,' said the inspector.

"'Yes, and I don't think he'll ever forgive me for not putting a stop to Jacob's game right away, as I should have done.'

"After an embarrassing silence, I asked Auriol if he could verify the time of Henri's departure.

"'Yes. He paid his bill at around 9 o'clock. I saw him leave with his sports bag.'

"'What did you do then?"

"'Nothing much,' replied Maurice, rubbing his neck thoughtfully. 'A bit of cleaning, then around 10 o'clock some workmen came.'

"'Right. We'd like to talk to your daughter now. That is, if she's in a fit state.'

"'I think it'll be all right,' replied Maurice, nodding his head. 'She's in her room. I'll let her know.'

"Shortly thereafter, we received the lovely Victorine. Her pale blue eyes were devoid of all expression, but even that fact couldn't diminish her elegant beauty framed in an opulent cascade of black curls.

"After we had explained the troubling details of our investigation, she wasted no time in telling us that she had rarely detested anyone as much as Jacob Amalric. His death, however tragic, was a deliverance for her, so much so that she had not yet fully recovered from the shock. She went on to say that, despite her decision, made on the spur of the moment, she probably would not have had the courage to go through with the wedding. Recently she had been joyfully imagining the discomfiture of her fiancé when she shouted 'No!' in front of the altar.

"To be frank, I was almost relieved to hear her talking like that. It seemed a normal healthy reaction to an unnatural situation. Nevertheless, we were left with the mystery at the heart of the matter. I asked her what she thought.

"'Jacob's ladder,' she said, breaking into a smile for the first time. 'Modesty forbids me from saying so, but I think he aimed too high when he decided to marry me. I was too inaccessible and he climbed too far to try and reach me – and he fell.'

"'Like the fall of Icarus,' I observed.

"'Exactly,' she replied, running her fingers through her jet black hair. 'I believe it was divine intervention.'

"The inspector reminded her gruffly that the justice of men required more substantial evidence, and he was the one charged with finding a rational explanation to the riddle. For that reason, he needed to know her whereabouts at the time of the crime.

"There was a defiant light in her eyes, and she favoured us with an ironic smile.

"'You'll have to look elsewhere, gentlemen. I have an alibi plated with the same metal as the famous ladder: that's to say, in gold. From 9 to 10 o'clock I was running errands in the village. The butcher, the grocer, the green-grocer; I even went to church and offered up a prayer, and ran into the vicar. I spoke to him, as the good lord had obviously intended me to do.'"

Merle paused before concluding, a nostalgic gleam in his eye.

"A beautiful child, young Victorine. I confess I was a little in love with her myself at the time. She had a lot of character – more, perhaps, than any of the men involved. From a psychological standpoint, she would have been the best equipped to have committed the murder, if that's what it was. But, as she pointed out, she had a cast-iron – or, rather, gold-plated – alibi. We confirmed it, of course. So, gentlemen, what do you think? It's not your everyday puzzle, I think you'll agree."

"A great impossible crime," agreed Dr. Twist enthusiastically. "A divine problem, one might say."

After pensively lighting a cigar, Superintendent Cullen observed with a calm smile:

"Only on the surface. An objective analysis of the facts will swiftly clear up the mystery."

"So you already have a solution?" enquired Major Merle, obviously intrigued.

"Yes. Or at least a rough idea. For obviously the 'divine' aspects of the story all come from one source: the brothers Amalric. The three other suspects – the innkeeper, the barman and the girl – all had good reason to want to kill the victim, but his brothers had an even stronger one: Jacob's inheritance, which, if I've understood correctly, was quite considerable."

"Quite right," agreed Merle. "His will was made out in their favour and represented quite a tidy sum."

"I imagine they took advantage of Jacob's ravings to put in place their diabolical plan. It's quite obvious that their account of the facts is a tissue of lies. There was no ladder reaching to the sky, no cry for help, no hideous scream, no sound of a fall. Just a simple fratricide, followed by some cock-and-bull story to cover their traces. The Amalric brothers were in it up to their necks – there's no other explanation."

"You know, I reached the same conclusion myself," replied Merle. "The problem was I couldn't explain the fall. I'm not going to go over the lie of the land again, I'll simply say that in the two or three days following the incident, we scoured the countryside thoroughly. But all in vain. Not the slightest clue there. And, of course, before accusing the Amalric brothers, we had to have proof."

"Did you really think of everything?" asked Cullen defiantly. "Couldn't one envisage, say, an improvised catapult throwing the victim up in the air? You know, like the natives in the bush. They bend a tree into an arc, tie the victim onto it loosely, and let go. The whiplash of the tree can easily catapult someone sixty feet in the air."

"We thought of that," said Merle, "but you need trees twice as big as any we found in the area."

"Well, all right," growled Cullen. "But for my money, those two brothers were the ones, however they did it. But we'd have to have been there to make any more sense of it. What do you think, Twist?"

The eminent detective, seemingly absorbed in contemplation of the fire, turned to his friend and shook his head.

"No, that wouldn't be necessary. Major Merle has given us all the clues we need. You actually solved the puzzle yourself, I believe?"

The major smiled in agreement:

"I did eventually work it out. What about you, Dr. Twist?"

"Of course. Your account was so precise that the solution became evident. Your insistence on the biblical aspects of the affair, and the clue of the dog-eared page made it clear to me that the brothers Amalric must be innocent.

"Why do you say that?" asked Cullen indignantly. "Do you mean to say they had nothing to do with it? And we should take their testimony at face value?"

Twist shrugged his shoulders:

"Do you seriously think they would have invented such a tall story if they had been guilty? No, they told the truth and nothing but the truth. They had nothing to do with their brother's murder. We have to look elsewhere. It's my belief that the guilty party conceived his trap several days before the murder, and may even have taken certain preparatory steps, after having heard Jacob's rants about his strange dream and his intention to marry Victorine. He sought, not just revenge on the detestable Amalric family in general, but specifically to prevent the marriage from happening – by ruining Jacob's dream and making him fall off his precious golden ladder. Henri's unexpected arrival on the scene merely hastened the diabolical plan. He burst the tyre in the middle of the night so as to delay Henri's arrival at the farm the next day to 10 o'clock, knowing full well that Jacob always took his daily walk an hour earlier."

"It's incredible," muttered Merle, scratching his head. "It took me nearly a week of sleepless nights to work it out, and you, sitting in an armchair, not having even visited the scene, have worked it out in fifteen minutes."

"It was the dog-eared page," said Twist, "that put me on the trail. The picture of Jesus sitting on the edge of the well, and Jacob's well to boot. It suddenly became as clear as day: Jacob didn't fall *from* a great height, he fell *down* a great height. He fell into the well. You even went out of your way to mention the well, near the abandoned farm near the top of the hill, with a crow sitting on the rim. You talked about it taking flight as you approached, vanishing in the blinding sunlight, which turned out to be the light of truth. The bottom of the well was almost certainly dry, given the previous drop in water levels you were careful to mention, and was probably very deep because of its location. All the murderer had to do was to throw down stones and sand taken from the banks of the pond, to cover the bottom; entice Jacob to the well under some pretext; knock him out and attach a rope around his waist; throw him to the bottom sixty feet below; and pull him back up. Afterwards, he simply dropped the shattered body where it was found. Excluding the preparation of the bottom of the well, which presumably occurred beforehand, the whole operation probably took less than half an hour. Obviously, only a man in robust health could have transported the body from the well to the pond, which already gives us a clue to the murderer's identity.

"Everything was in place for what followed. The murderer hid behind a rock. As soon as he heard the far-off noise of the motor car, he imitated Jacob's voice – a voice shrill from excitement is not hard to copy – so as to attract Mathias's attention. The older brother's irritation and indifference were entirely predictable. After Mathias went back indoors and Henri's car was close to the house, the killer let out a long and hideous scream. To create the heavy thud he must, I suppose, have dislodged a large boulder he had previously set up in an unstable position. All it needed then was for the two brothers to give their testimony, which nobody believed, and it was all over.

"The departure of the two brothers to alert the police gave him another idea, biblical but hardly divine. Up until then, his plan had proved a roaring success. The Amalric brothers had fallen for it hook, line, and sinker. Their bizarre testimony, added to the fact they stood to inherit a fortune, made them prime suspects. To put the last nail in their coffin, he decided to leave another clue, discreet but decisive. The police could hardly miss the dog-eared page he was going to leave in the bible sitting on the kitchen table, at the chapter on Jacob's well. He counted on their perspicacity so that the picture would provide the vital clue as to how the murder had been done. And he was right, wasn't he?"

Merle nodded his head and sighed:

"I admit I fell for it. At first, that is. After I'd understood the trick with the well, I was certain of the Amalrics's guilt. But that dog-eared page seemed too convenient. I had a feeling I was being manipulated."

Twist nodded his approval:

"You reasoned that if the Amalrics had put such a crafty plan in place to rid themselves of their brother, they wouldn't have left such an obvious clue behind."

"Exactly. And once I realised there was a plot against them, it wasn't very difficult to work out who was behind it: the only suspect who didn't have an alibi for that morning and who was strong enough to have carried the body some distance –"

"In other words, Julien the barman!" exclaimed Cullen.

"Well done, my old friend," said Twist with some irony. "There's no fooling you!"

"He admitted everything right away," added Merle, "and he got off relatively lightly: ten years behind bars – but not the same kind of bars!

"To be frank, his trial was hardly a model of impartial British justice. The Amalrics's bad reputation among the locals didn't hurt him, particularly as one jury member was related to one of the suicides – as I learned afterwards. Victorine's sacrifice (not to mention her beauty) also had an influence: The jury was visibly moved when she practically forgave Julien for the jealousy that had motivated him."

"So it was Julien that finally fell from Jacob's ladder," said Cullen, half-jokingly.

"One might say that," replied Merle. "But he paid the penalty, and it didn't stop him from trying a second ascension, successfully this time, because he got closer to heaven...."

"Let me guess," said the superintendent, with a knowing wink. "He ended up marrying the girl of his dreams after leaving prison."

"Actually, no. He took holy orders."

United Kingdom
Cyanide in the Sun
by Christianna Brand

Christianna Brand was born in Malaya and grew up in India. After a variety of jobs, including model and sales assistant, she settled on writing as a career after the modest success of her first novel *Death in High Heels*.

Like her prolific predecessors Carolyn Wells and L.T.Meade (see p 380), she wrote both mystery books and books for children. Her *Nurse Matilda* stories were adapted for the silver screen as *Nanny McPhee*.

The children's gain was the mystery fans' loss, for she wrote fewer than ten mystery novels, of which three *(Heads You Lose, Death of Jezebel* and *The Crooked Wreath/Suddenly in His Residence)* were impossible crimes. Many consider *Death of Jezebel*, where the victim is murdered at the top of a locked tower in full view of a theatre audience, one of the finest ever written.

Among her other novels, *Green for Danger, Tour de Force* and *London Particular (Fog of Doubt)* stand out, the first also having been successfully adapted for the screen, and the last being one of the few mystery novels where the solution is revealed on the very last line.

All of Brand's short stories are excellent, and can be found in the collections *Exeunt Murderers*, *Brand X*, and *The Spotted Cat*. The best is probably "The Gemminy Crickets Murder Case" (also "Murder Game"), another impossible crime.

"Cyanide in the Sun" one of two short stories written for the now-defunct British newspaper *The Daily Sketch* (the other being "Bank Holiday Murder") has not been reprinted since its original appearance in 1958.

The attractions of Scampton-on-Sea are many. And Mrs. Camp, plump proprietress of the Sunnyside Guest House, exploited them all but one.

(A+) BPR + O, wrote Mrs. Camp crisply across the tops of her letters, promising every comfort and happiness for prospective holidaymakers.

With much turning back and forth of the pages of the accompanying leaflets, they might discover what these cryptic letters stood for.

But nowhere would they find any mention of Scampton's major claim to fame – the Cyanide Murders.

Once she had them netted, however (terms payable in advance), Mrs. Camp regaled her guests freely with gossip upon this delightful theme.

She was particularly well-equipped to do so.

Widowed under distressing circumstances (her husband had choked on a crumb and suffocated himself) she had worked for many years as a district nurse before settling down to run Sunnyside.

And in this capacity had no less than three times been called to the scene of one of the now-famous murders. And once had been accidentally present.

Not that this was the full tally. Several others had taken place quite without benefit of Mrs. Camp's attentions.

On these, of course, she was less informative. "The first was just an old tramp," she explained rather disparagingly, doling out soup on the Saturday evening of their arrival to the new batch of guests sitting round the communal dining table.

"Quite well known in the town, he was. Sat down on a bench at the front to eat a sandwich, and suddenly….

"Frightful it was, they said. And they do arch up dreadfully, of course, dear.

"Let nobody tell you it's all over in a second…. Mind, I didn't see that one," admitted Mrs. Camp regretfully. "I'd gone up to London that day. But I can show you the very bench."

She paused to wipe a small splash of soup from her aproned bosom. "And in his hand a scrap of paper, just saying in block letters, PREPARE TO MEET THY DOOM."

"There's always a warning, isn't there?" said Miss Pratt. "I've read about it in the papers." She gave a shudder and put her soup spoon down suddenly in her half-finished plate of soup.

Miss Pratt had come down from London on the afternoon train.

She worked in one of the big stores in its medical and surgical department.

She had been, like Mrs. Camp, a nurse at one time, but had abruptly given it up and now dealt with medicines but not with invalids directly.

She was perhaps thirty-five; not pretty, but very fresh and spruce. If one is 35 and not pretty, the next best way to make oneself attractive is to be fresh and spruce. And Miss Pratt was as desirous as the next woman to make herself attractive.

"'Prepare to meet thy doom' – such a shocking message," said Miss Pratt. "They might at least have put it a little less horribly. Even 'Prepare to meet your end' would be better than 'doom.'"

"Only that might sound a bit like a whiting," said Mr. Culham. "Cooked with its tail in its mouth."

He smiled at Miss Pratt. And Miss Pratt's poor heart did a little somersault and was severely ordered back into place again. Mr. Culham was a married man.

Mrs. Camp continued to dole out with a pretty equal generosity horror and haricot mutton.

"Now the second murder, I did see. Helping out, I was, at the *fête* in the garden at the Old Ladies Home. And an old lady went that time."

Miss Jones gave a little shudder.

Miss Jones was a model, it seemed, free-lancing in London, and naturally must keep her figure and couldn't touch a potato. The bare idea had made her go pale.

She was an entrancingly pretty girl and considering her evident success at her glamorous job – for she seemed to have money to spend – very modest and simple.

Mrs. Camp, oblivious of the shudders, continued to regale them with details of the passing of the poor old lady and her Devonshire Split.

Mr. Culham looked at his wife in some alarm. Her white, peevish face – powdered whiter than ever to attract the more sympathy for her purely imaginary ailments – was more peevish than ever.

He knew that when they got to their room she would rail at him for bringing her to a place where such dreadful things could happen.

He plunged his head in his hands, his pale, soft hair sticking out spikily through his fingers in a little-boy way that made poor Miss Pratt's heart stand on end again.

"John," said Mrs. Culham sharply, "Don't sit there with your elbows on the table!"

Mrs. Gerald did not wait to get to her room before declaring her opinion about the suitability of Scampton for a holiday. "We should have been informed. I call it false pretences, Mrs. Camp, not warning us first."

"It's been in all the papers," protested Mrs. Camp. "And anyway there hasn't been a murder for months now. I daresay it's all over."

Mrs. Gerald was a monstrous old woman with a high colour and a high, hard, hooting voice. "Everywhere else will be booked," said Mrs. Culham, joining forces with her. "Or we should demand our money back and leave at once."

"A maniac at large!" cried Mrs. Gerald on a top note. "None of us is safe. We may all be murdered in our beds."

"We must be careful not to eat Devonshire splits in our beds," said Mr. Raie.

Hugo Raie was the sixth and last of Mrs. Camp's guests: a tall, thin young man with a permanently sorrowful expression which had quite gone to Sharon Jones's heart already. And a faintly foreign accent which by no means detracted from his interesting melancholy.

"But where iss this cyanide supposed to come from, Mrs. Camp? It iss not part of the natural attractions of Scampton. We do not breathe it in and out with the ozone?"

"The murders are not all in Scampton," said Mrs. Camp, anxious, perhaps, a bit late to retrieve the Sunnyside reputation for perfect hospitality.

"One was in the train. A girl, that was. All by herself in the carriage and not a corridor train. And it didn't stop anywhere.

"But when they got to London...."

She described with loving detail the scene when the train had arrived at the terminus. "And nothing to show for it but a roll and butter she'd bought at the last minute at the station buffet."

She stood up once more, serving spoon in hand. "A bit more pud, Mrs. Gerald, now do?"

If it was Mrs. Camp's plan to counter the lavishness of her table by putting off the appetites of her guests, she had found the perfect solution. Nobody by this time fancied a second helping of pud.

It was a slightly queasy little group that wandered out to the promenade on that first evening, averting their eyes from the bench, kindly pointed out by Mrs. Camp, where the tramp had expired.

All about them happy holidaymakers were strolling and laughing, evidently oblivious of the prevailing perils of their chosen resort.

"I think it's dreadful," insisted Mrs, Culham, her dark-rimmed eves blazing in her sick, white, peevish face. "We must leave tomorrow, John. You should never have brought me here."

"I don't think anyone will want to kill us," said John, mildly.

"Who would want to kill those others? A tramp, an old woman, a young girl, all the rest of them. It's a maniac, there's no motive in it, it's someone who gets a pleasure out of doing it...."

"So it might just as well be one of us, you mean?" said Miss Pratt in her pleasant, grave voice.

"What are the police doing about it?" said Mrs. Gerald. "That's what I'd like to know."

"Baffled," said Sharon Jones, and tried a little exchange of amused glances with Hugo Raie.

But young Mr. Raie was not laughing. "Do you think this iss funny?" he said. "For my part, I do not. I think it iss frightening.

"Here in England you don't believe in 'feelings,' in premonitions – you call it 'witchcraft' and you dismiss it. But in my country we believe in premonitions – and in witchcraft too.

"And I tell you frankly that I have 'feelings' about this horrible thing. I tell you frankly that standing here in the sunshine with the sands so yellow and the sea so blue and the sky so fresh and clear, I am cold inside and dark, and very much afraid."

And he swung about and cried out suddenly, on a sharp note of fear. "What did I tell you? It is witchcraft! Look there – look there!"

Very slowly, slowly and surely moving down the long, golden promenade, a black blot in the colour and movement and gaiety of the holiday crowds in their bright summer dress - an old, old man.

An old, old man, black as a carrion crow in his black suit and black hat and black-gloved hands. Carrying aloft a banner as black as himself.

And on the banner, in letters of gold, the words: PREPARE TO MEET THY DOOM.

They swung about and stood staring with thudding hearts and faltering breath, caught for a moment in that age-old web of darkness that the word "witchcraft" thrice repeated had spun about them.

And then – a shrug, a rather forced smile, a careless word.

For what was it after all?

An old man carrying a banner with a warning sent out by some killjoy religious sect.

But: "You see!" said Hugo Raie, with a touch of triumph. "You cannot say there is not something of witchcraft, even here."

And he stooped, carelessly, and picked up a scrap of paper from the ground. "Hass one of you dropped this?"

A scrap of paper – which had not been there a minute, half a minute, ago. Dropped by one of them: by one of the Culhams, by Miss Pratt, by old Mrs. Gerald, by Sharon Jones – by Hugo Raie himself.

A small scrap of paper, printed upon it in large, black, pencilled letters, PREPARE TO MEET YOUR END.

Within 24 hours one of the six people staring down at that scrap of paper was to die.

What Hugo Raie had said was true. It was a dreadful thing to be among gay holidaymakers in the blue and gold of a summer evening's sunshine by the sea – and to be dark and cold inside and very much afraid.

"A joke," said Mrs. Camp, dismissing it, when the huddled, uneasy little group, clinging together with some sort of forlorn trust in security in numbers, got back to Sunnyside.

"A trick – one of you trying to be funny."

"Or some stranger, perhaps, in the crowd," suggested Hugo Raie, doubtfully.

"No," said Sharon Jones.

"No?"

"Don't you see – it must have been one of us. One of you two," she said to the Culhams.

"Or Miss Pratt or you yourself, Mr. Raie. Or me. Because of the way it was put.

"'Prepare to meet thy doom'?"

"But it wasn't," said Sharon. "It usually was 'Prepare to meet thy doom.' But it wasn't this time: It was 'Prepare to meet your end.'

"And only six of us – not counting Mrs. Camp, who wasn't there – could have known that Miss Pratt had said only an hour before at supper that that would have been a less shocking way to phrase it."

"A joke," insisted Mrs. Camp again.

But next morning, round the Sunnyside breakfast table, five people sat ashen-faced. Mrs. Culham, the sixth of the party, being, as was her habit, still upstairs in bed.

For a letter arrived by the post, addressed in thick pencilled capital letters, that made Mrs. Camp gasp.

"It's the same! It's the letters on the message the old lady had. I saw it in her hand. And the others – they were reproduced in the newspapers, the other warning messages.

"After the murders, I mean – to see if anyone might recognise the writing and inform the police."

The envelope was addressed to Mrs. Culham.

"To Lena! To my wife!" cried John Culham, hardly able to believe his eyes. "Who on earth would want to do Lena any harm?"

"Why the tramp? Why the girl in the train? Why that poor Colonel Thomas?" said Mrs. Camp, unhappily shrugging. Colonel Thomas had been the Scampton Murderer's No. 5.

"Do you think I'd better open it?" said John Culham, at last. He looked round at them with agonised, anxious eyes. "My wife, she's so nervous already. Don't you think I'd better?"

And, after all, it might not be the murder message. It might be an ordinary letter. Why frighten her needlessly? They all agreed: "Yes, yes, open it yourself, before she comes down."

Inside the envelope – a scrap of paper. Bearing in the same block capitals five words: PREPARE TO MEET THY DOOM.

"I dare not tell her," said Mr. Culham. "She – well, she suffers from her nerves already. You've all seen her."

"If it's not a joke," said Sharon, her lovely blue eyes as wide and blue, in her terror, as a Siamese kitten's, "you do realise that it's one of us? One of US."

It was agreed at last to say nothing for the moment to the police: not to risk unnecessarily distressing Mrs. Culham. Joke or no joke, the sender of the notes was one of themselves.

Surely, then, it would be safest to keep together, so that the innocent might watch the guilty and so best guard Mrs. Culham.

Well, there was the girl in the train, the man at the theatre. To be out of Scampton, once one had received the warning, was by no means to be out of harm's way.

Better by far to stick together, to watch one another, to vet every mouthful of food Mrs. Culham ate.

***

The second Sunday in August is Landladies' Day in Scampton. By long tradition, the small private hotels and guesthouses entertain their guests to an evening picnic on the beach.

Each lady takes a hamper of food and drinks for her own little group.

To this junketing, Mrs. Culham, the only member of the Sunnyside party ignorant of the threat to her safety, in her whining way consented to go.

And true to their plan for her joint protection, the rest went too.

"I'll keep everything very, very simple," said Mrs. Camp, talking it over with the little Safety Committee. "No prepared stuff that might be doctored in advance. I can't be watching my kitchen every moment of the day.

"Everything fresh, still wrapped – just as I buy it. And some of you shall come with me to each of the shops. And nothing particularly marked for Mrs. Culham – everyone will take just what comes as it comes."

And no one person, she suggested, should wait on Mrs. Culham. "Each of us will do our bit – passing things, pouring the drinks, and so on."

It was clear that not much idle holidaymaking was coming the way of the Sunnyside guests for the next little while. Always excepting Mrs. Culham.

But none of them felt much inclined for jollifications anyway.

And the meal when it came was certainly simple enough. They sat in a ring on the hard, dry sand, all scuffed with the feet of the merrymakers, the checked tablecloth spread in the centre.

And all about them other little groups sat laughing and talking and carefree, each with its own presiding Mrs. Camp.

"Now," said Mrs. Camp. "Here's the loaf and some butter. And that's the lettuce in front of you, Miss Pratt, and a packet of ready-carved ham in front of Mr. Raie.

"So now you take the knife, Mr. Culham, and cut the loaf and pass each slice to me and I'll butter it.

"Miss Pratt can pop a piece of lettuce on it. Miss Jones can shake a little dressing on the lettuce from that bottle, and Mr. Raie shall lay a slice of ham on top of the lot.

"And Mrs. Gerald." said Mrs. Camp, determinedly gay, "shall be Queen of the Mustard Pot!

"Now – one, two, three: Off we go!"

They had eaten little lunch and not much tea, all watching Mrs. Culham's every mouthful as they ate.

Surely now they might relax a little under so foolproof a plan?

"I bags the crust!" cried Mrs. Camp, still dreadfully gay, as the first slice went its round.

If there's been any tampering with the ends of the loaf, her glance said to her fellow-conspirators, *that's my responsibility, and I shall take the outside to show good faith.*

The crust passed round was duly buttered, piled with salad, dressing, ham, and a dab of mustard.

Mrs. Culham watched with offended astonishment while their land-lady reached out her hand for it and took a large bite.

Mrs. Culham sat waiting with irritable impatience for her own slice.

Mr. Culham cut the slice. Mrs. Camp, using the same knife as before, digging the butter from the same part of the half-pound block as the first had come from, slapped on butter.

Miss Pratt forked a leaf of lettuce from the heap before her.

Sharon Jones shook a little dressing over it from the bottle.

Hugo Raie speared a slice of ham and laid it reverently on top of the lettuce.

Mrs. Gerald added a touch of mustard and passed the heaped open sandwich to her next-door neighbour.

All so safe, so simple, so utterly foolproof.

A moment of agonising uncertainty, a moment of petrified astonishment, an eternity of horror – all compressed within 60 seconds of watching that terrible, jerking, gasping marionette thrashing about in its death throes on the dry, scuffed golden sand.

Exactly one minute after taking her first mouthful, Mrs. Culham was dead.

***

Saturday, Sunday, Monday, Tuesday – it had settled down to be a wonderful August.

And the ninth of the Cyanide Murders was the only blot on the blue and gold of those shining summer days at Scampton-on-Sea.

Monday had begun a week of carnival – little damped, it seemed, by headlines screaming the news that the Scampton slayer had struck again.

But down at the end of the pier it was almost deserted. Sharon Jones leaned there on the wooden rail with Hugo Raie.

"It's so dreadful, so dreadful."

But one had said it so many times that the words and even the emotion itself had almost lost meaning.

"And so frightful for poor Mr. Culham."

"Also for poor Mrs. Culham," Hugo suggested drily.

"But they had him down at the police station for hours and hours."

"If a gentleman is not getting on so well with hiss wife," said Hugo in his soft, foreign voice, "and thiss wife suddenly dies –"

"How can you suggest such a thing," cried Sharon, horrified. "Mr. Culham has never even been in Scampton before. How could he possibly be the Cyanide Murderer?"

"Mr. Culham *says* he has never been in Scampton before.

"And I do not say he iss the Cyanide Murderer. Perhaps *a* cyanide murderer – but that's a different thing."

"But –"

"My dear Miss Jones – a maniac in Scampton kills off half a dozen people at random, first sending the message PREPARE TO MEET THY DOOM.

"This need not prevent someone else killing off one person or more, not at all at...random – warning message and all.

"Especially," added Hugo, "if the message can be conveniently prevented from ever reaching its destination. And the message to Mrs. Culham was prevented from reaching its destination."

"Why should poor John Culham do such a thing?" said Sharon.

"Have you not noticed," suggested Hugo in his young-old way, "that Mr. Culham looks upon Miss Pratt with a very friendly eye?"

"They never even saw one another before Monday."

"How do you know?" said Hugo, complacently.

"Well, I think you're perfectly horrid," said Sharon again.

"And anyway, as it happens he can't have done it. I know he can't. I watched him. He cut off the crust and passed it on the tip of the breadknife to Mrs. Camp.

"And then he just sat and waited with the knife sort of poised in the air, and then he cut the next slice and passed that on in exactly the same way. And the other hand didn't touch anything, not anything.

"So," said Sharon, triumphantly, "as you're such a great detective – where does that lead us?"

It led them, said the great detective quite unperturbed, to the only remaining corner of the triangle – it led them to Miss Pratt.

And so absorbed was Sharon in considering the case against Miss Pratt that she failed to observe that in his absorption, Mr. Hugo Raie had quite ceased to talk with a foreign accent.

The Rock Gardens, too, were deserted in favour of the carnival procession.

And here on a bench overlooking the formal (and really quite hideous) patterns of marigolds sat Mrs. Gerald and Mrs. Camp.

Mrs. Gerald was still in a high state of indignation at Mrs. Camp's having allowed her to come to Scampton at all.

"But I can't turn away business," pleaded Mrs. Camp, almost tearfully.

"And you must have read the papers. Anyway, you can't be the Maniac, can you?"

"I?" Mrs. Gerald's high nose flared more crimson than ever.

She got up and stood towering over stout little Mrs. Camp with uplifted parasol, as if for two pins she would strike her.

"I? The Maniac! Why it's you," squawked Mrs. Gerald, "who's the Maniac if anyone is.

"You're the only one that's been in Scampton all this time while these murders were going on."

"Any or all of you may have been in Scampton," said Mrs. Camp, calmly. "How do we know? None of us knows anything about the others."

"We know something about you," insisted Mrs. Gerald. "We know you were in Scampton. And very fishy, I call it, you being at the scene of the death so many times."

"I've been at the scene of more deaths than that, my dear," said Mrs. Camp. "I'm a trained nurse."

"Deaths, yes. These happened to be murders."

"I don't inquire first," said Mrs. Camp, still equably, "what my patients are proposing to die of. I just help them."

"Help them to die," agreed Mrs. Gerald.

"If you like to put it that way, yes," said Mrs. Camp. "Help them to die." But not, she added, by offering them doses of cyanide. With or without mustard.

"What do you mean?" cried Mrs. Gerald.

"So don't suggest silly things to me," said Mrs. Camp, "and I won't suggest them to you.

"I mean I buttered that slice of bread – same pound of butter, same knife, and all of you watching me. And you put mustard on the ham – same pot, same spoon, and all of us watching you.

"And as for her having been in Scampton at the time of the murders – two could play at that game also.

"And I have a good memory for faces," concluded Mrs. Camp.

"So you recognised her, too?" said Mrs. Gerald.

It wasn't quite what Mrs. Camp had meant. But she listened with growing enthusiasm to Mrs. Gerald's indictment of Miss Pratt.

And in the empty lounge at Sunnyside, Miss Pratt sat with poor, sad, anxious, remorse-stricken Mr. Culham.

"Dear Mr. Culham – you shouldn't reproach yourself. You and Mrs. Culham weren't happy."

"She changed," acknowledged Mr. Culham wretchedly. "We were happy enough at first, you know, but – she changed."

But his mind wandered away to the ever-recurring question: Who could have wanted to kill her?

"Me, Mrs. Camp, and yourself, Miss Pratt – we've been through it all so many times. Then there's little Miss Jones.

"All she did was to shake dressing from a bottle on to the lettuce."

"A proprietary brand. The bottle had never been opened."

"And young Raie. A slice of ham. Any slice of ham. Out of a foil-wrapped package he had never set eyes on. He just speared a piece and put it on to the bread."

"On to the lettuce," corrected Miss Pratt. "I put the lettuce on the bread."

"From a bundle of salad rolled in a damp table-napkin to keep it fresh."

"Which I, also, had never seen before," observed Miss Pratt.

"Of course, of course. I noticed," remarked John Culham, idly, "that on occasions you held the fork in your left hand."

"Yes, I'm left-handed," agreed Miss Pratt. But her mind was elsewhere.

She said, delicately: "Have you ever just wondered, Mr. Culham? I mean, your poor wife – always fancying herself ill and unhappy –"

"You mean suicide?" said John Culham bluntly. "But it's impossible. She wasn't truly distressed; she had nothing on earth to commit suicide *for*.

"And then in such a way! As if she – or anyone would!

"Everyone knows that a death from cyanide is dreadful. And after all those descriptions Mrs. Camp gave us...my wife was quite upset. She couldn't get them out of her mind – that wretched tramp on the bench, the old lady in her garden chair –"

"It was a bath chair," corrected Miss Pratt. "One of those old-fashioned ones, wicker-work...."

She had gone very pale, she spoke in a dreamy far-away voice. "She was – half in, half out of it.

"All – all crooked, arched up as you say, and – and froth you know, and –"

Suddenly the light came back to her eyes, she flung up her hand to her mouth.

"What have I been saying? I didn't mean to – to say anything. I just – just mean I pictured it all."

"You were there!" said John Culham. "You were at the Home when the old lady was murdered. You pretended you were never in Scampton before, but you were here when at least one of the murders happened."

And he caught at her wrist and pulled her hand away from her face and said: "Weren't you. Weren't you?"

It was the following morning that the second warning came: PREPARE TO MEET YOUR END

It was addressed to Miss Pratt.

Now it was Miss Pratt's turn to spend hours and hours with the police.

John Culham waited for her, leaning wretchedly over a low wall, watching with unseeing eyes while elderly gentlemen in white linen caps padded about the velvety bowling green.

She appeared at last, exhausted and much distressed. "They wanted me to go away, but I won't.

"We have the murderer in our midst, one of six people – you or Mrs. Camp or Mrs. Gerald, or one of those two young people, Hugo Raie or Sharon Jones.

"Or me, of course," said Miss Pratt, trying to smile. "And, incredible and impossible though it seems to say it here, in all this sunshine and colour and light-heartedness all around us – incredible though it seems, one of us is a murderer, a homicidal maniac.

"And he's out for blood – he or she, whichever it is. The mood is on him. He's killed and he wants to kill again.

"If it's not me, he'll go for someone else. I can be protected, but if I run away and hide he'll go for someone else.

"So I must stay. We must all stay. Once we disperse, the whole horrible business will start all over again. And what is more, we're repeating that picnic tonight – to trap the killer."

"No," said John Culham, violently. "NO!"

He consoled himself. "The killer will know it's a trap. You'll be safe. He daren't strike."

***

It was a dreadful day. At the insistence of the police, anxious to prevent panic, no mention of the warning note was permitted to reach the public outside Sunnyside.

Isolated among all the gay holidaymakers, the little group must carry their terrors in their own shrinking hearts.

Nor did they trust themselves now in one another's company. Solitary, they crept off to their long interviews with the police; solitary, they crept back to Sunnyside.

To lunch at the communal table was unthinkable. Each alone, they slunk into unfrequented shops and bought biscuits and buns to stave off hunger till the evening meal should come...looking fearfully over their shoulders, choosing only wrapped foods.

The lunch hour came and passed. Mrs. Camp, all by herself, presided at her dining table. She ate a good meal. But then the food had been prepared by herself, for herself.

Even she felt the need to be alone. She went up to her room and let out the strings of her corsets a bit, and kicked off her shoes and lay down on her bed.

The photograph of the late Mr. Camp gazed back at her as she lay. She got up and put him away in a drawer.

"You're better off out of the way for a bit, Tom," she said to it. "You get on my nerves, dear."

And John Culham in his room also lay wearily on his bed, and also stared at a photograph – and also addressed it.

"Don't look at me so reproachfully, Lena," he said. "It wasn't my fault. I just can't – can't help myself. I'm not to blame, truly."

Through the flimsy wall he could hear the sound of many matches striking the side of a box, and he wrenched away his wounded thoughts and wondered incuriously: letters, invitation cards, bridge scores in the process of feverish destruction would have answered him if he had been able to see through the wall as well as hear.

And above, in two little top rooms, two young people stared into two mirrors; and each thought: "I must not look so pale, they'll begin to suspect."

So Sharon Jones applied pink rouge, paused, and went to a drawer.

She prised up the lining paper and took a peep at a legal-looking document – or copy of a document – hidden there, hastily pushed it out of sight again and went back to her dressing table.

Hugo Raie sloshed half the contents of a bottle of brown-tinted lotion onto his forehead, cheeks, and chin.

Leaving off only to make an occasional dash to the window and peer out and up to where the lead guttering ran along the edge of the sloping roof.

But there was nothing to see there: not a sign, not the hint of a sign of that fat black pencil pushed away out of sight in a crack between guttering and roof – a thick black pencil with a very soft black lead in it.

***

So the long day passed. And suddenly the day was over and all too soon it was evening.

Wearily, anxiously, they trudged down to the picnic spot, spread the checked tablecloth, arranged themselves in a circle around it: not one of them without dread in his heart – murderer and all.

And in the shadows behind them, dodged behind rocks, crouched between the flower beds in the terraced cliff, armed with heaven-knows-what paraphernalia of telescopic lenses, tape recorders, first-aid sets, and all the rest of it were the police.

Mrs. Camp slowly opened her hamper. The last stage in the Scampton Cyanide Murders had begun.

The bread, fresh from the bakers, the bread knife, the unwrapped butter, the lettuce, the unopened bottle of dressing, the ham, the mustard pot.

Mrs. Camp, her round cheeks not so healthily pink as usual, shoved the loaf over to John Culham.

"We'd better begin."

But suddenly John Culham couldn't. He couldn't. "You all seem to forget it was my wife who died. How can I sit here, how can I go through that same routine?"

"I'll change places with you," said Miss Pratt. "I'll take over the bread."

The crust was sliced off, buttered, garnished, and came round full circle.

"The order has changed a bit, of course," Hugo Raie pointed out.

"With Mrs. Culham not – not here, the numbers are different. Who's eating the crust this time? Who's eating the first slice?"

"I'm eating the first slice," said Mrs. Pratt quietly. "I'm the one threatened. That must be as it was before.

"It was the first slice that Mrs. Culham ate and it'll be the first slice that I eat. It's all arranged.

"Anyone for the crust?"

No one seemed violently eager to take advantage of this offer. There was a short silence. Then into the silence a voice said casually: "All right – I'll eat the crust."

As they had sat on that Sunday night, struck silent and motionless with tension while slowly and firmly Mrs. Camp had eaten her way through the garnished crust, so now they sat again, absolutely silent, absolutely still.

And slowly Mrs. Camp's pink mouth opened, white teeth parted, thrust forward, bit into bread and salad and mustard.

And suddenly all the night was filled with screaming: with one word screamed out between rapidly tensing jaws, through foam-spattered lips – one word jerked out in an eternity of agony that yet lasted only for one single threshing, writhing, arching, screaming minute of pain and horror and then was absolutely still.

One word: "LEFT-HANDED!"

And the night was filled with the sound of men's voices shouting, and the men's boots running over the hard, dry sand towards them.

The cries of the startled holiday crowds all about them on the beach.

But at the storm centre, five people stood petrified to stone. Just staring. Staring at the writhing thing that writhed slower and slower even as, speechless with horror, they gazed upon it, and at last it was still.

Would never move again, would never speak again.

And would never kill again. The Cyanide Murderer of Scampton-on-Sea was dead.

And only one clue to that death. "Left-handed."

Mr. and Mrs. John Culham – that quiet, rather melancholy, very devoted couple talked to no one about the Scampton murders except each other.

For, to them, it was not a matter for juicy gossip and scandal. Nine people were dead, among them the first Mrs. Culham. And now the murderer herself...

The infamous Mrs. Camp, Maniac, was dead.

Her husband had died "under distressing circumstances" – had choked on a crumb of bread, been ignored as supposedly fooling. But had not been fooling...had suffocated and died.

Had died leaving her (already, no doubt, mentally unbalanced) with a grudge against the world which had failed to save him.

She had taken up her nursing again and gradually accumulated, as the years went by, tiny doses of stolen poison, adding up at last to enough to kill – and kill – and kill again.

At first she had gone cautiously, had not cared what victim she had selected, had not waited for him to die in agony to avenge that other death.

A tramp, well known in the district, with a set routine of habits such as many tramps acquire.

Shuffling along the promenade, searching the litter bins for scraps of food.

And his murderer was innocently away for a day in London. And the old lady at the garden *fête* where kind Campy was helping matron – in the refreshment tent.

And the girl in the train, oblivious in the scrum round the buffet counter of the small, dumpy figure buying a similar roll just next to her.

And the Colonel, hastening away from her friend and fellow landlady, Mrs. Boyle's – having broadcast his intention of taking his mother on the following Saturday to a matinee.

A tray of tea and bread and butter – passed so willingly along the row of stalls by the helpful hands of the unobtrusive little woman who had so shortly afterwards departed.

"Always bread," said Mrs. Culham. "Always bread."

To nobody, not even her husband, had the erstwhile Miss Pratt confided that one flash of inspiration that had come to her as – left-handed – she cut that loaf.

"I wonder if any one of us, even the police, would ever have guessed," mused Mr. Culham, "if she hadn't cried out as she died, 'Left-handed.'"

"I wonder," said Mrs. Culham, meekly.

For – why tell? Why say anything about it – about that one moment of inspiration as, left-handed, she had cut the loaf.

About that split-second decision as the whole plot unfolded itself to her.

Shall I cry out and stop her eating the crust and save her? Shall I save her from death by the hangman's rope? But – if she should escape from that? She is a murderess nine times over. Is this not the moment to make sure she does not escape?

"She got more daring with each murder, I suppose," said John Culham. "And, of course, she preferred to see it happening.

"But for that, and the fact that you're left-handed, the murders might still be continuing.

"Just a loaf of bread," he said, shaking his head at the ingenuity of it. "And a breadknife."

An innocent loaf. Bought openly at the baker's unwrapped, untouched. Don't cut it yourself – pass it to someone else, to anyone, it doesn't matter.

And, of course, the knife it's to be cut with.

All eyes on the loaf. Who looks at the knife?

For if you slice a loaf with a knife coated with poison – the poison will get on to *two* slices of bread.

But, of course, if you coat only one side of the knife with the poison – that's different.

You hold the knife in your right hand. You smear the side of the blade nearest to you with the poison. The loaf is held with the left hand, the knife cuts away the crust – which is innocent of poison.

But the next slice has been smeared with the poison on the near side of the blade.

What's more, the knife has been cleaned by contact with the bread, and now shows no trace of poison.

All so splendidly foolproof. Except that Miss Pratt – as she then had been – was left-handed.

So Miss Pratt held the loaf with her right hand and the knife in her left, and the poisoned blade came next to the crust.

And Mrs. Camp claimed the crust – and opened her smiling pink mouth and sank her white teeth into white bread and golden butter and pale green lettuce and pale pink ham with its white fat glistening.

And all in one moment of horror, the long, grim saga of the Scampton Murders was ended.

Real Life Impossibility: United States
The Incomprehensible Drunkenness of Louis Calhern

Louis Calhern and Marlon Brando met on the set of *Julius Caesar*, where Calhern played the title role. Despite the considerable difference in their ages and status (Calhern appeared in more than 60 films, but never achieved stardom), they became bosom pals and drinking partners. During one of their drinking bouts, Calhern confided the following story, which Brando related in his autobiography:

Calhern had been cast in a Broadway play and, on opening night, the finicky producers warned all the actors that they would be required to stay sober for every night of the run. When it became obvious that Louis Calhern had no intention of following orders, the producers rented a room in an actor's club in the city. There, they locked him up alone, after having thoroughly searched the room, and took away the key.

The next day they were furious to discover the actor blind drunk, and ordered an investigation. It transpired that the door had not been opened, the club owner having personally sworn that his own key had not left his private office. Furthermore, the room was on the fourth floor, overlooking a courtyard, and with no fire escape reachable from the room. Every night the room was searched before Calhern was locked in, and every morning he was found drunk. Despite his employers' best efforts, the drinking continued until the show closed and no one discovered Calhern's secret.

On the first night of his internment, he had seen a bellboy walking around in the courtyard and had thrown him a twenty-dollar bill, with instructions to buy him a bottle of whisky and a straw, and to keep the change. When the boy came up to his room, Calhern simply asked him to open the bottle, put one end of the straw into it, and pass the other end through the keyhole. And each night, while the boy stood outside the door, Louis Calhern consumed an entire bottle of neat whisky.

Sweden
Windfall
by Ulf Durling

Ulf Durling was trained as a physician, eventually becoming a teacher of psychiatry and director of the Danderyd hospital north of Stockholm.

In 1971 he wrote *Gammal Ost* (translated as *Old Cheese*, a reference to the Swedish expression "revenge for old cheese"), which won the Swedish Academy of Crime Fiction's award for best genre debut. After nearly twenty novels and many short stories, the SACF honoured him with the title of Grand Master.

In 2015, *Gammal Ost* was published by LRI as *Hard Cheese*. *CADS* (Crime and Detective Stories) magazine called it "quite simply...the funniest book I've read in a long time," and *Crime Fiction Lover* named it to its 2016 Top Ten Nordic Noir List.

"Windfall" is a characteristically Durling story, with a clever solution coming from a totally unexpected quarter.

Evidence as well as Beauty is in the Eye of the Beholder.
(Freely adapted from an old saying)

Earlier today, when Andreas called me on the phone, he sounded eager as well as secretive. Obviously he had something up his sleeve.

I arrived at his home half an hour later and my suspicions were soon confirmed. He certainly had a quite different problem on his mind than the subject he introduced after a few minutes of small talk. As my opinion on his official matters is of no interest to him, I wondered immediately why he began to describe the sermon he was preparing for next Sunday morning's service as *locum tenens* for our present vicar, his successor. It would, he said, deal with God's visitations and the propensity of human beings towards disobeying his commandments. Inspired by the abundant crops during this autumn, he planned to mention the Garden of Eden and Adam's and Eve's –

"Please," I cut him off. "Come to the point!"

"Touché," he said with a sly smile. "But in fact it was the forbidden fruit theme which opened my eyes and helped me understand what really happened at Örneholm in 1934! I assume you've heard of the tragedy?"

"Not a lot. I'd left Kisa by then and afterwards my father didn't talk about it much."

"Because he had been blind to the truth and his involvement turned out to be a failure! Talking about the case was too embarrassing for him."

"Wait a minute!" I protested. "He was a good policeman and –"

"Yes, but…anyhow, yesterday I solved the damned riddle!"

He leant back in his armchair with an almost intolerable air of self-satisfaction.

For uninformed readers – many of whom may not even know that Kisa is situated in the southeast of Sweden – it will be necessary to relate his summary of the events and also give a short introduction to the two of us, Andreas and me.

We had been as thick as thieves in school, but chose different paths afterwards. Andreas followed in the family footsteps and studied theology. I chose, like my father, to serve the judicial system.

Parallel tracks: heredity and environment. I ended my career as police commissioner far from here, and whom should I find more than ten years ago, after my divorce and return to my native town, but the dean and bachelor Andreas Somenius!

We look and act differently, but extremes have a tendency to meet. The stereotypical policeman is supposed to be hardboiled and well-disciplined; the clergyman is supposed to have a humble disposition and be pear-shaped after all those cake parties and wedding dinners. In our case it is the other way round. Andreas is lanky and somewhat hot-tempered while I am as round as an Edam cheese and as mild as a Brie.

Thank goodness we are both fairly hale and healthy. In contrast to me, he is doing fine all by himself, while I need some practical assistance. Though his situation is enviable, I've no reason to complain, thanks to the excellent care at Dove's Nest, my municipal lodging.

And so, at about seven o'clock, with an advanced stage of twilight outside the window, Andreas proceeded to fill in the many gaps in my knowledge of the sad story to which he had alluded:

"Sometime after lunch that faraway Friday, the baron and ex-troop colonel Rutger von G. was found dead. He was very old, and departing life in a tranquil way at his age is expected and even desirable, but further information soon complicated the picture.

"Rutger von G. at his estate in Örneholm was as brick-hard as he was stone-deaf, an ultra-conservative man on bad terms with almost everyone in the community. That his teenage niece Alicia had put up with staying under his roof was probably due to the fact that she had no alternative, her own family having been scattered by the many wrathful winds of fate. When not touring the countryside on horseback, she spent most of her time playing patience and reading poetry.

"The third member of the family was as estranged as the poor girl. The habitual drunkard and good-for-nothing Klaus von G., a distant relative of the baron, was widely considered to be out of his senses.

"The family escutcheon hangs at the House of Nobility in Stockholm. It represents a spade between two eagles in profile. In appearance, they are said to look like a couple of magpies anxiously guarding a silver spoon likely to be stolen at any moment.

"There was also a cook at hand and a lackey, Ivar Bäck, who once had been an officer's orderly for von G. in Småland's cavalry.

"It's relevant to the story that the day labourers of the manor, occasional or permanent, were badly treated by their employer. He was especially disobliging to his stable boys. The last one had been sacked after less than a month of toil and struggle.

"During the last few weeks, von G. had been in the habit of sitting under an apple tree in his garden. Every morning early, he would stagger there for the purpose of recovering from a cold that had kept him bedridden for some time. He sat in an easy chair in the shade of the foliage and enjoyed the warmth of the Indian summer, wrapped in a dressing gown and with his moth-eaten wig stuck on his head like a fur cap. The breakfast put on the table every day consisted of sandwiches, eggs, coffee, and a glass of Calvados. After the meal he was in the habit of shutting his eyes and thinking who-knows-what scurrilous thoughts.

"The reason for him wearing a postiche was that, to his embarrassment, he had long ago turned completely bald. He used it in a futile attempt to look attractive and tempting in the eyes of any female who caught his eye. Her own desires and consent for intimate pleasure were of absolutely no concern to him, nor was her voluntary co-operation.

"Had he known that later on it would be considered sexy to be bald – like Kojak and Picasso – he could have experienced more unforced success in his earlier years with numerous chambermaids and other females within his reach, by using more subtle seduction techniques, such as lollipops or bribes, rather than harsh and explicit orders.

"On that particular day, just like any other, nobody in the household took any more notice of him than was strictly necessary. For it was preferable to avoid being near him and thus escape his malicious comments and choleric outbursts.

"The one in the menagerie who most appreciated von G.'s forenoon siestas was Caro, also called Karon, since each meeting with his master gave a foretaste of Hades. Exhausted and frequently flogged, the poor creature stayed mostly in his backyard kennel, but did begin to bark whenever an unauthorized individual approached, whereupon he came hurtling out like a rocket for the purpose of biting the intruder's throat.

"But that day nothing had been heard from Karon, not even a muffled growl.

"Nobody would have noticed anything, had not a cold front arrived and heavy clouds sailed in from the east, causing Alicia and Klaus to go outside and reluctantly check the baron. They found him sitting upright but askew, with his right arm dangling down from the elbow rest and his glass of spirits still untouched.

"Bäck immediately took command. He had the table cleared away, carried von G. to lie in state in the Gustavian parlour and sent for the local physician, who arrived within half an hour.

"After having inspected the corpse without any remarkable findings, the doctor casually decided that no autopsy was required and wrote out a death certificate. 'Natural causes,' it said. A vague breeze had extinguished a nearly breathless flame of life.

"Whereupon something unexpected happened. Hey, presto! A police officer appeared!"

"Dad!"

"Right you are. And he behaved in a rather peculiar way!

“The news about the death had reached him through the grapevine. And now that he was on the spot, he carefully examined the ground around and under the apple tree, scratched his chin and stared straight out into space. He kept silent, and after a while he disappeared.”

“Strange,” I said. “Did they ever get to know how Rutger von G. met his destiny?”

“Yes, in due course.

“The reason for your father’s appearance was gossip he had heard, to the effect that a drunken young rascal in Kisa had talked loudly about killing von G. Thus, when the rumour of his death reached him, Max Axelson, Senior, quickly went to Örneholm, believing the promised act of violence had actually taken place. However, since there were no apparent signs of any crime having taken place, he was forced to drop his suspicions.

“Not surprisingly, the brawler turned out to be none other than the stable boy who had recently been sacked by the baron. But when he was eventually caught, he was able to prove convincingly that he’d been sleeping off the effects of booze in his mother’s home for the last twenty-four hours.

“That was a pity, because he belonged to those who were familiar to Karon and certainly would have aroused his attention.’

“The dog that didn’t bark in the daytime,” I noted. “That was the remarkable thing!”

“What?”

“That Karon didn’t bark. Beyond the people of the estate, nobody could enter the place unnoticed. Very clever of my father – who, as far as I know had never read ‘Silver Blaze’ by Conan Doyle.’

“To cut a long story short: The corpse was taken away, the bell of the estate promptly tolled subdued strokes, and the flag flew at half-mast.

“Except for Karon nobody mourned the deceased. The mongrel was seen prowling the manor in wider and wider circles, lop-eared and lost. Was he searching for the scent of his master? Could he, after all, have attributed the countless lashes, slaps, and kicks over the years as an expression of some kind of tough love?

"Everything would have been resolved fairly satisfactorily," Andreas concluded, "had it not been for – Maxi, my friend, guess what!"

I made a helpless gesture.

"Had it not been for a neighbour who, the same evening, had committed suicide leaving a letter in which he admitted the murder of von G.!

"It was an unambiguous confession," Andreas added. "The truth of it could simply not be questioned."

"But what about motive and *modus operandi*? Why and how? And, in particular, how did he manage to pass under the radar of Karon, the guardian of the home estate, with the most infallible nose in the region? By means of voodoo or a homemade ray gun?"

"An impossible crime, a mystery.

"Your father had continued fumbling in the dark and had found nothing, so the investigation was eventually discontinued."

At this point Andreas remembered his duties as a host. A bowl of apples stood on the table between us and when he leant back after having pushed it towards me, he suddenly grimaced and touched the small of his back.

"Demons of darkness!" he shouted. "My lumbago is killing me! From now on I'm incapable of moving an inch. But maybe I can take a catch."

"Excuse me?"

"As we did when we played baseball at school. Two teams, one out and one in. We – no, it doesn't matter. Do me a favour and throw one of the red apples to me. They are Red Delicious from the ICA Supermarket."

I obeyed him. He seized the fruit and took a bite out of it.

"The drama at Örneholm, Act Two," he resumed, while the ornamental timepiece behind him struck eight o'clock. "Ready?"

"Ready."

"Very well, after what happened later that night in October 1934, Johannes Somenius and the county administrator Max Axelson, our respective fathers, often discussed the affair without ever getting anywhere close to the truth. Why? Because they didn't have access to a vital clue that clears everything up! A clue, my friend, that was waiting for me yesterday at the ICA Supermarket, where I well and truly had my eyes opened! But before I go on, you have to meet David Mendel."

"Who's that? A strange name by the way."

"Yes. And, curiously enough it suggests the solution of the Örneholm mystery! Here we go! It turned out that the background of the self-accusing man was uncertain. Maybe Mendel was an immigrant, certainly to some people his features hinted of a Jewish origin. In such a case he could have come from Germany, where there were harsh times for him and many others. At the age of thirty, and after years of rather loose living, he had been lucky enough to meet God. Finding salvation, he had become acquainted with my father, and decided to build up both body and soul through physical training – *mens sana in corpore sano*."

"And how did he strengthen his bodily resilience?"

"Mainly by gymnastics, sit-ups, weightlifting, and plenty of tennis. But the spiritual part was the most important to him. My father supported everyone who openly tried to find a firm ground for their faith, especially if they did so along spacious roads and complicated roundabout ways. Our parish lies, as you know, on the outskirts of the so-called Bible Belt. And if you give that concept a more geographical than a symbolical meaning, you can say that spirituality neither should be like a tight belt or a choke collar, but – ahem, sorry, I am not in the pulpit now! Anyhow, dad liked him. He described him as an ugly duckling transformed into a white swan.

"They kept regular company before that black Friday in 1934. That explains why Somenius got to know almost immediately about Mendel's death, which occurred at Lidhult, a cottage near to the Örneholm estate previously reserved for forest keepers.

"Even before the tragedy took place, he knew a lot about Mendel, among other things that he was very much in love with Miss Alicia! Who, furthermore, reciprocated his feelings. Great joy, but even greater disappointment, since a common future between them was impossible. Baron Rutger von G., Alicia's guardian, had expressly opposed their alliance and turned a deaf ear to the girl's desperate appeals. He had forbidden her to see "that bloody dark-haired one." That is what the bewigged baron called anyone who didn't look Swedish, whether the person wore a *kippa* or a fez or any other kind of headgear. Or, for that matter, no headgear at all."

"Did Alicia respect his ban?" I asked.

"No. She –"

"Aha! A revolting teenager, a little sister of Lady Chatterley! The woman of birth and the man of the people, right?"

"Not at all. On the contrary, honourable Miss Alicia had no end of virtue and David was very civilized when courting her. But they met secretly during clandestine walks in the evenings. Both, of course, waited eagerly for the dragon to die so that they could at last legalise their relationship."

"Whereupon Mendel couldn't take it anymore? He raced ahead of the grim reaper and –'

"It wasn't as simple as that. Nevertheless you're on the right track, for he could have fantasised along those lines. If only someone – or he himself – could get rid of the baron.... Now listen carefully!

"Next day it was discovered that the two young people – well, David was a middle-aged youngster – had planned to meet on that Friday evening, weather permitting. Alicia, irrespective of what was expected of her, would certainly have slipped over to Lidhult to inform David of the fortunate news, had she had the opportunity. But Klaus scotched that plan by asking Bäck to drive her to the nearest town, Vimmerby, in order to summon some prominent members of the family society to a memorial service at Örneholm, at which Alicia would be expected to be present, in order to create the right mood with piano music and lamentations. To withdraw from such an obligation was out of the question.

"She had accepted her guardian's death with composure. But when she got the news of David's death, she collapsed in such a dramatic manner that nobody could have doubted what he had meant to her.

"Curiously enough, it had been thanks to her that Mendel's body had been discovered. For at the end of her day of family duty, she had written a sealed note to him and sent it to Lidhult. The runner, a farmer's girl, found his front door unlocked and, when nobody answered her knock, she entered and found a note inside the threshold, which caused her to run for assistance:

DEAREST ALICIA, I WILL NEVER BE ABLE TO PAY FOR MY CRIME. ONLY GOD CAN FORGIVE ME MY ENORMITY. YOU WERE THE BEST THING THAT HAPPENED TO ME IN MY LIFE, MY ROSE OF SHARON, PLEASE PRAY FOR MY SOUL. DAVID

When Andreas quoted the contents of David's letter so accurately it became obvious to me that all his information about the case must have been conveyed to him by his late father, Reverend Johannes Somenius, who in turn had got it from Senior. Thanks to his remarkable memory, my friend was also able to recite the exact words of Alicia's own message to her sweetheart before she learnt of his death:

MY OWN, MY TREASURE! AT LAST WE ARE FREE! YOU AND I AND WE FOREVER. YOUR ALICIA

"But, even before the message was sent, David already knew what had happened at Örneholm. The commotion over there and the flag lowered to half-mast must have confirmed his worst fears. By the time Alicia's letter was delivered, it was too late.

"Investigating Mendel's death that evening, your father determined that he had stabbed himself in the stomach and bled to death in his kitchen. He decided not to check Lidhult and its surroundings there and then, but to return at dawn. It was a wise decision because rain was pouring down, the darkness had deepened and the wind had increased. It would have been meaningless to stumble about in the wet with a kerosene lantern, trying to perform a crime-scene investigation.

"Fortunately, by the next morning the rain had stopped, the sun was shining and little birds were chirping in the bushes.

"But what did he find? Nothing of the slightest interest. The medical examiner, barely awake and resenting being grilled again about his observations at Örneholm the day before, testified that the deceased baron bore no marks of external injury: no pinpricks, bruises, wounds, or swellings. There were indeed signs of death, i.e. livor mortis – discolouration of the skin as a result of congestion in the lower body parts – but such signs appear quite soon postmortem, after just a few hours.

"Why all this nagging and skepticism? Did they distrust him? Aggrieved and not properly rested, the poor doctor had hardly been able to make even his un-Latinised language intelligible.

"The cook was similarly angry. Would she have acted on behalf of an unknown person and put something in her master's coffee or – what an accusation! Had she not indulged herself with a cup from the same jug and later permitted herself to consume a sandwich – one of three that her master had not managed to eat – and that without any side effects.

"With cheeks rosy with indignation, she threatened to quit. "Pick on Klaus instead of me," she had screamed. "He who constantly knocks back every drinkable drop within reach!"

"Then they were told that the day before, with people cackling around the carcass like dizzy chickens, she had seen Klaus secretly draining the glass of Calvados that the baron had left untouched!

"Did Axelson have anything else on his mind, she had roared, or could he please leave her alone?

"Whereupon he declared himself to be very sorry, asked for a cup of coffee – and, if possible, one of her famously tasty cinnamon buns – and fled.

"And since Klaus had survived the purloined drink, he could not possibly be suspected. Why first sharpen it with arsenic or prussic acid – on his own initiative or Mendel's – and then drink it? Otherwise he had most probably wished his old relative would kick the bucket, in the hope of inheriting the whole estate, particularly the wine cellar.

"Thus Axelson was faced with a dilemma. How on earth could David Mendel be guilty of murder? With Karon mute and everything else taken into account, there appeared to be no way that von G. could have been reached at his breakfast table.

"At last he decided that there must have been some kind of overheating in Mendel's brain. The poor devil had simply fallen victim to a misconception."

"You mean that the crime was a delusion on his part?"

"Well, how else to look at it? In spite of the confession, opportunity was missing and the method and means had eluded your father. When it came to the motive, however, lots of people had wished him a violent end – raped women, illegitimate children whom he had refused to accept, maltreated subalterns, deceived business associates, and dismissed servants."

Then Andreas recounted a recent visit he had paid to the scene of the tragedy, which had taken place just a week ago. He had hoped the Örneholm of today would inspire him to a solution of the mystery. But, to his disappointment, the mansion had been demolished and a conference centre now stood in its place. The new owner had bought every hectare within sight and created an eighteen-hole golf course.

"It was a fiasco," he summarised. "Not a single apple tree in sight!"

That his words were heavy with meaning would shortly be revealed.

"What happened to the survivors who once took part in the tragedy?" I asked.

"Alicia soon departed the scene. Rumour had it she had gone to a health resort in Switzerland.

"The other players left within a month: The cook returned to the peasantry from whence she had been recruited, Ivar Bäck went to Eksjö and enlisted as quartermaster at the town's hotel, and Klaus von G. was confined to Saint Gertrud's asylum in Västervik."

With a trace of irony, I asked about the animals.

"Two thoroughbreds with accompanying accessories, pedigrees, and harnesses, had been taken over by a stud farm as a part payment for one of the baron's many debts, and an Ardennes cart horse had gone to slaughter. As for Karon, nobody cared. When Örneholm was abandoned he was simply left to starve to death in his doghouse."

Now my patience was exhausted.

"Okay, enough is enough! How did the murderer do it?"

"Well, Justice is blind, at least Lady Justitia. But with a little additional help from me, even he who wanders in darkness, as you do, can –"

"Skip the gibberish," I hissed, trying to conceal my impatience by playing a tough cop like Dick Tracy. "Spit it out, for God's sake!"

"By all means! Let's use our imagination then, and go back to Friday, the eleventh of October, 1934. You are David Mendel and it's two or three o'clock in the afternoon, long after breakfast. You'll soon be meeting your sweetheart. It's getting cold, the wind is blowing up. You start to get worried. Maybe your meeting will be cancelled. When you go out on the porch of your cottage in order to assess the meteorological situation, you see black clouds in the sky beyond the fence between your lots – yours is very small, your neighbour's is as large as two tennis courts. And, not far away from the boundary of your lot—fifty metres or so—sits your worst enemy. Apparently he's asleep, still weak from the sickness which, according to Alicia, almost killed him. What goes through your mind?"

"I –"

Andreas held up his hand. He was doing the talking, not I.

"That it would be great if the old bastard kicked the bucket, and sooner rather than later. If he would just stay out there a little longer, and catch a cold which would turn into pneumonia, then...."

He interjected one of those pauses he uses so often during his official duties.

"But," he continued, "the thought has only just occurred to you when you are overcome by pangs of conscience. Such a reaction is not consistent with the Christian message of love and your own nature. Thus you must say mea culpa and atone for your sinful fancies. How? By warning the baron about the impending danger, since obviously nobody else will. But again, how? Do you have a good method or modus operandi? You can't go over there and wake him up. Karon would attack you straight away. And you can't wake up a deaf old man by screaming. What else can you do?"

He looked at me enquiringly. I didn't have to pretend to be mystified, because I was, and I shook my head to his obvious satisfaction.

"Maxi, my dear friend, you have to wake him up through remote control!"

"Through what? How?"

"Consider the situation! You're standing by your fence and what do you notice? Small red globes in the grass, very near the baron. They have been hanging loosely above him, lost their grip, and fallen to the ground. You get a bright idea. Everywhere in the region people cultivate apple varieties, as you do yourself, and now it is autumn and harvest time. If you throw one of yours and aim carefully at the crown of the baron's tree, you could trigger his own apples to fall. Furthermore your shot would lose momentum among the branches, change direction and also drop down. Doubtless von G. will be hit and wake up. The drop height of the apples is only a few metres, so he won't be hurt. And never mind if the windfall strikes his skull, the wig protects it. Eureka! You can breathe freely again!"

"Are you out of your mind? Nobody could...never! Fifty metres or more?"

"Oh, yes. Tennis gives fantastic fitness. Strong biceps, a hard and accurate forehand..."

I stared at him.

"But unfortunately you fail. Your throw is too low. It's a direct hit on the baron and when you see von G. start to slump to the side, you rapidly withdraw in order not to be seen by him."

"Wait a minute. There were no signs of injury on the body! If he had been strongly hit by an apple there should certainly have been some –"

"No, my dear Watson. He was effectively protected from superficial skin damage by the thick dressing gown, remember? And there are no bruises on a corpse after the heart has stopped beating and blood is no longer circulating. Now, back to putting yourself in David's shoes....

"At first you believe that your commendable mission has been fulfilled: that your target has just felt an inexplicable thud on his shoulder or one side of his chest, and that he will soon get to his feet and toddle off. But later, after one or two hours, you are seized by doubt. Fear creeps in: What could have happened if your...? So you take another look and what do you see? A crowd of people on Örneholm's terrace, a uniformed policeman by the garden table, the flag flying at half-mast. It all speaks for itself. You've killed the old man!"

"Instead of waking up von G., he brought about the opposite effect?"

"Exactly. And there's more to come. You realise that conclusive evidence of your guilt exists on the scene of the crime – shouting your name and calling you to account, even if you were to deny any responsibility. Which a person of your high moral standard wouldn't do. So you give up. You have – albeit with the best of intentions – got yourself into an irreparable mess. You will be caught, sentenced, and imprisoned for the rest of your life. In a flash you've wrecked your honour, your self-esteem, and your future. You write a few lines to the woman you love but have unwittingly betrayed. You take a knife and commit hara-kiri."

It sounded plausible. David had acted like the Japanese samurai when they lose face. They choose that ritual method as a way of escaping ignominy and degradation.

After a long silence, I ventured:

"There's just one thing…."

"Yes?"

"Well, somehow I have the feeling that von G. already had passed away long before the apple was thrown. Otherwise livor mortis could not possibly have appeared."

Andreas looked somewhat disappointed. I suspect he had hoped to surprise me, but had been beaten to the punch.

"You're right," he muttered. "The baron had probably been dead for hours! And that makes David's mistake even more tragic. All would have been fine if he just had understood that his small nuclear weapon, his sort of pomegranate missile, had only moved the position of von G.'s mortal remains in the chair. It was not the sudden movement of a living person he had seen, but the apparent turning around of a corpse, which had been shaken when the apple hit it, so that the arm fell to the side and the centre of gravity of the body was displaced and – yes, what is it?"

"What about the evidence you mentioned? If my father had examined every inch of the area so meticulously...?"

"He missed it because of his Daltonism. I guess you are familiar with that little flaw, am I right?"

His words filled me with confusion and resentment.

"Good grief! How can you know that he –"

"Since I began to realise that you suffered from it as well. It was during a school dance a long time ago. Two girls in a parallel class attracted us. "Let's invite them to dance," I suggested. "You go for the one in green, okay?" Your reply still echoes in my brain. "Perfect," you said, "she's the prettiest!" But tastes differ. So I got quite bewildered when you walked over to the girl in a red blouse and bowed, because at that time I knew nothing about colour blindness. Well, ten minutes ago I arranged a test by asking you to take a red apple from the fruit dish. After some hesitation you gave me one, without understanding that they were all the same colour. They're all green: Golden, not Red Delicious. Do you want a dram?"

He got to his feet, surprisingly undisturbed, and disappeared.

There I sat as if naked and unmasked. He'd known of my carefully guarded secret for over sixty years!

I've often wondered how I was accepted into the police, despite my defect – trifling enough in the daily life, but surely not in the police. Were the entrance requirements less strict in those days? Or had my dad intervened?

The condition was described for the first time by John Dalton in the beginning of the nineteenth century. The common form is about red and green. Between seven and eight percent of the population – most of them males – are affected, many being unaware of it. There's a genetic factor operating, sometimes very strongly, as it was in my case.

The return of Andreas kept me from more brooding on the subject. He brought a bottle of whisky and two glasses with ice cubes.

"How about the conclusive evidence?" I asked sternly.

"Thank you for reminding me. David simply realised that a green apple from his tree was left on the ground near the table among all the baron's red ones, immediately revealing from whence it must have been thrown. And who was the only person living at a – why not call it a 'throwable' distance? Only he, and thus he would be inexorably linked to the crime!"

He took a deep breath and continued:

"But behold! Due to his disability, Axelson was unable to see the difference between the green and red windfalls. So David would not have been suspected, even if the old man had died of unnatural causes – which your father first suspected, until he terminated his murder investigation when the stable boy turned out to have a watertight alibi. But of this, and the young drunkard's threats against von G., David knew nothing at all.

Therefore he thought himself to be guilty of homicide and was convinced that he would very soon be arrested. Furthermore he had a strong motive for the deed. No wonder he panicked. Weighed down with guilt and desperately unhappy, he saw his own death as the only solution and – well, Maxi, how about a quick nightcap?"

That was an offer I couldn't refuse.

While we were drinking, my host found an EP and put it into his record player. Soon the strains of the love song "Little Green Apples" could be heard. Though the lyrics had nothing to do with the fates of Alicia and David, it certainly had an obvious bearing on the theme of our evening together.

We drank and listened, over and over again. His eyes were filled with tears and I had a lump in my throat. Did he remember the school girl dressed in red, or some later infatuation? My thoughts were centred on my ex-wife, who once was the apple of my eye.

Andreas was slumped deeply in his chair. He blew his nose in some embarrassment, glanced furtively at me and cleared his throat:

"Pull yourself together. Don't yield to your sentimentality. Bottoms up and then off you go! Your leave from Cuckoo's Nest is running out and –"

"Dove's, if you don't mind. I live at Dove's Nest."

He shrugged his shoulders.

"Whatever. Now a good night's sleep would –"

"Wait a minute!"

I'd been struck by a thought.

"Yes?"

"David Mendel," I said. "Didn't you imply that the solution to the riddle was sort of included in his name? Does it allude to the German genetic researcher Gregor Mendel, considering that colour-blindness often has a hereditary aspect?"

"Correct. Also remember David in the Bible, who succeeded in felling Goliath with a stone! The similarity with the power relationship between Lidhult and Örneholm is striking, isn't it? Not to mention the approach."

"But in the Old Testament David used an aid. It was thanks to a sling that he –"

Andreas glanced meaningfully at his watch and rose.

"Yes, yes. Don't be so finicky. Human beings can be weak and imperfect. At a pinch we must find a little extra strength. Sometimes we get it as a gift from above, sometimes we use some practical tool or another which happens to be at hand. By the way, his name was Jan Karlsson. I baptised him David Mendel to put you a bit off the track.

"According to my father, von G. must have been mistaken about David's lineage because of his racial prejudices. In fact Alicia's admirer was the fruit of a joint venture between Linnea Karlsson, captain's mate on the M/S Ada of Gothenburg, and a harbour charmer in San Juan, Puerto Rico, as executive partners.

"End of story. Well, how about calling it a day? We are not fit for rocking around the clock any more. Right, amigo?"

We bade a brotherly good-bye to each other.

Outside there was a Stygian darkness and elements of coolness as well as sprinkles of rain in the air.

More than two hours ago I'd decided on making a report on the Örneholm tragedy, and the sooner I did it the better. There were many details to be integrated in the text, and nowadays my memory capacity is somewhat unreliable.

I got home at about half past nine and, without further delay, sat down at my writing table. The first lines were already formulated in my mind:

Earlier today, when Andreas called me on the phone, he sounded eager as well as secretive. Obviously he'd had something up his sleeve.

Kisa in October 1984
Max(imilian) Axelson, Jr.
Former Police Commissioner

Czech Republic
The Case of the Horizontal Trajectory
by Joseph Škvorecký

Joseph Škvorecký, born in what is now the Czech Republic, but a resident in Canada after the Russian invasion of 1968 until his death in 2012, won the Neustadt International Prize for Literature and the Governor General's Award. He was a Guggenheim Fellow, a Chevalier of France's Ordre des Arts et des Lettres, and was nominated for the Nobel Prize in Literature in 1982.

He wrote two sets of classical detective short stories about Czech detective Lieutenant Boruvka, and also conceived and executed *Sins for Father Knox*, in which each short story deliberately violates one of the famous rules for writing detective stories laid down by Monsignor Ronald Knox. Several of Škvorecký's tales are locked room mysteries. "The Case of the Horizontal Trajectory" is his best.

"Report on the Clarification of the Case of the Horizontal Trajectory." Lieutenant Boruvka, who had a fondness for flowery titles, was dictating to the young policewoman with the massive chignon at the nape of her neck. "On the morning of May 20, 19 – "

"Lieutenant, sir – "

"Well, what is it?"

"Excuse me, sir, but how do you spell *horizontal*?"

"You ought to know that," said the lieutenant rudely. His churlishness was an effort to cover up a variety of conscience pangs which he felt in connection with this particular policewoman, and a recent evening when he, a married man, had made a date with her, only to stand her up in favour of an interesting murder case. "Didn't you take a secretarial course?"

"Yes, but – "

"Then write it right."

"Yes, sir. But horizontal – "

The lieutenant slammed his notepad abruptly onto the desktop, and substituted a note of unpleasant sarcasm for the rudeness in his tone: "You know what! Look it up in the dictionary. And now, let's go on."

The policewoman bowed her head on her long graceful neck, and concentrated on the typewriter keyboard. The lieutenant felt a twinge of pain somewhere near his heart, and that might explain the blast in his voice as he continued: "On the morning of May 20 at 7:25 a.m., Mrs. Barbara Potesil telephoned the station to report a murder committed at number thirty-two Neruda Street. The victim was found, by the officers arriving on the scene, recumbent in bed with a pointed object sticking out of the left eye of the head resting on the right ear in a position perpendicular to the axis of the body, and its handle pointing at the window."

"I don't understand," squeaked the policewoman.

"Do you want me to say it in French?" growled the lieutenant. "The old woman was flat on her back, her head was turned to the right, with something like a dagger in her eye, that's all. What's so hard to understand about that?"

But when he recalled the scene, he had to admit that he was not being too clear. It wasn't even a dagger, really, that was stuck in the wrinkled old woman's right eye, and so the lieutenant barked at the policewoman to insert a footnote to the effect that a drawing of the murder weapon was attached. Later on, he made the drawing himself.

And then, with his eyes half-shut, he recalled the situation as he had seen it.

The old woman lay stretched out straight as a string precisely in the middle of the big double bed, with a thin little pillow under her head. Behind her, hanging over the head of the bed, within the reach of the bony hands, was a push-button switch on a cord. The handle of the odd weapon was pointed like a terrible index finger, directly at the window of the house across narrow old Neruda Street. In that window stood a bearded old man, observing the activity of the police officers with curiosity. The room – it was a spacious room on the third floor of a narrow eighteenth-century house – was full of antique furniture and all sorts of knickknacks, lamps, candlesticks, vases, reminiscent more of the storeroom of an antique shop than a bedroom. There was a sourish smell in the air, in spite of the wide-open window.

"So this is the way you found her, professor?" Lieutenant Boruvka asked the long-legged man with the disconcerted expression who was standing behind him.

"Yes, that's right. My sister-in-law brought her breakfast up for her, but she didn't respond to the knocking. The door was locked on the inside, and we were afraid that something had, had happened during the night. It's possible, you know, she was eighty-five, and, well, my sister-in-law didn't know what to do, she was so upset – so I sent her for our neighbour, and when he came, we broke down the door and –"

He nodded his head towards the old carved door, now hanging crookedly from its hinges.

"And then you sent your sister-in-law to phone for us. You didn't touch anything?"

"Not a thing. Our neighbour was here all along, weren't you, Mr. Kemmer?"

A grey-haired man in a striped shirt, who had been standing to one side, nodded his head. "I didn't want to leave the professor here by himself," he said.

"You didn't open that window?"

"No. Mother always slept with the window open, from spring till autumn. She believed in fresh air," said the professor.

"And always flat on her back like this?"

"Just like that. She used to say that sleeping on your left side puts pressure on your heart, and sleeping on your right puts pressure on your liver. And that a person should always sleep with as little as possible under his head."

"So you might say that she was fussy?"

The professor – his name was Peter Potesil – smiled sadly. "In some things, she was extremely fastidious. I should say that she kept to a very strict regimen."

"And it paid off," sounded from behind them. Unasked, a thin woman, who had perhaps once been handsome, spoke up. "Eighty-five. That's an age we'll never live to see."

Sergeant Malek turned to her sharply. "What makes you think so?" he asked dangerously.

"For heaven's sake, the worries, the rush – she lived a calm life. Nothing was allowed to disturb her comfort!"

"Barbara!" Another man, resembling the professor but not quite so tall, rebuked her. "She isn't alive any more – "

"No, let her go on," the sergeant broke in. "This is an official interrogation. What is it you were saying, ma'am?"

The woman made a face. "Take a look at this apartment," she said, and there was hatred in her voice. "Two little cubbyholes, a dining room, and this room, big as it is. This was hers – and the cubbyholes were ours. And Paul and I have three little children and Peter and Mary have two. And we weren't even allowed to use the dining room for a living room, she was used to having dinner there, she was used to sitting around there afternoons.

"What's the use of talking. It's just as simple as that – old people are sometimes unbearable."

Malek gave the lieutenant a meaningful glance. The lieutenant returned it. The case was beginning to be clear. Far too clear. The only thing that wasn't clear was the locked door.

"Let's go over it again," sighed the lieutenant. "You, professor, your wife, and two children live in the little room facing the courtyard, and you, doctor, your wife, and three children in the larger room facing out into the street. And your mother lived here in this big room."

"Yes," nodded Dr. Paul Potesil, and swallowed.

"Jim," said the lieutenant. He looked around the room. It was a high-ceilinged room in an old-fashioned house, and from the dirty ceiling hung a variety of cobwebs and antique chandeliers.

There were bronze lamps and candlesticks on the tables and stands, and dusty alabaster statuettes, a pendulum clock stood on top of the secretaire, and a number of old paintings hung on the walls. A storeroom. The man in the window opposite was leaning out and staring shamelessly across the street.

"Jim," repeated the lieutenant. "Who was the last one to see the victim alive?"

It turned out that it was Dr. Potesil. About nine o'clock in the evening, he brought her a glass of milk. That glass of milk was part of the old lady's daily health regimen, and the two families alternated regularly in carrying it out. Dr. Potesil placed the glass of milk on the table by his mother's bed, and left. He heard her lock the door behind him – as usual – and turn the key a second time as was her habit. Then he retired to the pub on the corner. For some time now, he had found evenings at home unbearable. Lieutenant Boruvka understood.

"So the last person to see her was you. The rest of the family saw her last at dinner?"

"No," volunteered Professor Potesil. "When she went to her room after dinner, I went to the kitchen for a glass of water, and she called me to her room."

"What for?"

"No real reason, actually. She told me some sort of crazy, mixed-up story about how the children had hidden her eyeglasses somewhere, and how the colonel had put them up to it, and then she gave me a lecture on rearing children."

"And then you left, and afterwards your brother went in with her glass of milk?"

"That's right."

"Hmm," growled the lieutenant again, and fixed his gaze on the bearded man in the house across the street. Was it the lieutenant's imagination, or had the fellow really grinned at him?

"One more thing," the lieutenant turned to the neighbour in the striped shirt. "When you broke down the door this morning, was the light in the room off or was it on?"

"It was off." The witness was certain. "We didn't touch a thing, and certainly not the light switch."

The lieutenant cast another look at the inquisitive fellow with the beard across the way.

"Who's that?" he asked the professor.

"That's the colonel," he replied with a smile. "The one who is supposed to put my children up to all kinds of mischief. He's retired, and staying with his widowed daughter across the street. He and my mother used to have terrible arguments."

Malek and the lieutenant exchanged glances.

"Arguments! What about? You mean they used to visit each other?"

"No, they would just argue from window to window," said the professor with just the slightest indication of a smile on his lips. "And what they argued about, heaven knows. Probably out of boredom. For that matter, ask the colonel yourself."

Malek gave the lieutenant another significant look.

"Yes, we'll do that," said the lieutenant. "We'll just do that. And now would you all go into the next room, please?"

"It is perfectly obvious," declared Malek, once the door had closed behind them. "The old battle-axe was taking up space in the apartment, and they needed to get rid of her. And they set it up so it would look as if the old man across the street did it: the room locked on the inside, the murder weapon ideal for throwing – did you notice the heavy lead front end, streamlined, and the dural-aluminium rear? Why it's just as if it were copied from a game of darts. Only lethal. And arguments across the street – "

"But the room really was locked on the inside," the lieutenant interrupted him softly.

"That's their story."

"And the neighbour's."

"Look Joe," grinned Malek, "if we take them in one by one, and try a little cross-examination, I bet we'll put an end to the locked room. They had a deal on with the neighbour."

"I don't know," said Lieutenant Boruvka. "Well, have him come in here."

"Yes indeed, the door was locked," nodded the man with the grey hair. "I looked through the keyhole myself and saw the key on the inside before we knocked down the door."

All of a sudden, the sergeant wheeled on him: "You're lying! How could the door be locked on the inside if somebody murdered her in there?"

"Don't raise your voice at me, officer," said the man in the striped shirt calmly. "And take a look out of the window. Maybe somebody could have climbed along the ledge."

Malek flushed and looked at the lieutenant uncertainly. The lieutenant nodded. Malek went to the window and leaned out.

"The doctor's wife asked me to help them with the door. I can't help it, it was really locked."

Malek returned from the window looking rebellious. “Perfectly smooth wall,” he said. “Nearest window three yards away. Do you think a fly could have done it?”

“That's up to you to find out,” the neighbour cut across the sergeant. “All I can do is swear that the door was locked and the bolt was shot.”

Both of the policemen turned inadvertently to the massive carved door. There it was, hanging by a single screw, the bolt proving that the door had been locked on the inside.

“Could it really have been the colonel across the way?” wondered Malek. “But could a person have thrown it all that way? And with an aim like that? No, somebody's trying to make fun of us.”

“It doesn't seem like fun to me,” growled Lieutenant Boruvka, and he looked at the dead woman. “But to throw this all the way across the street...” He weighed the murder weapon in his hand. Dr. Seifert had removed it from the victim’s eye, and now it was carefully wrapped in a napkin. “...that’s something I find pretty hard to believe. Unless—” he stopped in mid-sentence. The sergeant, irritated, urged him to finish it.

“Unless what?”

“Have you read ‘The Aluminium Dagger’ by Austin Freeman?”

“Oh no,” grimaced the sergeant, “not another detective mystery.”

“Oh, yes, another one. The situation was just like this one, and the murderer shot an aluminium dagger across the street out of an old musket.”

“For crying out loud!”

Lieutenant Boruvka sighed. “I don’t know what you mean. But we’ll go and take a look at the colonel.”

The bearded man was overjoyed at the arrival of the police. “Come in, do come in, gentlemen. I’m at your service, indeed I am. So you say somebody went and murdered the old crone, did they? Serves her right. He should have done it long agon.”

“It isn’t nice to talk like that,” frowned the lieutenant.

“Nice, Schmice, she was a crotchety old hag and it serves her right.”

“You hated her,” asked Malek foxily.

The old man wrinkled his nose, and his face, or what could be seen of his face beyond the borders of his full tangled beard, lit up with a joyous smile. “Am I a suspect?” he asked with unconcealed delight. “Am I really suspected of murder?”

"I didn't say anything of the kind," said Lieutenant Boruvka.

"But I had a reason to kill her," the old man insisted. "I wanted to kill her any number of times. You see that shotgun?" He pointed at a beautiful old double-barrelled shotgun hanging on the wall. "Many's the time I had a longing to load 'er up and—"

"When was the last time you saw her alive?" the lieutenant interrupted him.

The old man squinted cunningly. "Why, before I murdered her," he said.

"And when was that?"

"Last night," he said with alacrity. "I just got back from watching TV – my daughter has the TV set in the kitchen next door – and what do you know? – the light was on across the street. The old battle-axe was standing by the door with her son, the tall one, and she was talking at him hard. Then he went out. The old crone pottered around the room a little; that's when I took the shotgun down off the wall –." The old man rubbed his hands, and his eyes were shining. "But that's when the other son came in my sights; he had some milk for her or something.

"Anyway, so I had to wait a while until she drank it up. But I had my shotgun loaded here on the windowsill. Well, and then the old crone got into bed" – the old man's cheeks were blazing with excitement – "I took aim, and just when I had her monkey face in the sights, she turned her head and looked right at me with those stingy eyes of hers. And that's what she shouldn't have done, gentlemen. I might have changed my mind, but when I saw the old skinflint look me straight in the eye, well" – the old man indicated the motion with his index finger – "I pulled the trigger, and that was that!"

Sergeant Malek approached the old man, who stretched out his wrists eagerly.

"That's it, handcuffs, and make it snappy. And will you walk me through the Old Town on foot? So everybody sees me?" he asked hopefully. "Do you think the evening paper will – "

The sergeant, fascinated, actually reached into his pocket.

"Just a minute, Paul," murmured the lieutenant, and looked sombrely at the old man. "Tell me one thing, Colonel, if you shot her with your shotgun, how did you turn off the light in her bedroom?"

The bearded man looked at the old criminologist, disappointed, and the smile slowly faded. "Well, what do you know?" he said regretfully. "That's something I didn't think of. Well, you know how it is, General, every murderer makes a mistake somewhere." But the lieutenant couldn't get rid of the idea of the miracle shot, and so, before he went to lunch, he borrowed a text on ballistics from the station library. Back at his desk, he opened it hopefully. But right on the first page, he found the words, "With x and y as the vertical and horizontal axes respectively, co-ordinates for the points determining the parabolic trajectory of a missile in a vacuum as follows:

$$X(^0) = v_0 \times \cos \psi \times t$$
$$Y(^0) = v \times \sin \psi \times t\ G/2\ t^2$$ "

So, disappointed, he closed the book, and went home for lunch. At home, after an unpleasant exchange over schoolwork with his daughter Zuzana, he began to think. Then, as a punishment for his daughter, who had an afternoon lesson in preparatory mathematics, he gave her the following problem to solve there: How much atmospheric pressure would it take to expel a missile weighing half a kilogram from a muzzle with a diameter of 21.6 millimetres, in order that it attain a velocity of 6 metres per second at a distance of 12 metres?

Zuzana, unversed in mathematics, and thus incapable of judging whether the problem was easy or hard, took off for her preparatory maths lesson, under the guidance of Paul Lavecky, D.Sc. She didn't have the slightest idea that her father was relying less on her mathematical talent than on the effective assistance of the said learned gentleman.

All of the data concerning the weight and diameter of the death weapon, and its velocity upon impact, had been obtained by the lieutenant at the police laboratory earlier that day.

"Nonsense," said Dr. Seifert. "It hit the head fairly slowly, five or six metres per second at the very most. Otherwise that old skull would have looked a whole lot different, if a bomb like that had hit it any faster. It'd be shattered to bits. No, Joe, somebody must have simply tossed it."

"Besides," said Dr. Hejda, the police lab chemist, "There aren't any traces of gunpowder on it."

The lieutenant looked at him timidly. "And what if – you know the way suicides do it sometimes – what if he poured water in the barrel first – then the traces of explosive – "

"Nonsense," the ballistics expert Jandacek interrupted him. "If you want to shoot a missile that weighs over a pound, you need a small cannon, and not a shotgun. The calibre is all right, but I'm telling you, it'd have to have been a cannon. A shotgun wouldn't have been able to take it."

The lieutenant didn't let himself be put off. "Or – that would eliminate traces of gunpowder – something, in the order of an airgun – "

He didn't finish saying what he had started. Jandacek burst out laughing, and, from his sitting position on the edge of the lieutenant's desk, he fell across it onto his back.

"Great jumping Jehosephat," he bubbled. "Never, I say never, say that aloud. Particularly not in front of the chief. Or else he'll send you to keep an eye on pickpockets in the White Swan department store, if nothing worse."

The blushing lieutenant stopped asking questions. It was all nonsense. He added to the conversation that had just taken place the absurd mystery of the light in the old lady's bedroom: How could the murderer have turned it off when – according to the testimony of Dr. Potesil and that of the prison-hungry colonel – it had been on. And nobody could hit a target like that in the dark. It must be nonsense, somebody is making fun of us, the lieutenant thought to himself in the words of Sergeant Malek. This case belongs among my fantastic cases, the ones that nobody believes when I tell them, rather than in the station files.

But on the other hand, there were certain things that appeared to confirm the lieutenant's ballistic hypothesis. The locked door, and the concierge's testimony that at about nine o'clock she had heard a bang that shook the old house in Neruda Street, a report that sounded, in retrospect, for all the world like a gunshot. A noise that a number of other perfectly reliable witnesses had also heard. But it might, the lieutenant told himself, have been the backfire of one of the cars which, mounting the steep old-fashioned street, had to be given plenty of throttle.

When Zuzana had left for her preparatory maths lesson, the lieutenant settled down in the chair at his desk with a painful sigh. Nothing could be done for the present but meditate and wait for the final results of the autopsy and the lab tests. And the lieutenant preferred to meditate at home. He leaned back comfortably in his chair, closed his eyes, folded his hands behind his head, and turned his face towards the ceiling. On the inside of his eyelids, he projected the odd storeroom with the spartan sleeping facilities in the midst of it, several bronze candelabras hanging from the ceiling, statuettes of alabaster shepherdesses. He could see the wrinkled old face with the handle of the curious weapon sticking up out of one eye, the face contorted in a death cramp. He shivered. It was like the dust jacket on an American murder mystery. And the handle of the weapon pointing straight out of the window...

Suddenly he opened his eyes and stared at the abstract painting on the ceiling, the result of an absentminded bather on the floor above who had left the bathwater running. He closed his eyes again, opened them, then he humped out of his chair and pounced on Zuzana's bookshelf in the corner of the room. Once, long ago, in a praiseworthy attempt at being educational, he had hung a portrait of Comenius over the bookcase, which had more recently been joined by the photograph of another man with a beard, this time a much younger one, holding a banjo. Lieutenant Boruvka dug about furiously among his daughter's schoolbooks until he found what he was looking for. It was a book covered with wrapping paper, which in turn was covered with monstrous little drawings, and incomprehensible notes like “At five, you know where!” or “Right?” (in an unfamiliar handwriting); “Right” (Zuzana's handwriting); “That's great!” (the former handwriting); “Isn't it?” (Zuzana's hand again). Almost lost among the scrolls and scribbles was the book's title, Second Year Physics. The lieutenant took it to his desk and flipped the pages until something caught his eye. He pulled up a notepad, picked up a pencil, and within the course of the next hour, filled the page with the calculations.

He had just come up with a ten-mile altitude, and crossed it out disgustedly, when Zuzana arrived home from her maths lesson.

“Did you do the problem I gave you?” he asked in as severe a tone as he could muster. Zuzana pursed her lips.

“No, Daddy,” she replied.

“And why not, pray?”

“We had the principal teaching us today, because Professor Lavecky had to miss class on account of a voluntary brigade. And the principal said,” she explained, “that although he is aware of the fact that the science of ballistics is near and dear to you as a criminologist, nonetheless, he as a teacher has an obligation to guide us towards the idea of peaceful co-existence among all the nations of the world, and so he thinks that it would not be proper to teach us mathematics on problems of ballistics."

"Is that what he said?" asked the lieutenant pointedly. He wondered whether that intolerant choleric individual hadn't fallen victim to the attack of pacifism only after he had looked up the equations:

$$x(^0) = v_o \times \cos\psi \times t \text{ and } y(^\circ) = v_o \ \sin \psi \times t - G/2 \times t^2.$$

He didn't say it aloud, though, and continued interrogating his daughter.

"What did you cover today?"

"Equations in one unknown."

"How did you do?"

"Not bad," said Zuzana, and looked her father straight in the eye.

"Well, we'll see how you did," said her father ominously. "Sit down and take a pencil and a piece of paper. And now, write. From what altitude—"

"But Daddy, I wanted to watch TV. There's a programme with—"

"Quiet, sit down and write!"

"But Daddy—"

"No TV until you work out a problem," decided her father. "We'll soon find out whether or not you know anything about equations with one unknown. Write!"

"But—"

"YOU HEARD ME!" roared Lieutenant Boruvka in a mighty voice. The unusually forcible volume surprised Zuzana to the point of making her sit down obediently at her desk in the corner, and, with a tearful look at the bearded banjo player, take down what her father dictated : "From what altitude must an object weighing 500 grammes fall in order to achieve an impact velocity of six metres per second. Got it?"

"Yes, Daddy," whined Zuzana.

"Now work it out. I'll go in the other room and watch TV so you couldn't say that I was in your way here."

That last sentence was not quite honest. His departure for the other room was based on a plan founded on the full knowledge of Zuzana's psyche, particularly where problems in mathematics were concerned.

The room with the TV was empty. Mrs Boruvkova was out with Joey at a party, and when the lieutenant had shut the door behind him, he remained standing there with an ear laid quietly to its painted surface. His calculations had been correct —not the ones on paper, resulting in 18 kilometres, but the ones concerning his daughter's activity within the ensuing minutes.

A soft sound could be heard through the door, resembling the whirring given off by an old pendulum clock when you are winding it. It sounded six consecutive times, each time lasting less than a second. There was a brief silence, and then Zuzana could be heard, speaking softly.

“Oliver? HO—Say, he gave me a problem to work—that's right, a maths problem—he says I can't watch TV until I do it—but Oliver, Ollie, say you're a pal—it's nothing at all for you—all right, thanks, grab a pencil and some paper, and hurry up, he's next door gawking at that blonde blues singer of his.”

Behind the door, “he” bridled at the mention of the blues singer. He had hoped that his interest in TV programmes in which the said blonde performed had gone unnoticed by his daughter. Apparently it hadn't.

“All right, are you ready?—then take it down: from what altitude must an object weighing 500 grammes fall—” dictated Zuzana in a soft voice, and the lieutenant listened. Under different circumstances, he would have taken drastic steps against this underhand manner of obtaining knowledge, but this time...

“What?” he heard her say, “what do you say?—the weight is unnecessary? The formula for free fall is the same regardless of mass? Well, you know him. He's forgotten his multiplication tables already. He doesn't need them for those murderers of his.”

Behind the door, the lieutenant blushed a little, and went to sit down in the armchair in front of the TV set. He sat there for a good quarter of an hour and forgot to turn it on. Then he heard the sounds reminiscent of the winding of an old cuckoo clock again, and Zuzana speaking in a quiet voice again. Then there was a long silence, interrupted only by the scratching of a blunt pencil on a pad of paper. “Thanks, Ollie, you're a darling!” she whispered finally, and then there was a silence following the tinkle of the phone being hung up. The lieutenant, engrossed in thought, wondered morbidly how he must appear to his daughter, and realised that he must seem like an old man, and that that undoubtedly is the way he appears to another young woman, not too many years older than Zuzana and possessing a regal chignon—he was rescued from these unpleasant thoughts by the squeak of the door and Zuzana's voice, the soft one that she used for wheedling: "I've got it, Daddy."

"You have? Well, all right, let's see!" He almost ripped the paper out of her hand, and immersed himself in the calculations.

"Can I turn it on now? The answer is right," purred Zuzana.

Her father nodded absent-mindedly. When Zuzana flicked the switch on the TV set and settled down blissfully on the hassock beside her father's armchair, the lieutenant got up and walked, with the air of a sleepwalker, to his study.

There, he placed the sheet of paper on his desk under the lamp.

In Zuzana's neat handwriting, the computations started in the same way his had, but then continued differently.

The lieutenant stared for a long time at the result, so very different from the one he had arrived at, and he growled reluctantly, "That could be right."

His eyes grew sadder. In the hallway, he put on his raincoat and hat, and he left the apartment in a hurry. As he shut the door, he could hear the bearded banjo player insisting that the yellow rose of Texas was the only girl for him, in Czech. But not even this encouraging statement succeeded in cheering him up.

Constable First Class Sintak opened the door to the apartment in Neruda Street for the lieutenant, and saluted respectfully.

"Have you come to make an arrest, Lieutenant?" he asked, gravely.

"Maybe," replied the lieutenant, and disappeared behind the door of the room where the dead old woman had been found that morning.

He turned the light switch by the door, and looked around. One of the chandeliers, refurbished as an electric light fixture, had been turned on. It was the big one in the centre of the room, over the round polished dining-table. The old lady had apparently had a weakness for chandeliers—there were all of five of them hanging from the ceiling of the room.

One of them hung directly over the bed.

Lieutenant Boruvka sighed and approached the bed. He stood there for a while, staring at it, and thinking about something. Then he looked up at the ceiling, and the heavy bronze chandelier hanging over the bed. It had two arms with light bulbs attached, and above them was a sort of a stand, displaying the figurine of some classic god or other. Maybe it was Mercury. The lieutenant didn't know, didn't really care.

His hand went out slowly to the push-button switch on a cord hanging over the head of the bed, within the reach of the person lying in bed.

He pressed it, and both arms lit up. The little god glowed.

For some time the lieutenant gazed at that vestige of the late Baroque period, electrified for the twentieth century. The electric cord wound around the shiny rod that supported the stand with the little god. He couldn't take his eyes off it. Several times he made a motion as if he wanted to climb up on to the bed, but each time he changed his mind again. The round face expressed something akin to inner suffering. It seemed that Lieutenant Boruvka was afraid of something. Perhaps it was the disappointment he would feel if the fantastic thing he had tricked his daughter's classmate into figuring out for him proved wrong. Or rather, if it proved correct.

Finally, he took courage. He switched off the light, took off his shoes, and climbed on to the bed. When he straightened up, the cowlick on top of his head touched the bottom part of the chandelier, where there was a bronze rosette. Once again, he became thoughtful, and once again he stared at the rosette, but it was not with admiration, although it was a beautiful asymmetrical work, with the face of a cherub in the middle.

He reached up, touched the cherub inquisitively with his forefinger, carefully; then with thumb and forefinger, he grasped its little bronze nose, and pulled.

The cherub tipped open. It was fastened on one side to the lower part of the chandelier with a spring that obviously did not date back to the Baroque period. And above it, at the base of the shiny rod that supported the god's stand, gaped a round hole reminiscent of the bore of a 12-gauge shotgun.

The lieutenant's expression grew even more mournful. He reached up and twisted the statuette of the god.

It turned. It was fastened to the stand with a screw. He removed it carefully, and found that it was hollow, and that its hollow had concealed two fat coils that gave off a coppery sheen in the fading light of evening.

The contemptuous opinion of his daughter to the contrary, the lieutenant still recalled enough elementary physics to recognise an electromagnet when he saw it.

"The electromagnet was placed inside the chandelier," he dictated with despicable superciliousness to the young policewoman, "parenthesis 'drawing attached' end parenthesis--here is the drawing."

He tossed his drawing of the chandelier on to the desk in front of the girl at the typewriter.

He allowed a pause long enough for her to admire his drawing abilities to the full, and then he went on dictating: "All right then, the electromagnet was placed inside the chandelier by Professor Potesil, who, as we determined, is a professor of physics. He also fastened the spring on to the cherub. He had plenty of opportunity to do so, as, according to the previous testimony of Mrs Barbara Potesil, she was in the habit of spending her afternoon in the dining-room."

"Who was?" asked the policewoman.

"The victim, naturally. And thus the bedroom was empty. Potesil, moreover, admits that earlier that evening he had entered the bedroom of the victim—wait a minute, put victim-to-be or something like that, but make sure it doesn't look sloppy—and loosened the light bulbs in the chandelier. He had determined earlier by means of experiments conducted at times when the old woman had retired to the dining-room during the daytime that the mouth of the rod in the chandelier opens directly over the pillow where the old woman, who was generally known to be extremely fastidious, was in the habit of placing her head when she—"

"Full stop?" suggested the policewoman.

"All right," replied the lieutenant, irritated. "Put a full stop after 'head'. And let's get going. After dinner of the fateful day, the professor followed the old woman out of the dining-room, and upon determining that the chandelier over the bed didn't work—"

"Who, lieutenant? The professor or the old woman?"

"The old woman of course. He knew it! Anyway, when she determined that the light didn't work, she called the professor into her room. He tightened the two light bulbs, which lit up, and simultaneously covertly slipped the projectile into the tube. The electromagnet, which was connected to the regular electrical circuit by means of the cord to the switch that controlled the light, but insulated from the bulbs, of course, the electromagnet held the murder weapon in the tube by means of the iron plate affixed to the end of it by means of a screw that—"

"Full stop?" asked the policewoman.

"Full stop," growled Lieutenant Boruvka. "When subsequently the subsequently murdered—no, wait a minute—when subsequently the later victim—the late victim no, that's not it, put: Later when the old woman went to bed, and reached behind her by memory for the switch and turned off the light, the power supply to the electromagnet was interrupted which caused the projectile to be released, opening the hole covered by the cherub by its own weight—" The lieutenant paused, sensing a misplaced qualifying clause, and then, quickly, said, "—full stop."

"The projectile, released, fell on to the victim's head at a velocity of six metres per second. In view of the sharpness of the point and the weight of the weapon, and the age of the victim parenthesis eight-five years and seven months end parenthesis the impact was fatal. The weight of the handle turned the victim's head to the right and made it appear that the weapon had been thrown through the open window. Furthermore the professor knew that the murdered woman—no, put that his victim was in the habit of getting up after his brother and his wife—no, better put down between his and wife—else put the wife first, in front of the brother, that's it, like this: after his wife and his brother left the apartment; and so he was counting on the crime being discovered by his sister-in-law when she brought the old woman breakfast. In order to make sure of another non-partisan witness, he had the unsuspecting neighbour called to help break down the door to the locked room.

The lieutenant gave a satisfied pause, and looked over the policewoman's shoulder. He intentionally ignored the long, lovely neck and the chignon.

"There," he said. "And at the end, put Motive with a capital

M, colon, the crisis produced by the housing shortage in the family of Professor Potesil and Doctor Potesil, his brother."

Lieutenant Boruvka sat back, musing over the argument that he and the sergeant had had over that. Sergeant Malek known as an inveterate supporter of capital punishment and famous for being indomitable with regard to murderers, had softened up when analysing this case, and had said:

"You know, Joe, it's a nasty business, it really is. But I sort of feel for them. The old gal was as old as Methuselah, no earthly good to anybody at all. There's a housing shortage, and what does an old woman like that need all that room for? And those people lived like sardines."

Surprisingly the lieutenant, an out-and-out opponent of capital punishment, and a collector of extenuating circumstances of all varieties, frowned.

"But they were people," he said, "not sardines."

"Exactly," said Malek, significantly.

"Exactly," said Lieutenant Boruvka, equally significantly.

Malek thought that his superior was voicing agreement. But the lieutenant was possessed by the idea of how he would be treated, as the possessor of a three-roomed apartment, where with some small interruptions he had already spent eighteen years of his life—no matter what kind of a life, it was a life, and that was what mattered—and how long had that fussy old woman lived in that store-room of hers? How would he be treated when he was really old, and no earthly use to anybody at all—?

"Was there anything else, lieutenant?" He heard the velvety and somewhat stiff voice of the policewoman.

He immediately assumed a disgruntled frown.

"No, give it here. Let me see."

He took the sheets of paper from her, and they seemed to be typed with heavier strokes than usual. He glanced at the title: Report on the Classification of the Case of the Vertical Trajectory.

He was furious.

"Why did you put vertical? I remember quite clearly dictating horizontal?"

The policewoman, offended, tossed her head on her lovely long neck, and said, "You know what, lieutenant? Look up horizontal in the dictionary."

Real Life Impossibility: Barbados
The Moving Coffins

In 1808 Thomas Chase of Barbados acquired for his family's use a burial vault in Christ Church, Barbados. Sadly, he had occasion to use the vault almost immediately, as his infant daughter Mary was interred there in 1808, and another daughter, Dorcas, was interred in 1812.

Later in 1812 Chase himself died, and on August 9 of that year the vault was opened. At this time the coffins of Mary and Dorcas were found to have been moved, with Mary's apparently flung all the way to the other end of the vault. Thomas Chase was interred, and Mary's and Dorcas's coffins replaced.

Other family deaths in 1816 and 1819 occasioned the opening of the vault several more times, with various coffins found to have been moved each time. After the 1819 incident, the marble slab sealing the entrance was cemented shut. Even so, on the reopening of the tomb in 1820 all but one of the caskets were in disarray, and Dorcas Chase's coffin had a hole in the side, out of which protruded the bones of one arm.

After this the Chase Vault was abandoned, and all the caskets were relocated elsewhere. Theories of flooding and earthquakes that might account for the mysterious disruptions were investigated but no substantiation was ever found, and the mystery remains today.

Ireland
The Mystery of the Sleeping-Car Express
by Freeman Wills Crofts

Freeman Wills Crofts was one of the giants of the detective story world in the first half of the 20th century, and was at one time considered one of the "Big Five," the others being H.C. Bailey, Agatha Christie, R. Austin Freeman, and Dorothy Sayers.

His twin specialities were plots involving detailed transportation plans, usually on boats or trains, and the analysis and breaking of apparently ironclad alibis. Two of his books, *The End of Andrew Harrison* and *Sudden Death*, are good locked room mysteries, but some of the "alibi" mysteries also qualify, when the alibi seems impossible to break. A good example is *Tragedy at the Hollow.*

The problem in this story is clearly a locked room, described thus: "That is to say, inspector, you have proved the murderer was in the coach at the time of the crime, that he was not in it when it was searched, and that he did not leave it in the interval." A pretty problem aboard an English train in 1909.

No one who was in England in the autumn of 1909 can fail to remember the terrible tragedy which took place in a North-Western express between Preston and Garlisle. The affair attracted enormous attention at the time, not only because of the arresting nature of the events themselves, but even more for the absolute mystery in which they were shrouded.

Quite lately a singular chance has revealed to me the true explanation of the terrible drama, and it is at the express desire of its chief actor that I now take upon myself to make the facts known. As it is a long time since 1909, I may, perhaps, be pardoned if I first recall the events which came to light at the time.

One Thursday, then, early in November of the year in question, the 10:30 p.m. sleeping-car train left Euston as usual for Edinburgh, Glasgow, and the North. It was generally a heavy train, being popular with businessmen who liked to complete their day's work in London, sleep while travelling, and arrive at their northern destination with time for a leisurely bath and breakfast before office hours. The night in question was no exception to the rule, and two engines hauled behind them eight large sleeping-cars, two firsts, two thirds, and two vans, half of which went to Glasgow, and the remainder to Edinburgh.

It is essential to the understanding of what follows that the composition of the rear portion of the train should be remembered. At the extreme end came the Glasgow van, a long eight-wheeled, bogie vehicle, with Guard Jones in charge. Next to the van was one of the third-class coaches, and immediately in front of it came a first class, both labeled for the same city. These coaches were fairly well filled, particularly the third class. In front of the first class came the last of the four Glasgow sleepers. The train was corridor throughout, and the officials could, and did, pass through it several times during the journey.

It is with the first-class coach that we are principally concerned, and it will be understood from the above that it was placed in between the sleeping car in front and the third-class behind, the van following immediately behind the third. It had a lavatory at each end and six compartments, the last two, next to the third-class, being smokers, the next three non-smoking, and the first, immediately beside the sleeping car, a Ladies Only. The corridors in both it and the third-class coach were on the left-hand side in the direction of travel – that is, the compartments were on the side of the double line.

The night was dark as the train drew out of Euston, for there was no moon and the sky was overcast. As was remembered and commented on afterwards, there had been an unusually long spell of dry weather and, though it looked like rain earlier in the evening, none fell till the next day, when, about six in the morning, there was a torrential downpour.

As the detectives pointed out later, no weather could have been more unfortunate from their point of view, as, had footmarks been made during the night, the ground would have been too hard to take good impressions, while even such traces as remained would more than likely have been blurred by the rain.

The train ran to time, stopping at Rugby, Grewe, and Preston. After leaving the latter station Guard Jones found he had occasion to go forward to speak to a ticket collector in the Edinburgh portion. He accordingly left his van in the rear and passed along the corridor of the third-class carriage adjoining.

At the end of this corridor, beside the vestibule joining it to the first-class, were a lady and gentleman, evidently husband and wife, the lady endeavouring to soothe the cries of a baby she was carrying. Guard Jones addressed some civil remark to the man, who explained that their child had been taken ill, and they had brought it out of their compartment as it was disturbing the other passengers.

With an expression of sympathy, Jones unlocked the two doors across the corridor at the vestibule between the carriages and, passing on into the first-class coach, re-closed them behind him. They were fitted with spring locks, which became fast on the door shutting.

The corridor of the first-class coach was empty, and as Jones walked down it he observed that the blinds of all the compartments were lowered, with one exception – that of the Ladies Only. In this compartment, which contained three ladies, the light was fully on, and the guard noticed that two out of the three were reading.

Continuing his journey, Jones found that the two doors at the vestibule between the first-class coach and the sleeper were also locked, and he opened them and passed through, shutting them behind him. At the sleeping-car attendant's box, just inside the last of these doors, two car attendants were talking together. One was actually inside the box, the other standing in the corridor. The latter moved aside to let the guard pass, taking up his former position as, after exchanging a few words, Jones moved on.

His business with the ticket collector finished, Guard Jones returned to his van. On this journey he found the same conditions obtaining as on the previous – the two attendants were at the rear end of the sleeping car, the lady and gentleman with the baby in the front end of the third-class coach, the first-class corridor deserted, and both doors at each end of the latter coach locked. These details, casually remarked at the time, became afterwards of the utmost importance, adding as they did to the mystery in which the tragedy was enveloped.

About an hour before the train was due at Carlisle, while it was passing through the wild moorland country of the Westmorland highlands, the brakes were applied – at first gently, and then with considerable power. Guard Jones, who was examining parcel waybills in the rear end of his van, supposed it to be a signal check, but as such was unusual at this place, he left his work and, walking down the van, lowered the window at the left-hand side and looked out along the train.

The line happened to be in a cutting, and the railway bank for some distance ahead was dimly illuminated by the light from the corridors of the first- and third-class coaches immediately in front of his van. As I have said, the night was dark and, except for this bit of bank, Jones could see nothing ahead. The railway curved away to the right, so, thinking he might see better from the other side, he crossed the van and looked out of the opposite window, next the up line.

There were no signal lights in view, nor anything to suggest the cause of the slack, but as he ran his eye along the train he saw that something was amiss in the first-class coach. From the window at its rear end figures were leaning, gesticulating wildly, as if to attract attention to some grave and pressing danger. The guard at once ran through the third-class to this coach, and there he found a strange and puzzling state of affairs.

The corridor was still empty, but the centre blind of the rear compartment – that is, the first reached by the guard – had been raised. Through the glass Jones could see that the compartment contained four men. Two were leaning out of the window on the opposite side, and two were fumbling at the latch of the corridor door, as if trying to open it. Jones caught hold of the outside handle to assist, but they pointed in the direction of the adjoining compartment, and the guard, obeying their signs, moved on to the second door.

The centre blind of this compartment had also been pulled up, though here, again, the door had not been opened. As the guard peered in through the glass he saw that he was in the presence of a tragedy.

Tugging desperately at the handle of the corridor door stood a lady, her face blanched, her eyes starting from her head, and her features frozen into an expression of deadly fear and horror. As she pulled she kept glancing over her shoulder, as if some dreadful apparition lurked in the shadows behind. As Jones sprang forward to open the door his eyes followed the direction of her gaze, and he drew in his breath sharply.

At the far side of the compartment, facing the engine and huddled down in the corner, was the body of a woman. She lay limp and inert, with head tilted back at an unnatural angle into the cushions and a hand hanging helplessly down over the edge of the seat. She might have been thirty years of age, and was dressed in a reddish-brown fur coat with toque to match. But these details the guard hardly glanced at, his attention being riveted to her forehead. There, above the left eyebrow, was a sinister little hole, from which the blood had oozed down the coat and formed a tiny pool on the seat. That she was dead was obvious.

But this was not all. On the seat opposite her lay a man, and, as far as Guard Jones could see, he also was dead.

He apparently had been sitting in the corner seat, and had fallen forward so that his chest lay across the knees of the woman and his head hung down towards the floor. He was all bunched and twisted up – just a shapeless mass in a grey frieze overcoat, with dark hair at the back of what could be seen of his head. But under that head the guard caught the glint of falling drops, while a dark, ominous stain grew on the floor beneath.

Jones flung himself on the door, but it would not move. It stood fixed, an inch open, jammed in some mysterious way, imprisoning the lady with her terrible companions. As she and the guard strove to force it open, the train came to a standstill. At once it occurred to Jones that he could now enter the compartment from the opposite side.

Shouting to reassure the now almost frantic lady, he turned back to the end compartment, intending to pass through it on to the line and so back so that containing the bodies. But here he was again baffled, for the two men had not succeeded in sliding back their door. He seized the handle to help them, and then he noticed their companions had opened the opposite door and were climbing out onto the permanent way.

It flashed through his mind that an up-train passed about this time and, fearing an accident, he ran down the corridor to the sleeping car, where he felt sure he would find a door that would open. That at the near end was free, and he leaped out onto the track. As he passed he shouted to one of the attendants to follow him, and to the other to remain where he was and let no one pass. Then he joined the men who had already alighted, warned them about the up-train, and the four opened the outside door of the compartment in which the tragedy had taken place.

Their first concern was to get the un-injured lady out, and here a difficult and ghastly task awaited them. The door was blocked by the bodies, and its narrowness prevented more than one man from working. Sending the car attendant to search the train for a doctor, Jones clambered up, and, after warning the lady not to look at what he was doing, he raised the man's body and propped it back in the corner seat.

The face was a strong one with clean-shaven but rather coarse features, a large nose, and a heavy jaw. In the neck, just below the right ear, was a bullet hole which, owing to the position of the head, had bled freely. As far as the guard could see, the man was dead. Not without a certain shrinking, Jones raised the feet, first of the man, and then of the woman, and placed them on the seats, thus leaving the floor clear except for its dark, creeping pool. Then, placing his handkerchief over the dead woman's face, he rolled back the end of the carpet to hide its sinister stain.

"Now, ma'am, if you please," he said, and keeping the lady with her back to the more gruesome object on the opposite seat, he helped her to the open door, from where willing hands assisted her to the ground.

By this time the attendant had found a doctor in the third-class coach, and a brief examination enabled him to pronounce both victims dead. The blinds in the compartment having been drawn down and the outside door locked, the guard called to those passengers who had alighted to resume their seats, with a view to continuing their journey.

The fireman had meantime come back along the train to ascertain what was wrong and to say the driver was unable completely to release the brake. An examination was therefore made, and the telltale disc at the end of the first-class coach was found to be turned, showing that someone in that carriage had pulled the communication chain. This, as is perhaps not generally known, allows air to pass between the train pipe and the atmosphere, thereby gently applying the brake and preventing its complete release. Further investigation showed that the slack of the chain was hanging in the end smoking compartment, indicating that the alarm must have been operated by one of the four men who travelled there. The disc was then turned back to normal, the passengers reseated, and the train started, after a delay of about fifteen minutes.

Before reaching Carlisle, Guard Jones took the name and address of everyone travelling in the first- and third-class coaches, together with the numbers of their tickets. These coaches, as well as the van, were thoroughly searched, and it was established beyond any doubt that no one was concealed under the seats, in the lavatories, behind luggage, or, in fact, anywhere about them.

One of the sleeping-car attendants having been in the corridor in the rear of the last sleeper from the Preston stop till the completion of this search, and being positive no one except the guard had passed during that time, it was not considered necessary to take the names of the passengers in the sleeping cars, but the numbers of their tickets were noted.

On arrival at Carlisle the matter was put into the hands of the police. The first-class carriage was shunted off, the doors being locked and sealed, and the passengers who had travelled in it were detained to make their statements. Then began a most careful and searching investigation, as a result of which several additional facts became known.

The first step taken by the authorities was to make an examination of the country surrounding the point at which the train had stopped, in the hope of finding traces of some stranger on the line. The tentative theory was that a murder had been committed and that the murderer had escaped from the train when it stopped, struck across the country and, gaining some road, had made good his escape.

Accordingly, as soon as it was light, a special train brought a force of detectives to the place, and the railway, as well as a tract of ground on each side of it, were subjected to a prolonged and exhaustive search. But no traces were found. Nothing that a stranger might have dropped was picked up, no footsteps were seen, no marks discovered. As has already been stated, the weather was against the searchers.

The drought of the previous days had left the ground hard and unyielding, so that clear impressions were scarcely to be expected, while even such as might have been made were not likely to remain after the downpour of the early morning.

Baffled at this point, the detectives turned their attention to the stations in the vicinity. There were only two within walking distance of the point of the tragedy, and at neither had any stranger been seen. Further, no trains had stopped at either of these stations; indeed, not a single train, either passenger or goods, had stopped anywhere in the neighbourhood since the sleeping-car express went through. If the murderer had left the express, it was, therefore, out of the question that he could have escaped by rail.

The investigators then turned their attention to the country roads and adjoining towns, trying to find the trail – if there was a trail – while it was hot. But here, again, no luck attended their efforts. If there were a murderer, and if he had left the train when it stopped, he had vanished into thin air. No traces of him could anywhere be discovered.

Nor were their researches in other directions much more fruitful.

The dead couple were identified as a Mr. and Mrs. Horatio Llewelyn, of Gordon Villa, Broad Road, Halifax. Mr. Llewelyn was the junior partner of a large firm of Yorkshire iron-founders. A man of five-and-thirty, he moved in good society and had some claim to wealth. He was of kindly, though somewhat passionate disposition and, so far as could be learnt, had not an enemy in the world. His firm was able to show that he had had business appointments in London on the Thursday and in Garlisle on the Friday, so that his travelling by the train in question was quite in accordance with his known plans.

His wife was the daughter of a neighbouring merchant, a pretty girl of some seven-and-twenty. They had been married only a little over a month, and had, in fact, only a week earlier returned from their honeymoon. Whether Mrs. Llewelyn had any definite reason for accompanying her husband on the fatal journey could not be ascertained. She also, so far as was known, had no enemy, nor could any motive for the tragedy be suggested.

The extraction of the bullets proved that the same weapon had been used in each case – a revolver of small bore and modern design. But as many thousands of similar revolvers existed, this discovery led to nothing.

Miss Blair-Booth, the lady who had travelled with the Llewelyns, stated she had joined the train at Euston, and occupied one of the seats next the corridor. A couple of minutes before starting the deceased had arrived, and they sat in the two opposite corners. No other passengers had entered the compartment during the journey, nor had any of the three left it; in fact, except for the single visit of the ticket collector shortly after leaving Euston, the door into the corridor had not been even opened.

Mr. Llewelyn was very attentive to his young wife, and they had conversed for some time after starting, then, after consulting Miss Blair-Booth, he had pulled down the blinds and shaded the light, and they had settled down for the night. Miss Blair-Booth had slept at intervals, but each time she wakened she had looked round the compartment, and everything was as before. Then she was suddenly aroused from a doze by a loud explosion close by.

She sprang up, and as she did so a flash came from somewhere near her knee, and a second explosion sounded. Startled and trembling, she pulled the shade off the lamp, and then she noticed a little cloud of smoke just inside the corridor door, which had been opened about an inch, and smelled the characteristic odour of burnt powder. Swinging round, she was in time to see Mr. Llewelyn dropping heavily forward across his wife's knees, and then she observed the mark on the latter's forehead and realized they had both been shot.

Terrified, she raised the blind of the corridor door which covered the handle and tried to get out to call assistance. But she could not move the door, and her horror was not diminished when she found herself locked in with what she rightly believed were two dead bodies. In despair she pulled the communication chain, but the train did not appear to stop, and she continued struggling with the door till, after what seemed to her hours, the guard appeared, and she was eventually released.

In answer to a question, she further stated that when her blind went up the corridor was empty, and she saw no one till the guard came.

The four men in the end compartment were members of one party travelling from London to Glasgow. For some time after leaving they had played cards, but, about midnight, they too had pulled down their blinds, shaded their lamp, and composed themselves to sleep. In this case also, no person other than the ticket collector had entered the compartment during the journey. But after leaving Preston the door had been opened. Aroused by the stop, one of the men had eaten some fruit, and having thereby soiled his fingers, had washed them in the lavatory. The door then opened as usual. This man saw no one in the corridor, nor did he notice anything out of the common.

Sometime after this all four were startled by the sound of two shots. At first they thought of fog signals, then, realizing they were too far from the engine to hear such, they, like Miss Blair-Booth, unshaded their lamp, raised the blind over their corridor door, and endeavoured to leave the compartment. Like her they found themselves unable to open their door, and, like her also, they saw that there was no one in the corridor.

Believing something serious had happened, they pulled the communication chain, at the same time lowering the outside window and waving from it in the hope of attracting attention. The chain came down easily as if slack, and this explained the apparent contradiction between Miss Blair-Booth's statement that she had pulled it, and the fact that the slack was found hanging in the end compartment. Evidently the lady had pulled it first, applying the brake, and the second pull had simply transferred the slack from one compartment to the next.

The two compartments in front of that of the tragedy were found to be empty when the train stopped, but in the last of the non-smoking compartments were two gentlemen, and in the Ladies Only three ladies. All these had heard the shots, but so faintly above the noise of the train that the attention of none of them was especially arrested, nor had they attempted any investigation. The gentlemen had not left their compartment or pulled up their blinds between the time the train left Preston and the emergency stop, and could throw no light whatever on the matter.

The three ladies in the end compartment were a mother and two daughters, and had got in at Preston. As they were alighting at Carlisle they had not wished to sleep, so they had left their blinds up and their light unshaded. Two of them were reading, but the third was seated at the corridor side, and this lady stated positively that no one except the guard had passed while they were in the train.

She described his movements – first, towards the engine, secondly, back towards the van, and a third time, running, towards the engine after the train had stopped – so accurately in accord with the other evidence that considerable reliance was placed on her testimony. The stoppage and the guard's haste had aroused her interest, and all three ladies had immediately come out into the corridor and had remained there till the train proceeded, and all three were satisfied that no one else had passed during that time.

An examination of the doors which had jammed so mysteriously revealed the fact that a small wooden wedge, evidently designed for the purpose, had been driven in between the floor and the bottom of the framing of the door, holding the latter rigid. It was evident therefore that the crime was premeditated and the details had been carefully worked out beforehand. The most careful search of the carriage failed to reveal any other suspicious object or mark.

On comparing the tickets issued with those held by the passengers, a discrepancy was discovered. All were accounted for except one. A first single for Glasgow had been issued at Euston for the train in question, which had not been collected. The purchaser had therefore either not travelled at all, or had got out at some intermediate station. In either case, no demand for a refund had been made.

The collector who had checked the tickets after the train left London believed, though he could not speak positively, that two men had then occupied the non-smoking compartment next to that in which the tragedy had occurred, one of whom held a Glasgow ticket, and the other a ticket for an intermediate station. He could not recollect which station nor could he describe either of the men, if indeed they were there at all.

But the ticket collector’s recollection was not at fault, for the police succeeded in tracing one of these passengers, a Dr. Hill, who had got out at Crewe. He was able, partially at all events, to account for the missing Glasgow ticket. It appeared that when he joined the train at Euston, a man of about five-and-thirty was already in the compartment. This man had fair hair, blue eyes, and a full moustache, and was dressed in dark well-cut clothes. He had no luggage, but only a waterproof and a paper-covered novel. The two travellers had got into conversation, and on the stranger learning that the doctor lived at Crewe said he was alighting there also, and asked to be recommended to a hotel. He then explained that he had intended to go on to Glasgow and had taken a ticket to that city, but had since decided to break his journey to visit a friend in Chester next day. He asked the doctor if he thought his ticket would be available to complete the journey the following night, and if not, whether he could get a refund.

When they reached Crewe, both these travellers had alighted, and the doctor offered to show his acquaintance the entrance to the Crewe Arms, but the stranger, thanking him, declined, saying he wished to see to his luggage. Dr. Hill saw him walking towards the van as he left the platform.

Upon interrogating the staff on duty at Crewe at the time, no one could recall seeing such a man at the van, nor had any inquiries about luggage been made. But as these facts did not come to light until several days after the tragedy, confirmation was hardly to be expected.

A visit to all the hotels in Crewe and Chester revealed the fact that no one in any way resembling the stranger had stayed there, nor could any trace whatever be found of him.

Such were the principal facts made known at the adjourned inquest on the bodies of Mr. and Mrs. Llewelyn. It was confidently believed that a solution to the mystery would speedily be found, but as day after day passed away without bringing to light any fresh information, public interest began to wane, and became directed into other channels.

But for a time controversy over the affair waxed keen. At first it was argued that it was a case of suicide, some holding that Mr. Llewelyn had shot first his wife and then himself; others that both had died by the wife's hand. But this theory had only to be stated to be disproved.

Several persons hastened to point out that not only had the revolver disappeared, but on neither body was there powder blackening, and it was admitted that such a wound could not be self-inflicted without leaving marks from this source. That murder had been committed was therefore clear.

Rebutted on this point, the theorists then argued that Miss Blair-Booth was the assassin. But here again the suggestion was quickly negatived. The absence of motive, her known character, and the truth of such of her statements as could be checked were against the idea. The disappearance of the revolver was also in her favour. As it was not in the compartment nor concealed about her person, she could only have rid herself of it out of the widow. But the position of the bodies prevented access to the window, and, as her clothes were free from any stain of blood, it was impossible to believe she had moved these grim relics, even had she been physically able.

But the point that finally demonstrated her innocence was the wedging of the corridor door. It was obvious she could not have wedged the door on the outside and then passed through it. The belief was universal that whoever wedged the door fired the shots, and the fact that the former was wedged an inch open strengthened that view, as the motive was clearly to leave a lot through which to shoot.

Lastly, the medical evidence showed that if the Llewelyns were sitting where Miss Blair-Booth stated, and the shots were fired from where she said, the bullets would have entered the bodies from the direction they were actually found to have done.

But Miss Blair-Booth's detractors were loath to recede from the position they had taken up. They stated that of the objections to their theory only one – the wedging of the doors – was overwhelming. And they advanced an ingenious theory to meet it. They suggested that before reaching Preston, Miss Blair-Booth had left the compartment, closing the door after her, that she had then wedged it, and that, on stopping at the station, she had passed out through some other compartment, re-entering her own through the outside door.

In answer to this it was pointed out that the gentleman who had eaten the fruit had opened his door after the Preston stop, and if Miss Blair-Booth was then shut into her compartment she could not have wedged the other door. That two people should be concerned in the wedging was unthinkable. It was therefore clear that Miss Blair-Booth was innocent, and that some other person had wedged both doors, in order to prevent his operations in the corridor being interfered with by those who would hear the shots.

It was recognized that similar arguments applied to the four men in the end compartment – the wedging of the doors cleared them also.

Defeated on these points the theorists retired from the field. No further suggestions were put forward by the public or the daily press. Even to those behind the scenes the case seemed to become more and more difficult the longer it was pondered.

Each person known to have been present came in turn under the microscopic eye of New Scotland Yard, but each in turn had to be eliminated from suspicion, till it almost seemed proved that no murder could have been committed at all. The prevailing mystification was well summed up by the chief at the Yard in conversation with the inspector in charge of the case.

"A troublesome business, certainly," said the great man, "and I admit that your conclusions seem sound. But let us go over it again. There must be a flaw somewhere."

"There must, sir. But I've gone over it and over it till I'm stupid, and every time I get the same result."

"We'll try once more. We begin, then, with a murder in a railway carriage. We're sure it was a murder, of course?"

"Certain, sir. The absence of the revolver and of powder blackening and the wedging of the doors prove it."

"Quite. The murder must therefore have been committed by some person who was either in the carriage when it was searched, or had left before that. Let us take these two possibilities in turn. And first, with regard to the searching. Was that efficiently done?"

"Absolutely, sir. I have gone into it with the guard and attendants. No one could have been overlooked."

"Very good. Taking first, then, those who were in the carriage. There were six compartments. In the first were the four men, and in the second Miss Blair-Booth. Are you satisfied these were innocent?"

"Perfectly, sir. The wedging of the doors eliminated them."

"So I think. The third and fourth compartments were empty, but in the fifth there were two gentlemen. What about them?"

"Well, sir, you know who they were. Sir Gordon M'Clean, the great engineer, and Mr. Silas Hemphill, the professor of Aberdeen University. Both utterly beyond suspicion."

"But, as you know, Inspector, no one is beyond suspicion in a case of this kind."

"I admit it, sir, and therefore I made careful inquiries about them. But I only confirmed my opinion."

"From inquiries I also have made I feel sure you are right. That brings us to the last compartment, the Ladies Only. What about those three ladies?"

"The same remarks apply. Their characters are also beyond suspicion and, as well as that, the mother is elderly and timid, and couldn't brazen out a lie. I question if the daughters could either. I made inquiries all the same, and found not the slightest ground for suspicion."

"The corridors and lavatories were empty?"

"Yes, sir."

"Then everyone found in the coach when the train stopped may be definitely eliminated?"

"Yes. It is quite impossible it could have been any that we have mentioned."

"Then the murderer must have left the coach?"

"He must, and that's where the difficulty comes in."

"I know, but let us proceed. Our problem then really becomes – how did he leave the coach?"

"That's so, sir, and I have never been against anything stiffer."

The chief paused in thought, as he absently selected and lit another cigar. At last he continued, "Well, at any rate, it is clear he did not go through the roof or the floor, or any part of the fixed framing or sides. Therefore he must have gone in the usual way – through a door. Of these, there is one at each end and six at each side. He therefore went through one of these fourteen doors. Are you agreed, inspector?"

"Certainly, sir."

"Very good. Take the ends first. The vestibule doors were locked?"

"Yes, sir, at both ends of the coach. But I don't count that much. An ordinary carriage key opened them and the murderer would have had one."

"Quite. Now, just go over again our reason for thinking he did not escape to the sleeper."

"Before the train stopped, sir, Miss Bintley, one of the three in the Ladies Only, was looking out into the corridor, and the two sleeper attendants were at the near end of their coach. After the train stopped, all three ladies were in the corridor, and one attendant was at the sleeper vestibule. All these persons swear most positively that no one but the guard passed between Preston and the searching of the carriage."

"What about these attendants? Are they reliable?"

"Wilcox has seventeen years' service, and Jeffries six, and both bear excellent characters. Both, naturally, came under suspicion of the murder, and I made the usual investigation. But there is not a scrap of evidence against them, and I am satisfied they are all right."

"It certainly looks as if the murderer did not escape towards the sleeper."

"I am positive of it. You see, sir, we have the testimony of two separate lots of witnesses, the ladies and the attendants. It is out of the question that these parties would agree to deceive the police. Conceivably one or other might, but not both."

"Yes, that seems sound. What, then, about the other end – the third-class end?"

"At that end," replied the inspector, "were Mr. and Mrs. Smith with their sick child. They were in the corridor close by the vestibule door, and no one could have passed without their knowledge. I had the child examined, and its illness was genuine. The parents are quiet persons, of exemplary character, and again quite beyond suspicion. When they said no one but the guard had passed I believed them. However, I was not satisfied with that, and I examined every person that travelled in the third-class coach, and established two things: first, that no one was in it at the time it was searched who had not travelled in it from Preston; and secondly, that no one except the Smiths had left any of the compartments during the run between Preston and the emergency stop. That proves beyond question that no one left the first-class coach for the third after the tragedy."

"What about the guard himself?"

"The guard is also a man of good character, but he is out of it, because he was seen by several passengers as well as the Smiths running through the third-class after the brakes were applied."

"It is clear, then, the murderer must have got out through one of the twelve side doors. Take those on the compartment side first. The first, second, fifth, and sixth compartments were occupied, therefore he could not have passed through them. That leaves the third and fourth doors. Could he have left by either of these?"

The inspector shook his head.

"No, sir," he answered, "that is equally out of the question. You will recollect that two of the four men in the end compartment were looking out along the train from a few seconds after the murder until the stop. It would not have been possible to open a door and climb out onto the footboard without being seen by them. Guard Jones also looked out at that side of the van and saw no one. After the stop these same two men, as well as others, were on the ground, and all agree that none of these doors were opened at any time."

"Hmm," mused the chief, "that also seems conclusive, and it brings us definitely to the doors on the corridor side. As the guard arrived on the scene comparatively early, the murderer must have got out while the train was running at a fair speed. He must therefore have been clinging on to the outside of the coach while the guard was in the corridor working at the sliding doors. When the train stopped all attention was concentrated on the opposite, or compartment, side, and he could easily have dropped down and made off. What do you think of that theory, inspector?"

"We went into that pretty thoroughly, sir. It was first objected that the blinds of the first and second compartments were raised too soon to give him time to get out without being seen. But I found this was not valid. At least fifteen seconds must have elapsed before Miss

Blair-Booth and the men in the end compartment raised their blinds, and that would easily have allowed him to lower the window, open the door, pass out, raise the window, shut the door, and crouch down on the footboard out of sight. I estimate also that nearly thirty seconds passed before Guard Jones looked out of the van at that side. As far as time goes he could have done what you suggest. But another thing shows he didn't. It appears that when Jones ran through the third-class coach, while the train was stopping, Mr. Smith, the man with the sick child, wondering what was wrong, attempted to follow him into the first-class. But the door slammed after the guard before the other could reach it, and, of course, the spring lock held it fast. Mr. Smith therefore lowered the end corridor window and looked out ahead, and he states positively no one was on the footboard of the first-class. To see how far Mr. Smith could be sure of this, on a dark night we ran the same carriage, lighted in the same way, over the same part of the line, and we found a figure crouching on the footboard was clearly visible from the window. It showed a dark mass against the lighted side of the cutting. When we remember that Mr. Smith was specially looking out for something abnormal, I think we may accept his evidence."

"You are right. It is convincing. And, of course, it is supported by the guard's own testimony. He also saw no one when he looked out of his van."

"That is so, sir. And we found a crouching figure was visible from the van also, owing to the same cause – the lighted bank."

"And the murderer could not have got out while the guard was passing through the third-class?"

"No, because the corridor blinds were raised before the guard looked out."

The chief frowned.

"It is certainly puzzling," he mused. There was silence for some moments, and then he spoke again. "Could the murderer, immediately after firing the shots, have concealed himself in a lavatory and then, during the excitement of the stop, have slipped out unperceived through one of these corridor doors and, dropping on the line, moved quietly away?"

"No, sir, we went into that also. If he had hidden in a lavatory he could not have got out again. If he had gone towards the third-class the Smiths would have seen him, and the first-class corridor was under observation during the entire time from the arrival of the guard till the search. We have proved the ladies entered the corridor immediately after the guard passed their compartment, and two of the four men in the end smoker were watching through their door till considerably after the ladies had come out."

Again silence reigned while the chief smoked thoughtfully. "The coroner had some theory, you say?" he said at last.

"Yes, sir. He suggested the murderer might have, immediately after firing, got out by one of the doors on the corridor side – probably the end one – and from there climbed on the outside of the coach to some place from which he could not be seen from a window, dropping to the ground when the train stopped. He suggested the roof, the buffers, or the lower step. This seemed likely at first sight, and I tried therefore the experiment. But it was no good. The roof was out of the question. It was one of those high curved roofs – not a flat clerestory – and there was no handhold at the edge above the doors. The buffers were equally inaccessible. From the handle and guard of the end door to that above the buffer on the corner of the coach was seven feet, two inches. That is to say, a man could not reach from one to the other, and there was nothing he could hold on to while passing along the step. The lower step was not possible either. In the first place it was divided – there was only a shot step beneath each door – not a continuous board like the upper one – so that no one could pass along the lower while holding on to the upper, and secondly, I couldn't imagine anyone climbing down there, and knowing that the first platform they came to would sweep him off."

"That is to say, inspector, you have proved the murderer was in the coach at the time of the crime, that he was not in it when it was searched, and that he did not leave it in the interval. I don't know that that is a very creditable conclusion."

"I know, sir. I regret it extremely, but that's the difficulty I have been up against from the start."

The chief laid his hand on his subordinate's shoulder. "It won't do," he said kindly. "It really won't do. You try again. Smoke over it, and I'll do the same, and come in and see me again tomorrow."

But the conversation had really summed up the case justly. My Lady Nicotine brought no inspiration and, as time passed without bringing to light any further facts, interest gradually waned till at last the affair took its place among the long list of unexplained crimes in the annals of New Scotland Yard.

And now I come to the singular coincidence referred to earlier whereby I, an obscure medical practitioner, came to learn the solution of this extraordinary mystery. With the case itself I had no connection, the details just given being taken from the official reports made at the time, to which I was allowed access in return for the information I brought. The affair happened in this way.

One evening just four weeks ago, as I lit my pipe after a long and tiring day, I received an urgent summons to the principal inn of the little village near which I practised. A motorcyclist had collided with a car at a crossroads and had been picked up terribly injured. I saw almost at a glance that nothing could be done for him; in fact, his life was a matter of a few hours. He asked coolly how it was with him, and, in accordance with my custom in such cases, I told him, inquiring was there anyone he would like sent for. He looked me straight in the eyes and replied:

"Doctor, I want to make a statement. If I tell it to you will you keep it to yourself while I live and then inform the proper authorities and the public?"

"Why, yes," I answered, "but shall I not send for some of your friends or a clergyman?"

"No," he said, "I have no friends, and I have no use for parsons. You look a white man; I would rather tell you."

I bowed and fixed him up as comfortable as possible, and he began, speaking slowly in a voice hardly above a whisper.

"I shall be brief for I feel my time is short. You remember some few years ago a Mr. Horatio Llewelyn and his wife were murdered in a train on the North-Western some fifty miles south of Carlisle?"

I dimly remembered the case. "The Sleeping-Car Express Mystery the papers called it?" I asked.

"That's it," he replied. "They never solved the mystery and they never got the murderer. But he's going to pay now. I am he."

I was horrified at the cool, deliberate way he spoke. Then I remembered that he was fighting death to make his confession and that, whatever my feelings, it was my business to hear and record it while yet there was time. I therefore sat down and said as gently as I could, "Whatever you tell me I shall note carefully, and at the proper time shall inform the police."

His eyes, which had watched me anxiously, showed relief.

"Thank you. I shall hurry. My name is Hubert Black, and I live at 24 Westbury Gardens, Hove. Until ten years and two months ago I lived at Bradford, and there I made the acquaintance of what I thought was the best and most wonderful girl on God's earth – Miss Gladys Wentworth. I was poor, but she was well off. I was diffident about approaching her, but she encouraged me till at last I took my courage in both hands and proposed. She agreed to marry me, but made it a condition our engagement was to be kept secret for a few days. I was so mad about her I would have agreed to anything she wanted, so I said nothing, though I could hardly behave like a sane man from joy."

"Some time before this I had come across Llewelyn, and he had been very friendly, and had seemed to like my company. One day we met Gladys, and I introduced him. I did not know till later that he had followed up the acquaintanceship."

"A week after my acceptance there was a big dance at Halifax. I was to have met Gladys there, but at the last moment I had a wire that my mother was seriously ill, and I had to go. On my return I got a cool little note from Gladys saying she was sorry, but our engagement had been a mistake, and I must consider it at an end. I made a few inquiries, and then I learnt what had been done. Give me some stuff, doctor; I'm going down."

I poured out some brandy and held it to his lips.

"That's better," he said, continuing with gasps and many pauses: "Llewelyn, I found out, had been struck by Gladys for some time. He knew I was friends with her, and so he made up to me. He wanted the introduction I was fool enough to give him, as well as the chances of meeting her he would get with me. Then he met her when he knew I was at my work, and made hay while the sun shone. Gladys spotted what he was after, but she didn't know if he was serious. Then I proposed, and she thought she would hold me for fear the bigger fish would get off. Llewelyn was wealthy, you understand. She waited till the ball, then she hooked him, and I went overboard. Nice, wasn't it?"

I did not reply, and the man went on, "Well, after that I just went mad. I lost my head and went to Llewelyn, but he laughed in my face. I felt I wanted to knock his head off, but the butler happened by, so I couldn't go on and finish him then. I needn't try to describe the hell I went through – I couldn't, anyway. But I was blind mad, and lived only for revenge. And then I got it. I followed them till I got a chance, and then I killed them. I shot them in that train. I shot her first and then, as he woke and sprang up, I got him too."

The man paused.

"Tell me the details," I asked, and after a time he went on in a weaker voice, "I had worked out a plan to get them in a train, and had followed them all through their honeymoon, but I never got a chance till then. This time the circumstances fell out to suit. I was behind him at Euston and heard him book to Carlisle, so I booked to Glasgow. I got into the next compartment. There was a talkative man there, and I tried to make a sort of alibi for myself by letting him think I would get out at Crewe. I did get out, but I got in again, and travelled on in the same compartment with the blinds down. No one knew I was there. I waited till we got to the top of Shap, for I thought I could get away easier in a thinly populated country. Then, when the time came, I fixed the compartment doors with wedges, and shot them both. I left the train and got clear of the railway, crossing the country till I came on a road. I hid during the day and walked at night till after dark on the second evening I came to Carlisle. From there I went by rail quite openly. I was never suspected."

He paused, exhausted, while the Dread Visitor hovered closer.

"Tell me," I said, "just a word. How did you get out of the train?"

He smiled faintly.

"Some more of your stuff," he whispered, and when I had given him a second dose of brandy he went on feebly and with long pauses which I am not attempting to reproduce. "I had worked the thing out beforehand. I thought if I could get out on the buffers while the train was running and before the alarm was raised, I should be safe. No one looking out of the windows could see me, and when the train stopped, as I knew it soon would, I could drop down and make off. The difficulty was to get from the corridor to the buffers. I did it like this: I had brought about sixteen feet of fine, brown silk cord, and the same length of thin silk rope. When I got out at Crewe I moved to the corner of the coach and stood close to it by way of getting shelter to light a cigarette. Without anyone seeing what I was up to I slipped the end of the cord through the bracket handle above the buffers. Then I strolled to the nearest door paying out the cord, but holding on to its two ends. I pretended to fumble at the door as if it was stiff to open, but all the time I was passing the cord through the handle–guard, and knotting the ends together. If you've followed me you'll understand this gave me a loop of fine silk connecting the handles at the corner and the door. It was the colour of the carriage, and was nearly invisible. Then I took my seat again.

"When the time came to do the job, I first wedged the corridor doors. Then I opened the outside window and drew in the end of the cord loop and tied the end of the rope to it. I pulled one side of the cord loop and so got the rope pulled through the corner bracket handle and back again to the window. Its being silk made it run easily, and without marking the bracket. Then I put an end of the rope through the handle-guard, and after pulling it tight, knotted the ends together. This gave me a loop of rope tightly stretched from the door to the corner.

"I opened the door and then pulled up the window. I let the door close up against a bit of wood I had brought. The wind kept it to, and the wood prevented it from shutting."

"Then I fired. As soon as I saw that both were hit I got outside. I kicked away the wood and shut the door. Then, with the rope for handrail, I stepped along the footboard to the buffers. I cut both the cord and the rope and drew them after me, and shoved them in my pocket. This removed all traces."

"When the train stopped I slipped down on the ground. The people were getting out at the other side so I had only to creep along close to the coaches till I got out of their light, then I climbed up the bank and escaped."

The man had evidently made a desperate effort to finish, for as he ceased speaking his eyes closed, and in a few minutes he fell into a state of coma which shortly preceded his death.

After communicating with the police I set myself to carry out his second injunction, and this statement is the result.

Australia
Dead Man in the Scrub
by Mary Fortune

Mary Fortune was born in Belfast and arrived in the Australian goldfields in 1855, moving from town to town, which is doubtless why she chose the pseudonym Waif Wander when she started to write. From 1865 to 1908 she contributed "The Detective's Album" to the *Australian Journal,* making her among the earliest women detective writers in the world. In all, she wrote more than 500 self-contained crime tales, making her series the longest running in the early history of crime fiction, and possibly the earliest example of the police procedural – predating Georges Simenon, Hilary Waugh, and Ed McBain by more than sixty years.

"The Dead Man in the Scrub" appeared in 1867. Because of the author's chosen style, it is not treated as a locked-room (or, rather, locked-tent) mystery, but it is one nonetheless.

Some years ago, at the close of what had been a hot summer, two men, who had worked unsuccessfully for some months on a diggings in the Loddon District, determined to go and "prospect" in a scrub some four or five miles off. It was a lonely and out-of-the-way place – far from any road or settlement whatever – and, as far as the mates knew, had never been penetrated by a human foot. In this opinion, however, a few miles' tramp convinced them they had been mistaken, for, after succeeding in making their way through the tangled vegetation for about two miles, they came upon a small spot of partially cleared ground, where there were evident traces of man's labour. Two or three shallow holes had been sunk, and at a small water hole, not far off, the stuff had been evidently cradled. Looking around for some appearance of a home or pathway near this spot – for of course the man or men who had been working here must have had some place to live in; it was not likely workers would tramp that weary scrub twice in the day – they fancied that in one particular place the vegetation seemed to be less dense. But seeing no way toward that place, they made one slowly with the tomahawk, and after cutting and untangling hundreds of feet of the mallee vine, they came upon a little white tent, almost hidden in the very heart of the bushes. Here an awful scene awaited them, and if you have not heard something of the same sort yourself, I need not attempt to give you any idea of the sound made by millions of those horrible flies that collect around and revel in the decomposition of any animal life in Australia. Inside the tent, which was quite closed up, a continuous buzz, suggestive of innumerable myriads of flies, met the ears of the horrified mates, who were now quite certain that death, in some shape, inhabited this little white calico home in the mallee; indeed another of the senses already assured them that their fortitude would most likely be severely tried by the sight in store for them. What to do was the question; the tent, as I have already said, was fastened, the door being apparently secured closely inside while the slight movement one of the men made in ascertaining this fact seemed to disturb the feasters upon the dead. They rose in such terrible clouds that through the thin calico one could see them, as they came buzzing in millions against its sides.

"What are we to do?" asked one.

"Go back to Leggat's and tell the police," replied his mate. "Tell the police what, man?" inquired the first speaker, "for all we know it may be a dog's carcase that's inside."

His mate shook his head: "A dog wouldn't stay in a closed tent to die, Bill, but at any rate I wouldn't like to open the place without a policeman."

"You know the dog might have been chained up; a digger might leave his dog to watch inside, and maybe something prevented his coming back," observed Bill.

"Maybe," replied the mate dubiously, "but at any rate we can't stop here much longer, I can't stand it."

Bill walked around the tent, and at the back observed a small hole near the wall-plate, which he slightly enlarged with his fingers, and so enabled himself to peep into the interior. He gave but one glance, and then drawing back with horror ejaculated, "Oh God, that's awful!"

"What is it?" eagerly enquired the other.

"Oh, it's a man lying there dead – rotten! Look for yourself, and come away for God's sake! I feel like fainting!"

Well these men tramped back these miles, and told me at the camp, and we returned, in a spring cart, to the lonely place.

To avoid meddling with the door, I tore up a width of the calico, and entered to witness the most piteous and horrible sight I had seen for a long time. A man, or the remains of what had been a man, lay extended upon the floor, but in such an advanced state of decomposition as to be almost unrecognisable. He was fully dressed, and in good sound digger's clothes: His boots were nearly new, his trousers quite respectable. He had on a blue Guernsey shirt, over a good flannel one, but of course, in consequence of the fearful state of the body, even these articles were not to be identified. The poor fellow lay as if he had fallen out of his bunk, which was close by, one arm under his forehead, but the head, detached by decomposition, had fallen partially away, and not a feature was recognisable; the abundant black hair alone being remarkable. Upon his bunk were good blankets, and in the tent was a billy, and one or two other little cooking utensils, but there was not the slightest appearance of anything to eat, or anything whatever which might have held provisions – not a scrap of paper, not a crumb of bread. Having observed this, I turned my attention to the fastening of the opening, which, in every original tent, forms the entrance, and I was astonished to find that it had really been nailed up from the inside; a stone and a few broken tacks still lay upon the ground near it, and I could readily perceive that the former had been used as a hammer. The first idea that suggested itself to my professional mind was that of suicide, and suicide most likely induced by want, remembering the absence of anything like food in the place – or, that the poor fellow had really died of starvation, and had fastened the door with the hope of preventing his body from being devoured by dingoes, before it was discovered.

I had not time to speculate about it just at that moment, however, as my duty obliged me to remove the remains and give information to the coroner of the district as early as possible. And so, with great difficulty, we succeeded in enveloping the remains of the poor miner, in one of his own blankets, and, after carrying them some distance, depositing them in the cart. A jury was empanelled, an inquest was held, which resulted in an open verdict of "Found dead," for the condition of the body rendered it impossible for a postmortem to be of the slightest service, and the poor fellow was buried. No one knew anything about him – no person had been aware of a digger being in the scrub, and the general impression was my first one, that he had perished of want.

I say my first one, for I soon altered my opinion, although it was not likely to be of the slightest service to the interests of justice that I did so. Almost as a matter of form, I suppose, I went to remove the tent, which had become the property of Government. It was of so little value as to be scarcely worth the trouble, but I was glad of an opportunity to examine the place at my leisure. Well, there was nothing, absolutely nothing in the tent but what I have already mentioned, and a matchbox under the blankets on the bunk, which contained half a dozen matches, and at the bottom, pushed into the smallest space, a small piece, about a square inch, of some woollen material, apparently new. I did not believe at all that this unfortunate man had died a natural death. I was firmly convinced in my own mind that there had been foul play, and yet, had I been asked to give a reason for that conviction, I must have been silent, I had none to give. Yet, with all that, I looked for traces of murder, just as if I was absolutely certain it had been committed. The door was nailed inside: Well, supposing the poor fellow himself had not nailed it, where did the person who had find egress? Might he not have ripped a seam of the calico, and sewed it again outside? I set to work and examined the seams carefully. The tent had apparently been made by a woman, no man or tentmaker was likely to have taken the trouble to stitch so neatly, and besides the seams were all on the inside, except in one corner, where, for about two feet in length, a much rougher seam had been made upon the outside.

"Here, then," I convinced myself, "the murderer has got out, fastening the door inside, to leave it to be supposed that the man himself must have accomplished it."

I pulled down the tent, and removed every little article in it, and, as they were few, I had soon done, and took a last look around before I left. As I have before stated, the scrub was growing almost closely around the tent. From the length of time that had elapsed since the owner lay dead inside, the little space was untrodden, and the creeping mallee vine had enwrapped itself over and over, and under and around every near stick. Examining closely the circumscribed space of the tenting spot, I perceived a portion of a dirty rag of some sort, peeping out from the vegetation, and drawing it forth, I was possessor of a pair of old trousers, which, from the size of the dead man, might have belonged to him; they were of a large size, and he had been a tall man. There was nothing particular about them, a pair of old cast-offs evidently, nothing in the pockets, and no difference in them whatever from any other pair of old trousers in the world, only that from the portion least worn, at the back of the leg, a square piece had been taken for some purpose or other. It was no accidental tear, for the piece had been cut out, and the cut extended across the side seam, where it was quite certain it would not have torn. So, interested in these old rags, I carefully folded them up with the rest of the dead man's property, and proceeded campwards. Months passed on, indeed, I may say years; it must have been nearly three years before I fell over the clue to the death-tenanted home in the untrodden mallee. I had meanwhile been removed, and was, at the time I resume my story, stationed at Walhalla, a prosperous reefing township, and a great improvement upon the old alluvial "rush": The tent was the great exception, the slab and bark erection most common, while there were many of weatherboard, and zinc roofing. In short, Walhalla was such a mining township as we may see anywhere today. In passing backwards and forwards I had often noticed a snug hut that lay upon my way, or rather I had remarked the clean, bright, good-looking woman who lived there, and as it is our business to know as much as possible about everything and everybody, I was aware that she was the wife of a man named Jerry Round, who worked as wages-man in one of the Companies. There were no children about this hut, but the woman, who might have been some twenty-five years old, was always busy. I think she took in washing.

One day, then, about this time, I was passing this hut early in the forenoon of a Saturday. Mrs. Round was apparently having a grand clean out, and the dust was flying in all directions. I was going straight on as usual, when out of the door came flying a pair of dirty old trousers, which, after passing within an inch of my nose, fell directly upon the pathway before me, and there, as they lay sprawling out, covered with the dirt of a week's underground work, I saw upon the knee of one of the legs the identical patch missing from the old pair which I had still safely stowed at home in the camp! I could have almost sworn to it the first moment my eyes lighted upon it; the pattern and colour were peculiar, and I had been too much interested not to have closely marked both, but when I came to perceive that in the patch was the very side-seam of my trousers, I had no doubt in the world about it. I stooped down, in a puzzled, bewildered sort of way, wondering to myself how that patch came upon these trousers, and what connection it had with the dead man in the malice, and how it would all end, when, just as I was carefully, and with as little detriment to myself as I could, picking up the pants at arm's length, Mrs. Round herself rushed out in a state of great excitement.

"Good gracious me, sir, I hope you don't think I threw the old things at you a'purpose! I didn't know anyone was passing, and they were in my way when I was sweeping, and so I "chucked" them out! I hope you will excuse it, sir!"

"Oh, you need not bother your head about that, Mrs. Round," I replied, still holding the articles in my hand. "I guessed how it was when I saw the dust flying out of the door, but I was just taking a fancy to this patch here. If you've done with the old trousers, I am sadly in need of a bit of woollen rag to clean up my traps, and this would be the very thing."

"Lord, to be sure, sir. Jerry wore them down in the shaft until they would hardly hang together, but anything most is good enough for working on them drives. But wouldn't a bit of old flannel be better, sir? I could give you lots of flannel."

"No, Mrs. Round," I replied, handing her the trousers, "these bright buckles of ours want such a lot of rubbing you see, flannel lasts no time, while a piece of that good woollen trousering would be worth twice as much to me, so if you'll just be good enough to rip it off for me, I'll owe you a heap of thanks!"

"And welcome, sir," she replied, going towards the hut to procure a pair of scissors, and I followed her to the door, holding, when she returned, the trousers while she ripped the piece off.

"It's been a good piece of stuff, Mrs. Round," I remarked, as she clipped and cut. "You could not buy such a good bit of trousering on the diggings now."

"No, sir," replied the woman, a shade coming over her face, "it's a bit of a pair that came from England long ago; my first husband bought them before we left home, and many a happy gathering of friends they were at!"

"Your first husband? Is it possible you've been married twice? You're very young for that."

"Jerry and I have only been married a matter of two years," she said, adding, with an effort to change the conversation, "Anyone can tell it was a man that sewed this. I expect Jerry put it on while he and poor Jim were working together; it's as hard to take off as if it was nailed on."

"And where were you then, while Round and Jim were working together?" I asked, guessing at once that "poor Jim" meant the dead first husband.

"I was in New Zealand, sir. They came back to a rush at Carngham, and I never saw him again, he died at Sailor's Gully."

"And you married his mate?"

"Yes, sir."

There was the shadow of old memories in the poor woman's face, as she simply gave me this information, and I had not the heart to grieve her by questions that might perhaps excite her curiosity, as well as put Round on his guard, and so, for the present, I said no more. The patch I carried home safely, and found, as I had expected, that it was indeed the very piece which had been cut out of the dead man's trousers, and I was, of course, quite certain that the dead man of the mallee was none other than the "poor Jim" of Mrs. Round.

What story did Round tell about his death, I could not but wonder, and I thought long about the best means of finding this out. The conclusion I came to was to ask Mrs. Round herself, and make some reasonable excuse for so doing. So the very first time I went that way, I made it my business to time my walk down the road so that I met her coming from a hole with a bucket of water, and as she set it down to rest herself, I stopped before her for a moment.

"Do you know, Mrs. Round," I said, affecting an air of great interest, "I have been puzzling my head ever since I saw you last about your first husband. I believe I knew him, and your mentioning his name as Jim made me almost sure of it. I believe I have seen these very same trousers on him a dozen times! You said he worked at Carngham, but he didn't die there, did he?"

"No, sir, the poor fellow died at some little out-of-the-way gully back of Bendigo, him and Jerry were prospecting, and when Jim was taken bad, Jerry had to bring a doctor six miles through the scrub to him. But it was no use, and after he died Jerry brought the news over to me, and bad news it was, I tell you."

"Well, well! It is strange how things come about!" I ejaculated, "When I saw poor Jim last, I had no idea that I should make your acquaintance through a patch of a pair of his old pantaloons!"

"It was a sore grief to me, sir," said Mrs Round, with a sigh, as she again lifted her pail, "to hear that he was dead, and without my hand to smooth his blankets, or give him a drink! We were very fond of each other, and, and to tell the truth," she added, lifting her eyes to mine for one moment, "I don't know how ever I came to marry Jerry at all, for poor Jim never liked him, though he was his mate!"

"Twas instinct," I repeated to myself, as I proceeded on my way. "Little cause the poor fellow had to like him! I dare say if Mrs. Round liked she could give me a good reason for this wretch murdering the poor unsuspicious husband, so that he might go and inherit his place in the affections of the betrayed wife."

And so I was going on, thinking moodily over the affair, when my attention was attracted by a great commotion among the deep workings: People were running and shouting to one another, and all were tending toward one place, so, hastening my steps, I went in that direction too, and soon found that a frightful mining calamity had taken place, one of the drives had fallen in! From the men who had escaped I learned that the drive had fallen in only at the further end, and that, warned by the cracking of the timber, all had escaped in time, save one – it was Jerry Round.

I went down into the drive, where every exertion was being made to extricate the unfortunate man from the most terrible position that can be conceived: He was not buried, that would have been a merciful fate in comparison with what he endured, and my heart sickened as I looked at him. The drive had partially collapsed, and two steps more towards the shaft would have saved him, but those two steps he did not get time to make. One of the cap-pieces of the timbering had fallen right across his body, the fallen earth partially supporting it, and partially also covering his body. His head, however, was quite exposed, his eyes protruding in his great agony, and for a few minutes he was even able to speak, urging the workers for God's sake to hasten. But there was no need for that, every man worked as if his own existence depended upon speed, and, indeed, they could not be certain that at any moment further breaks would not take place in the shaken timbering, and place themselves in the same position from which they were endeavouring to rescue their wretched mate. A very few moments and he was extricated. But the torture he was enduring had become unbearable before that; he was insensible when they carried him upon a stretcher to his own hut, which was not far away, and where his wife met him, quite unprepared for the sight so horrible. Yet she met it with far greater composure than one might have anticipated. The medical men who were immediately summoned declared the case of Round to be hopeless. His internal injuries precluded any expectation of a change, save the last great one, and so Mrs. Round, the doctor, and I watched the bruised and broken remnant of humanity stretched out upon his own comfortable bed, comfortable, alas, to him no longer, but we only watched to see the last faint breathing cease, to return no more. He was a dark, stoutly built man, his hair and whiskers were black as night; one of his arms, broken in two places, lay in a twisted, unnatural position beside him, and his nerveless head, rolled over helplessly to one side, was covered with blood from a wound upon his temple, from which the crimson drops, still oozing, fell down over his white face, making the whole picture more horrible. Poor Mrs. Round wept silently, wiping meanwhile the blood gently from his face, and the death damp from his forehead.

The time was not far off now. By his side sat the doctor, holding his fingers upon the wrist of the dying man, and at that moment he gave me a slight nod, unnoticed by the wife. He felt in the fluttering pulse indications of the last struggle. I was about to try and send Mrs. Round upon some excuse or an errand, for the purpose of saving her the last scene, when Round opened his eyes, and with a gaze full of consciousness, rested them upon the face of his wife.

"Oh Ellen, I am dying!" he gasped, faintly, and with horror. "I am dying, and I murdered poor Jim!" And with this last confession the last breath went away too. He was dead!

Mrs. Round turned round from her dead husband and stared at me; some instinctive certainty, I have no doubt, she felt, that I had something to do with the truth of these last words, some recollection, no doubt, of our late conversation, and a multitude of old ones, with which I had nothing whatever to do, would be sure to lend their aid in overcoming the poor woman, for the light of life faded out of her white face. She had fainted.

There was nothing that touches so mutually the feelings of a whole mining community as a sudden death from one of those fearful and frequent underground accidents, to which their calling is so liable, and which, indeed, the carelessness of the miner himself makes so much more frequent, and therefore Jerry Round was followed to the grave by every man in the place who could manage to leave his employment. Little guessed the mourners how guilty was the poor broken mortal, whose shattered remains they followed, and as I watched the sad procession winding away among the rocks and trees, true to the instincts of my profession, I quietly speculated how many of these very mourners would be likely to come within my jurisdiction, if the secrets of all hearts were known.

As I was making these heartless speculations, as you may think them, I was smoking a cigar, and leaning upon the fence which surrounded our Police camp, and the black coffin had scarcely disappeared away on the bush track when Mrs. Round herself stood before me. Poor little woman, she looked very ill, and was, at the moment I speak of, as calm-looking and nearly as white as if she had already lain down in the narrow peaceful resting place to which they were bearing her husband. She impressed me with the idea of rigidity. It seemed as if she had hard work to keep herself calm, and, the effort over-produced the appearance.

“Mr. Mark, I am going away to Melbourne tomorrow,” she said, laying her hand emphatically upon my arm. “I am going, with the few pounds we had saved, home to my friends in England. Before I go it is your duty, before God, to tell me all you know of my husband Jim!”

“Perhaps it is,” I replied, gently, “but of what use can it be to harrow your feelings by retailing the crimes of the past? Death has covered them all up now!”

“But death hasn't covered me up!” she replied. “And death hasn't as yet covered up all the thoughts that have no guide unless you tell me the truth.”

I felt that she was right, and I led her into the barrack-room, where my traps were, and where I unfolded the pair of old pants which I had got near the dead man in the mallee, and with the piece she had so lately given me herself, I handed them to her. She recognised them at once, said she would have known them among a hundred, from some mending of her own upon them, and then she listened, weepingly, while I told her all about the little tent in the scrub, and its death-tenant.

"And was there no more?" she asked. "Was there nothing else you could have brought? Oh, poor Jim! Poor murdered Jim!"

"There was this," I said, giving her the matchbox, with the little bit of stuff in it. "And this," I added, handing her a lock of the poor fellow's dark hair, which I had cut off, and folded in a bit of paper.

Poor Mrs. Round opened it, and looked at the hair, and then, after all the horrors she had heard, she pressed it to her lips. Alas! It was more than I could have done, had it belonged to the dearest and nearest I had in the world! For it had far more than usual of the smell of death, which the hair of the dead always has. How could it be otherwise, considering the state of the head from which I had taken it? The piece of stuff in the matchbox, too, how well she knew it!

"I sent it to him in a letter from New Zealand," she said, "to show him the sort of dress I had bought with the first money he sent me from Victoria!"

And so ends the story of poor Jim. His wife left the next day, as she had said, taking with her all she had left of the young husband she had followed from her home in old England, and that all was an old matchbox, a pair of worn and dilapidated trousers, and a lock of black death-tainted hair!

Real Life Impossibility: Austria Bridge to Death

In chapter XXXI of S.S. Van Dine's *The Greene Murder Case* (1928), the cerebral dilettante Philo Vance read from volume II of Dr. Hans Gross's celebrated *Handbook for Examining Magistrates, Police Officials, and Military Policemen, etc*. (1893):

"Early one morning the authorities were informed that the corpse of a murdered man had been found. At the spot indicated the body was discovered of a grain merchant, A. M., supposed to be a well-to-do man, face downward with a gunshot wound behind his ear. The bullet, after passing through the brain, had lodged in the frontal bone above the left eye. The place where the corpse was found was in the middle of a bridge over a deep stream. Just when the inquiry was concluding and the corpse was about to be removed for the postmortem, the investigating officer observed quite by chance that on the decayed wooden parapet of the bridge, almost opposite to the spot where the corpse lay, there was a small but perfectly fresh dent which appeared to have been caused by a violent blow on the upper edge of the parapet of a hard and angular object. He immediately suspected that the dent had some connection with the murder. Accordingly he determined to drag the bed of the stream below the bridge, when almost immediately there was picked up a strong cord about fourteen feet long with a large stone at one end and at the other a discharged pistol, the barrel of which fitted exactly the bullet extracted from the head of A. M. The case was thus evidently one of suicide. A. M. had hung the stone over the parapet of the bridge and discharged the pistol behind his ear. The moment he fired he let go the pistol, which the weight of the stone dragged over the parapet into the water."

More recently, *The Dallas Morning News,* on July 16, 2008 reported the death of one Thomas Hickman whose body had been discovered 4 months earlier near Albuquerque, N.M. Authorities initially thought the Red Lobster executive had been kidnapped and shot in the back of the head, but eventually concluded that Mr. Hickman committed suicide. The first clue was the bundle of white helium balloons, with the gun still attached, found snagged on bushes and cactus near Mr. Hickman's body; the grip of the gun had been removed and the trigger guard ground down to make the weapon as light as possible so it would float far away after being fired.

Investigators were also able to show that he purchased the balloons and the gun, and they found shavings from the gun in his garage.

Partway through the investigation, one of the investigators recalled seeing a television show in which balloons were used in a suicide. They obtained a copy of an October 2003 episode of the television drama *CSI: Crime Scene Investigation* and noticed that there were several similarities between that show and Mr. Hickman's case, but were not sure if Mr. Hickman ever saw the program.

United States
The Hidden Law
by Melville Davisson Post

Post was at one time championed by Ellery Queen as one of the four best detective short story writers of all time, along with Edgar Allan Poe, Arthur Conan Doyle, and G.K. Chesterton. Other critics, including Francis M. Nevins, Jr. and Howard Haycraft, have praised him highly. But while they continue to be published one hundred years later, his stories never had the same popular success of the other "Big Four" writers.

This may be due to the stern, unhumorous tone in the Uncle Abner stories, Post's best-known works. Abner is a righteous and religious West Virginian, solving local crimes in the backwoods in the middle of the nineteenth century. He's given to flowery oratory which can seem like heavy reading today, but Post used this dialogue to mask the brilliant and out-in-the-open clues he left for his readers.

Post was an innovator. The Uncle Abner stories are the first historical mysteries, the tales about the scheming Randolph Mason are the first "crooked lawyer" mysteries, and he was an early proponent of the impossible crime, with several original solutions.

But there was little innovation in his most famous tale. "The Doomdorf Mystery," one of the most famous locked-room stories of all time, has had perhaps a little more praise than it deserves, as the exact same brilliant solution had been used twenty years earlier by M. McDonnell Bodkin in "Murder by Proxy." Post admittedly put the notion to much better use.

"The Hidden Law" is an Uncle Abner story, and this tale of gold stolen from a locked and guarded house hits all the high points: a tale of nature and Man, avarice and fear, the ringing tones of Abner's Biblical disapproval – and a very high impossibility quotient.

We had come out to Dudley Betts's house and were standing in a bit of meadow. It was an afternoon of April; there had been a shower of rain, and now the sun was on the velvet grass and the white-headed clover blossoms. The sky was blue above and the earth green below, and swimming between them was an air like lotus. Facing the south upon this sunny field was a stand of bees, thatched with rye-straw and covered over with a clapboard roof, the house of each tribe a section of a hollow gum-tree, with a cap on the top for the tribute of honey to the human tyrant. The bees had come out after the shower was gone, and they hummed at their work with the sound of a spinner.

Randolph stopped and looked down upon the humming hive. He lifted his finger with a little circling gesture.

"'Singing masons building roofs of gold,'" he said. "Ah, Abner, William of Avon was a great poet."

My uncle turned about at that and looked at Randolph and then at the hive of bees. A girl was coming up from the brook below with a pail of water. She wore a simple butternut frock, and she was clean-limbed and straight like those first daughters of the world who wove and spun. She paused before the hive and the bees swarmed about her as about a great clover blossom, and she was at home and unafraid like a child in a company of yellow butterflies. She went on to the spring house with her dripping wooden pail, kissing the tips of her fingers to the bees. We followed, but before the hive my uncle stopped and repeated the line that Randolph had quoted:

"'Singing masons building roofs of gold' – and over a floor of gold and pillars of gold." He added, "He was a good riddle maker, your English poet, but not so good as Samson, unless I help him out."

I received the fairy fancy with all children's joy. Those little men singing as they laid their yellow floor, and raised their yellow walls, and arched their yellow roof! Singing! The word seemed to open up some sunlit fairy world.

It pleased Randolph to have thus touched my uncle.

"A great poet, Abner," he repeated, "and more than that; he drew lessons from nature valuable for doctrine. Men should hymn as they labor and fill the fields with song and so suck out the virus from the curse. He was a great philosopher, Abner, William of Avon."

"But not so great a philosopher as Saint Paul," replied Abner, and he turned from the bees toward old Dudley Betts, digging in the fields before his door. He put his hands behind him and lifted his stern bronze face.

"Those who coveted after money," he said, "have pierced themselves through with many sorrows. And is it not the truth? Yonder is old Dudley Betts. He is doubled up with aches, he has lost his son, he is losing his life, and he will lose his soul – all for money. 'Pierced themselves through with many sorrows,' as Saint Paul said it, and now, at the end he has lost the hoard that he slaved for."

The man was a byword in the hills – mean and narrow, with an economy past belief. He used everything about him to one end and with no thought but gain. He cultivated his fields to the very door, and set his fences out into the road, and he extracted from those about him every tithe of service. He had worked his son until the boy had finally run away across the mountains. He had driven his daughter to the makeshifts of the first patriarchal people-soap from ashes, linen from hemp, and the wheel and the loom for the frock upon her limbs.

And like every man under a single dominating passion, he grew in suspicion and in fear. He was afraid to lend out his money lest he lose it. He had given so much for this treasure that he would take no chance with it, and so kept it by him in gold.

But caution and fear are not harpies to be halted; they wing on. Betts was dragged far in their claw-feet. There is a land of dim things that these convoys can enter. Betts arrived there. We must not press the earth too hard, old, forgotten peoples believed, lest evil things are squeezed out that strip us and avenge it. And ancient crones, feeble, wrapped up by the fire, warned him: The earth suffered us to reap, but not to glean her. We must not gather up every head of wheat. The earth or dim creatures behind the earth would be offended. It was the oldest belief. The first men poured a little wine out when they drank and brought an offering of their herds and the first fruits of the fields.

It was written in the Book. He could get it down and read it.

What did they know that they did this? Life was hard then; men saved all they could. There was some terrible experience behind this custom, some experience that appalled and stamped the race with a lesson!

At first Betts laughed at their warnings; then he cursed at them, and his changed manner marked how far he had got. The laugh meant disbelief, but the curse meant fear.

And now, the very strangest thing had happened: The treasure that the old man had so painfully laid up had mysteriously vanished clear away. No one knew it. Men like Betts, cautious and secretive, are dumb before disaster. They conceal the deep mortal hurt as though to hide it from themselves.

He had gone in the night and told Randolph and Abner, and now they had come to see his house.

He put down his hoe when we came up and led us in. It was a house like those of the first men, with everything in it homemade – hand-woven rag carpets on the floor and hand-woven coverlets on the beds, tables and shelves and benches of rude carpentry. These things spoke of the man's economy. But there were also things that spoke of his fear: The house was a primitive stockade. The door was barred with a beam, and there were heavy shutters at the window; an ax stood by the old man's bed and an ancient dueling pistol hung by its trigger-guard to a nail.

I did not go in, for youth is cunning. I sat down on the doorstep and fell into so close a study of a certain wasp at work under a sill that I was overlooked as a creature without ears, but I had ears of the finest and I lost no word.

The old man got two splint-bottom chairs and put them by the table for his guests, and then he brought a blue earthen jar and set it before them. It was one of the old-fashioned glazed jars peddled by the hucksters, smaller but deeper than a crock, with a thick rim and two great ears. In this he kept his gold pieces until on a certain night they had vanished.

The old man's voice ran in and out of a whisper as he told the story. He knew the very night, because he looked into his jar before he slept and every morning when he got out of his bed. It had been a devil's night – streaming clouds drove across an iron sky, a thin crook of a moon sailed, and a high bitter wind scythed the earth.

Everybody remembered the night when he got out his almanac and named it. There had been noises, old Betts said, but he could not define them. Such a night is full of voices; the wind whispers in the chimney and the house frame creaks. The wind had come on in gusts at sunset, full of dust and whirling leaves, but later it had got up into a gale. The fire had gone out and the house inside was black as a pit. He did not know what went on inside or out, but he knew that the gold was gone at daylight, and he knew that no living human creature had got into his house. The bar on his door held and the shutters were bolted. Whatever entered, entered through the keyhole or through the throat of the chimney that a cat would stick in.

Abner said nothing, but Randolph sat down to an official inquiry:

"You have been robbed, Betts," he said. "Somebody entered your house that night."

"Nobody entered it," replied the old man in his hoarse, half-whispered voice, "either on that night or any other night. The door was fast, Squire."

"But the thief may have closed it behind him."

Betts shook his head. "He could not put up the bar behind him, and besides, I set it in a certain way. It was not moved. And the windows –I bolt them and turn the bolt at a certain angle. No human touched them."

It was not possible to believe that this man could be mistaken. One could see with what care he had set his little traps – the bar across the door precisely at a certain hidden line, the bolts of the window shutters turned precisely to an angle that he alone knew. It was not likely that Randolph would suggest anything that this cautious old man had not already thought of.

"Then," continued Randolph, "the thief concealed himself in your house the day before the robbery and got out of it on the day after."

But again Betts shook his head, and his eyes ran over the house and to a candle on the mantelpiece.

"I look," he said, "every night before I go to bed."

And one could see the picture of this old, fearful man, looking through his house with the smoking tallow candle, peering into every nook and corner. Could a thief hide from him in this house that he knew inch by inch? One could not believe it. The creature took no chance; he had thought of every danger, this one among them, and every night he looked! He would know, then, the very cracks in the wall. He would have found a rat.

Then, it seemed to me, Randolph entered the only road there was out of this mystery.

"Your son knew about this money?"

"Yes," replied Betts, "'Lander knew about it. He used to say that a part of it was his because he had worked for it as much as I had. But I told him," and the old man's voice cheeped in a sort of laugh, "that he was mine."

"Where was your son Philander when the money disappeared?" said
Randolph.

"Over the mountains," said Betts. "He had been gone a month." Then he paused and looked at Randolph. "It was not 'Lander. On that day he was in the school that Mr. Jefferson set up. I had a letter from the master asking for money.... I have the letter," and he got up to get it.

But Randolph waved his hand and sat back in his chair with the aspect of a brooding oracle.

It was then that my uncle spoke.

"Betts," he said, "how do you think the money went?"

The old man's voice got again into that big crude whisper.

"I don't know, Abner."

But my uncle pressed him.

"What do you think?"

Betts drew a little nearer to the table.

"Abner," he said, "there are a good many things going on around a man that he don't understand. We turn out a horse to pasture, and he comes in with handholds in his mane.... You have seen it?"

"Yes," replied my uncle.

And I had seen it, too, many a time, when the horses were brought up in the spring from pasture, their manes twisted and knotted into loops, as though to furnish a handhold to a rider.

"Well, Abner," continued the old man in his rustling whisper, "who rides the horse? You cannot untie or untwist those handholds – you must cut them out with shears – with iron. Is it true?"

"It is true," replied my uncle.

"And why, eh, Abner? Because those handholds were never knotted in by any human fingers! You know what the old folk say?"

"I know," answered my uncle. "Do you believe it, Betts?"

"Eh, Abner!" he croaked in the guttural whisper. "If there were no witches, why did our fathers hang up iron to keep them off? My grandmother saw one burned in the old country. She had ridden the king's horse, and greased her hands with shoemaker's wax so her fingers would not slip in the mane – shoemaker's wax! Mark you that, Abner!"

"Betts," cried Randolph, "you are a fool; there are no witches!"

"There was the Witch of Endor," replied my uncle. "Go on, Betts."

"By gad, sir!" roared Randolph, "If we are to try witches, I shall have to read up James the First. That Scotch king wrote a learned work on demonology. He advised the magistrate search on the body of the witch for the seal of the devil; that would be a spot insensible to pain, and, James said, 'Prod for it with a needle.'"

But my uncle was serious.

"Go on, Betts," he said. "I do not believe that any man entered your house and robbed you. But why do you think that a witch did?"

"Well, Abner," answered the old man, "who could have got in but such a creature? A thief cannot crawl through a keyhole, but there are things that can. My grandmother said that once in the old country a man awoke one night to see a gray wolf sitting by his fireside. He had an ax, as I have, and he fought the wolf with that and cut off its paw, whereupon it fled screaming through the keyhole. And the paw lying on the floor was a woman's hand!"

"Then, Betts," cried Randolph, "it's damned lucky that you didn't use your ax, if that is what one finds on the floor."

Randolph had spoken with pompous sarcasm, but at the words there came upon Abner's face a look of horror. "It is," he said, "in God's name!"

Betts leaned forward in his chair.

"And what would have happened to me, Abner, do you think, if I had used my ax? Would I have died there with the ax in my hand?"

The look of horror remained upon my uncle's face. "You would have wished for that when the light came; to die is sometimes to escape the pit."

"I would have fallen into hell, then?"

"Aye, Betts," replied my uncle, "straightway into hell!"

The old man rested his hands on the posts of the chair. "The creatures behind the world are baleful creatures," he muttered in his big whisper.

Randolph got up at that.

"Damme!" he said. "Are we in the time of Roger Williams, and is this Massachusetts, that witches ride and men are filched of their gold by magic and threatened with hell fire? What is this cursed foolery, Abner?"

"It is no foolery, Randolph," replied my uncle, "but the living truth."

"The truth!" cried Randolph. "Do you call it the truth that creatures, not human, able to enter through the keyhole and fly away, have Betts's gold, and if he had fought against this robbery with his ax he would have put himself in torment? Damme, man! In the name of common sense, do you call this the truth?"

"Randolph," replied Abner, and his voice was slow and deep, "it is every word the truth."

Randolph moved back the chair before him and sat down. He looked at my uncle curiously.

"Abner," he said, "you used to be a crag of common sense. The legends and theories of fools broke on you and went to pieces. Would you now testify to witches?"

"And if I did," replied my uncle, "I should have Saint Paul behind me."

"The fathers of the church fell into some errors," replied Randolph.

"The fathers of the law, then?" said Abner.

Randolph took his chin in his hand at that. "It is true," he said, "that Sir Matthew Hale held nothing to be so well established as the fact of witchcraft for three great reasons, which he gave in their order, as became the greatest judge in England: First, because it was asserted in the Scriptures; second, because all nations had made laws against it; and, third, because the human testimony in support of it was overwhelming. I believe that Sir Matthew had knowledge of some six thousand cases. But Mr. Jefferson has lived since then, Abner, and this is Virginia."

"Nevertheless," replied my uncle, "after Mr. Jefferson, and in Virginia, this thing has happened."

Randolph swore a great oath.

"Then, by gad, sir, let us burn the old women in the villages until the creatures who carried Betts's treasure through the keyhole bring it back!"

Betts spoke then. "They have brought some of it back!"

My uncle turned sharply in his chair.

"What do you mean, Betts?" he said.

"Why this, Abner," replied the old man, his voice descending into the cavernous whisper. "On three mornings I have found some of my gold pieces in the jar. And they came as they went, Abner, with every window fastened down and the bar across the door. And there is another thing about these pieces that have come back: They are mine, for I know every piece, but they have been in the hands of the creatures that ride the horses in the pasture – they have been handled by witches!" He whispered the word with a fearful glance about him. "How do I know that? Wait, I will show you!"

He went over to his bed and got out a little box from beneath his cornhusk mattress – a worn, smoke-stained box with a sliding lid. He drew the lid off with his thumb and turned the contents out on the table.

"Now look," he said. "Look, there is wax on every piece! Shoemaker's wax, mark you – eh, Abner! My mother said that the creatures grease their hands with that so their fingers will not slip when they ride the barebacked horses in the night. They have carried this gold clutched in their hands, see, and the wax has come off!"

My uncle and Randolph leaned over the table. They examined the coins.

"By the Eternal!" cried Randolph. "It is wax! But were they clean before?"

"They were clean," the old man answered. "The wax is from the creatures' fingers. Did not my mother say it?"

My uncle sat back in his chair, but Betts strained forward and put his fearful query:

"What do you think, Abner, will all the gold come back?"

My uncle did not at once reply. He sat for some time silent, looking through the open door at the sunny meadowland and the far-off hills. But finally he spoke like one who has worked out a problem and got the answer.

"It will not all come back," he said.

"How much, then?" whispered Betts.

"What is left," replied Abner, "when the toll is taken out."

"You know where the gold is?"

"Yes."

"And the creatures that have it, Abner," Betts whispered, "they are not human?"

"They are not human!" replied my uncle.

Then he got up and began to walk about the house, but not to search for clues to this mysterious thing. He walked like one who examines something within himself – or something beyond the eye – and old Betts followed him with his straining face. And Randolph sat in his chair with his arms folded and his chin against his stock, as a skeptic overwhelmed by proof might sit in a house of haunted voices. He was puzzled upon every hand. The thing was out of reason at every point, both in the loss and in the return of these coins upon the table, and my uncle's comments were below the soundings of all sense. The creatures who now had Betts's gold could enter through the keyhole! Betts would have gone into the pit if he had struck out with his ax! A moiety of this treasure would be taken out and the rest returned! And the coins testified to no human handling! The thing had no face, nor aspect of events in nature. Mortal thieves enjoyed no such supernatural powers. These were the attributes of the familiar spirit. Nor did the human robber return a percent upon his gains!

I have said that my uncle walked about the floor. But he stopped now and looked down at the hard, miserly old man.

“Betts,” he said, “this is a mysterious world. It is hedged about and steeped in mystery. Listen to me! The Patriarchs were directed to make an offering to the Lord of a portion of the increase in their herds. Why? Because the Lord had need of sheep and heifers? Surely not, for the whole earth and its increase were His. There was some other reason, Betts. I do not understand what it was, but I do understand that no man can use the earth and keep every tithe of the increase for himself. They did not try it, but you did!”

He paused and filled his big lungs.

“It was a disastrous experiment.... What will you do?”

“What must I do, Abner?” the old man whispered. “Make a sacrifice like the Patriarchs?”

“A sacrifice you must make, Betts,” replied my uncle, “but not like the Patriarchs. What you received from the earth you must divide into three equal parts and keep one part for yourself.”

“And to whom shall I give the other two parts, Abner?”

“To whom would you wish to give them, Betts, if you had the choice?”

The old man fingered about his mouth.

“Well,” he said, “a man would give to those of his own household first – if he had to give.”

“Then,” said Abner, “from this day keep a third of your increase for yourself and give the other two-thirds to your son and your daughter.”

“And the gold, Abner? Will it come back?”

“A third part will come back. Be content with that.”

“And the creatures that have my gold? Will they harm me?”

“Betts,” replied my uncle, “the creatures that have your gold on this day hidden in their house will labor for you as no slaves have ever labored – without word or whip. Do you promise?”

The fearful old man promised, and we went out into the sun.

The tall straight young girl was standing before the spring-house, kneading a dish of yellow butter and singing like a blackbird. My uncle strode down to her. We could not hear the thing he said, but the singing ceased when he began to talk and burst out in a fuller note when he had finished – a big, happy, joyous note that seemed to fill the meadow.

We waited for him before the stand of bees, and Randolph turned on him when he came.

"Abner," he said, "what is the answer to this damned riddle?"

"You gave it, Randolph," he replied. "'Singing masons building roofs of gold.'" And he pointed to the bees. "When I saw that the cap on one of the gums had been moved I thought Betts's gold was there, and when I saw the wax on the coins I was certain."

"But," cried Randolph, "you spoke of creatures, not-human creatures that could enter through the keyhole – "

"I spoke of the bees," replied my uncle.

"But you said Betts would have fallen into hell if he had struck out with his ax!"

"He would have killed his daughter," replied Abner. "Can you think of a more fearful hell? She took the gold and hid it in the bee cap. But she was honest with her father. Whenever she sent a sum of money to her brother she returned an equal number of gold pieces to old Betts's jar."

"Then," said Randolph, with a great oath, "there is no witch here with her familiar spirits?"

"Now that," replied my uncle, "will depend upon the imagery of language. There is here a subtle maiden and a stand of bees!"

France
House Call
by Alexandre Dumas

Alexandre Dumas, *père*, (not to be confused with Alexandre Dumas, *fils*) was one of the world's greatest writers of adventure stories, such as *The Three Musketeers, Twenty Years After*, and *The Count of Monte Cristo,* as well as historical novels such as *La Reine Margot.*

His writing made him wealthy early in life, and he spent freely on travel, women, and an extensive estate.

Dumas is known to have frequently used collaborators, but in the absence of evidence we assume this locked room story, about the abduction of a girl from her locked room in a boarding school, is his work alone. "House Call" is adapted from chapters seventy-three and seventy-four of *Les Mohicans de Paris* (1854) and is the earliest recorded example of one of the most frequently used locked-room tricks.

It is historic in another sense also, as the first appearance of the time-honored phrase "*Cherchez la femme*."

Mina, Justin's fiancée, has been abducted from her room in Madame Desmarets's boarding school. Justin's friend Salvator has enlisted the help of M. Jackal, the mysterious head of the Sûreté.

As for M. Jackal, having learnt from Salvator that Justin was the fiancé, he greeted the young man earnestly and asked if anyone had come in through the garden or the window.

"Nobody, monsieur," replied Justin.

"Are you sure?"

"Here's the key to the garden."

"And the key to Mademoiselle Mina's room?"

"The door is locked from the inside."

"Ah!" said M. Jackal.

And, partaking of an enormous pinch of snuff, he added:

"We'll see about that."

Then, preceded by Justin, he reached a sort of parlour situated between the courtyard and the garden, from which led the corridor to Mina's room.

Looking around him, he enquired:

"Who is the mistress of this establishment?"

At that moment, Madame Desmarets entered the room.

"Here I am, messieurs," she said.

"The people I was awaiting from Paris, madame," said Justin.

"Did you know anything about Mina's disappearance before the arrival of monsieur?" enquired M. Jackal, indicating Justin.

"No, monsieur. I'm not even sure there has been a disappearance," replied Madame Desmarets in a voice trembling with emotion, "because we haven't entered her room yet."

"Rest assured, we'll go in shortly," said M. Jackal.

And, pulling his glasses down to the end of his nose, he looked over the lenses at Madame Desmarets. The lenses seemed to be there more to hide his eyes than to improve his vision; putting them back in place, he shook his head.

Salvator and Justin stood there, waiting impatiently for the interrogation to continue.

"Would the messieurs care to go into the salon?" asked Madame Desmarets. "It would be more comfortable there."

"Thank you, madame," replied M. Jackal, looking around him again and noting that he had instinctively, like a consummate general, established camp in an excellent position.

"And now, madame," he continued, "put yourself in the place of a responsible boarding school headmistress who is missing one of her residents, and think very carefully before answering my questions."

"Oh, monsieur, I couldn't be more painfully affected than I am now," said Madame Desmarets, wiping away a tear, "and as for thinking before I answer, that won't be necessary because I will only speak the truth."

M. Jackal made a small sign of approval and continued.

"At what time do the residents go to bed, madame?"

"At eight o'clock in winter, monsieur."

"And what about your assistants?"

"At nine o'clock."

"Do any of them stay up later than the others?"

"Only one."

"And at what time does she go to bed?"

"Around eleven-thirty or midnight."

"Where does she sleep?"

"On the first floor."

"Above Mademoiselle Mina's room?"

"No, the person on watch has a room overlooking the dormitory and the street, whereas poor little Mina's room looks out over the garden."

"And you, madame. Where do you reside?"

"In a room on the first floor, adjacent to the salon and overlooking the street."

"So none of your windows overlooks the garden?"

"My bathroom window does."

"At what time did you go to sleep last night?"

"At about eleven o'clock, roughly."

"Ah!" said M. Jackal. "Now we'll do a tour of the house. Come with me, Monsieur Salvator. You, Monsieur Justin, stay here and keep Madame company."

One obeyed M. Jackal as one obeyed an army general.

Salavator followed behind. Justin stayed with Madame Desmarets who collapsed onto a chair, sobbing her heart out.

"That woman had nothing to do with it," said M. Jackal as he went down the front steps and crossed the courtyard to the street door.

"How can you tell?" asked Salvator.

"By the tears," replied M. Jackal. "The guilty ones tremble but don't cry."

M. Jackal examined the house.

It was situated on the corner of a street and a deserted, paved alleyway.

M. Jackal set off down the alleyway like a bloodhound on the scent.

To his left, for a length of about fifty feet, rose the garden wall of the boarding school. Above the wall could be seen the tops of trees.

M. Jackal proceeded along the base of the wall with great concentration.

Salvator followed M. Jackal.

The detective indicated the alleyway with a toss of his head.

"Alleys like that are very bad at night. They seem to have been designed for abductions and cat burglaries."

After about twenty-five feet, M. Jackal bent down and picked up a small piece of plaster that had been broken off the top of the wall – then another, and a third.

He examined them carefully, then wrapped them in his handkerchief.

Then, picking up a broken piece of tile, he threw it back over the wall, so it landed on the other side.

"Is that where they went over?" asked Salvator.

"We'll find out soon enough," replied M. Jackal. "Meanwhile, let's go back inside."

They found Justin and Madame Desmarets where they had left them.

"Well?" asked Justin.

"We're working on it," said M. Jackal.

"For mercy's sake, monsieur, have you found anything, any clues?"

"You're a musician, young man, so you must know the saying 'Don't play faster than the violin.' I'm the violin; follow me, but don't get ahead of me.... Monsieur Justin, the garden key, if you please."

The young man handed over the key and, walking along the corridor, said:

"This is the door to Mina's room."

"Fine, fine. Everything in its turn. We'll go in there later."

And M. Jackal opened the door to the garden.

He stopped at the entrance, absorbing in one sweeping glance the several places he would examine in more detail later. "Right!" he said. "Here we have to exercise precaution and walk as if on eggshells. Follow me if you wish, but in the following order: me first,

Monsieur Salvator second, Monsieur Justin third, and Madame Desmarets fourth. Now, fall in behind me!"

It was obvious that M. Jackal was headed towards the portion of the garden wall that he had previously examined from the other side. But, instead of cutting diagonally across the garden, he followed the path that ran along the wall, which obliged him to make a right angle to reach the desired point.

Just before starting out, he cast a glance over his glasses at the window of Mina's room; the shutters were closed.

"Hmm!" he exclaimed, as he set off.

The path, made from yellow sand, offered nothing of interest, but after having travelled roughly twenty-five feet after the right-angled turn he stopped, and with a silent laugh picked up the broken tile he had previously thrown over the wall to act as a point of reference. He pointed out to Salvator the fresh footprint in the adjacent flower bed.

"Here we are!" he said.

Not only the eyes of Salvator, but also those of Justin and Madame Desmarets followed the direction of M. Jackal's finger.

"So you think the poor child was taken out this way?" asked Salvator.

"There's no doubt about it," replied the detective.

"My God! My God!" murmured Madame Desmarets. "An abduction in my boarding school!"

"Monsieur, in heaven's name give us some certitude."

"Oh, certitude," exclaimed M. Jackal. "Look for yourself, my friend, and you'll find it."

As Justin was looking, M. Jackal, who felt he was on the right track, pulled his snuffbox out of his pocket and gave his nose a mighty dose, all the while examining the ground from under his glasses and Madame Desmarets from over them.

"But, monsieur, what exactly do you see?" asked Justin impatiently.

"Those two holes in the ground, connected by a straight line."

"Don't you recognise the print of a ladder?" Salvator asked Justin.

"Bravo! That's what it is," said Justin. "But what's the straight line?"

"Go on, tell him," said M. Jackal to Salvator.

"It's the bottom rung of the ladder, which sank about an inch into the ground because of the humidity of the soil."

"Now," continued M. Jackal, "we have to find out how many men were on the ladder to drive the vertical uprights half a foot into the ground and the horizontal rung an inch."

"Let's examine the footprints," said Salvator.

"Be careful. Prints can be very confusing. Two men can have walked in the same footprint. There are crafty fellows who have made it a speciality."

"So what are you going to do?"

"It's very simple."

Then, turning to the boarding school headmistress, who could no more follow what was happening than if it had been explained in Arab or Sanskrit, he asked:

"Madame, is there a ladder on the premises?"

"There's one that the gardener uses."

"Where is it?"

"Under the shed, probably."

"And the shed?"

"Over there."

"Stay there, I'll fetch it myself."

M. Jackal lightly jumped about a metre and a half to avoid touching the paths and flower beds where numerous footprints could be seen and which he, following his own method, did not wish to examine until later.

He returned shortly with the ladder.

"Let's make sure of one thing right away," he said.

He raised the ladder and aligned the uprights with the holes in the flower bed.

"Good!" he said. "Here's the first exhibit. This is almost certainly the ladder that was used. The uprights and the holes line up perfectly."

"But aren't all ladders made to approximately the same dimensions?" asked Salvator.

"This one is slightly wider than normal. The gardener has an apprentice, or a student, or a son, isn't that the case, Madame Desmarets?"

"He has a twelve-year-old son, monsieur."

"There we are! His son helps him and he bought a ladder wide enough so that the boy can go up alongside him while he works."

"Monsieur," said Justin. "I beg you, let's get back to Mina."

"We're getting there, but we're taking a detour."

“Yes, but the detour is costing us time.”

“My dear sir,” replied the detective, “in this kind of case time doesn’t matter. There are two possibilities: Either the fellow who has taken your fiancée has left France and is too far away for us to catch him or he has hidden her somewhere near Paris, in which case we’ll know where he is within three days.”

“Oh, I do so hope you’re right, Monsieur Jackal. But you were saying you were about to find out how many men were involved in the abduction.”

“That’s exactly what I’m trying to do, monsieur.”

So saying, M. Jackal carried the ladder to a spot roughly one metre from where the first print was found, placed it against the wall, and climbed the first few rungs, stopping at each to assess the depth to which the ladder had sunk into the ground. It never exceeded three inches.

From a position halfway up the ladder, M. Jackal could see the whole garden; he noticed a man on the doorstep of the entrance to the corridor.

“Hello there, friend!” he shouted. “Who may you be?”

“I’m Madame Desmarets’s gardener,” the man replied.

“Madame,” said M. Jackal, “please go over there to verify that man’s identity and bring him over here, being careful to follow the same path we used.”

Madame Desmarets obeyed.

“I tell you, Monsieur Justin – and I repeat, Monsieur Salvator – that woman had nothing to do with the child’s abduction.”

Madame Desmarets returned with the gardener, who was quite astonished to find a stranger in his garden, standing on his ladder.

“My friend,” asked M. Jackal, “did you work in the garden yesterday?”

“No, monsieur. Yesterday was Mardi Gras, and in an establishment as respectable as Madame Desmarets’s, one doesn’t work on holidays.”

“Fine. And the day before yesterday?”

“Oh, that was Lundi Gras, and on Lundi Gras I rest.”

“And the day before that?”

“The day before that was Dimanche Gras, an even bigger holiday than Mardi Gras.”

“So you haven’t worked here for the past three days, is that correct?”

"Monsieur," replied the gardener solemnly, "I have no wish to be eternally damned."

"Fine. All I wanted to know was whether your ladder was in the shed for the last three days?"

"My ladder isn't in the shed," observed the gardener. "You're standing on it."

"This man is bursting with intelligence," commented M. Jackal. "But I'm quite sure he had nothing to do with the abduction.... Please climb the ladder."

The man looked at Madame Desmarets and read in her eyes that he needed to obey the intruder.

"Do as monsieur tells you," she said.

The gardener climbed three rungs.

"More," said M. Jackal.

The gardener continued his climb.

"What do you think?" asked M. Jackal of Salvator.

"It's sinking, but not as far as the rung," the other replied.

"You can come down, my friend," said M. Jackal to the gardener.

The man obeyed.

"There, I'm down," he said.

"I must say," observed M. Jackal, "this man doesn't say much, but what he does say is to the point!"

The gardener laughed; he was flattered by what he took to be a compliment.

"Now, my friend," continued M. Jackal, "take Madame Desmarets in your arms."

"Oh!" exclaimed the gardener

"What are you saying, monsieur?" asked Madame Desmarets.

"Take madame in your arms," repeated M. Jackal.

"I would never dare!" said the gardener.

"And I forbid you to do it, Pierre!" exclaimed the headmistress of the boarding school.

M. Jackal climbed a few rungs, then jumped back down.

"Climb to where I was, my friend," he said to the gardener.

The gardener went up without difficulty to the rung where M. Jackal had been standing. Meanwhile M. Jackal approached Madame Desmarets, placed one arm around her shoulders and the other around her knees, and lifted her into the air before she had time to realise his intention.

"But monsieur! But monsieur!" cried Madame Desmarets. "What are you doing?"

"Suppose, madame, that I am in love with you and I carry you off."

"That's some supposition," said the gardener, perched on the ladder.

"But monsieur! But monsieur!" repeated Madame Desmarets.

"Rest assured, madame," continued M. Jackal. "It's only, as our friend Pierre observed, a supposition."

And, carrying Madame Desmarets in his arms, he climbed four or five rungs.

"It's going in!" said Salvator, watching the ladder uprights, which were pushing further down into the soil.

"Going in as far as the lowest rung?" asked M. Jackal.

"Not quite."

"Put your foot on the second rung," said M. Jackal.

Salvator obliged.

"This time," he said, "it's at exactly the same point as the other.

"Good," replied the detective. "Let's all get down."

He came down first, placed Madame Desmarets in an upright position, told Pierre to stand where he was on the path, and, pulling the ladder out of the ground, where it had left the same trace as the other, said:

"My dear Monsieur Justin, Madame Desmarets is slightly heavier than Mademoiselle Mina, and I am slightly lighter than the man who carried her, so that all evens out."

"Which means...?"

"That your fiancée was abducted by three men: Two carried her on the ladder while the third kept it in place by putting his foot on it."

"Ah!" said Justin.

"Now," continued M. Jackal, "we shall attempt to establish the identities of the three men."

"Ah, I understand," said the gardener. "One of our residents has been abducted."

Lowering his glasses, M. Jackal looked long and hard at Pierre, and said:

"Madame Desmarets, don't ever think of getting rid of this lad. He's a glittering jewel of intelligence."

Then he turned to the gardener and said:

"My friend, you may take your ladder back to where we found it. We shan't need it anymore."

While the gardener headed off in the direction of the shed, M. Jackal, his glasses pushed up on his forehead and his nose full of snuff, examined the footprints.

Pulling out of his pocket an instrument that seemed half penknife and half pruning knife, he opened one of its nine or ten blades and cut off a small branch with which he started to measure the markings on the ground.

"Observe the tracks," he said. "They go from the wall to the window and back. The kidnappers seemed so well informed about the habits of the residents that they didn't feel the need for excessive precautions. But –." He looked embarrassed. "But," he repeated, "look at the shoes. They are exactly the same length and exactly the same width. Is it possible that, once they were in the garden, only one of them did the job while the others looked on?"

"The shoes are exactly the same length and width," retorted Salvator. "But they don't belong to the same foot."

"Aha! And how can we tell that?"

"From the nails in the sole, which are aligned differently."

"My goodness, it's true!" exclaimed M. Jackal. "One of the left shoes has the nails arranged in a triangle. One of our men is a freemason."

Salvator blushed modestly.

M. Jackal either didn't see it or pretended not to.

"Plus which," Salvator continued, "one of the two men had a limp in his right leg: As you can see, the shoe is worn more on that side than the other."

"That's true, too," said the detective. "Were you ever in the police force?"

"No," said Salvator. "But I am – or rather, I was – a hunter."

"Shush!" said M. Jackal.

"What is it?" asked Salvator.

"There's a third footprint.... A very distinctive one, with no resemblance to the flat-footed ones we were just looking at. Definitely the foot of a man of the world: an aristocrat, a nobleman, or an abbot."

"A nobleman, I think, Monsieur Jackal."

"Why must it be a nobleman? I'd rather like to see an abbot mixed up in this business," said the detective, an admirer of Voltaire.

"I'm afraid you're going to be denied that pleasure."

"And why is that?"

"Because abbots don't go around on horseback any more, and the man who left this print is a horseman. You can see the spur marks behind the heel of the boot."

"It's true!" exclaimed M. Jackal. "Heavens, my dear fellow, you're almost as good as a professional detective.

"That's because I spend a good part of my life observing," replied Salvator.

"So then help me trace these tracks back to the window."

"That won't be difficult."

Sure enough, the tracks of the shoes and boots led straight there.

Justin followed them, hanging on their every word and following their glances. The poor young man was like a miser who had lost a treasure he had guarded jealously for many years, and who, on the brink of finding it again, saw more intelligent souls discover the thieves before he did.

As for Madame Desmarets, she was completely bewildered and stood there stock still, staring into space.

When they arrived at the window, they found the prints had cut deeper into the ground there than elsewhere.

"I was told that you, Madame Desmarets, or you, Monsieur Justin, tried to open Mademoiselle Mina's door?" asked M. Jackal.

"We did, monsieur," they replied in unison.

"And you found it locked with a bolt?"

"It was Mina's habit to lock herself in at night," replied Madame Desmarets.

"So, they must have got in through the window."

"Hmm. The shutters seem to be pretty firmly in place," observed Salvator.

"Oh, it's not difficult to get a shutter open," said M. Jackal, trying his hand.

"Aha!" he continued. "Not only is it shut, it's hooked on the inside."

"Not as easy as you thought?" asked Salvator, slyly.

"You're sure the door's bolted shut?" asked the detective, addressing himself to Justin.

"Oh, yes, Monsieur, I pushed it with all my force."

"Maybe it was only locked with a key?"

"The upper part of the door sticks to the frame just as much as the middle part."

"Tut, tut, tut, tut," said M. Jackal to himself. "If the shutters were hooked up on the inside and the door was bolted, the people who did this must really know their stuff."

He shook the shutters again.

"I only know two men capable of getting out of locked doors and windows, and if one wasn't in prison in Brest and the other in Toulon, I'd say it was either Robichon or Gibassier who pulled this off."

"So there's a way of getting out through a locked door?" asked Salvator.

"My dear fellow, there's even a way of getting out of a room without a door, as one of my predecessors, the late M. Latude, proved. Luckily, not everyone knows how to do it."

Then, after partaking generously of snuff, he announced:

"Let's go back inside the house, madame."

So saying, and without bothering about the niceties of who should go first, he led the way up to the door of Mina's room.

"You obviously must have a duplicate key for every room, madame," said M. Jackal.

"Yes, but that's not much use if the door is bolted."

"Fetch it anyway, madame."

Madame Desmarets disappeared for a short while and returned with the key.

"Here it is," she said.

M. Jackal inserted the key in the lock and tried to turn it.

"The other key is on the inside, but it hasn't been turned twice."

Then he added, as if talking to himself:

"That proves the door was locked from the outside."

"But, if the bolt has been shot," asked Salvator, "how did the kidnappers manage to do it from the outside?"

"I'll show you that in a minute, young man. It's Gibassier who devised the method, for which he only got five years hard labour, instead of ten. It was a second offence, but it wasn't considered to be breaking and entering. Now, please find me a locksmith."

The locksmith duly arrived, armed with a crowbar, and prised the door upwards.

It burst open under the pressure.

Everyone prepared to rush into the room.

M. Jackal, arms outstretched, barred their entry.

"Calm down! Everything hangs on the initial examination. Our investigation is hanging by a thread," he said with a smirk, as if enjoying a private joke.

Then, going in alone, he examined the lock and the bolt.

He seemed dissatisfied with this first inspection.

Whereupon he removed his glasses – which, apparently, had been the only obstacle to lynx-like vision – and a triumphant smile immediately appeared on his lips as he seized an almost invisible object between thumb and forefinger and brandished it in the air.

"Aha!" he exclaimed happily. "When I told you our investigation was hanging by a thread...here it is!"

The witnesses were indeed able to make out a thin filament of silk thread, about fifteen centimetres long, which had been trapped between the iron of the bolt and the wood of the door.

"And they were able to close the door with that?" asked Salvator.

"Yes," replied M. Jackal. "Except the actual thread was half a metre long, and what you see here is a small piece which broke off and was not noticed."

The locksmith was watching M. Jackal with astonishment.

"Well," he said, "I thought I knew every method of opening and closing a door, but it looks as though I'm just a beginner."

"I'll be happy to teach you something, my friend," replied M. Jackal. "I'll show you how it works. You fold the thread in two – silk is better than cotton, because it's stronger – and you loop it around the knob of the bolt. The thread has to be long enough so that, when the door is closed, the two ends can be gathered from the outside. When you tug on the two ends, the loop tugs on the bolt and the job is done. Except sometimes the thread breaks and gets trapped under the bolt. That's when M. Jackal arrives and says: 'If that devil Gibassier wasn't in clink, I would have bet on him.'"

"Monsieur Jackal," said Justin, who clearly had only a faint interest in the subject, "however important this may be in advancing the progress of science, we really need to get into the room."

"Quite right, dear Monsieur Justin," replied the detective.

And everyone entered the room.

"Aha!" exclaimed M. Jackal. "Footprints from the door to the bed and from the bed to the window."

Then, taking a quick look at the bed and the adjacent table, he announced:

"So. The child went to bed and read some letters."

"Oh! My letters," exclaimed Justin. "Darling Mina!"

"Then," continued M. Jackal, "she blew out the candle; up to that point, everything was all right."

"How do you know she extinguished the candle herself?" asked Salvator.

"Observe closely: The wick is still curved from being blown out, and to judge from the shape of the curve, the gust of air came from the direction of the bed. Let's go back to the footprints, please. Monsieur Salvator, look at this one with your hunter's eyes."

Salvator bent down.

"Ah! Ah!" he exclaimed. "Here's something new: a woman's foot!"

"What did I tell you, Monsieur Salvator? 'Cherchez la femme!' As you say, a woman's foot... And, upon my word, a resolute woman, not walking on tiptoe, but pressing firmly on the sole and the heel."

"Yes," replied Salvator, "and a woman concerned about her appearance. She kept to the garden paths, so as not to dirty her boots. Notice how the print is traced in yellow sand without any hint of mud."

"Monsieur Salvator, Monsieur Salvator," exclaimed the detective. "What a pity you chose your current profession! You can be my aide-de-camp anytime you want. Don't move!"

M. Jackal left the room, went down into the garden, walked along the sandy path to the foot of the ladder, and returned.

"That's it," he said. "The woman left the house, followed the path, stopped at the ladder, and retraced her steps. Now I'm going to tell you what happened. I couldn't be more sure if I'd seen it with my own eyes."

Everyone listened attentively.

"Mademoiselle Mina came into the house at the usual hour, very sad but calm; she went to bed – look, the bed has hardly been slept in! – and read some letters. She cried while reading them – look at her handkerchief: It's crumpled like that of someone who's been crying...."

"Oh! Give it to me! Give it to me!" exclaimed Justin.

And, without waiting for M. Jackal to give it to him, he picked it up and pressed it to his lips.

"So she went to bed," continued M. Jackal, "she read, and she cried. But, because you can't read if you can't cry any more, she felt the need to sleep and blew out the candle. Did she sleep, or didn't she? It doesn't matter. However, once the candle was out, this is what happened. Someone knocked at the door –."

"Who, monsieur?" asked Madame Desmarets.

"Ah! You want to know more than I do myself, dear madame! Who? Maybe I'll be able to tell you shortly. The woman, in any case."

"The woman?" murmured Madame Desmarets.

"The wife, the daughter, the mother: When I say woman, I'm referring to the species, not to anyone in particular. So the woman knocked on the door, and Mina got up and opened it."

"But why would Mina open the door without knowing who was knocking?" asked Madame Desmarets.

"Who told you she didn't know who it was?"

"She wouldn't have opened it to an enemy."

"No, but to a friend? Ah, Madame Desmarets, am I to be the one to reveal to you that in boarding schools there are friends who are also terrible enemies? So Mina opened the door to her friend. Standing behind this friend was the young man in riding boots and stirrups. And standing behind the young man in riding boots and stirrups was the man with the triangular pattern of nails in his soles. How did little Mina sleep?"

"I don't understand," said Madame Desmarets, to whom the question was addressed.

"I meant: What clothes did she wear at night?"

"In winter she wore a shirt and a large dressing gown."

"Good! So they stuffed a handkerchief in her mouth, wrapped her in a shawl or a bedcover – look there at the foot of the bed, her stockings and shoes, and on the chair, her dress and petticoat – and they took her out through the window like that."

"Through the window?" asked Justin. "Why not through the door?"

"Because they would have had to go along the corridor and someone may have heard them. In any case, it was simpler for the two men in the room to hand the child over to the man waiting in the garden. Come to think of it, the fact that the shutters and windows were so securely shut is further proof that she was taken out that way and that she didn't go of her own free will."

M. Jackal indicated where a large piece had been torn out of the muslin curtain by a hand that had grabbed hold of it.

"So that's what happened. The child was taken out through the window, and then passed over the wall. After that, the person still left on the premises put the ladder back in the shed, went back into the house, locked the windows and shutters on the inside, looped a silk thread around the bolt knob, closed the door, pulled on the thread, and went peacefully to bed."

"But while she was going in and out of the dormitory she must have been seen."

"Have you any other residents occupying their own room like Mademoiselle Mina?"

"Only one."

"Then she's the one who carried it out. My dear Monsieur Salvator, we've found the woman!"

"What? You think it's Mina's friend who is the cause of all this?"

"I didn't say the cause, I said the accomplice."

"Suzanne!" exclaimed Madame Desmarets.

"Madame," said Justin, "believe me, it must be the case."

"But what put that idea in your head, monsieur?"

"The dislike I felt for that young woman the first time I saw her. Oh, madame! It was like a premonition that something awful would happen because of her. As soon as monsieur started talking about a woman," continued Justin, indicating M. Jackal, "I thought of her. I didn't dare accuse her, but I suspected her. For heaven's sake, monsieur, bring her here and confront her."

"No," replied M. Jackal. "Let's not bring her here, let's go to her. Madame, please lead us to the young woman's room."

Madame Desmarets, who, in the face of the relentless M. Jackal, had lost all will to resist, went ahead wordlessly and pointed the way.

The room was situated on the first floor at the end of the corridor.

"Knock on the door, madame," instructed M. Jackal.

Madame Desmarets knocked, but there was no reply.

"She may be on the eleven o'clock break," said Madame Desmarets. "Should I call her?"

"No," replied M. Jackal. "Let's look at her room first."

"There's no key in the door."

"But you have duplicate keys for all the doors. Isn't that what you told me?"

"Yes, monsieur."

"Well then, go and find the spare key for Mademoiselle Suzanne's room, and if you happen to see her, not a word about what we've found. On your head be it."

Madame Desmarets indicated that they could count on her discretion and went downstairs. A few seconds later she returned with the key, which she handed to M. Jackal.

The door was opened.

"Messieurs," said M. Jackal. "Wait for me in the corridor. Madame Desmarets and I will make the inspection."

The two of them went in.

"There," said Madame Desmarets, indicating a closet.

M. Jackal opened the door and found a pair of blue sapphire boots on a shelf inside. He inspected the sole, which had traces of the yellow sand from the garden path along its entire length.

"Do the residents go into the orchard?" he asked Madame Desmarets.

"No, monsieur," came the reply. "The orchard, which overlooks a deserted alleyway, is not locked, but is strictly out of bounds."

"That's good," said M. Jackal, putting the boots back in their place. "I know what I wanted to know. Now, where do you think Mademoiselle Suzanne is at this moment?"

"In all likelihood, she's in the playground."

"And which room in your establishment overlooks the playground?"

"The salon."

"Then let's go to the salon, madame."

So saying, he walked out of Mademoiselle Suzanne's room, leaving Madame Desmarets to lock the door.

"Well?" asked Salvator and Justin in unison.

"Well," replied M. Jackal, partaking of a huge pinch of snuff. "I think we've found the woman!"

Real Life Impossibility: Switzerland
Death of the Empress Elisabeth

In 1898, Elisabeth, Empress of Austria-Hungary, was walking along the promenade at Lake Geneva before boarding the steam ferry to Montreux when, without warning or apparent motive, the anarchist Luigi Lucheni plunged a needle file into her heart. Because of the very thin nature of the wound, the Empress did not realise that she had been fatally injured and witnesses saw her walk unaided to her cabin, where she collapsed. Well-meaning helpers loosened her corset, whereupon she died due to the sudden release of the pressure that had been stanching the flow of blood.

It is not known whether she locked the cabin door behind her – which would have created the appearance of a locked-room murder. At least one prominent French locked-room expert, Roland Lacourbe, believes that this notorious event was the inspiration for Gaston Leroux's seminal *The Mystery of the Yellow Room* (1907), named by John Dickson Carr as the greatest locked-room mystery ever written. It also bears an unmistakable resemblance to the central crime in Maurice Leblanc's short story "Therese and Germaine" (1922). In Georgette Heyer's *Envious Casca* (1969), the villain took his inspiration directly from reading an account of Empress Elizabeth's death that he found in the library.

Argentina
The Twelve Figures of the World
by Jorge Luis Borges and Adolfo Bioy Casares

Like Edward D. Hoch, the Argentinian Jorge Luis Borges built his mystery reputation entirely on short stories, and wrote very few at that. But what stories! In "The Garden of Forking Paths" he gave us an almost mythic tale of fate and determinism with ideas from physics and Eastern religion overlaying a grim tale of espionage. In "Death and the Compass" he again combines his favourite themes of the labyrinth, religion, and detection into a perfect surprise-ending tale.

Those elements are again present in "The Twelve Figures of the World," co-written by Adolfo Bioy Casares and using a principle well known to magicians and mentalists. Although written as a parody, the impossible problem and solution are handled quite rigorously.

Borges, like Skvorecky and another celebrated mystery writer, Graham Greene, was nominated for the Nobel Prize in Literature, but never won.

To the memory of Jose S. Alvarez

Capricorn, Aquarius, Pisces, Aries, Taurus, thought Achilles Molinari in his sleep. Then came a moment of uncertainty. He saw the Scales, the Scorpion. Realizing his mistake, he woke with a start.

The sun had warmed his face. On the night table, perched atop a copy of the Bristol Almanac and a handful of lottery tickets, his alarm clock showed twenty to ten. Still reciting the signs, Molinari got up. He looked out of the window. There on the street corner stood the unknown man.

Molinari smiled knowingly. Ambling down the corridor, he returned with his razor, a brush, a sliver of yellow soap, and a cup of steaming water. He flung the window open wide, stared down at the unknown man with exaggerated calm, and slowly, whistling the tango "Marked Card," began to shave.

Ten minutes later Molinari was on the street, wearing his brown suit on which he still owed the Rabuffi chain of Great English Tailor Shops the final two payments. He strolled to the corner. At once, the man became absorbed in the posted lottery results.

Molinari, accustomed by now to this dreary pretense, went on to the corner of Humberto I. A bus pulled up; he boarded it. To make it easier for the man tailing him, Molinari sat at the front. Two or three blocks farther on, he glanced around. The unknown man, easily recognizable by his dark glasses, was reading a newspaper. Before reaching downtown, the bus had filled up. Molinari could have gotten off without being detected, but he had a better plan. He stayed on until the Palermo Beer Gardens: There, never once looking back, he made his way north, skirting the penitentiary wall, and entered the front gate. He thought he was behaving normally, but before reaching the armed guards he threw away a cigarette that he had just lit. He spoke briefly to a man in shirtsleeves behind a counter. A prison officer accompanied him to cell 273.

Fourteen years earlier, Agustin R. Bonorino, the butcher, while taking part in a carnival parade in Belgrano rigged out as an Italian, received a fatal conk on the head. It was common knowledge that the seltzer bottle that had laid him low had been wielded by one of the goons in the gang known as the Holy Hoofs. But since the Holies were useful during elections, the police decided that the culprit was Isidro Parodi, who some claimed was an anarchist, by which they meant an oddball. Actually, Isidro Parodi was neither. He owned a barbershop in Barracas, on the Southside of Buenos Aires, and he had been unwise enough to have let a room to a police clerk from the Eighth Precinct, who owed him a year's back rent. This conjunction of adverse circumstances had sealed Parodi's fate. The evidence of witnesses (all of whom belonged to the Holy Hoofs) was unanimous; Parodi was sentenced to twenty-one years. A sedentary life had worked a change in the homicide of 1919; he was now in his forties, sententious and fat, and had a shaved head and unusually wise eyes. These eyes were now fixed on young Molinari.

"What can I do for you, my friend?"

The tone was not overly cordial, but Molinari knew that Parodi was not averse to visits. Besides, any reaction of Parodi's was less important than Molinari's need to find a confidant and a counselor. Slowly and efficiently, Parodi brewed maté in a small blue mug.

He offered some to Molinari. Molinari, though impatient to explain the irreversible adventure that had turned his life upside down, knew it was pointless to try to hurry Isidro Parodi. Molinari astounded himself by the ease with which he launched into a casual discussion of the racetrack and how it was rigged nowadays so that nobody could tell who was going to win anymore. Don Isidro paid no attention. Taking up his favorite gripe, he railed on and on against the Italians, who had wormed their way into everything – not excluding the state penitentiary.

"Now it's full of foreigners of the most dubious pedigree," he said, "and nobody knows where they come from."

Molinari, who was prone to nationalistic sentiments, joined battle to say that he was fed up with Italians and Druses, not to mention English capitalists, who had filled Argentina with railways and meat-packing plants. Only yesterday he'd walked into the All-Star Pizza Parlor, and the first thing he set eyes on was an Italian.

"Tell me," said Don Isidro, "this Italian that's on your mind – is it a man or a woman?"

"Neither," replied Molinari, to the point. "Don Isidro, I have killed a man."

"They say I killed one too, and yet look at me. Take it easy. This business of the Druses is complicated, but as long as no clerk in the Eighth Precinct has it in for you, maybe your hide can be saved."

Molinari was taken aback. Then he remembered that his name had been linked to the mystery of Ibn Khaldun's villa by an unscrupulous newspaper – a newspaper that was a breed apart from the dynamic daily for which Molinari reported on soccer as well as the nobler sports. He recalled that Parodi kept his mind sharp and, thanks to his astuteness and the generous oversight of Assistant Chief Grondona, always submitted the afternoon papers to intelligent scrutiny. In fact, don Isidro was not unaware of the recent demise of Ibn Khaldun. Nonetheless, he asked Molinari to explain what had happened, requesting him not to speak fast, since he was becoming a bit hard of hearing. Molinari, almost relaxed, told this story:

"Believe me, I'm a modern guy, a man of my times. I've seen a thing or two, but I also enjoy a bit of meditation. It seems to me that mankind has gone beyond the stage of materialism. Holy Communion and the mobs who attended the recent Eucharistic Congress left me with something unforgettable. As you said last time – and believe you me, your words didn't fall on deaf ears – life's enigma has to be solved. Look, fakirs and yogis, with their breathing exercises and their gimmicks, know a thing or two. As a good Catholic, I've renounced the Honor and Patria Spiritualist Institute, but I'm convinced that the Druses form a forward-looking community and are closer to the mystery than many who go to Mass every Sunday. For instance, Dr. Ibn Khaldun had a real showplace out in Villa Mazzini, with a fabulous library. I first met him at Radio Phoenix on Arbor Day. He made a really meaningful speech, and he praised me for an article of mine that someone had sent him. He took me to his house, lent me serious books, and invited me to a party he was giving. The female element was missing, but these cultural exchanges are something, let me tell you. People accuse the Druses of believing in idols, but in their assembly room there's a metal statue of a bull that must be worth a king's ransom. Every Friday the Akils – they're the initiates – gather around the bull. A while ago, Dr. Ibn Khaldun wanted me to be initiated. I didn't see how I could refuse; I wanted to be on good terms with the old guy, and man doesn't live by bread alone. The Druses are a closed group; some of them didn't think a Westerner was worthy of entering the brotherhood. To give one example, Abdul Hassam, the owner of a fleet of trucks that carry frozen meat, recalled that the number of the chosen is fixed and that it's not in the bylaws to make converts. The treasurer, Izz-al-Din, was opposed too. But he's a nobody who spends his whole day at a desk scribbling figures in a ledger. Dr. Ibn Khaldun laughed off him and his books. Still, these reactionaries, with their outdated prejudices, kept trying to cut the ground from under me, and I wouldn't hesitate to come right out and say that indirectly they're to blame for everything. The eleventh of August I had a letter from Ibn Khaldun, informing me that on the fourteenth I'd be put through a pretty stiff test, for which I had to prepare myself."

"And what did you have to do to prepare yourself?" asked Parodi.

"Well, as I'm sure you know, three days on nothing but tea, learning the signs of the Zodiac – in their correct order – the way they appear in the Bristol Almanac. I asked for sick leave at the Sanitation Department, where I work mornings. At first, it surprised me that the ceremony was to take place on a Sunday and not on a Friday, but the letter explained that for an examination as important as this one the Lord's day was more appropriate. I was told to turn up at the villa before midnight. All Friday and Saturday I was relatively calm, but on Sunday I woke up with a bad case of nerves. You see, Don Isidro, now that I think about it I'm sure I already had a premonition of what was going to happen. But I didn't cave in. I spent the whole day with the book in my hand. It was comical. Every five minutes I looked at my watch to see if I could have another glass of tea. I don't know why the watch; I had to drink anyway. My throat was parched, and it cried out for liquid. And then, although I had been waiting and waiting for the hour of the examination, I went and missed the train out of Retiro. The one I took, the eleven-eighteen, was slower than the one I should have been on.

"Despite being well rehearsed, I kept studying the Almanac on the train. I was annoyed by a gang of idiots arguing about how the Millionaires trounced the Chacarita Juniors, and, believe you me, they didn't know a thing about soccer. I got off at Belgrano R. The villa's located about thirteen blocks from the station. I thought the walk was going to refresh me; instead, it left me bushed. Following Ibn Khaldun's instructions to the letter, I phoned him from the bar at the corner of Rosetti Street.

"In front of the villa was a line of parked cars; the house was lit up as if for a wake, and from a long way off you could hear the sound of voices. Ibn Khaldun was waiting for me in the doorway. It struck me that he had aged. I'd always seen him by day; only that night did I realize that with his beard and all he looked a bit like D'Annunzio. Here's one of life's little ironies. Worried half out of my wits over the examination, I go and notice a foolish thing like that. We made our way along the brick walk that went around the house and entered by a back door. Izz-al-Din was in the office, standing beside the files."

"It's fourteen years now that I've been filed away," remarked Don Isidro sweetly. "But this office – describe the place a little."

"Well, it's very simple. The office is on the upper floor. A stairway comes down directly into the assembly room. That's where the Druses were, about a hundred and fifty of them, all veiled and dressed in white robes, standing around the metal bull. The files are in an alcove off the office – it's an inner room. I've always maintained that in the long run a room without a proper window is unhealthy. You feel the same, don't you?"

"Don't talk to me about rooms without windows. Since settling here on the Northside I'm fed up with blank walls. Describe the office."

"It's a big room. There's an oak desk with an Olivetti on it, some really comfortable armchairs that you sink down to your ears in, one of those Turkish pipe things that seemed to be broken but still worth a mint, a crystal chandelier, a kind of futuristic-looking Oriental carpet, a bust of Napoleon, a library of serious books – Cesare Cantù's *World History*, *The Wonders of the World and of Man*, *The International Library of Famous Authors*, the *Daily Mirror Yearbook*, Peluffo's *Illustrated Gardener*, *The Treasure of Youth*, Lombroso's *Criminal Woman*, and who knows what else.

"Izz-al-Din was nervous. Right away I found out why; he'd gone back to work on his books. There was an enormous stack of them on the table. Dr. Ibn Khaldun, concerned about my examination, wanted to get rid of Izz-al-Din and he said to him, 'Don't worry. I'll look into your books later tonight.'

"I don't know whether Izz-al-Din believed him or not. He left to put on his robe to go down with the others. He never once glanced at me. As soon as we were alone, Dr. Ibn Khaldun said to me, 'Have you fasted faithfully? Have you learned the twelve figures of the world?'

"I assured him that since ten o'clock on Thursday night – earlier that evening, in the company of some drumbeaters for the new sensibility, I had eaten a light stew and some roast beef at the Wholesale Market – I'd had nothing but plain tea.

"Then Ibn Khaldun asked me to recite the names of the twelve figures. I recited them without a single mistake; he made me repeat the list five or six times. Finally, he said to me, 'I see you've carried out your instructions. This wouldn't have been enough, however, had you not been diligent and brave. I know that you are, and I've decided to ignore your detractors. I shall put you to a single test – the most perilous and difficult of all. Thirty years ago, in the mountains of

Lebanon, I myself performed it, but my masters assigned me other easier tests beforehand. I found a coin at the bottom of the sea, a forest made of air, a chalice at the center of the earth, a saber condemned to Hell. You will not seek four magical objects; you shall seek out the four masters who make up the veiled tetragon of the Godhead. Right now, entrusted with a pious mission, they are gathered around the metal bull, praying with their brothers, the Akils, who are also veiled. No mark distinguishes them, but your heart will recognize them. I command you to bring Yusuf. You will descend to the auditorium, remembering in their exact order the twelve figures of the heavens. When you reach the last figure, the sign of Pisces, you shall return to the first, which is Aries, and so on in rotation. Thrice you will weave a circle round the Akils and your steps will lead you to Yusuf – so long as you have not changed the order of the figures. You will tell him, "Ibn Khaldun summons," and you will bring him here. Then I shall command you to bring the second master, then the third, then the fourth.'

"Luckily, reading and rereading the Bristol Almanac so many times had engraved the twelve figures in my mind, but to make a mistake all you need is to be told not to. I was not daunted, I assure you, but I had a premonition. Ibn Khaldun shook my hand, told me his prayers would be with me, and I started down the stairs into the gathering. I was very busy with the figures; as if that weren't enough, those white backs, those bowed heads, those smooth masks, and that sacred bull I'd never before seen close up made me uneasy. Still, I circled three times without a mistake, and I found myself behind a person in a sheet who looked to me exactly like all the others. But as my mind was working on the signs of the Zodiac, I had no time to think, and I said, 'Ibn Khaldun summons.' The man followed me. I kept the signs in mind as we climbed the stairway and entered the office. Ibn Khaldun was praying; he made Yusuf enter the alcove, and almost immediately he turned again and said to me, 'Now bring Ibrahim.' I went back to the assembly, made my three turns, stopped behind another man in a sheet, and said, 'Ibn Khaldun summons.' Leading him, I returned to the office."

"Whoa, my friend, whoa," said Parodi. "Are you sure that while you were weaving your three circles no one left the office?"

"Look, I can tell you positively. I admit I was concentrating on the figures and all that, but I'm not that foolish. I didn't take my eyes off that door. Nobody went in or came out.

"Ibn Khaldun took Ibrahim by the arm and ushered him into the other room. Then he said to me, 'Now bring Izz-al-Din.' A strange thing, Don Isidro, the first two times I had all the confidence in the world; this time I lost my nerve. I went down, I walked around the Druses three times, and I returned with Izz-al-Din. I was absolutely exhausted. On the stairway my sight blurred. I figured it was my kidneys acting up. Everything seemed different – even the man beside me. Ibn Khaldun himself had so much faith in me by now that I found him playing a game of solitaire instead of praying. He herded Izz-al-Din into the alcove and, speaking like a father, said to me, 'This exercise has worn you out. I shall seek the fourth initiate – Kahlil.'

"Fatigue is the enemy of concentration, but as soon as Ibn Khaldun went out, I put my nose to the gallery railing and spied on him. He made his three turns without any ado, took Kahlil by the arm, and brought him back up. I said that the alcove had no other door than the one that opened into the office. Well, Ibn Khaldun entered that door with Kahlil; straightaway he came out with the four veiled Druses. He made the sign of the cross, because these Druses are very devout people. Then he told them in good Argentine to take off their veils. You'll say I've made all this up, but there was Izz-al-Din with that foreign face of his, and Kahlil, the assistant manager of Dyno-Rod Pipe, Drain, and Hygiene Services, and Yusuf, the brother-in-law of a man who talks through his nose, and Ibrahim, Ibn Khaldun's partner, unshaven and white as a corpse. A hundred and fifty identical Druses, and here were the four masters!

"Dr. Ibn Khaldun almost embraced me. But the others were the sort that hate to show their feelings, and being full of superstitions and taboos they wouldn't let him twist their arms. They got angry with him in Druse. Poor Ibn Khaldun tried hard to convince them, but in the end he had to submit. He said he would put me to another test, an extremely difficult one this time, but that in this test the lives of all of them and maybe the fate of the world would be at stake.

"'We'll blindfold you with this veil,' he said. 'We'll put this long rod in your hand, and each of us will hide in some corner or other of the house or garden. You'll wait here until the clock strikes twelve. Then you'll search for us, one by one, guided by the figures. These signs rule the world. While the examination lasts, we shall entrust you with the order of the figures. The entire cosmos will be in your power. If you do not change the order of the Zodiac, our fate and the fate of the world will continue on their predetermined course. If you make a mistake – if, for instance, after Libra you come up with Leo or Scorpio – the master you seek will perish, and the whole wide world will fall victim to the menace of wind and water and fire.'

"Everyone agreed, except for Izz-al-Din. He'd stuffed himself with so much salami that his eyes were half shut, and he was so flustered that on leaving he shook hands with us all, one by one – a thing he never does.

"They handed me a bamboo rod, blindfolded me, and scattered. I was alone. I was petrified! I had to imagine the figures without changing their order; I had to wait for the stroke of twelve, which I was sure would never come, knowing all the while that I'd have to find my way through that house. Suddenly the place seemed not only interminable but completely unfamiliar. Without trying to, I kept thinking about the stairway, the landings, the furniture I'd bump into, the cellars, the courtyard, the skylights. And I heard all sorts of things – the branches of the trees in the garden; some footsteps upstairs; the Druses, who were leaving the house; Abd-al-Malik's Isotta starting up. You know, he's the one who won the Raggio Olive Oil raffle. Well, everybody was leaving and there I was, all alone in the mansion, with those Druses hiding God knows where. When midnight struck I nearly jumped out of my skin! I set out with my wand – me, a young man, still in the prime of life – walking like a cripple, like a blind man, if you know what I mean. I immediately turned left. The brother-in-law of the guy that talks through his nose has a lot of savoir faire, and I thought I'd find him under the table. At this time, clear as a bell, I saw Libra, Scorpio, Sagittarius, and all those illustrations. I forgot the first landing and kept stumbling. Then I entered the conservatory. Suddenly I was lost. I couldn't find either the door or the walls. What else would you expect after three days on plain tea, not to mention the strain of concentration? Still, I took myself in hand and headed for the dumbwaiter, suspecting that one of them might have hidden himself in the coalbin. But these Druses, no matter how educated they are, haven't our native Argentine cunning. I went back to the assembly room. I tripped over a three-legged table used by some of the Druses who still believe in spiritualism – as if they were back in the Middle Ages. I felt that all the eyes in the oil paintings were staring at me. You'll probably laugh – my younger sister always said I have something of the mad poet in me. But I was on my toes, and at once I discovered Ibn Khaldun. I stretched out an arm and there he was. Without much trouble we found the stairway, which turned out to be a lot closer than I thought, and we entered the office. On our way, we didn't exchange a single word. I was too busy concentrating on the signs. I left him and went to look for another Druse. Just then I heard a stifled laugh. For the first time, a doubt crossed my mind. I began to think they were laughing at me. Suddenly I heard a cry. I'd swear I made no mistake with the signs. But what with my anger and then my surprise I may have mixed them up – I never try to hide the truth. I turned around and, prodding with my rod, I went back into the office. I tripped over something on the floor. I squatted down. My hand touched hair; I felt a nose, eyes. Without realizing what I was doing, I tore off the blindfold.

"Ibn Khaldun lay on the floor, his mouth covered with saliva and blood. I touched him; he was still warm but he was already a corpse. There was no one in the room. I saw the rod, which had fallen from my hand. Blood stained the tip of it. Only then did I see I had killed him. When I heard the laugh and the cry, I must have become momentarily confused and changed the order of the figures. That cost a man his life – maybe even the lives of the four masters. I looked over the gallery and called out. Nobody answered. In a panic, I ran through the back part of the house, mumbling to myself, 'The Ram, the Bull, the Twins,' trying to keep the world in one piece. Despite the fact that the grounds were nearly a block long, I was at the garden wall in no time. Tullido Ferrarotti always said I had a future in the middle-distance events, but that night I turned into a champion high-jumper. With one leap I cleared the wall, which is close to six feet high. Picking myself up from the ditch and brushing off the pieces of broken glass that clung to me, I found I was coughing. From the villa poured a column of smoke, thick and black as mattress stuffing. Out of condition or not, I sprinted like I used to in the old days. When I reached Rosetti Street I turned around. The sky was lit up like Independence Day. The house was burning – that's what a mix-up in the figures could do! Just the thought of it made my mouth drier than a parrot's tongue. Catching a glimpse of a cop on the corner, I did an about-face, then dashed across some open lots. What a disgrace that we still have them in this city! As a good Argentine it hurt me, let me tell you, and what with shaking off a pack of dogs I was quite dizzy. All it takes is one to start barking for all the others to deafen you. Out there in those Westside neighborhoods you're not safe walking around, and there's no police of any kind. But after a while, seeing I was on Charlone Street, I calmed down. A right, then a left, and I found myself at the wall of the Chacarita. A bunch of hooligans standing on a street corner began chanting, 'The Ram, the Bull,' and making noises unfit for a human mouth. What could I do? I gave them a wide berth. Would you believe it took some time before I realized I was repeating the names of the signs out loud? I lost my way again. You know how it is out in that part of the city. They don't know a thing about urbanization, and all the streets end up in a labyrinth. The idea of looking for transportation didn't even occur to me. My shoes were a mess. I got home just about the time the trash men were making their rounds. I was sick with exhaustion; I think I was even running a temperature. I threw myself down on my bed, but so as not to lose my concentration on the figures I wouldn't let myself fall asleep.

"At noon I asked for sick leave from both the newspaper and the Sanitation Department. That was when my neighbor poked his head in – he's on the road for Brylcreem – and he insisted on taking me to his room for a spaghetti feed. I'm opening my heart to you now. At first I felt a little better. My friend has a bit of the old savoir faire, and he uncorked a nice little local muscatel. But I was in no mood for deep conversation. Using the excuse that the sauce sat on my stomach like lead, I retired to my room. I didn't go out all day. Still, not being a hermit and worried stiff about what had happened the night before, I asked the landlady to bring me a copy of the afternoon paper. I skipped the sports page, plunged straight into the crime news, and saw the photographs of the holocaust. At twelve-thirty in the morning a fire of vast proportions had broken out in the Villa Mazzini home of Dr. Ibn Khaldun. Despite the brave efforts of the Fire Department, the property was gutted by the flames, its owner, the distinguished member of the Syrio-Lebanese community, also perishing in the blaze. Dr. Ibn Khaldun was a pioneer in the importation of linoleum substitutes. I was horror-stricken. Baudizzone, who's always sloppy in his reporting, had made several errors. For example, he completely overlooked the religious ceremony and said that that night they had met to read the minutes and to reelect officers. A little before the disaster, the Messrs. Kahlil, Yusuf, and Ibrahim had left the premises. They claimed that up until midnight they had been engaged in amicable conversation with the deceased, who, far from foreseeing the tragedy that would put an end to his days and would reduce to ashes a residence characteristic of our city's western zone, displayed his usual esprit. The cause of the great conflagration was still to be determined.

"I'm not afraid of work, but from then on I haven't been back to the paper or to the department. I've been in a terrible state. Two days later, I was paid a visit by an affable gentleman, who questioned me about my part in the requisition of brooms and mops for the personnel canteen at the government warehouse on Bucarelli Street. Then he changed the subject and spoke of foreign communities, and he was especially interested in the Syrio-Lebanese. He vaguely promised to come back again, but he never did. Instead, a total stranger installed himself on my street corner, and he follows me everywhere, hiding behind dark glasses. I know you aren't a man to be taken in by the police or by anybody else. Help me, Don Isidro. I'm desperate!"

"I'm neither a wizard nor a magician – I don't go around solving riddles. I won't deny you a helping hand, however. But there's one condition. Promise me you'll do everything I tell you."

"Whatever you say, Don Isidro."

"Good. We'll begin right now. Recite in order the figures of the Almanac."

"Aries, Taurus, Gemini, Cancer, Leo, Virgo, Libra, Scorpio, Sagittarius, Capricorn, Aquarius, Pisces."

"Fine. Now say them backward."

Molinari, his face pale, mumbled, "Riesa, Rustau – "

"Can the pig Latin. Now change the order and say the figures any way you like."

"Change the order? You haven't understood me, Don Isidro. That can't be done!"

"No? Give the first sign, the last, and next to last."

On the brink of terror, Molinari obeyed. Then he looked wildly around him.

"Good. Now that you've emptied your head of this nonsense, off you go to the paper. And don't worry about a thing."

Speechless, redeemed, dumbfounded, Molinari left the jail. Outside, the man was waiting for him.

A week later, Molinari told himself that he couldn't wait any longer, he'd have to pay a second visit to the penitentiary. Still, having to face Parodi troubled him, for Parodi had seen through his vanity and his pitiful gullibility. It galled him that a man of his sophistication should let himself be bamboozled by a pack of foreign fanatics! At the same time, the appearances of the affable gentleman had become more frequent and more sinister. He spoke not only of the Syrio-Lebanese but also of the Druses of Lebanon. And his conversation was enriched by new subjects – for example, the abolition of torture in 1813, the merits of an electric prod recently imported from Bremen by the Criminal Investigation Division, and so forth.

One rainy morning, Molinari caught the bus at the corner of Humberto I. When he got off in Palermo, the unknown man got off too. He had graduated from dark glasses to a blond beard.

As usual, Parodi received Molinari with a certain curtness. The older man had the tact not to refer to the Villa Mazzini mystery. He launched into a theme that was almost obsessive with him – what a man could do with a solid knowledge of cards. He called to mind the teachings of Lynxie Rivarola, who was hit by a chair and died just as he drew a second ace of spades from a special device he had up his sleeve. Complementing the anecdote, Parodi brought out a greasy pack of cards, had Molinari shuffle them, and asked him to lay out the cards, face down.

"My dear friend," said Parodi, "you who have magic powers are going to hand this poor old man the four of hearts."

"I've – I've never pretended to have magic powers," stammered Molinari. "You know very well, sir, that I've cut all ties with those fanatics."

"You've cut that deck too. Give me the four of hearts. Don't be afraid. It's the first card you'll reach for."

His hand shaking, Molinari picked up a card at random and gave it to Parodi.

"Wonderful," Parodi said, glancing at it. "Now you're going to give me the jack of spades."

Molinari picked and offered another card. "The seven of clubs."

Molinari handed Parodi a card.

"The exercise has tired you. I'll pick the last card for you. It's the king of hearts."

Casually, Parodi drew a card and added it to the three previous ones. Then he told Molinari to turn them up. They were the king of hearts, the seven of clubs, the jack of spades, and the four of hearts.

"Don't be so amazed," said Parodi. "Among these cards is one that's marked – the first I asked for, but not the first you gave me. I asked for the four of hearts; you gave me the jack of spades. I asked for the jack of spades; you gave me the seven of clubs. I asked for the seven of clubs; you gave me the king of hearts. Then I said you were tired and that I would pick the fourth card myself – the king of hearts. I picked the four of hearts, the marked card.

"Ibn Khaldun did the same. He ordered you to seek out Druse number one, and you brought him number two. He asked for number two, and you brought him three. He asked for three and you brought him four. He told you he'd find number four himself, and he brought number one. Number one was Ibrahim, his closest friend. Ibn Khaldun had no trouble recognizing him even among the crowd. You see – this is what happens to people who get themselves mixed up with foreigners. You told me yourself that the Druses are a closed society. You were right, and the most closed of them all was Ibn Khaldun, the dean of the community. The rest were satisfied just to make fun of a native Argentine; it was Ibn Khaldun who wanted to rub it in. He told you to appear on a Sunday, and you said yourself that Friday was the day of his services. To give you a case of nerves he put you on a three-day diet of tea and the Bristol Almanac. On top of that, he made you walk I don't know how many blocks. He plunged you into the midst of a gathering of Druses who were got up in bedsheets and, as if you needed more confusing, he made up the business of the figures of the Almanac. The man was having his fun. He hadn't yet looked over Izz-al-Din's account books – nor would he ever. Those were the books they were talking about when you entered. You thought they were speaking about mere novels and poetry. Who knows what fiddling the treasurer had done. But what's certain is that he killed Ibn Khaldun and burned down the house so that no one would ever see those books. He said goodbye to you all, he shook hands – a thing he never did – to make you think he had left. He hid nearby, waited for the others to leave – by then they'd have had enough of the joke – and when you, with the rod and blindfold, were looking for Ibn Khaldun, Izz-al-Din went back to the office. When you returned with the old man, the two of them laughed to see you walking around like a blind man. You went out to find a second Druse. Ibn Khaldun followed you so that you would find him again; you made four trips, bumping into things and bringing the same person back each time. The treasurer then knifed him in the back; you heard the cry. While you were going back to the room, feeling your way, Izz-al-Din fled, setting fire to the books. After that, to justify the disappearance of the books, he set fire to the house."

Pujato, Province of Santa Fe, December 27, 1941

Greece
Rhampsinitos and the Thief
by Herodotus

Herodotus was a Greek historian born in Halicarnassus in the Persian Empire who lived in the fifth century BC (c. 484–c. 425 BC), a contemporary of Socrates. Cicero called him "The Father of History." He was the first known historian to break from Homeric tradition and treat historical subjects as methods of investigation – specifically by collecting his materials systematically and critically, and then arranging them into a historiographic narrative.

The tale of Rhampsinitos and the Thief was told to Herodotus during his travels in Egypt, and he set it down for later use.

It is surely the oldest locked room story ever published, and the author can be forgiven if the solution is one which most present-day writers would disdain to use.

After Proteus, Rhampsinitos received in succession the kingdom, who left as a memorial of himself that gateway to the temple of Hephaistos which is turned towards the West, and in front of the gateway he set up two statues, in height five-and-twenty cubits, of which the one which stands on the North side is called by the Egyptians Summer and the one on the South side Winter; and to that one which they call Summer they do reverence and make offerings, while to the other which is called Winter they do the opposite of these things.

This king, they said, got great wealth of silver, which none of the kings born after him could surpass or even come near to, and wishing to store his wealth in safety he caused to be built a chamber of stone, one of the walls whereof was towards the outside of his palace. And the builder of this, having a design against it, contrived as follows, that is, he disposed one of the stones in such a manner that it could be taken out easily from the wall either by two men or even by one. So when the chamber was finished, the king stored his money in it, and after some time the builder, being near the end of his life, called to him his sons (for he had two) and to them he related how he had contrived in building the treasury of the king, and all in forethought for them, that they might have ample means of living. And when he had clearly set forth to them everything concerning the taking out of the stone, he gave them the measurements, saying that if they paid heed to this matter they would be stewards of the king's treasury.

So he ended his life, and his sons made no long delay in setting to work, but went to the palace by night, and having found the stone in the wall of the chamber they dealt with it easily and carried forth for themselves a great quantity of the wealth within.

And the king happening to open the chamber, he marvelled when he saw the vessels falling short of the full amount, and he did not know on whom he should lay the blame, since the seals were unbroken and the chamber had been close shut; but when upon his opening the chamber a second and a third time the money was each time seen to be diminished, for the thieves did not slacken in their assaults upon it, he did as follows: Having ordered traps to be made he set these round about the vessels in which the money was, and when the thieves had come as at former times and one of them had entered, then so soon as he came near to one of the vessels he was straightway caught in the trap. And when he perceived in what evil case he was, straightway calling his brother he showed him what the matter was, and bade him enter as quickly as possible and cut off his head, for fear lest being seen and known he might bring about the destruction of his brother also. And to the other it seemed that he spoke well, and he was persuaded and did so; and fitting the stone into its place he departed home bearing with him the head of his brother.

Now when it became day, the king entered into the chamber and was very greatly amazed, seeing the body of the thief held in the trap without his head, and the chamber unbroken, with no way to come in by or go out. And being at a loss he hung up the dead body of the thief upon the wall and set guards there, with charge if they saw any one weeping or bewailing himself to seize him and bring him before the king. And when the dead body had been hung up, the mother was greatly grieved, and speaking with the son who survived she enjoined him, in whatever way he could, to contrive means by which he might take down and bring home the body of his brother, and if he should neglect to do this, she earnestly threatened that she would go and give information to the king that he had the money.

So as the mother dealt hardly with the surviving son, and he though saying many things to her did not persuade her, he contrived for his purpose a device as follows: Providing himself with asses he filled some skins with wine and laid them upon the asses, and after that he drove them along, and when he came opposite to those who were guarding the corpse hung up, he drew towards him two or three of the necks of the skins and loosened the cords with which they were tied. Then when the wine was running out, he began to beat his head and cry out loudly, as if he did not know to which of the asses he should first turn; and when the guards saw the wine flowing out in streams, they ran together to the road with drinking vessels in their hands and collected the wine that was poured out, counting it so much gain, and he abused them all violently, making as if he were angry, but when the guards tried to appease him, after a time he feigned to be pacified and to abate his anger, and at length he drove his asses out of the road and began to set their loads right. Then more talk arose among them, and one or two of them made jests at him and brought him to laugh with them, and in the end he made them a present of one of the skins in addition to what they had.

Upon that they lay down there without more ado, being minded to drink, and they took him into their company and invited him to remain with them and join them in their drinking, so he (as may be supposed) was persuaded and stayed.

Then as they in their drinking bade him welcome in a friendly manner, he made a present to them also of another of the skins, and so at length having drunk liberally the guards became completely intoxicated, and being overcome by sleep they went to bed on the spot where they had been drinking.

He then, as it was now far on in the night, first took down the body of his brother, and then in mockery shaved the right cheeks of all the guards, and after that he put the dead body upon the asses and drove them away home, having accomplished that which was enjoined him by his mother.

Upon this the king, when it was reported to him that the dead body of the thief had been stolen away, displayed great anger, and desiring by all means that it should be found out who it might be who devised these things, did this (so at least they said, but I do not believe the account): He caused his own daughter to sit in the stews, and enjoined her to receive all equally, and before having commerce with any one to compel him to tell her what was the most cunning and what the most unholy deed which had been done by him in all his lifetime, and whosoever should relate that which had happened about the thief, him she must seize and not let him go out.

Then as she was doing that which was enjoined by her father, the thief, hearing for what purpose this was done and having a desire to get the better of the king in resource, did thus: From the body of one lately dead he cut off the arm at the shoulder and went with it under his mantle, and having gone in to the daughter of the king, and being asked that which the others also were asked, he related that he had done the most unholy deed when he cut off the head of his brother, who had been caught in a trap in the king's treasure chamber, and the most cunning deed in that he made drunk the guards and took down the dead body of his brother hanging up, and she when she heard it tried to take hold of him, but the thief held out to her in the darkness the arm of the corpse, which she grasped and held, thinking that she was holding the arm of the man himself, but the thief left it in her hands and departed, escaping through the door.

Now when this also was reported to the king, he was at first amazed at the ready invention and daring of the fellow, and then afterwards he sent round to all the cities and made proclamation granting a free pardon to the thief, and also promising a great reward if he would come into his presence. The thief accordingly trusting to the proclamation came to the king, and Rhampsinitos greatly marvelled at him, and gave him this daughter of his to wife, counting him to be the most knowing of all men; for as the Egyptians were distinguished from all other men, so was he from the other Egyptians.

Real Life Impossibility: Germany
Mass Murder in the Basement

Herr Konrad was a truck driver in Berlin in the 1880s. His wife and five children were found dead in their cellar and it was immediately assumed it was a case of murder-suicide on the part of the mother. The ponderous cellar door had no keyhole nor any space around the molding, and was securely bolted on the inside. There was not the slightest aperture anywhere and the door fitted so tightly around the frame that a piece of paper could not have been passed through any crevice.

However, the examining magistrate, using a powerful lens, eventually found a barely discernible hole just above the bolt on the inside of the door. There was no corresponding hole on the outside, but he found a small spot where the paint seemed fresher. Inserting a heated hatpin through the hole on the inside, he pushed out a hole in the exact centre of the painted spot. A piece of horsehair and a slight film of wax were found attached to the hatpin. Konrad had bored a tiny hole through the door above the bolt, looped a piece of horsehair over the bolt's knob, and slipped the two ends through the hole. By pulling upwards on the bolt-knob until the horsehair loop was disengaged, he was able to withdraw the horsehair through the hole, which he then filled up with wax and painted over.

Konrad was found guilty and executed. He may have got the idea from a mystery novel, probably *Nena Sahib* (1858) by Hermann Goedsche, writing as “Sir John Retcliffe.”

Outer Space
The Martian Crown Jewels
by Poul Anderson

Poul Anderson was one of the giants of science-fiction writing in the mid-to-late 20th century, contributing short stories to all of the major pulp magazines and writing many respected novels. He won seven Hugo awards (the fan-voted award for best novel), and three Nebula awards (the writer-voted award for best novel), and was named a Grand Master by the Science Fiction Writers of America.

Less well known is that he also wrote a half-dozen or so mystery short stories for *Ellery Queen's Mystery Magazine, Alfred Hitchcock's Mystery Magazine,* and *The Saint Mystery Magazine.*

In this story he takes on the difficult task of melding mystery and science fiction, explaining how the Martian crown jewels were stolen from an unmanned spacecraft in flight, and producing an alien pastiche of Sherlock Holmes!

"The Martian Crown Jewels" previously appeared in Asimov, Greenberg, and Waugh's *Tantalizing Locked Room Mysteries* and has an original solution to the disappearing object problem.

The signal was picked up when the ship was still a quarter million miles away, and recorded voices summoned the technicians. There was no haste, for the ZX28749, otherwise called the Jane Brackney, was right on schedule, but landing an unmanned spaceship is always a delicate operation. Men and machines prepared to receive her as she came down, but the control crew had the first order of business.

Yamagata, Steinmann, and Ramanowitz were in the GCA tower, with Hollyday standing by for an emergency. If the circuits should fail – they never had, but a thousand tons of cargo and nuclear-powered vessel, crashing into the port, could empty Phobos of human life. So Hollyday watched over a set of spare assemblies, ready to plug in whatever might be required.

Yamagata's thin fingers danced over the radar dials. His eyes were intent on the screen. "Got her," he said. Steinmann made a distance reading and Ramanowitz took the velocity off the Dopplerscope. A brief session with a computer showed the figures to be almost as predicted.

"Might as well relax," said Yamagata, taking out a cigarette. "She won't be in control range for a while yet."

His eyes roved over the crowded room and out its window. From the tower he had a view of the spaceport: unimpressive, most of its shops and sheds and living quarters being underground. The smooth concrete field was chopped off by the curvature of the tiny satellite. It always faced Mars, and the station was on the far side, but he could remember how the planet hung enormous over the opposite hemisphere, soft ruddy disc blurred with thin air, hazy greenish-brown mottlings of heath and farmland. Though Phobos was clothed in vacuum, you couldn't see the hard stars of space: the sun and the floodlamps were too bright.

There was a knock on the door. Hollyday went over, almost drifting in the ghostly gravity, and opened it. "Nobody allowed in here during a landing," he said. Hollyday was a stocky blond man with a pleasant, open countenance, and his tone was less peremptory than his words.

"Police." The newcomer, muscular, round-faced, and earnest, was in plain clothes, tunic, and pajama pants, which was expected; everyone in the tiny settlement knew Inspector Gregg. But he was packing a gun, which was not usual, and looked harried.

Yamagata peered out again and saw the port's four constables down on the field in official spacesuits, watching the ground crew. They carried weapons. "What's the matter?" he asked.

"Nothing...I hope." Gregg came in and tried to smile. "But the Jane has a very unusual cargo this trip."

"Hmm?" Ramanowitz's eyes lit up in his broad plump visage. "Why weren't we told?"

"That was deliberate. Secrecy. The Martian crown jewels are aboard." Gregg fumbled a cigarette from his tunic.

Hollyday and Steinmann nodded at each other. Yamagata whistled. "On a robot ship?" he asked.

"Uh-huh. A robot ship is the one form of transportation from which they could not be stolen. There were three attempts made when they went to Earth on a regular liner, and I hate to think how many while they were at the British Museum. One guard lost his life. Now my boys are going to remove them before anyone else touches that ship and scoot 'em right down to Sabaeus."

"How much are they worth?" wondered Ramanowitz.

"Oh...they could be fenced on Earth for maybe half a billion UN dollars," said Gregg. "But the thief would do better to make the Martians pay to get them back – no, Earth would have to, I suppose, since it's our responsibility." He blew nervous clouds. "The jewels were secretly put on the Jane, last thing before she left on her regular run. I wasn't even told till a special messenger on this week's liner gave me the word. Not a chance for any thief to know they're here, till they're safely back on Mars. And that'll be safe!"

Ramanowitz shuddered. All the planets knew what guarded the vaults at Sabaeus.

"Some people did know, all along," said Yamagata thoughtfully. "I mean the loading crew back at Earth."

"Uh-huh, there is that." Gregg smiled. "Several of them have quit since then, the messenger said, but of course, there's always a big turnover among spacejacks – they're a restless bunch." His gaze drifted across Steinmann and Hollyday, both of whom had last worked at Earth Station and come to Mars a few ships back. The liners went on a hyperbolic path and arrived in a couple of weeks; the robot ships followed the more leisurely and economical Hohmann A orbit and needed 258 days. A man who knew what ship was carrying the jewels could leave Earth, get to Mars well ahead of the cargo, and snap up a job here – Phobos was always shorthanded.

"Don't look at me!" said Steinmann, laughing. "Chuck and I knew about this – of course – but we were under security restrictions. Haven't told a soul."

"Yeah. I'd have known it if you had," nodded Gregg. "Gossip travels fast here. Don't resent this, please, but I'm here to see that none of you boys leaves this tower till the jewels are aboard our own boat."

"Oh well. It'll mean overtime pay."

"If I want to get rich fast, I'll stick to prospecting," added Hollyday.

"When are you going to quit running around with that Geiger in your free time?" asked Yamagata. "Phobos is nothing but iron and granite."

"I have my own ideas about that," said Hollyday stoutly.

"Hell, everybody needs a hobby on this godforsaken clod," declared Ramanowitz. "I might try for those sparklers myself, just for the excitement – " He stopped abruptly, aware of Gregg's eyes.

"All right," snapped Yamagata. "Here we go. Inspector, please stand back out of the way, and for your life's sake don't interrupt us."

The Jane was drifting in, her velocity on the carefully pre-calculated orbit almost identical with that of Phobos. Almost, but not quite – there had been the inevitable small disturbing factors, which the remote-controlled jets had to compensate, and then there was the business of landing her. The team got a fix and were frantically busy.

In free fall, the Jane approached within a thousand miles of Phobos, a spheroid 500 feet in radius, big and massive, but lost against the incredible bulk of the satellite. And yet Phobos is an insignificant airless pill, negligible even beside its seventh-rate planet. Astronomical magnitudes are simply and literally incomprehensible.

When the ship was close enough, the radio directed her gyros to rotate her, very, very gently, until her pickup antenna was pointing directly at the field. Then her jets were cut in, a mere whisper of thrust. She was nearly above the spaceport, her path tangential to the moon's curvature. After a moment Yamagata slapped the keys hard, and the rockets blasted furiously, a visible red streak up in the sky. He cut them again, checked his data, and gave a milder blast.

"Okay," he grunted. "Let's bring her in."

Her velocity relative to Phobos's orbit and rotation was now zero, and she was falling. Yamagata slewed her around till the jets were pointing vertically down. Then he sat back and mopped his face while Ramanowitz took over; the job was too nerve-stretching for one man to perform in its entirety. Ramanowitz sweated the awkward mass to within a few yards of the cradle. Steinmann finished the task, easing her into the berth like an egg into a cup. He cut the jets and there was silence.

"Whew! Chuck, how about a drink?" Yamagata held out unsteady fingers and regarded them with an impersonal stare.

Hollyday smiled and fetched a bottle. It went happily around. Gregg declined. His eyes were locked to the field, where a technician was checking for radioactivity. The verdict was clean, and he saw his constables come soaring over the concrete, to surround the great ship with guns. One of them went up, opened the manhatch, and slipped inside.

It seemed a very long while before he emerged. Then he came running. Gregg cursed and thumbed the tower's radio board. "Hey, there! Ybarra! What's the matter?"

The helmet set shuddered a reply: "Señor...Señor Inspector...the crown jewels are gone."

Sabaeus is, of course, a purely human name for the old city nestled in the Martian tropics, at the juncture of the "canals" Phison and Euphrates. Terrestrial mouths simply cannot form the syllables of High Chlannach, though rough approximations are possible. Nor did humans ever build a town exclusively of towers broader at the top than the base, or inhabit one for twenty thousand years. If they had, though, they would have encouraged an eager tourist influx; but Martians prefer more dignified ways of making a dollar, even if their parsimonious fame has long replaced that of Scotchmen. The result is that though interplanetary trade is brisk and Phobos a treaty port, a human is still a rare sight in Sabaeus.

Hurrying down the avenues between the stone mushrooms, Gregg felt conspicuous. He was glad the airsuit muffled him. Not that the grave Martians stared; they varkled, which is worse.

The Street of Those Who Prepare Nourishment in Ovens is a quiet one, given over to handicrafters, philosophers, and residential apartments. You won't see a courtship dance or a parade of the Lesser Halberdiers on it – nothing more exciting than a continuous four-day argument on the relativistic nature of the null class or an occasional gunfight. The latter are due to the planet's most renowned private detective, who nests here.

Gregg always found it eerie to be on Mars, under the cold deep-blue sky and shrunken sun, among noises muffled by the thin oxygen-deficient air. But for Syaloch he had a good deal of affection, and when he had gone up the ladder and shaken the rattle outside the second-floor apartment and had been admitted, it was like escaping from a nightmare.

"Ah, Krech!" The investigator laid down the stringed instrument on which he had been playing and towered gauntly over his visitor. "An unexbectet bleas sure to see hyou. Come in, my tear chab, to come in." He was proud of his English – but simple misspellings will not convey the whistling, clicking Martian accent. Gregg had long ago fallen into the habit of translating it into a human pronunciation as he listened.

The Inspector felt a cautious way into the high, narrow room. The glowsnakes which illuminated it after dark were coiled asleep on the stone floor, in a litter of papers, specimens, and weapons; rusty sand covered the sills of the Gothic windows. Syaloch was not neat except in his own person. In one corner was a small chemical laboratory. The rest of the walls were taken up with shelves, the criminological literature of three planets – Martian books, Terrestrial micros, Venusian talking stones. At one place, patriotically, the glyphs representing the reigning Nest-mother had been punched out with bullets. An Earthling could not sit on the trapezelike native furniture, but Syaloch had courteously provided chairs and tubs as well; his clientele was also triplanetary. Gregg found a scarred Duncan Phyfe and lowered himself, breathing heavily into his oxygen tubes.

"I take it you are here on official but confidential business." Syaloch got out a big-bowled pipe. Martians have happily adopted tobacco, though in their atmosphere it must include potassium permanganate. Gregg was thankful he didn't have to breathe the blue fog.

He started. "How the hell do you know that?"

"Elementary, my dear fellow. Your manner is most agitated, and I know nothing but a crisis in your profession would cause that in a good stolid bachelor. Yet you come to me rather than the Homeostatic Corps...so it must be a delicate affair."

Gregg laughed wryly. He himself could not read any Martian's expression – what corresponds to a smile or a snarl on a totally non-human face? But this overgrown stork –

No. To compare the species of different planets is merely to betray the limitations of language. Syaloch was a seven-foot biped of vaguely storklike appearance. But the lean, crested, red-beaked head at the end of the sinuous neck was too large, the yellow eyes too deep; the white feathers were more like a penguin's than a flying bird's, save at the blue-plumed tail; instead of wings there were skinny red arms ending in four-fingered hands. And the overall posture was too erect for a bird.

Gregg jerked back to awareness. God in Heaven! The city lay gray and quiet; the sun was slipping westward over the farmlands of Sinus Sabaeus and the desert of the Aeria; he could just make out the rumble of a treadmill cart passing beneath the windows – and he sat here with a story which could blow the Solar System apart!

His hands, gloved against the chill, twisted together. “Yes, it's confidential, all right. If you can solve this case, you can just about name your own fee.” The gleam in Syaloch's eyes made him regret that, but he stumbled on: “One thing, though. Just how do you feel about us Earthlings?”

“I have no prejudices. It is the brain that counts, not whether it is covered by feathers or hair or bony plates.”

“No, I realize that. But some Martians resent us. We do disrupt an old way of life – we can't help it, if we're to trade with you – “

“K'teh. The trade is on the whole beneficial. Your fuel and machinery – and tobacco, yesss – for our kantz and snull. Also, we were getting too...stale. And of course space travel has added a whole new dimension to criminology. Yes, I favor Earth.”

“Then you'll help us? And keep quiet about something which could provoke your planetary federation into kicking us off Phobos?”

The third eyelids closed, making the long-beaked face a mask. “I give no promises yet, Gregg.”

“Well...damn it, all right, I'll have to take the chance.” The policeman swallowed hard. “You know about your crown jewels, of course.”

“They were lent to Earth for exhibit and scientific study.”

“After years of negotiation. There's no more priceless relic on all Mars – and you were an old civilization when we were hunting mammoths. All right. They've been stolen.”

Syaloch opened his eyes, but his only other movement was to nod.

“They were put on a robot ship at Earth Station. They were gone when that ship reached Phobos. We've damn near ripped the boat apart trying to find them – we did take the other cargo to pieces, bit by bit – and they aren't there!”

Syaloch rekindled his pipe, an elaborate flint-and-steel process on a world where matches won't burn. Only when it was drawing well did he suggest: “Is it possible the ship was boarded en route?”

"No. It isn't possible. Every spacecraft in the System is registered, and its whereabouts are known at any time. Furthermore, imagine trying to find a speck in hundreds of millions of cubic miles, and match velocities with it – no vessel ever built could carry that much fuel. And mind you, it was never announced that the jewels were going back this way. Only the UN police and the Earth Station crew could know till the ship had actually left – by which time it'd be too late to catch her."

"Most interesting." Syaloch puffed hard.

"If word of this gets out," said Gregg miserably, "you can guess the results. I suppose we'd still have a few friends left in your Parliament – "

"In the House of Actives, yesss...a few. Not in the House of Philosophers, which is of course the upper chamber."

"It could mean a twenty-year hiatus in Earth-Mars traffic – maybe a permanent breaking off of relations. Damn it, Syaloch, you've got to find those stones!"

"Hm-m-m. I pray your pardon. This requires thought." The Martian picked up his crooked instrument and plucked a few tentative chords. Gregg sighed and attempted to relax. He knew the Chlannach temperament; he'd have to listen to an hour of minor-key caterwauling.

The colorless sunset was past, night had fallen with the unnerving Martian swiftness, and the glowsnakes were emitting blue radiance when Syaloch put down the demifiddle.

"I fear I shall have to visit Phobos in person," he said. "There are too many unknowns for analysis, and it is never well to theorize before all the data have been gathered." A bony hand clapped Gregg's shoulder. "Come, come, old chap. I am really most grateful to you. Life was becoming infernally dull. Now, as my famous Terrestrial predecessor would say, the game's afoot – and a very big game indeed!"

A Martian in an Earthlike atmosphere is not much hampered, needing only an hour in a compression chamber and a filter on his beak to eliminate excess oxygen and moisture. Syaloch walked freely about the port clad in filter, pipe, and tirstokr cap, grumbling to himself at the heat and humidity. He noticed that all the humans but Gregg were reserved, almost fearful, as they watched him – they were sitting on a secret which could unleash red murder.

He donned a spacesuit and went out to inspect the Jane Brackney. The vessel had been shunted aside to make room for later arrivals, and stood by a raw crag at the edge of the field, glimmering in the hard spatial sunlight. Gregg and Yamagata were with him.

"I say, you have been thorough," remarked the detective. "The outer skin is quite stripped off."

The spheroid resembled an egg which had tangled with a waffle iron: an intersecting grid of girders and braces above a thin aluminum hide. The jets, hatches, and radio mast were the only breaks in the checkerboard pattern, whose depth was about a foot and whose squares were a yard across at the "equator."

Yamagata laughed in a strained fashion. "No. The cops fluoroscoped every inch of her, but that's the way these cargo ships always look. They never land on Earth, you know, or any place where there's air, so streamlining would be unnecessary. And since nobody is aboard in transit, we don't have to worry about insulation or air-tightness. Perishables are stowed in sealed compartments."

"I see. Now where were the crown jewels kept?"

"They were supposed to be in a cupboard near the gyros," said Gregg. "They were in a locked box, about six inches high, six inches wide, and a foot long." He shook his head, finding it hard to believe that so small a box could contain so much potential death.

"Ah...but were they placed there?"

"I radioed Earth and got a full account," said Gregg. "The ship was loaded as usual at the satellite station, then shoved a quarter mile away till it was time for her to leave – to get her out of the way, you understand. She was still in the same free-fall orbit, attached by a light cable – perfectly standard practice. At the last minute, without anyone being told beforehand, the crown jewels were brought up from Earth and stashed aboard."

"By a special policeman, I presume?"

"No. Only licensed technicians are allowed to board a ship in orbit, unless there's a life-and-death emergency. One of the regular station crew – fellow named Carter – was told where to put them. He was watched by the cops as he pulled himself along the cable and in through the manhatch." Gregg pointed to a small door near the radio mast. "He came out, closed it, and returned on the cable. The police immediately searched him and his spacesuit, just in case, and he positively did not have the jewels. There was no reason to suspect him of anything – good steady worker – though I'll admit he's disappeared since then. The Jane blasted a few minutes late and her jets were watched till they cut off and she went into free fall. And that's the last anyone saw of her till she got here – without the jewels."

"And right on orbit," added Yamagata. "If by some freak she had been boarded, it would have thrown her off enough for us to notice as she came in. Transference of Momentum between her and the other ship."

"I see." Behind his faceplate, Syaloch's beak cut a sharp black curve across heaven. "Now then, Gregg, were the jewels actually in the box when it was delivered?"

"At Earth Station, you mean? Oh, yes. There are four UN Chief Inspectors involved, and HQ says they're absolutely above suspicion. When I sent back word of the theft, they insisted on having their own quarters and so on searched, and went under scop voluntarily."

"And your own constables on Phobos?"

"Same thing," said the policeman grimly. "I've slapped on an embargo – nobody but me has left this settlement since the loss was discovered. I've had every room and tunnel and warehouse searched." He tried to scratch his head, a frustrating attempt when one is in a spacesuit. "I can't maintain those restrictions much longer. Ships are coming in and the consignees want their freight."

"Hnachla. That puts us under a time limit, then." Syaloch nodded to himself. "Do you know, this is a fascinating variation of the old locked-room problem. A robot ship in transit is a locked room in the most classic sense." He drifted off into a reverie.

Gregg stared bleakly across the savage horizon, naked rock tumbling away under his feet, and then back over the field. Odd how tricky your vision became in airlessness, even when you had bright lights. That fellow crossing the field there, under the full glare of sun and floodlamps, was merely a stipple of shadow and luminance – what the devil was he doing, tying a shoe of all things? No, he was walking quite normally –

"I'd like to put everyone on Phobos under scop," said Gregg with a violent note, "but the law won't allow it unless the suspect volunteers – and only my own men have volunteered."

"Quite rightly, my dear fellow," said Syaloch. "One should at least have the privilege of privacy in his own skull. And it would make the investigation unbearably crude."

"I don't give a fertilizing damn how crude it is," snapped Gregg. "I just want that box with the crown jewels safe inside."

"Tut-tut! Impatience has been the ruin of many a promising young police officer, as I seem to recall my spiritual ancestor of Earth pointing out to a Scotland Yard man who – hmm – may even have been a physical ancestor of yours, Gregg. It seems we must try another approach. Are there any people on Phobos who might have known the jewels were aboard this ship?"

"Yes. Two men only. I've pretty well established that they never broke security and told anyone else till the secret was out."

"And who are they?"

"Technicians, Hollyday and Steinmann. They were working at Earth Station when the Jane was loaded. They quit soon after – not at the same time – and came here by liner and got jobs. You can bet that their quarters have been searched!"

"Perhaps," murmured Syaloch, "it would be worthwhile to interview the gentlemen in question."

Steinmann, a thin redhead, wore truculence like a mantle; Hollyday merely looked worried. It was no evidence of guilt – everyone had been rubbed raw of late. They sat in the police office, with Gregg behind the desk and Syaloch leaning against the wall, smoking and regarding them with unreadable yellow eyes.

"Damn it, I've told this over and over till I'm sick of it!" Steinmann knotted his fists and gave the Martian a bloodshot stare. "I never touched the things and I don't know who did. Hasn't any man a right to change jobs?"

"Please," said the detective mildly. "The better you help the sooner we can finish this work. I take it you were acquainted with the man who actually put the box aboard the ship?"

"Sure. Everybody knew John Carter. Everybody knows everybody else on a satellite station." The Earthman stuck out his jaw. "That's why none of us'll take scop. We won't blab out all our thoughts to guys we see fifty times a day. We'd go nuts!"

"I never made such a request," said Syaloch.

"Carter was quite a good friend of mine," volunteered Hollyday.

"Uh-huh," grunted Gregg. "And he quit too, about the same time you fellows did, and went Earthside and hasn't been seen since. HQ told me you and he were thick. What'd you talk about?"

"The usual." Hollyday shrugged. "Wine, women, and song. I haven't heard from him since I left Earth."

"Who says Carter stole the box?" demanded Steinmann. "He just got tired of living in space and quit his job. He couldn't have stolen the jewels – he was searched, remember?"

"Could he have hidden it somewhere for a friend to get at this end?" inquired Syaloch.

"Hidden it? Where? Those ships don't have secret compartments." Steinmann spoke wearily. "And he was only aboard the Jane a few minutes, just long enough to put the box where he was supposed to." His eyes smoldered at Gregg. "Let's face it: The only people anywhere along the line who ever had a chance to lift it were our own dear cops."

The Inspector reddened and half rose. "Look here, you – "

"We've got your word that you're innocent," growled Steinmann. "Why should it be any better than mine?"

Syaloch waved both men back. "If you please. Brawls are unphilosophic." His beak opened and clattered, the Martian equivalent of a smile. "Has either of you, perhaps, a theory? I am open to all ideas."

There was a stillness. Then Hollyday mumbled: "Yes. I have one."

Syaloch hooded his eyes and puffed quietly, waiting. Hollyday's grin was shaky. "Only if I'm right, you'll never see those jewels again."

Gregg sputtered.

"I've been around the Solar System a lot," said Hollyday. "It gets lonesome out in space. You never know how big and lonesome it is till you've been there, all by yourself. And I've done just that – I'm an amateur uranium prospector, not a lucky one so far. I can't believe we know everything about the universe, or that there's only vacuum between the planets."

"Are you talking about the cobblies?" snorted Gregg.

"Go ahead and call it superstition. But if you're in space long enough...well, somehow, you know. There are beings out there – gas beings, radiation beings, whatever you want to imagine, there's something living in space."

"And what use would a box of jewels be to a cobbly?"

Hollyday spread his hands. "How can I tell? Maybe we bother them, scooting through their own dark kingdom with our little rockets. Stealing the crown jewels would be a good way to disrupt the Mars trade, wouldn't it?"

Only Syaloch's pipe broke the inward-pressing silence. But its burbling seemed quite irreverent.

"Well – " Gregg fumbled helplessly with a meteoric paperweight. "Well, Mr. Syaloch, do you want to ask any more questions?"

"Only one." The third lids rolled back, and coldness looked out at Steinmann. "If you please, my good man, what is your hobby?"

"Huh? Chess. I play chess. What's it to you?" Steinmann lowered his head and glared sullenly.

"Nothing else?"

"What else is there?"

Syaloch glanced at the Inspector, who nodded confirmation, and then replied gently:

"I see. Thank you. Perhaps we can have a game sometime. I have some small skill of my own. That is all for now, gentlemen."

They left, moving like things of dream through the low gravity.

"Well?" Gregg's eyes pleaded with Syaloch. "What next?"

"Very little. I think...yesss, while I am here I should like to watch the technicians at work. In my profession, one needs a broad knowledge of all occupations."

Gregg sighed.

Ramanowitz showed the guest around. The Kim Brackney was in and being unloaded. They threaded through a hive of spacesuited men.

"The cops are going to have to raise that embargo soon," said Ramanowitz. "Either that or admit why they've clamped it on. Our warehouses are busting."

"It would be politic to do so," nodded Syaloch. "Ah, tell me...is this equipment standard for all stations?"

"Oh, you mean what the boys are wearing and carrying around? Sure. Same issue everywhere."

"May I inspect it more closely?"

"Hmm?" Lord, deliver me from visiting firemen! thought Ramanowitz. He waved a mechanic over to him. "Mr. Syaloch would like you to explain your outfit," he said with ponderous sarcasm.

"Sure. Regular spacesuit here, reinforced at the seams." The gauntleted hands moved about, pointing. "Heating coils powered from this capacitance battery. Ten-hour air supply in the tanks. These buckles, you snap your tools into them, so they won't drift around in free fall. This little can at my belt holds paint that I spray out through this nozzle."

"Why must spaceships be painted?" asked Syaloch. "There is nothing to corrode the metal."

"Well, sir, we just call it paint. It's really gunk, to seal any leaks in the hull till we can install a new plate, or to mark any other kind of damage. Meteor punctures and so on." The mechanic pressed a trigger and a thin, almost invisible stream jetted out, solidifying as it hit the ground.

"But it cannot readily be seen, can it?" objected the Martian. "I, at least, find it difficult to see clearly in airlessness."

"That's right, Light doesn't diffuse, so...well, anyhow, the stuff is radioactive – not enough to be dangerous, just enough so that the repair crew can spot the place with a Geiger counter."

"I understand. What is the half-life?"

"Oh, I'm not sure. Six months, maybe? It's supposed to remain detectable for a year."

"Thank you." Syaloch stalked off. Ramanowitz had to jump to keep up with those long legs.

"Do you think Carter may have hid the box in his paint can?" suggested the human.

"No, hardly. The can is too small, and I assume he was searched thoroughly." Syaloch stopped and bowed. "You have been very kind and patient, Mr. Ramanowitz. I am finished now, and can find the Inspector myself."

"What for?"

"To tell him he can lift the embargo, of course." Syaloch made a harsh sibilance. "And then I must get the next boat to Mars. If I hurry, I can attend the concert in Sabaeus tonight." His voice grew dreamy. "They will be premiering Hanyech's Variations on a Theme by Mendelssohn, transcribed to the Royal Chlannach scale. It should be most unusual."

It was three days afterward that the letter came. Syaloch excused himsef and kept an illustrious client squatting while he read it. Then he nodded to the other Martian. "You will be interested to know, sir, that the Estimable Diadems have arrived at Phobos and are being returned at this moment."

The client, a Cabinet Minister from the House of Actives, blinked. "Pardon, Freehatched Syaloch, but what have you to do with that?"

"Oh...I am a friend of the Featherless police chief. He thought I might like to know."

"Hraa. Were you not on Phobos recently?"

“A minor case.” The detective folded the letter carefully, sprinkled it with salt, and ate it. Martians are fond of paper, especially official Earth stationary with high rag content. “Now, sir, you were saying?”

The parliamentarian responded absently. He would not dream of violating privacy – no never – but if he had X-ray vision he would have read:

“Dear Syaloch,

“You were absolutely right. Your locked-room problem is solved. We've got the jewels back, everything is in fine shape, and the same boat which brings you this letter will deliver them to the vaults. It's too bad the public can never know the facts – two planets ought to be grateful to you – but I'll supply that much thanks all by myself, and insist that any bill you care to send be paid in full. Even if the Assembly had to make a special appropriation, which I'm afraid it will.

“I admit your idea of lifting the embargo at once looked pretty wild to me, but it worked. I had our boys out, of course, scouring Phobos with Geigers, but Hollyday found the box before we did. Which saved us a lot of trouble, to be sure. I arrested him as he came back into the settlement, and he had the box among his ore samples. He has confessed, and you were right all along the line.

“What was that thing you quoted at me, the saying of that Earthman you admire so much? 'When you have eliminated the impossible, whatever remains, however improbable, must be true.' Something like that. It certainly applies to this case.

“As you decided, the box must have been taken to the ship at Earth Station and left there – no other possibility existed. Carter figured it out in half a minute when he was ordered to take the thing out and put it aboard the Jane. He went inside, all right, but still had the box when he emerged. In that uncertain light nobody saw him put it 'down' between four girders right next to the hatch. Or as you remarked, if the jewels are not in the ship, and yet not away from the ship, they must be on the ship. Gravitation would hold them in place. When the Jane blasted off, acceleration pressure slid the box back, but of course the waffle-iron pattern kept it from being lost; it fetched up against the after rib and stayed there. All the way to Mars! But the ship's gravity held it securely enough even in free fall, since both were on the same orbit.

"Hollyday says that Carter told him all about it. Carter couldn't go to Mars himself without being suspected and watched every minute once the jewels were discovered missing. He needed a confederate. Hollyday went to Phobos and took up prospecting as a cover for the search he'd later be making for the jewels.

"As you showed me, when the ship was within a thousand miles of this dock, Phobos gravity would be stronger than her own. Every spacejack knows that the robot ships don't start decelerating till they're quite close, that they are then almost straight above the surface, and that the side with the radio mast and manhatch – the side on which Carter had placed the box – is rotated around to face the station. The centrifugal force of rotation threw the box away from the ship, and was in a direction toward Phobos rather than away from it. Carter knew that this rotation is slow and easy, so the force wasn't enough to accelerate the box to escape velocity and lose it in space. It would have to fall down toward the satellite. Phobos Station being on the side opposite Mars, there was no danger that the loot would keep going till it hit the planet.

"So the crown jewels tumbled onto Phobos, just as you deduced. Of course Carter had given the box a quick radioactive spray as he laid it in place, and Hollyday used that to track it down among all those rocks and crevices. In point of fact, its path curved clear around this moon, so it landed about five miles from the station.

"Steinmann has been after me to know why you quizzed him about his hobby. You forgot to tell me that, but I figured it out for myself and told him. He or Hollyday had to be involved, since nobody else knew about the cargo, and the guilty person had to have some excuse to go out and look for the box. Chess playing doesn't furnish that kind of alibi. Am I right? At least, my deduction proves I've been studying the same canon you go by. Incidentally, Steinmann asks if you'd care to take him on the next time he has planet leave.

"Hollyday knows where Carter is hiding, and we've radioed the information back to Earth. Trouble is, we can't prosecute either of them without admitting the facts. Oh, well, there are such things as blacklists.

"Will have to close this now to make the boat. I'll be seeing you soon – not professionally, I hope!

"Admiring regards, Inspector Gregg"

But as it happened, the Cabinet minister did not possess X-ray eyes. He dismissed unprofitable speculation and outlined his problem.

Somebody, somewhere in Sabaeus, was farniking the hats, and there was an alarming zaksnautry among the hyukus. It sounded to Syaloch like an interesting case.

Lebanon
Leaving No Evidence
by Dudley Hoys

The impossible disappearance of a person is one of the most intriguing "locked room" situations for readers. At the same time there is relatively little room for innovation and it is difficult to pull off successfully. In this terrifying short short Dudley Hoys expertly takes on the challenge and succeeds brilliantly.
(Frank) Dudley Hoys, son of an English fishmonger, was an English army veteran (Lieutenant, Machine Gun Corps), a writer, and a playwright. He spent many years as a Cumberland hill farmer and wrote several books about the lake country. He was also a prolific short story writer and a frequent contributor to *The 20-Story Magazine, Hutchinson's Magazine, The Strand Magazine,* and *The Passing Show*, from which this 1938 story comes.

"They vanish," said Fahmi, solemnly. He snapped his thick fingers. "Like that, Mister."

Corland, the American, laughed. "Poppycock! Where to?"

Fahmi shrugged. He had the eyes of a humorous and not quite respectable spaniel. For once there was dread in them and that intrigued Corland. It made him more determined than ever to get his way.

"How do they vanish? Why do they vanish?"

Standing there respectfully, Fahmi said not a word. In his tarboosh and heavy brown burnoose, an ebony walking stick in his hand, he loomed with a sly magnificence against the cobalt of the bay below.

"Come on, Fahmi. Out with it."

"Mister, it gets them...."

"What gets them?"

"The Thing," whispered Fahmi. His eyes rolled and the bluish whites were startling against the oily, brown skin.

Corland grinned. Sure, this was funny. He had almost come to accept Fahmi as Western. Tough, sardonic, hard-boiled. He had picked the man up in Cairo while on this world tour, enjoyed the public – and private – delights of Egypt under his guidance, brought him up through Palestine and across the border to Beirut. With no morals, no scruples, and a pretty wit, he seemed a prince of dragomans. And now here he was behaving like some superstitious old mossback from the Middle Ages.

"See here, Fahmi, we're hiking."

"There is rack railway. Mister," said Fahmi, stubbornly. "Step aside at Baalbek for vast Roman ruins, including largest hewn block of stone in world. Thence – "

"Cut it out. We're hiking."

Fahmi said: "I am born in Lebanon. I live there until twenty. I know. Nine thousand feet no great height. Slope no great difficulty. In summer – a walk." He laughed and wagged an expressive hand. "But in winter, no countrymen of mine will cross." He leaned forward intensely. "I tell you something. Many have tried and most them—" His fingers snapped again.

"But how the heck do they vanish? How? Fall down a ravine or...?"

Fahmi's head shook slowly. "One moment they are there. The next they are not. The Thing gets them."

"There now," said Corland, not at all impressed. He fished a map out of his pocket, spread it on the table, and ran his fingernail along a pencilled route. "We can drive as far as that village."

"My village!" said Fahmi, squinting over his shoulder. "Where I was born. The last village below the snow line."

"Reckon you know the layout then. Stop there the night and push off about eight in the morning. Take a look at the Cedars of Lebanon on the way. Then up and over. I've calculated we should be at the top by two." His fingernail slid on. "There's a village here on the other side we can put up the next night. That's my programme."

"Not goo-ood."

"You're a mule," said Corland, genially, "but you'll budge for dollars."

"But, Mister, if anything should happen – "

"The Thing won't pinch you," said Corland, gaily, "you're too much of a twister."

"Damn honest man," said Fahmi, with a look of injured dignity.

"Oh, yeah? Think I don't know you haven't been running a kinda half-commission racket ever since I picked you up? When I bought all that stuff in the Mouski in Cairo – " Corland laughed heartily. "I'm not blaming you. Part of your game."

Fahmi considered his employer, earnestly. Corland was tall and broad, with thick greying brown hair and owlish spectacles.

"Mister, if anything happened to you – "

"Say. We'll chance it," said Corland, lightly.

Fahmi made a gesture of resignation. "One guide needed, and one man to carry belongings."

"OK. You fix that."

"I get men from my own village." Corland nodded carelessly.

Fahmi the sleek, the salacious, the sophisticated, shivered a little.

"Remember, Mister, I have given warning."

Unlike the limp stuff of cities and plains, the mountain air had a cold, taut, fragrant taste. Corland sucked it into his lungs and stared about him. The little village where he had spent the night perched on the edge of a blue-shadowed ravine.

Corland was charmed. This was real travel. Liners and cocktail bars and luxury meant nothing. Today he was going to sample the genuine article, a stiff climb up these dazzling slopes. On top he'd melt snow, make coffee, and fry thick rashers, sizzling rashers. Jiminy, he could savour it already.

Fahmi was coming along from the end of the village with the two men, Arzuf and Faraja. Arzuf was fat, with the blue eyes and fair hair of the west. Faraja had a dark sallowness. Both wore long crude coats of untanned skin. They were getting twenty dollars apiece for the job and Corland only chuckled at the thought of this extortion. Another racket of Fahmi's. According to him, of course, it had been difficult to find anybody at all and these two had only been tempted to face the wrath of The Thing by offering a high price.

Fahmi touched his forehead. Arzuf and Faraja picked up the small loads. They looked sombre, unwilling.

"Tell 'em," said Corland, "this is a hike, not a funeral."

It was fairly level going at first, along a track that ran between boulders, skirted a rocky wall and debouched upon a shallow depression dark with the Cedars of Lebanon, legitimate descendants of the originals of King Solomon.

Above them, the slopes sharpened under a white crispness of snow, and as the party ascended, Arzuf moved off to the left and Faraja to the right.

"What's the idea?" asked Corland.

Fahmi blinked. "It is wise. Together, The Thing might get us all. But if we are separated – "

Corland giggled. "Sure," he said, kindly.

After that his talk became infrequent. In this rarefied atmosphere he needed his breath for the steepish climb. But his eyes were full of exhilarated comment. The glittering, uptilted purity of the snow, the vivid, winter blue of the sky, the cold and perfect silence, the sense of high isolation – his past travels couldn't touch this. Queer how the scrunch, scrunch of their boots didn't seem to break the silence. In fact, it accentuated the mountain hush.

Fahmi was puffing. Corland smiled to himself. Do the old villain good, a chunk of exercise.

Then Corland stopped dead and the breath whistled up shrilly in the back of his throat. Arzuf had vanished.

For a moment he stood in stunned disbelief. The man couldn't have vanished. It was downright impossible.

Fahmi's head turned. At once the bluish whites of his eyes glistened with terror. He stared and stared at the nothingness where a few moments before had been the solid flesh of Arzuf.

Corland's practical mind was reeling. How could a man vanish on a stretch of virgin snow? There, away to the left, were his footprints broad and deep – thirty yards away, ending abruptly. Just ending.

Fahmi cried out hoarsely and to the right, stopped and turned round. He gazed at the emptiness and his dark face was a mask of fear.

Fahmi was calling to Faraja, but Faraja remained rooted to the spot where he had halted.

"Mister, he will not come here. He says The Thing must be close to us."

"It's bunk," said Corland, with all the anger of a frightened man. "Are you trying to tell me that man Arzuf's been whisked away into space by some...some...?"

Fahmi shrugged his shoulders. The hand holding the ebony stick was trembling.

Corland shouted: "We've got to do something, d'you hear?" From far off the words came back, thin and, somehow, jeering. It was only a trick of the heights, an echo, but it frayed the edges of sanity and deterred him from shouting again. The acute, listening silence was preferable to echoes.

His jaw set, he began to plod towards those ended footprints. Fahmi lumbered after him, grabbed his arm.

"No, Mister!" he begged. "Not goo-ood. Keep away."

"Don't be a fool!" said Corland, roughly.

Fahmi clung to his arm. "Am not a fool, Mister, You have seen. Arzuf has been taken. Do not let yourself be taken."

"But we've got to do something!"

Fahmi shook his head. "What can we do?"

"We can't leave the poor guy," began Corland, and swallowed over the blank futility of the remark.

"I ask Faraja," said Fahmi and called out in the local dialect.

Faraja's guttural words, floating back over the snow, had the urgent, warning quality of a bird's alarm call.

"He says, we go on. Not so far as going back."

Corland lit a cigarette. He turned his smouldering, unquiet eyes towards the summit. About six or seven hundred feet above, it had a peaceful, smiling, white beauty, tinted by the gold of the wintry sun. He thought he could read in the gentle smoothness of the snow something sly and horrible.

Then he looked to the left and quickly looked away. It didn't do to dwell on those ended footprints.

"We go on, Mister?" said Fahmi, hoarsely.

Corland clenched his hands and nodded. There was no more to be said.

The scrunching of their boots re-entered the silence. Corland caught himself jerking his head continually, from Fahmi to Faraja and back. That annoyed him. He wasn't going to play up to this weakness.

With a dogged bravado he started to whistle one of Sousa's marches. It was not easy. The angle of ascent and the lack of air pressure were an increasing strain. His whistle dropped to a whisper. Every twenty yards or so it was necessary to halt and gain a fresh supply of breath, yet the physical urge in him was to hurry, hurry. He would have liked to run.

He glanced at Fahmi, who was keeping level with him. Fahmi had a dazed and desperate expression. His eyes gazed straight in front of him with a glassy eagerness as if he, too, craved to run.

The summit was close now. Perhaps two hundred feet. Up there, with coffee boiling and the friendly smell of bacon, a man's brain would go right. Sure it would.

Fahmi moaned and stopped. In the instant Corland knew what to expect. Shuddering, he stared to the right.

Faraja had gone. Beyond the sudden end of his broad footprints the snow lay virgin white.

"Where are you? For God's sake! Where are you?" Without knowing it, Garland was screaming.

The echo returned. "Where are you? For God's sake! Where are you?"

Fahmi's fingers were plucking convulsively at his mouth. Madness hovered near.

"Stop that!" Corland had him by the elbow. "Stop that! There's the two of us left. We've got to fight it!"

Fahmi moaned again. Corland, on guard, shuffled in a complete circle, glaring as if to challenge some unseen abomination. The snow smiled at him.

Fahmi picked up his fallen stick with a mechanical action. He was still moaning.

"We go on, Mister!" he babbled. "We must go on! All who have vanished have been taken this side. Never the other. Only let us reach the top – "

Grotesquely, they were holding hands tightly. They were scrambling, half-running, slipping, tugging at each other, their breathing growing harsher, like the gusty whining of animals.

In a last frantic burst they reached the summit. Fahmi's knees gave way under him and he collapsed in the snow. Gasping for breath, Corland pulled out his flask and forced it between the man's teeth.

Presently Fahmi's lips moved.

"Who shall tell their wives, Mister, and their children?"

Corland bowed his face in his hands. "I was a fool, a fool. Why didn't I listen to you?...Fahmi, how could it have happened?"

"Arzuf lost," whimpered Fahmi, "Faraja lost. Their wives and children – "

"My fault." Corland's throat worked. "I shall have to do something for them. I can't give them back their husbands. But money – " His voice broke.

Three weeks later, as Corland's representative, Fahmi arrived at the village with the equivalent of ten thousand dollars. Two men greeted him. They were Arzuf and Faraja.

Fahmi counted out half the sum and handed it over. The rest he retained as his rake-off. A modest percentage, since he had been the author and stage manager of the whole affair. Business completed, he accompanied them up the mountainside on an expedition after hares. They wore the long skin coats and carried ancient guns.

Their method was to get well above the snow line, then reverse their coats and lie flat beneath them on the ground, their legs tucked in. In that way an unsuspecting quarry might come close enough for a certain shot.

Many dead white mountain hares had gone to the making of those coats. With their furry sides against the snow, they were almost invisible to their living brethren. In this blanched dazzle they would have been quite invisible to a short-sighted American.

Real Life Impossibility: Scotland
Houdini Defeated

At the height of his fame Harry Houdini was performing his daring escape act around the world to packed houses. So it was in Scotland from 1915–1920, during which time he regularly sold out a week's worth of shows at the Gaiety and the Empire Palace.

Always a master of publicity, Houdini attracted attention to his shows there by inviting poor children to attend and receive a free pair of boots. In addition local residents were invited to bring locks and strong boxes to try to defeat his escapology skills.

In one of his standard publicity stunts, Houdini boasted that he could get out of any jail cell within thirty minutes, provided he was permitted to enter wearing his street clothes. Of course this meant it was easy for him to conceal a set of lock picks with which to work.

But in one such case in Scotland, Houdini found himself struggling against a lock with which he was generally familiar. After thirty minutes he was still unable to unlock the door.

After two hours Houdini leaned heavily against the door with exhaustion – and it opened!

The cell had never been locked in the first place.

India
The Venom of the Tarantula
by Sharadindu Bandyopadhyay

Sharadindu Bandyopadhyay was a Bengali composer, poet, screenwriter, and novelist. He began writing the stories about his amateur detective, Byomkesh Bakshi, in 1932. In recent years Bakshi has seen a resurgence in popularity, appearing in many movie, radio, television, and even video game adaptations.

In addition to the story here, Badyopadhyay also wrote a second locked-room mystery, “Iron Biscuits,” starring his second series detective, Feluda.

“The Venom of the Tarantula” is a clever story about how a dying old drug addict is getting his supply when he never leaves his bedroom and everything coming in and out is inspected.

It was almost under duress that I got Byomkesh to leave the house.

For the last month he had been concentrating on a complicated forgery case. He would sit with a pile of papers all day and try to conjure up the image of the criminal from it all.

As the mystery thickened, so did his conversation trickle gradually to silence. I noticed that this endless ploughing through papers, sitting in the library day after day, wasn't doing his health any good. But every time I brought this up, he would say, “Oh no, I am quite all right.”

That evening I said, “I am not going to take no for an answer. We're going for a walk. You need at least a couple of hours respite in the day.”

“But...”

“No buts. Let's go to the lake. Your forger won't give you the slip in two hours.”

“Oh, all right.” He pushed the papers away and set off, but it wasn't difficult to guess that his mind hadn't let go of the problem at hand.

While walking by the lake I suddenly spotted a long-lost friend of mine. We had studied together until the Intermediate class – then he had entered the medical college. I hadn't seen him since. I called out to him, “Hey, you're Mohan, aren't you? How are you doing?”

He turned around and exclaimed delightedly, “Ajit! It is you! It's been so long. So tell me, how is everything?”

After exchanging excited greetings I introduced him to Byomkesh.

Mohan said, “So you are Byomkesh Bakshi. Delighted to make your acquaintance. I did suspect at times that the Ajit Badyopadhyay who writes about your exploits is our old friend, Ajit. But I wasn't quite sure.”

I said, “So what are you up to nowadays?”

Mohan replied, “I have my practice here in Calcutta.”

We strolled about and spoke of this and that. An hour passed pleasantly. I noticed that during the conversation Mohan opened his mouth a couple of times as if to say something, but then stopped himself. Byomkesh must have noticed it, too, because at one point he smiled and said, “Please go ahead and say what you want to say.”

Mohan said, a little shyly, “There is something that I want to ask you, but I am hesitant. Actually it is such a trivial problem that it seems unfair to bother you with it. Yet – “

I said, "That's all right, tell us. If nothing else, it will at least serve the purpose of delivering Byomkesh for a short while from the hands of that forger."

"Forger?"

I explained.

Mohan said, "I see! But perhaps Byomkeshbabu will laugh at what I have to say."

"If it is amusing I shall certainly laugh," said Byomkesh, "but from your manner it doesn't seem to be a laughing matter. Instead it appears that a certain problem has kept you pondering – you are desperate to find a solution to it."

Mohan said excitedly, "You are absolutely right. Perhaps it is very simple – but for me it has become an irresoluble conundrum. I am not entirely stupid – I think I have my fair share of common sense – yet, you'll be surprised to know how an ailing old man, who is paralysed to boot, is duping me every single day. It isn't just me; he is defeating his entire family's attempts at strict vigilance."

In the course of the conversation we had sat down on a bench. Mohan said, "Let me tell you about it as briefly as possible. I am the family physician in a very affluent household. The family goes back a long way to when the city was just coming up. In addition to other incomes and assets they own a market from which they earn a massive monthly amount as rent. So you can gauge their financial standing.

"The master of this house is Nandadulalbabu. He is actually my only patient in that household. In his heyday he was such a profligate that by the time he reached the age of fifty his health gave up on him. His body plays host to a plethora of diseases. He has long been rendered immobile from arthritis. Now there are signs of paralysis as well. There is a saying among us doctors that there is nothing strange about man's death; it is the fact that he is alive at all that is a source of wonder. This patient of mine is a prime example of that.

"Words fail me in trying to describe the character of Nandadulalbabu to you. Foul-mouthed, mistrustful, crafty, malicious – in brief, I have never seen a meaner nature than his. He has a wife and a family, but he isn't on good terms with anyone. He would like to continue along the same depraved lines as he did in his youth. But his vitality has sapped and his health doesn't permit such excesses any longer. Hence, he bears great bitterness and envy towards everyone –

as if they were responsible for his condition. He is always looking for ways and means to pull a fast one on someone to prove his ability.

"His body is weak and he has a heart condition too – hence he cannot leave his room. He sits there in his den, heaping unspeakable indignities upon the entire universe with every sentence he speaks and filling page after page with writing. He has a misplaced notion that he is an unparalleled litterateur; so, now in black, now in red ink, he writes and writes. He is terribly upset with the publishers – he believes that they are in on the conspiracy against him and therefore refuse to publish his work."

Curious, I asked, "What does he write?"

"Fiction. Or it may even be autobiographical. Only once did I glance at a page of the stuff; never again have I been able to look at it. After you've read that filth, even a holy oblation won't cleanse you. I am certain that even today's young experimental writers would have a fit if they read it."

Byomkesh gave a slight smile and said, "I can see the character before my eyes. But what exactly is the problem?"

Mohan offered a cigarette to each of us, lighted one for himself and said, "Perhaps you think that such a special character cannot possibly have any more qualities, right? But that is not so. He has another terrific trait – to add to his wonderful health, he has a dangerous addiction."

He took a couple of puffs on his cigarette and continued, "Byomkeshbabu, you are always dealing with such people; the most inferior class of the society is regular fare to you. I am sure you are familiar with alcohol, marijuana, cocaine, and many other such kinds of addictions. But have you heard of anyone being addicted to spider juice?"

I gasped out loud, "Spider juice? What on earth is that?"

Mohan said, "There is a certain breed of spiders from whose bodies a venomous juice is extracted – "

Almost as if speaking to himself, Byomkesh muttered, "Tarantula dance! It used to be practised in Spain – the spider's bite would make people cavort! It's a deadly poison! I have read about it but I haven't come across anyone using it in this country."

Mohan said, "You are absolutely right – tarantula. The use of tarantula extract is very prevalent among the hybrid Hispanic tribes of South America. The venom of the tarantula is a deadly poison, but if used in small quantities it can provide a tremendous thrill to the nervous system. As you can guess, this venom is very tempting to someone who cannot live without a constant state of nervous excitement. But continuous use of this stuff can prove to be fatal. The user would be sure to die of a fit of palsy.

"I am almost certain that Nandadulalbabu had picked up this beautiful addiction at some point in his youth. Later, when his body became totally unfit, he couldn't let go of it. It was about a year ago that I came in as his family physician, and at that time he was a confirmed addict to spider venom. The first thing I did was to prohibit this; I told him that if he wanted to live he would have to give up the drug.

"There was quite a tussle over this – he wouldn't let go of it and I simply wouldn't let him have it. Finally I said, "I shall not let the stuff enter your house. Let me see how you lay your hands on it." He gave a sly smile and said, "Is that so? All right, I shall go on having it – let me see how you stop me." And thus, war was declared.

"The rest of the family was, quite obviously, on my side and so it was quite easy to set up a strong barricade system within the house. His wife and children took turns in guarding his room so that there was no means of the drug reaching him. He himself is practically immobile. So he is unable to go out of the house and collect it for himself. After making such rigorous arrangements to prevent him from getting at the drug, I began to feel a sense of immense satisfaction.

"But it was all in vain. In spite of all our precautions he continued to consume the drug. No one could figure out his means of gaining access to it. At first I suspected that someone within the house was secretly supplying the drug to him. So one day, I myself kept guard for the entire day. But amazingly, right under my nose he took the drug at least thrice. I could determine this by checking his pulse, but I could not figure out when and how he did it.

"Since then I have searched every nook and cranny of his room, I have stopped any outsider from coming into contact with him, and yet I have been unsuccessful in stopping him from getting his narcotic fix. This is where things stand.

"Now, my problem is that I need to locate how that man gets hold of the spider venom and how exactly he tricks everyone and consumes it."

Mohan stopped. I couldn't tell if Byomkesh had become unmindful during the monologue, but as soon as Mohan stopped speaking, he stood up and said, “Ajit, let us go home. I have suddenly thought of something and if my guess is right, then….”

I realized that the forger was on his mind again. It was possible that the last part of Mohan's story had entirely slipped by him.

A little disconcerted, I said, “Perhaps you weren’t paying attention to Mohan's tale – “

“No, no. Of course I have heard him carefully. It is a most amusing problem and I must say I am also quite intrigued by it, but right now it will be difficult for me to make the time. It is a rather difficult case that I am handling now….”

Perhaps Mohan felt a little offended, but he concealed the emotion and said, “Oh, of course, in that case just let it go. It certainly isn’t right to bother you with such trivial matters. But, you know, if this mystery could be solved, perhaps the man's life could be saved. What can be more frustrating than watching a man – albeit a sinner – die a slow death right before your eyes, simply by consuming poison?”

A trifle abashed, Byomkesh said, “I didn't say I wouldn't look into it. It will take me at least a couple of hours’ cogitation to solve this riddle. It would also help if I could see the man himself. But I may not be able to make it today. It will certainly be a crime to let an unusual man like Nandadulalbabu die. And I shall not let that happen – you may be sure of that. But I need to return to my room right now. I think I may have been able to pin down the forger – I need to take another good look at the papers. Therefore, let Nandadulalbabu continue to consume his poison in peace for just another night – from tomorrow on, I shall put a spanner in his works.”

Mohan laughed and said, “That is fine with me. Please give me a time that's convenient for you and I shall arrange for the car to pick you up.”

Byomkesh gave it a moment's thought and said, “I have an idea – it may even help lessen your anxiety for now. Let Ajit accompany you and take a good look around. After hearing his report I should be able to give you the answer to your riddle either tonight or tomorrow morning.”

It was impossible not to notice the shadow of disappointment that crossed Mohan's face at the suggestion that I should go with him instead of Byomkesh. Byomkesh noticed it too and laughed, “Since Ajit is an old friend of yours, perhaps you do not have much faith in him. But please do not lose heart; in the company of greatness his faculties have now become so unusually sharp that a few examples of his perceptiveness might astonish you. It may even happen that he will solve your problem all by himself and not need my assistance at all."

But even such high praise couldn't convince Mohan. His face reflected the despondency of an angler who fishes through the day in the hope of hooking a big one and then manages to land only a lowly bluegill. He said, "All right then, let Ajit come along. But if he isn't able to – "

"Most certainly, in that case you can count on me."

Byomkesh called me aside and said, "Take good notice of everything – and don't forget to inquire about incoming mail."

I had seen Byomkesh solve many a complex mystery and even aided him in some cases. Observing him over the years, I had even picked up some of his modes of investigation. So, I thought to myself, could it be so difficult to solve this simple problem? As a matter of fact, Mohan's mistrust of my capabilities had hurt my pride and I felt a little headstrong urge to solve this mystery all by myself. My mind made up, I followed Mohan away from the lake with resolute steps. A bus ride brought us to our destination. It was already dark. The streetlamps had been lit. Mohan walked ahead, showing the way. We walked down a lane off Circular Road; after a few minutes he pointed to a big house with an iron fence around the compound and said, "This is the place."

It was an old house, built in the baroque style. In front of the iron gate a watchman sat on a stool. He saluted Mohan and let him through. Then he noticed me, and, after casting a suspicious glance my way, said, "Sir, you are not – "

Mohan smiled and said, "It's all right watchman, he is with me."

"Very good, sir." The watchman stepped aside. We entered the courtyard of the house. As we crossed it and stepped onto the veranda, a young man of about twenty stepped out. "Is that you, doctor? Do come in." Then he raised questioning eyes at me. "This is...?"

Mohan took him aside, said something to him, and the young man replied, "Certainly, of course, do let him come and see."

Mohan then introduced us. The young man's name was Arun; he was Nandadulalbabu's eldest son. We followed him into the house. After passing two doors, Arun knocked on the third. At once a querulous, hoarse voice answered from within, "Who's there? What is it? Don't bother me now, I am writing."

Arun said, “Father, the doctor has come. Abhay, please open the door.”

The door was opened by a youth – probably Arun’s younger brother – who looked to be about eighteen. All of us filed into the room. Arun asked Abhay quietly, “Has he had it again?”

Abhay wanly nodded his head.

Upon entering the room my eyes fell first on the bed, which was placed in the centre of the room. Upon it, clutching a pen, slouched the gaunt Nandadulalbabu, leaning against a pillow and glaring at us with eyes burning with hostility. There was a fluorescent light overhead and another table lamp was placed upon a bedside table, so I could observe the man very clearly. His age was probably on the right side of fifty but all the hair on his head had become grey and his skin had taken on a pallid hue. His structure was bony, with not an ounce of extra flesh on his angular face. The cheekbones seemed to be piercing through his skin and his sharp, slightly crooked nose was jutting out over his lips. The eyes were glittering from an unusual excitement. But within them there lurked the obvious signs that the ebb of the excitement would turn them back into expressionless fish eyes. His lower lip hung limply. All in all, the entire face had a famished, discontented expression stamped upon every single pore.

As I stared at this ghostly physiognomy for some time, I noticed that his left hand gave a jerk from time to time, as if it had a life that was independent of the rest of the body and had decided to tango all on its own. Those who have seen a dead frog's limbs jump up when they come in contact with electric current may perhaps be able to visualize this nervous twitch.

Nandadulalbabu was staring at me, too, with vicious eyes, and soon, in that sharp, cackling voice, he ranted, “Doctor! Who is this with you? What does the man want? Tell him to buzz off – at once – now....”

Mohan glanced at me and nodded to indicate that I shouldn't take my host's profanities to heart. He then moved the pile of papers that lay scattered on the bed to make some space, sat down, and took his patient's pulse in his hand.

Nandadulalbabu sat with a perverted grin stuck on his face and alternated his gaze between me and the doctor. His left hand continued to jerk erratically.

Finally Mohan let go of his wrist and said, “So you have taken it again?”

"You bet I have – what bloody business is it of yours?"

Mohan bit his lip and then continued, "You are only doing yourself harm with this. But you wouldn't understand that. You have let the venom addle your brain."

Nandadulalbabu made a diabolical face and mocked, "Is that so? I have addled my brain, eh? But you still have a lot of grey matter in there, don't you? So why can't you catch me out? You have placed your guards all around me – so how is it that you can't get to me?" He laughed in a vicious and obscene fashion.

Exasperated, Mohan stood up and said, "It is impossible to have a conversation with you. I suppose I should just leave you to yourself."

Nandadulalbabu continued cackling in that irritating manner and said, "Shame on you, doctor, you call yourself a man? Catch me if you can, or suck on one of these and let me have my fun." And he waved both his thumbs right under our noses.

Such gross and crude behaviour in front of his sons began to seem unbearable to me. Mohan had probably reached the end of his tether too because he said, "All right Ajit, look around and take whatever notes you need to take. This is becoming impossible to tolerate."

All of a sudden the victory dance of the thumbs came to a stop. Nandadulalbabu raised his reptilian eyes towards me and demanded sourly, "Who the hell are you and what are you doing in my house?" When he got no answer from me, he continued, "A smart aleck, are you? Well, you better listen – your tricks won't work on me, you get it? Better get out of here as fast as you can or else I'll call the police. Bunch of rogues, scoundrels, and thieves, every single one of them!" He included Mohan in his sweeping glance as well. Although he couldn't quite figure out Mohan's reasons for bringing me there, he was obviously deeply suspicious of my presence.

Quite embarrassed, Arun whispered into my ear, "Please ignore all that he says. Once he consumes the drug, he is completely out of his mind."

How terrible is the venom that aggravates and brings to the foreground all that is mean and ugly in a person's nature, I thought. And how would anyone check the moral degeneration of a person who consumes this venom willingly and of his own accord?

Byomkesh had instructed me to take note of everything carefully. So I tried to quickly make a mental inventory going around the room. The room was quite large and sparsely furnished. There was just the bed, a few chairs, an almirah, and a bedside table. There was a lamp and some blank sheets of paper and a few other writing accessories on the table. The written sheets were scattered all over the place. I picked up a sheaf. But after reading a few lines I shuddered and had to put them down. Mohan was right. The writing would have made Emile Zola blush. To make matters worse, Mr. Litterateur had actually underscored the "juicier" sections of the material in red ink to draw attention to them. In truth, I could not recall ever having come into contact with a dirtier or a more repugnant mind.

Revolted, I looked up at the man and found that he had gone back to his penmanship. The Parker pen was rapidly filling up the sheet of paper with scrawls. In a little pen stand which stood on the bedside table, another crimson Parker fountain pen rested, probably awaiting a lull in the writing when the underscoring would begin.

This is exactly what happened. As soon as he reached the end of the page, Nandadulalbabu laid down the black pen and picked up the red one, only to find that it had run out of ink. He filled it from a bottle of red ink that stood on the table, and went back to underscoring his sparkling gems with a solemn expression.

I turned away and began to inspect the other sections of his room. The almirah contained nothing except for a few half-empty bottles of medicine. Mohan said they had been prescribed by him. The room had two windows and two doors.

We had entered through one of these doors and I was told that behind the other lay the bathroom. I inspected that too; there was just the usual bath linen, soap, oil, toothpaste, etc. My queries about the windows revealed that they did not open out into the courtyard; in fact, they remained shut most of the time.

I tried to visualize how Byomkesh would have gone about it had he been there, but I drew a blank. I was just wondering whether to knock on the walls or not – might there be a secret vault or something? – when I suddenly noticed a silver essence-holder in one corner of a shelf in the wall. I examined it eagerly; it held some cotton wool and attar in some of the tiny compartments. I asked Arun in a whisper, "Is he in the habit of using essence?"

Hesitantly he shook his head and said, "I don't think so; if he had, we would have smelt it on him."

"How long has this been here?"

"Oh, for as long as I can remember. It was Father who had it brought."

I turned around and noticed that Nandadulalbabu had stopped writing and was gazing in my direction. Excited, I dipped some cotton wool in the attur and dropped it in my pocket. Then I took one last look around the room before walking out. Nandadulalbabu's eyes followed me; he had that mocking, grotesque smile pinned on his face.

We came out on the veranda and sat down. I said, "I would like to ask you all a few questions. Please give me honest answers without hiding anything."

Arun said, "Certainly, please go ahead."

I asked, "Do you keep a constant vigil on him? Who are the ones on guard?"

"Abhay, Mother, and I take turns in staying with him. We don't let any of the servants or outsiders go near him."

"Have you ever seen him consume the stuff?"

"No, we haven't seen him actually putting it in his mouth, but we have found out every time he has ingested it."

"Has anybody seen what it actually looks like?"

"When he used to take it openly, I did see it – it is a transparent liquid which used to be kept in a bottle for homeopathic medicine. He used to dilute a few drops of it in a glass of fruit juice."

"Are you certain that no bottles of that kind are still there in the room?"

"Absolutely certain. We have turned the place upside down."

"Then it obviously comes in from somewhere. Who brings it?"

Arun shook his head, "We don't know."

"Is there anybody else other than the three of you with access to that room? Please think carefully."

"No, there's nobody else. Just the doctor."

My inquisition ended. What else could I ask? As I sat there trying to come up with something else, Byomkesh's came to my mind and I started afresh, "Does he receive any letters?"

"No."

"Any parcels or anything else like it?"

Now Arun said, "Yes, once a week he receives a registered letter."

I leaned forward eagerly, "Where does it come from? Who sends it?"

Arun hung his head in embarrassment and spoke softly, "It comes from within Calcutta. A woman called Rebecca Light sends it."

I said, "Oh, I see. Has any one of you seen what it contains?"

"Yes," Arun said, looking towards Mohan.

I asked impatiently, "Well, what does it contain?"

"Blank paper."

"Blank paper?"

"Yes, just a few blank sheets of paper are stuffed in the envelope – there's nothing else."

Dumbly, I repeated, "Nothing else?"

"No."

I was speechless for a few moments and then asked again.

"Are you absolutely sure that the envelopes contain nothing else?"

Arun gave a slight smile and said, "Yes. Although Father signs and takes the letters from the postman, I open them myself. There is never anything but white sheets inside."

"Do you open the letter each and every time? Where do you do this?"

"In Father's room. That is where the postman brings the letter."

"But this is extremely strange. What is the meaning of sending empty sheets of paper by registered post?"

Arun shook his head and said, "I don't know."

I sat there a little longer like a dimwit, and finally, with a great big sigh, I rose to leave. The first mention of the registered letters had raised my hopes to think that perhaps I had hit upon the solution, but no, that particular door seemed locked and sealed. I understood that although the problem appeared to be quite simple, it was beyond my acumen. Appearances can be very deceptive. It was beyond my capabilities to take on the old geezer with his body riddled with poison and paralysis. What was required here was the razor-edged, crystal-clear intelligence of Byomkesh.

As I was leaving with a crestfallen look, promising to report everything to Byomkesh, something else occurred to me.

I asked, "Does Nandadulalbabu write letters to anyone?"

Arun said, "No, but he sends a money order every month."

"To whom?"

With shame writ all over his face, Arun murmured, "To the same Jewish woman."

Mohan explained, "Once she was Nandadulalbabu's – "

"I see. How much does he send her?"

"Quite a hefty sum. I don't know why, though."

The reply drifted to my lips: "Pension." But I held my tongue and quietly walked out. Mohan stayed back.

It was almost eight o'clock when I reached home. Byomkesh was in the library. He answered my knock immediately and held the door open, saying, "How was it? Is the mystery solved?"

"No." I walked into the room and sat down. Byomkesh had been examining a piece of paper through the thick lens of a magnifying glass. He gave me a piercing look and said, "Since when have you become this fashionable? Are you using attar nowadays?"

"I'm not wearing it, merely carrying it."

I reported everything to him in great detail. He listened attentively. In conclusion I said, "I couldn't solve it, my friend, so now you have to have a go at it. But I have a feeling that an analysis of this attar may reveal something – "

"Reveal what – the spider venom?" Byomkesh took the piece of cotton wool from my hands and held it to his nose, "Ah, wonderful essence. Pure, unadulterated amburi attar. Yes, you were saying something," he continued as he rubbed some of the attar onto his wrist. "What may be revealed?"

A little hesitantly I said, "Perhaps under the pretense of using attar Nandadulalbabu – "

Byomkesh laughed out loud, "Is it possible to hide the use of something that, by its smell alone, can alert people for miles around? Have you got any indication to believe that Nandadulalbabu actually wears this attar?"

"Well, no, I haven't, but – "

"No, my dear, you're barking up the wrong tree; try looking elsewhere. Try to think about how the stuff is smuggled into the room and how Nandadulalbabu consumes it in everyone's presence. Why do blank sheets of paper arrive by registered post? What is the reason for sending money to that woman?

"Have you figured that out?"

Dejected, I said, "I have thought about all these things, but the solution is beyond me."

"Think again, harder – nothing will come from nothing, you know. Think deeply, think intensely, think relentlessly," and so saying, he picked up the lens again.

I asked, "What about you?"

"I am thinking too. But it is going to be impossible to think intensely. My forger...." He leaned over the table.

I left the room and stretched out in the armchair in the living room and started to think again. For God's sake, this couldn't be all that difficult to solve. I was sure I could do it. To begin with, what was the significance of sending blank sheets by registered post? Was there something written on the sheets with invisible ink? If that were so, how would Nandadulalbabu benefit from it? His quota of venom could not be reaching him that way.

All right, let us assume that the venom somehow managed to get smuggled into the room from outside. But where did Nandadulalbabu hide it? Even a bottle of homeopathic medicine wasn't easy to conceal. He was constantly under surveillance by vigilant eyes. There was even the occasional raid on his room. How then did he do it? All this intense thinking heated up my brain; five cheroots were burnt to ashes, but I still could not find an answer to even one of these questions. I had almost given up hope when a marvellous idea occurred to me. I sat up straight in the armchair. Could this be possible? And yet – why ever not? It did sound a bit odd, but what other solution could there be?

Byomkesh always said that if there was a logical inference that could be made, even if it appeared improbable, one had to take it to be the only possible solution. In this case too this had to be, absolutely, the only possible explanation.

I was just going to go to Byomkesh when he himself came in. He took one look at my face and said, "What is it? Have you figured it out?"

"I just may have."

"Good. Tell me about it."

When it came to spelling it out, I felt some pangs of hesitancy, but I brushed them aside and proceeded. "Look, I just remembered seeing some spiders on the walls of Nandadulalbabu's room. I believe that he – just grabs them off the wall and gobbles them down?"

Byomkesh burst out laughing. "Ajit, you are an utter genius. You are matchless. Those house spiders on the wall – if someone ate those there would be some abrasive rashes on the body, but no addictive surges. Understand?"

A little huffily I said, "All right then why don't you explain?"

Byomkesh took a chair and put his feet up on the table. Indolently, he lit up a cheroot and asked:

"Have you understood why blank sheets come by post?"

"No."

"Did you figure out why the Jewish woman is paid every month?"

"No."

"Haven't you at least worked out why Nandadulalbabu needs to underline his obscene stories?"

"No. Have you?"

"Perhaps," Byomkesh took a long drag on the cheroot and said, his eyes closed, "but unless I am absolutely certain about one fact, it will not be fair to make any comment."

"What is that?"

"I need to know the colour of Nandadulalbabu's tongue."

It looked like he was pulling my leg. Brusquely I said, "Are you trying to be funny?"

"Funny!" Byoinkesh opened his eyes and saw my expression. "Are you offended? Honestly, I am not joking. Everything hinges upon the colour of Nandadulalbabu's tongue. If the colour of his tongue is red, then my guess is right, and if it is not – you didn't happen to notice it, did you?"

Irritated, I said, "No, it didn't occur to me to notice his tongue."

Byomkesh grinned and said, "Yet, that should have been the first thing to look at. Anyway, do something – call Nandadulalbabu's son and ask about it."

"He may think I am being facetious."

Byomkesh waved his arms and recited poetically, "Fear not, oh fear not, there is no need for thee to quail – "

I went into the next room, located the number and dialed it. Mohan was still there and it was he who answered. "I didn't tell you about it because I hadn't thought that piece of information mattered," he said. "Nandadulalbabu's tongue is a deep crimson in colour. It seems a bit unusual because he doesn't take much paan either. But why do you ask?"

I called Byomkesh. He asked, "It is red, right? Well then, it is solved."

He took the phone from me and said, "Doctor, it is good that I got hold of you. Your riddle has been solved. Yes, it was Ajit who solved it – I just helped him a bit. I was so busy with the forger – yes, I've got him too.... You don't have to do too much, just remove the bottle of red ink and the red fountain pen from Nandadulalbabu's room.... Yes, you got it. Please drop in sometime tomorrow and I shall explain everything. Goodbye. I shall certainly convey your gratitude to Ajit. Didn't I say that his intellect has grown really sharp nowadays?" Laughing to himself, Byomkesh put the receiver down.

After returning to the living room, I said, a trifle bashfully, “I think I am beginning to get it in bits and pieces, but please tell me in greater detail. How did you work it out?”

Byomkesh glanced at the clock and said, “It is time for dinner. Putiram will be here at any moment to announce it. All right, let me go over it briefly with you. You were on the wrong track from the very beginning. It was important to find out how the stuff entered the room. It doesn't have limbs of its own, hence obviously it was being brought in by someone. Who could that be? Five people have access to the room – the doctor, the two sons, the wife and one other person. The first four people would not deliberately bring the poison to Nandadulalbabu. So this was the work of the fifth person.”

“Who is the fifth person?”

“The fifth one is – the postman. He comes in once a week. It was through him that the poison entered the room.”

“But the envelopes contain nothing but blank sheets of paper.”

“That is the trick. Everyone thinks that the envelope might contain the stuff and so nobody pays attention to the postman.

The man is smart; he switches the red inkpot with ease. The point of sending blank sheets of paper by registered post is to give the postman access into Nandadulalbabu's room.”

“And then?”

“You made one more error in your judgement. The money that is sent to the Jewish woman – it's not a pension: that custom doesn't prevail anywhere. It is payment for the drug; the woman supplies it through the postman. So now you see, the venom comes into Nandadulalbabu’s hands and nobody even suspects how. But the room is under surveillance at all hours, so how would he consume it? This is where his writing comes in useful. The paper and ink is always at hand and there is no need to get up in order to take in the drug – the task can be accomplished from his seat on the bed. He writes with the black pen, highlights with the red one, and at every chance, sucks on the nib of the fountain pen. When the ink runs out he refills the pen. Now do you understand why the colour of his tongue is red?”

“But how did you know it would be the red one? Couldn’t it be the black one too?”

“Oh no, can't you see? The black ink is used much more profusely. Would Nandadulalbabu want any superfluous use of that precious stuff? Hence the highlighting – with the red ink.”

"I get it. So simple – " _

"Of course it is simple. But the brain that has come up with such a simple plan is not to be slighted. It is because of its simplicity that all of you were fooled."

"How did you figure it out?"

"Very easily. In this case two facts seemed to stand out as entirely unnecessary and therefore suspicious. One, the arrival of blank sheets by registered post, and two, Nandadulalbu's excessive writing and highlighting habit. When I began to mull over the real reasons for these two, I stumbled upon the solution. You see, my forger too – "

The telephone shrilled into action in the next room. Both of us hurried to it. Byomkesh picked it up and said, "Yes, who is it? Oh, Doctor, yes, tell me.... Nandadulalbabu is creating a racket? He is ranting and raving? Well, well, that was inevitable.... What was that? He is cursing Ajit? He is using the "f" and "b" words? That is very wrong, very wrong indeed. But if he cannot be shut up, it can't be helped. Of course Ajit doesn't take it to heart, he is well aware that good deeds seldom go uncriticized in this world! You have to take the brickbats with the bouquets – such is life. All right then, goodbye!"

United Kingdom
Sir Gilbert Murrell's Picture
by Victor L. Whitechurch

Some of the most ingenious impossible crimes feature unique situations never tackled before or since by any other writer. So it is with this story by English clergyman Victor L. Whitechurch. And although there have been many fine impossible murders and disappearances set in the railway milieu – *Murder on the Orient Express* by Christie, "The Lost Special" by Doyle, "Snowball in July" by Queen, and "Beware of the Trains" by Crispin – none of them is as ingenious as this fine caper mystery.

It is interesting to note that the eccentric behaviour of Whitechurch's detective, Thorpe Hazell, has become almost mainstream over time, as modern ideas about diet and exercise have validated the ideas that Whitechurch surely meant to appear eccentric and amusing.

The affair of the goods truck on the Didcot and Newbury branch of the Great Western Railway was of singular interest, and found a prominent place in Thorpe Hazell's notebook. It was owing partly to chance, and partly to Hazell's sagacity, that the main incidents in the story were discovered, but he always declared that the chief interest to his mind was the unique method by which a very daring plan was carried out.

He was staying with a friend at Newbury at the time, and had taken his camera down with him, for he was a bit of an amateur photographer as well as book lover, though his photos generally consisted of trains and engines. He had just come in from a morning's ramble with his camera slung over his shoulder, and was preparing to partake of two plasmon biscuits, when his friend met him in the hall.

"I say, Hazell," he began, "you're just the fellow they want here."

"What's up?" asked Hazell, taking off his camera and commencing some "exercises."

"I've just been down to the station. I know the stationmaster very well, and he tells me an awfully queer thing happened on the line last night."

"Where?"

"On the Didcot branch. It's a single line, you know, running through the Berkshire Downs to Didcot."

Hazell smiled, and went on whirling his arms round his head.

"Kind of you to give me the information," he said, "but I happen to know the line. But what's occurred?"

"Well, it appears a goods train left Didcot last night bound through to Winchester, and that one of the waggons never arrived here at Newbury."

"Not very much in that," replied Hazell, still at his "exercises," "unless the waggon in question was behind the brake and the couplings snapped, in which case the next train along might have run into it."

"Oh no, the waggon was in the middle of the trains."

"Probably left in a siding by mistake," replied Hazell.

"But the stationmaster says that all the stations along the line have been wired to, and that it isn't at any of them,"

"Very likely it never left Didcot."

"He declares there is no doubt about that."

"Well, you begin to interest me," replied Hazel, stopping his whirligigs and beginning to eat his plasmon. "There may be something in it, though very often a waggon is mislaid. But I'll go down to the station."

"I'll go with you, Hazell, and introduce you to the stationmaster. He has heard of your reputation."

Ten minutes later they were in the stationmaster's office, Hazell having re-slung his camera.

"Very glad to meet you," said that functionary, "for this affair promises to be mysterious. I can't make it out at all."

"Do you know what the truck contained?"

"That's just where the bother comes in, sir. It was valuable property. There's a loan exhibition of pictures at Winchester next week, and this waggon was bringing down some of them from Leamington. They belong to Sir Gilbert Murrell – three of them, I believe – large pictures, and each in a separate packing case."

"Hmm, this sounds very funny. Are you sure the truck was on the train?"

"Simpson, the brakesman, is here now, and I'll send for him. Then you can hear the story in his own words."

So the goods guard appeared on the scene. Hazell looked at him narrowly, but there was nothing suspicious in his honest face.

"I know the waggon was on the train when we left Didcot," he said in answer to inquiries, "and I noticed it at Upton, the next station, where we took a couple off. It was the fifth or sixth in front of my brake. I'm quite certain of that. We stopped at Compton to take up a cattle truck, but I didn't get out there. Then we ran right through to Newbury, without stopping at the other stations, and then I discovered that the waggon was not on the train. I thought very likely it might have been left at Upton or Compton by mistake, but I was wrong, for they say it isn't there. That's all I know about it, sir. A rum go, ain't it?"

"Extraordinary!" exclaimed Hazell. "You must have made a mistake."

"No, sir, I'm sure I haven't."

"Did the driver of the train notice anything?"

"No, sir."

"Well, but the thing's impossible," said Hazell. "A loaded waggon couldn't have been spirited away. What time was it when you left Didcot?"

"About eight o'clock, sir."

"All quite dark. You noticed nothing along the line?"

"Nothing, sir."

"You were in your brake all the time, I suppose?"

"Yes, sir – while we were running."

At this moment there came a knock at the stationmaster's door and a porter entered.

"There's a passenger train just in from the Didcot branch," said the man, "and the driver reports that he saw a truck loaded with packing cases in Churn siding."

"Well, I'm blowed!" exclaimed the brakesman. "Why, we ran through Churn without a stop – trains never do stop there except in camp time,"

"Where is Churn?" asked Hazell, for once at a loss.

"It's merely a platform and a siding close to the camping ground between Upton and Compton," replied the stationmaster, "for the convenience of troops only, and very rarely used except in the summer, when soldiers are encamped there."

"I should very much like to see the place, and as soon as possible," said Hazell.

"So you shall," replied the stationmaster. "A train will soon start on the branch. Inspector Hill shall go with you, and instruction shall be given to the driver to stop there, while a return train can pick you both up."

In less than an hour Hazell and Inspector Hill alighted at Churn. It is a lonely enough place, situated in a vast flat basin of the Downs, scarcely relieved by a single tree and far from all human habitation with the exception of a lonely shepherd's cottage some half a mile away.

The "station" itself is only a single platform, with a shelter and a solitary siding, terminating in what is known in railway language as a "dead end" – that is, in this case, wooden buffers to stop any trucks. This siding runs off from the single line of rail at points from the Didcot direction of the line.

And in this siding was the lost truck, right against the "dead end," filled with three packing cases, and labelled "Leamington to Winchester, via Newbury." There could be no doubt about it at all. But how it had got there from the middle of a train running through without a stop was a mystery even to the acute mind of Thorpe Hazell.

"Well," said the inspector when they had gazed long enough at the truck, "we'd better have a look at the points. Come along."

There is not even a signal box at this primitive station. The points are activated by two levers in a ground frame, standing close by the side of the line, one lever unlocking and the other shifting the same points.

"How about these points?" said Hazell as they drew near. "You only use them so occasionally, that I suppose they are kept out of action?"

"Certainly," replied the inspector, "a block of wood is bolted down between the end of the point rail and the main rail, fixed as a wedge – ah! There it is, you see, quite untouched, and the levers themselves are locked – here's the keyhole in the ground frame. This is the strangest thing I've ever come across, Mr. Hazell."

Thorpe Hazell stood looking at the points and levers sorely puzzled. They must have been worked to get that truck in the siding, he knew well. But how?

Suddenly his face lit up. Oil evidently had been used to loosen the nut of the bolt that fixed the wedge of wood. Then his eyes fell on the handle of one of the two levers, and a slight exclamation of joy escaped him.

"Look," said the inspector at that moment, "it's impossible to pull them off," and he stretched out his hand towards a lever. To his astonishment Hazell seized him by the collar and dragged him back before he could touch it.

"I beg your pardon," he exclaimed, "Hope I've not hurt you, but I want to photograph those levers first, if you don't mind."

The inspector watched him rather sullenly as he fixed his camera on a folding tripod stand he had with him, only a few inches from the handle of one of the levers, and took two very careful photographs of it.

"Can't see the use of that, sir," growled the inspector. But Hazell vouchsafed no reply.

"Let him find it out for himself," he thought.

Then he said aloud:

"I fancy they must have had that block out, inspector – and it's evident the points must have been set to get the truck where it is. How it was done is a problem, but if the doer of it was anything of a regular criminal, I think we might find him."

"How?" asked the puzzled inspector.

"Ah," was the response, "I'd rather not say at present. Now, I should very much like to know whether those pictures are intact."

"We shall soon find that out," replied the inspector, "for we'll take the truck back with us." And he commenced undoing the bolt with a spanner, after which he unlocked the levers.

"Hmm, they work pretty freely," he remarked as he pulled one.

"Quite so," said Hazell, "they've been oiled recently."

There was an hour or so before the return train would pass, and Hazell occupied it by walking to the shepherd's cottage.

"I am hungry," he explained to the woman there, "and hunger is Nature's dictate for food. Can you oblige me with a couple of onions and a broomstick?"

And she talks today of the strange man who "kept a swingin' o' that there broomstick round 'is 'ead and then eat them onions as solemn as a judge."

The first thing Hazell did on returning to Newbury was to develop his photographs. The plates were dry enough by the evening for him to print one or two photos on gaslight paper and to enclose the clearest of them with a letter to a Scotland Yard official whom he knew, stating that he would call for an answer, as he intended returning to town in a couple of days. The following evening he received a note from the stationmaster, which read:

DEAR SIR,

I promised to let you know if the pictures in the cases on that truck were in any way tampered with. I have just received a report from Winchester by which I understand that they have been unpacked and carefully examined by the Committee of the Loan Exhibition. The Committee are perfectly satisfied that they have not been damaged or interfered with in any way, and that they have been received just as they left the owner's hands.

We are still at a loss to account for the running of the waggon on to Churn siding or for the object in doing so. An official has been down from Paddington, and at his request, we are not making the affair public – the goods having arrived in safety. I am sure you will observe confidence in this matter.

"More mysterious than ever," said Hazell to himself. "I can't understand it at all."

The next day he called at Scotland Yard and saw the official.

"I've had no difficulty with your little matter, you'll be glad to hear," he said. "We looked up our records and very soon spotted your man."

"Who is he?"

"His real name is Edgar Jeffreys, but we know him under several aliases. He's served four sentences for burglary and robbery – the latter a daring theft from a train, so he's in your line, Mr. Hazell. What's he been up to, and how did you get that print?"

"Well," replied Hazell, "I don't quite know yet what he's been doing. But I should like to be able to find him if anything turns up. Never mind how I got the print – the affair is quite a private one at present, and nothing may come of it."

The official wrote an address on a bit of paper and handed it to Hazell.

"He's living there just now, under the name of Allen. We keep such men in sight, and I'll let you know if he moves."

When Hazell opened his paper the following morning he gave a cry of joy. And no wonder, for this is what he saw:

MYSTERY OF A PICTURE.

SIR GILBERT MURRELL AND THE WINCHESTER LOAN EXHIBITION.

AN EXTRAORDINARY CHARGE.

The Committee of the Loan Exhibition of Pictures to be opened next week at Winchester are in a state of very natural excitement brought about by a strange charge that has been made against them by Sir Gilbert Murrell.

Sir Gilbert, who lives at Leamington, is the owner of several very valuable pictures, among them being the celebrated "Holy Family," by Velasquez. This picture, with two others, was dispatched by him from Leamington to he exhibited at Winchester, and yesterday he journeyed to that city in order to make himself satisfied with the hanging arrangements, as he had particularly stipulated that "The Holy Family" was to be placed in a prominent position.

The picture in question was standing on the floor of the gallery, leaning against a pillar, when Sir Gilbert arrived with some representatives of the Committee.

Nothing occurred till he happened to walk behind the canvas, when he astounded those present by saying that the picture was not his at all, declaring that a copy had been substituted, and stating that he was absolutely certain on account of certain private marks of his at the back of the canvas which were quite indecipherable, and which were now missing. He admitted that the painting itself in every way resembled his picture, and that it was the cleverest forgery he had ever seen, but a very painful scene took place, the hanging committee stating that the picture had been received by them from the railway company just as it stood.

At present the whole affair is a mystery, but Sir Gilbert insisted most emphatically to our correspondent, who was able to see him, that the picture was certainly not his, and said that as the original is extremely valuable he intends holding the Committee responsible for the substitution which, he declares, has taken place.

It was evident to Hazell that the papers had not as yet got hold of the mysterious incident at Churn. As a matter of fact, the railway company had kept that affair strictly to themselves, and the loan committee knew nothing of what had happened on the line.

But Hazell saw that inquiries would be made, and determined to probe the mystery without delay. He saw at once that if there was any truth in Sir Gilbert's story the substitution had taken place in that lonely siding at Churn. He was staying at his London flat, and five minutes after he had read the paragraph had called a hansom and was being hurried off to a friend of his who was well known in art circles as a critic and art historian.

"I can tell you exactly what you want to know," said he, "for I've only just been looking it up, so as to have an article in the evening papers on it. There was a famous copy of the picture of Velasquez, said to have been painted by a pupil of his and for some years there was quite a controversy among the respective owners as to which was the genuine one – just as there is today about a Madonna belonging to a gentleman at St. Moritz, but which a Vienna gallery also claims to possess.

"However, in the case of "The Holy Family," the dispute was ultimately settled once and for all years ago, and undoubtedly Sir Gilbert Murrell held the genuine picture. What became of the copy no one knows. For twenty years all trace of it has been lost. There –

that's all I can tell you. I shall pad it out a bit in my article, and I must get to work on it at once. Good-bye."

"One moment – where was the copy last seen?"

"Oh! The old Earl of Ringmere had it last, but when he knew it to be a forgery he is said to have sold it for a mere song, all interest in it being lost, you see."

"Let me see, he's a very old man, isn't he?"

"Yes, nearly eighty – a perfect enthusiast on pictures still, though."

"Only said to have sold it," muttered Hazell to himself, as he left the house, "that's very vague – and there's no knowing what these enthusiasts will do when they're really bent on a thing. Sometimes they lose all sense of honesty. I've known fellows actually rob a friend's collection of stamps or butterflies. What if there's something in it? By George, what an awful scandal there would be. It seems to me that if such a scandal were prevented I'd be thanked all round. Anyhow, I'll have a shot at it on spec. And I must find out how that truck was run off the line."

When once Hazell was on the track of a railway mystery he never let a moment slip by. In an hour's time, he was at the address given him at Scotland Yard. On his way there he took a card from his case, a blank one, and wrote on it, "From the Earl of Ringmere." This he put into an envelope. "It's a bold stroke," he said to himself, "but, if there's anything in it, it's worth trying."

So he asked for Allen. The woman who opened the door looked at him suspiciously, and said she didn't think Mr. Allen was in.

"Give him this envelope," replied Hazell. In a couple of minutes she returned, and asked him to follow her.

A short, wiry-looking man, with sharp, evil-looking eyes, stood in the room waiting for him and looking at him suspiciously.

"Well," he snapped, "what is it – what do you want?"

"I come on behalf of the Earl of Ringmere. You will know that when I mention Churn," replied Hazell, playing his trump card boldly.

"Well," went on the man, "what about that?"

Hazell wheeled round, locked the door suddenly, put the key in his pocket, and then faced his man. The latter darted forward, but Hazell had a revolver pointing at him in a twinkling.

"You – detective!"

"No, I'm not – I told you I came on behalf of the Earl – that looks like hunting up matters for his sake, doesn't it?"

"What does the old fool mean?" asked Jeffreys.

"Oh! I see you know all about it. Now listen to me quietly, and you may come to a little reason. You changed that picture at Churn the other night."

"You seem to know a lot about it," sneered the other, but less defiantly.

"Well, I do – but not quite all. You were foolish to leave your traces on that lever, eh?"

"How did I do that?" exclaimed the man, giving himself away.

"You'd been dabbling about with oil, you see, and you left your thumbprint on the handle. I photographed it, and they recognised it at Scotland Yard. Quite simple."

Jeffreys swore beneath his breath.

"I wish you'd tell me what you mean," he said.

"Certainly. I expect you've been well paid for this little job."

"If I have, I'm not going to take any risks. I told the old man so. He's worse than I am – he put me up to getting the picture. Let him take his chance when it comes out – I suppose he wants to keep his name out of it, that's why you're here."

"You're not quite right. Now just listen to me. You're a villain, and you deserve to suffer, but I'm acting in a purely private capacity, and I fancy if I can get the original picture back to its owner that it will be better for all parties to hush this affair up. Has the old Earl got it?"

"No, not yet," admitted the other, "he was too artful. But he knows where it is, and so do I."

"Ah – now you're talking sense! Look here. You make a clean breast of it, and I'll take it down on paper. You shall swear to the truth of your statement before a commissioner for oaths – he need not see the actual confession. I shall hold this in case it is necessary, but if you help me to get the picture back to Sir Gilbert, I don't think it will be."

After a little more conversation, Jeffreys explained. Before he did so, however, Hazell had taken a bottle of milk and a hunch of wholemeal bread from his pocket, and calmly proceeded to perform "exercises" and then to eat his "lunch," while Jeffreys told the following story:

"It was the old Earl who did it. How he got hold of me doesn't matter. Perhaps I got hold of him – maybe I put him up to it – but that's not the question. He'd kept that forged picture of his in a lumber room for years, but he always had his eye on the genuine one. He paid a long price for the forgery, and he got to think that he ought to have the original. But there, he's mad on pictures.

"Well, as I say, he kept the forgery out of sight and let folks think he'd sold it, but all the time he was in hopes of getting it changed somehow for the original.

"Then I came along and undertook the job for him. There were three of us in it, for it was a ticklish business. We found out by what train the picture was to travel – that was easy enough. I got hold of a key to unlock that ground frame, and the screwing off of the bolt was a mere nothing. I oiled the points well, so that the thing should work as I wanted it to.

"One pal was with me – in the siding, ready to clap on the side brake when the track was running in. I was to work the points, and my other pal, who had the most awkward job of all, was on the goods train – under a tarpaulin in a truck. He had two lengths of very stout rope with a hook at each end of them.

"When the train left Upton, he started his job. Goods trains travel very slowly, and there was plenty of time. Counting from the back brake van, the truck we wanted to run off was No. 5. First he hooked No. 4 truck to No. 6 – fixing the hook at the side of the end of both trucks, and having the slack in his hand, coiled up.

"Then when the train ran down a bit of a decline he uncoupled No. 5 from No. 4 – standing on No. 5 to do it. That was easy enough, for he'd taken a coupling staff with him; then he paid out the slack till it was tight. Next he hooked his second rope from No. 5 to No. 6, uncoupled No. 5 from No. 6, and paid out the slack of the second rope.

"Now you can see what happened. The last few trucks of the train were being drawn by a long rope reaching from No. 4 to No. 6, and leaving a space in between. In the middle of this space No. 5 ran, drawn by a short rope from No. 6. My pal stood on No. 6, with a sharp knife in his hand.

"The rest was easy. I held the lever, close by the side of the line – corning forward to it as soon as the engine passed. The instant the space appeared after No. 6 I pulled it over, and No. 5 took the siding points, while my pal cut the rope at the same moment.

"Directly the truck had run by and off I reversed the lever so that the rest of the train following took the main line. There is a decline before Compton, and the last four trucks came running down to the main body of the train, while my pal hauled in the slack and finally coupled No. 4 to No. 6 when they came together. He jumped from the train as it ran very slowly into Compton. That's how it was done."

Hazell's eyes sparkled.

"It's the cleverest thing I've heard of on the line," he said.

"Think so? Well, it wanted some handling. The next thing was to unscrew the packing case, take the picture out of the frame, and put the forgery we'd brought with us in its place. That took us some time, but there was no fear of interruption in that lonely part. Then I took the picture off, rolling it up first, and hid it. The old Earl insisted on this. I was to tell him where it was, and he was going to wait for a few weeks and then get it himself."

"Where did you hide it?"

"You're sure you're going to hush this up?"

"You'd have been in charge long ago if I were not."

"Well, there's a path from Churn to East Ilsley across the downs, and on the right hand of that path is an old sheep well – quite dry. It's down there. You can easily find the string if you look for it – fixed near the top."

Hazell took down the man's confession, which was duly attested. His conscience told him that perhaps he ought to have taken stronger measures.

"I told you I was merely a private individual," said Hazell to Sir Gilbert Murrell. "I have acted in a purely private capacity in bringing you your picture."

Sir Gilbert looked from the canvas to the calm face of Hazell.

"Who are you, sir?" he asked.

"Well, I rather aspire to be a book collector; you may have read my little monogram on 'Jacobean Bindings'?"

"No," said Sir Gilbert, "I have not had that pleasure. But I must inquire further into this. How did you get this picture? Where was it? Who – "

"Sir Gilbert," broke in Hazell, "I could tell you the whole truth, of course. I am not in any way to blame myself. By chance, as much as anything else, I discovered how your picture had been stolen, and where it was."

"But I want to know all about it. I shall prosecute. I – "

"I think not. Now, do you remember where the forged picture was seen last?"

"Yes, the Earl of Ringmere had it – he sold it."

"Did he?"

"Eh?"

"What if he kept it all this time?" said Hazell, with a peculiar look.

There was a long silence.

"Good heavens!" exclaimed Sir Gilbert at length. "You don't mean that. Why, he has one foot in the grave – a very old man – I was dining with him only a fortnight ago."

"Ah! Well, I think you are content now, Sir Gilbert?"

"It is terrible – terrible! I have the picture back, but I wouldn't have the scandal known for worlds."

"It never need be," replied Hazell. "You will make it all right with the Winchester people?"

"Yes – yes – even if I have to admit I was mistaken, and let the forgery stay through the exhibition."

"I think that would be the best way," replied Hazell, who never regretted his action.

"Of course, Jeffreys ought to have been punished," he said to himself, "but it was a clever idea – a clever idea!"

"May I offer you some lunch?" asked Sir Gilbert.

"Thank you, but I am a vegetarian, and – "

"I think my cook could arrange something – let me ring."

"It is very good of you, but I ordered a dish of lentils and a salad at the station restaurant. But if you will allow me just to go through my physical training ante luncheon exercises here, it would save me the trouble of a more or less public display at the station."

"Certainly," replied the rather bewildered Baronet, whereupon Hazell threw off his coat and commenced whirling his arms like a windmill.

"Digestion should be considered before a meal," he explained.

Real Life Impossibility: France
The Impossible Theft of 1,000 Rare Books

In 2000 and 2001, hundreds of rare and priceless fifteenth-century manuscripts and books disappeared from the Mont Sainte-Odile abbey near Strasbourg, France. No one could determine how they were stolen.

The books seemed to be in a secure place. The abbey's library was isolated in the Vosges mountains, 2,500 feet above the Rhine. A guard stood watch in the single passage leading to the library's only door. The door was locked securely, and the windows were sealed from the inside.

After the first thefts were reported, the locks were changed – twice. Investigators lifted floorboards and tested walls and ceilings.

Finally, after an astounding 1,000 books were stolen, a police officer found that pressing a section of wall behind one of the bookcases in a certain way revealed a hidden doorway. This doorway concealed a rope ladder in a narrow opening leading to a workshop in a different part of the abbey.

The culprit was found after a video camera was deployed in the secret passage. A local teacher had been joining daily tours of the abbey's public areas, then sneaking off to the workshop that led to the secret passage.

Abbey authorities speculate that the passage was originally put in place to monitor nuns who used the library as their chapter room.

China/Taiwan
The Miracle on Christmas Eve
by Szu-Yen Lin

In contrast to Japan, China and Taiwan do not appear to have a strong tradition of impossible-crime stories. The Dutchman Robert Van Gulik wrote a series of stories about eighteenth-century magistrate Judge Dee partly in an attempt to stir the Chinese people's interest in their own detective heritage, but apparently to little avail. Of Van Gulik's work, *The Chinese Gold Murders* (1959), *The Chinese Maze Murders* (1962), and *The Red Pavilion* (1964) contain locked-room mysteries.

Szu-Yen Lin is a Taiwanese mystery writer who has written four novels and twenty short stories, most of which have also been published in simplified Chinese in China. He is mainly known for his adherence to Golden Age rules of mystery writing, though some of his works fall outside that category. He also writes critical and introductory articles concerning mystery fiction for publishers. "The Apparition of the Badminton Court" won the Mystery Writers of Taiwan Award in 2002, and an English-language translation appeared in *Ellery Queen's Mystery Magazine* in August 2014. The present story appeared in *EQMM* in May 2016.

His first full-length novel in English, *Death in the House of Rain,* will be published by Locked Room International in October 2017.

The boy turned over in bed, the first gleams of daylight caressing his forehead. The cold morning air brought him sharply back from hazy dreams to reality. He rubbed his eyes and stretched.

Pushing aside the heavy quilt, he sat up on the bed. The thin hands of the wall clock pointed to 5 a.m. His eyes turned to the nearby desk, on which a rectangular box stood among a mess of textbooks and drawing papers.

The boy got quickly out of bed and stood barefoot in front of the desk, leaving the rumpled quilt on the cold floor. He clasped the box tightly to his chest. Although the Japanese words on the box were enigmatic, the pictures beside them told him all he needed to know: they were of beautifully designed robots.

Holding the box, he ran into the corridor and shouted with great excitement, "Dad! Come see my Christmas gift from Santa Claus! It's the newest type of robot!"

He galloped at full speed to the other end of the corridor.

1.

Two soft knocks on the door disturbed the silence of the cold December morning.

"Come in." Ruoping put down the mystery novel he had been reading and adjusted his silver glasses.

He had been preparing for a symposium for the forthcoming Taipei International Book Exhibition, which is the fourth largest book fair in the world. A Japanese mystery writer who specialized in mysteries without crimes was participating in the panel Ruoping would be moderating, and he was trying to finish all of the author's books.

A young man entered. "Sorry for interrupting your work. I'm Meng-Hsing Ko. We talked on the phone."

"Nice to meet you." Ruoping arose from his swivel chair and nodded back. "Have a seat, please."

The man took off his jacket and seated himself nervously on the sofa.

"Since we have an appointment," said Ruoping, "the floor's all yours."

The visitor hesitated for a moment, then looked Ruoping straight in the eye and said:

"I'd like you to show me whether Santa Claus exists or not."

No. He was not out of his mind. Ruoping studied Ko's face closely. He might have burst out laughing, but for Ko's sincere demeanor. "Tell me more," he urged.

"I know this sounds crazy," smiled the visitor abashedly. "But that's exactly what I want you to do for me: to prove whether Santa Claus exists or not, especially on Christmas Eve sixteen years ago."

"Why that particular night?"

"Sorry, I wasn't clear," said Ko, scratching his neck. "Something inexplicable occurred that night, and I want to know whether it was due to Santa Claus or not."

"I understand. So please tell me what happened?"

Ko's uneasiness disappeared as he took up the role of storyteller.

"I've spent the past twenty-eight years in Hualien, except for my time at university. Hualien is a beautiful place full of beautiful memories. My mother passed away when I was three, so I was raised by my father and grandparents. Dad worked in a gas station when Mom left us, and had numerous jobs thereafter, including transporter, substitute teacher, and vendor. Then he made his name by selling soup buns, and for fifteen years this had been our livelihood. He ran a small shop three blocks away from home and employed a young man named Yen-Min as his assistant.

"Although Dad wasn't highly educated, he was very studious. He bought and read all sorts of books, and spent a lot of money buying me books and toys."

"Toys?"

"Yes. Most parents are happy to buy books for their children, but not toys. My dad wasn't like that. Each time I was attracted by a robot model in a toy shop, he would buy me one. I like to collect the robots which appear in cartoons, and all my classmates were envious of my collection."

"You had a great father."

"Yes, indeed. Everyone said so. He always wore a loving smile and was never hard on me. He would spend hours with me watching and discussing cartoons, never showing any signs of tiredness. He spent his whole life bringing his son happiness. There wasn't a better father in the world. But there is one thing I'm not sure about."

"What's that?"

"He told me interesting bedtime stories every night, from classical literature to science fiction. One night he told me the story of Santa Claus, who lives in the Arctic, and flies on a sleigh pulled by reindeer to deliver gifts every Christmas to children all over the world. They find gifts in their room when they wake up on Christmas morning. I liked this story very much and asked Dad whether I would receive a Christmas gift from Santa Claus.

"Of course," he said. "Christmas is coming soon. Why don't you wait and see?"

"I was seven years old then. On Christmas night, Dad urged me to turn in early, because Santa Claus would only come once children were sound asleep. I went to bed shortly after dinner and tried my best to fall asleep. When I opened my eyes again it was early in the morning. And my first thought was about my Christmas gift from Santa Claus.

"There was a box on the desk. It was the model of the most popular robot in a cartoon I watched every week. I jumped out of bed, grabbed the box, and ran joyfully to my dad's room."

"What did your father say?" asked Ruoping.

"He got out of bed slowly, smiled as usual, and said:

"See? I told you. Santa Claus will send you a gift every Christmas."

Then we opened the gift together. I ran around the house wildly all day long with my robot. Grandma thought I was possessed by a ghost!"

"I can imagine."

"I received a gift every Christmas after that. It always happened the same way: I would wake up in the morning to find the gift placed on the desk. Santa Claus knew pretty well what I really wanted each time and never disappointed me. Because of this, I became deeply convinced that he really did exist and he delivered gifts to me on those cold winter nights."

"So," asked Ruoping, "you believed in his existence in your childhood, but started to have doubts later on, is that it?"

Ko nodded. "I was just a kid then, and would believe in whatever my dad told me. I would have believed that ninja turtles lived in the sewers if he'd told me so. But later I started asking myself questions. How did Santa get into our house? Grandma was a cautious person and would lock all the windows and doors from the inside before going to bed. How did Santa Claus get in without breaking any locks?"

"Did you ask your father about this?"

"Yes. He told me it was because Santa knows magic. How can a lock be a problem to him if he can fly a sleigh in the sky? I was persuaded right away, and felt my question had been a serious offence to Santa. I put away my doubts for several years."

"But you began again at some point."

"Yes. When I look back now at that annual Christmas event, I know my father must have been the man behind the scenes, for two reasons. First, Santa Claus must be one of the family members because no one else could have broken into the house locked from the inside at night. Grandma was too crippled to enter my room without making any noise. That leaves Dad as the only suspect. Second, Santa Claus knew what type of robot I wanted each time. The only person who knew that was Dad, because we discussed robot cartoons almost every day. So it's pretty obvious."

"It seems that way."

"But there's one particular event which prevented me from drawing that conclusion."

"What event?"

"I was twelve at the time," said Ko in a dreamy tone, his eyes dimming with tears. "That Christmas Eve I witnessed a miracle which could only have been performed by Santa Claus, who knows magic."

"Miracle?" said Ruoping, eyes gleaming.

"What I'm going to tell you is the most baffling part of my story." Ko cleared his throat and explained.

2.

"My elementary school days were carefree and full of daydreams. My schoolwork was average and I wasn't very active socially, either. I was an ordinary school kid.

"It was one week before Christmas when I stood by the classroom window during a break, chatting with some classmates. It was cold outside, yet a few kids wearing less than enough clothes were out on the playground.

"'Christmas is coming soon,' I said excitedly.

"I told them briefly about my receiving a gift every Christmas, only to realize that none of them believed in Santa Claus. One of them was nicknamed Ant, who always laced his comments about people with invective. When I finished, he pulled a face and sneered:

"'Come on, that's a kid's story! You're a sixth-grader, not a sniveling baby!'

"'Santa Claus does exist! He sends me a gift every Christmas!'

"I clenched my little fists and repeated what I'd said, which made Ant and the others laugh even more.

"'You're so dumb. It had to be your father. He put the gift in your room when you were sleeping like a pig. They should send you back to kindergarten.'

"Everyone burst out laughing again. I was a meek and mild person. Their mocking brought me to the brink of tears. I clenched my fists again and returned to my seat and sat there with a long face until the class was dismissed.

"'Is Santa Claus waiting for you at home?'

"Ant and his followers pulled faces at me when I was about to leave the classroom. I rushed out quickly without saying goodbye to anyone. Passing through the school gate, I ran tearfully towards Dad's restaurant. Yen-Min, the young helper Dad had hired, was there. He hadn't gone to university after graduating from senior high school and had chosen to work for Dad, who trusted him and liked him a lot.

"'What happened, Meng-Hsing?' Yen-Min left the front desk quickly and came over to me. Dad heard us and walked out of the kitchen.

"'You didn't go home?' asked Dad, hands stained with the stuffing of soup buns.

"I poured out tearfully how I had been treated by the disbelievers in Santa Claus. Dad rubbed his hands against a towel and put his right hand over my head gently.

"'Never mind. They must be jealous of you because they didn't receive any gifts. Santa Claus doesn't send gifts to bad kids.'

"'Does Santa Claus really exist?' I raised my head, nose twitching, staring at him.

"'Ah?' Dad paused before answering with a smile. 'Of course he does. He sends you a gift every Christmas, doesn't he?'

"'But Ant said that was you. Is it true?' When I said this I could feel the reproachful tone in my voice. But Dad remained impassive.

"'I see. They don't believe it.' Dad sank into deep thought with his arms crossed on his chest. He spoke after a long minute. 'How about this? Invite them to dinner on Christmas night. They'll see Santa Claus through their own eyes.'

"'Will Santa Claus show up before so many people?'

"'Just ask them to come. Have they ever seen Santa's magic powers? They'll be stunned when they do!'

"'Santa's magic?' I stared. Merely thinking of Ant and the others being stunned by magic made me excited.

"'Ask them to come over next week. Now go home. I have business to do.'

"The next day I told Ant and his followers about this.

"'My father said if you want to see Santa Claus, come to dinner on Christmas Eve. We'll have soup buns together.'

"'See Santa Claus?' said Fatty, blowing his nose.

"'Stay overnight, and see Santa Claus's magic.'

"'Magic? Nonsense!' Ant grimaced at me.

"'If you don't come you won't get a Christmas gift.' Dad had told me to seduce them with gifts.

"'I want a gift.' Fatty rubbed his running nose with the back of his hand. 'Also, his father's buns are yummy. I'm in. How about you guys?'

"'Well...'

"I could see that Dad's buns were a big lure for Ant.

"'All right. I'll come. But if you lie to us, you'll have to give us fifty soup buns.'

"'A deal.'

"Finally a total of six boys decided to come. After class, I rushed to Dad's restaurant and let him know.

"'Six,' said Dad, kneading the dough in his hands, 'a perfect number.'

"'I'm still worried about this. Did you discuss this with Santa Claus? What if he doesn't want to show up?'

"'I have a plan. We don't need to discuss with him, and he doesn't need to show up, either. But we can still verify his existence.'

"'How?'

"'You'll see.'

"I didn't ask for further details, because I knew everything would be fine if Dad said so.

"Life at school remained the same before Christmas. Ant and the others kept teasing me about Santa Claus, but their eyes glittered when it came to the Christmas dinner.

"On Thursday, Christmas Eve, I heard someone knocking at the front door while I was helping Dad with dinner in the kitchen.

"Dad nodded to me. I rushed to the door and opened it. Five boys crowded in the hallway.

"Ant, Fatty, Stupid, Catty, Cracker – someone was missing?

"'Doraemon has a fever,' said Fatty, sniveling. 'He kept running around the playground with not enough clothes on.'

"'I'm Meng-Hsing's father. Welcome!' Dad's voice came from behind them.

"'Good evening!' chorused the kids.

"Dad surveyed them and smiled, 'Some of you are my regulars. You must be hungry. Come in and have dinner together.'

"'Hooray!' A horde of hungry young wolves rushed into the house.

"To my surprise, Dad didn't mention Santa Claus at all during dinner. Instead, he chatted with the boys about themselves, their families and school life. The atmosphere was cozy, but I felt nervous thinking of what was going to happen.

"After dinner, we watched Christmas TV shows and then played poker and chess. At nine o'clock sharp, Dad stood up and said, 'All right, time for today's special. You're here to see Santa's magic. Follow me and I'll let you know what we're going to do.'

"We followed Dad excitedly into the corridor. He stopped in front of the first door on the left.

"'This is Meng-Hsing's bedroom,' said Dad. 'I believe all of you are already familiar with the story of Santa Claus. Every Christmas he places Meng-Hsing's gift quietly in his room at night.'

"There was a commotion among the boys. Dad hushed them and continued, 'I know you don't believe it. Meng-Hsing asked me the same question: How did Santa Claus get into the house while all the doors and windows were locked from the inside? The answer is simple: because he knows magic and can get in and out of a sealed space with ease.'

"'Impossible!' said Ant, toning down his language in the presence of an adult.

"'Agreed,' echoed Fatty, 'it sounds like a cartoon.'

"'Then let's have a test,' said Dad mysteriously. 'Let's assume Santa Claus will come tonight, and try to increase the difficulty of his mission.'

"'What do you mean?' the kids asked with one accord.

"'Tonight, if we all sleep in the corridor, in front of the door of Meng-Hsing's room, then nobody can get into the room without our noticing, right?'

"'How come?' asked Stupid, scratching his head.

"'Because he will need to step over us.'

"'But what if he does it lightly and cautiously?' I asked.

"'Good question. How about this? We seal the doorframe with adhesive tapes. The visitor will need to remove the tapes if he wants to get in. Removing long tapes makes a loud noise. And if that happens we'll know.' Dad reached into his pocket and produced a bunch of keys. 'The key to Meng-Hsing's room is one of these keys. After locking the room later I'll put the keys under Ant's pillow. That way nobody can get the key without disturbing Ant.'

"'But why me?'

"'You are the most die-hard disbeliever in Santa Claus, aren't you? If somehow the gift can still find its way into the sealed room, I assume that would change you into a believer?'

"'Well...'

"'I see your point.' Fatty cut in before Ant could reply. 'Meng-Hsing's father wants to show us that Santa Claus can make the impossible possible.'

"'That's right, smart guy!' nodded Dad. 'We make the room impossible to get in. If we still find gifts delivered into the room tomorrow morning, that will be sufficient proof of the existence of Santa Claus.'

"I suddenly saw the light. In this case, there was no need to have a word with Santa Claus in the first place and we didn't need to worry about whether he was happy to expose himself or not.

"'But,' asked Fatty, sucking his thumb, 'could it be that you have put the gifts in the room before we find them?'

"Dad smiled. 'So I'll let you search the room first. You'll need to check whether there are hidden gifts or secret passages inside.'

"Dad nodded at me for consent. I nodded back. He then opened the door and turned on the light inside the room.

"'So this is Meng-Hsing's room!' the kids exclaimed.

"There was a window right opposite the door, and my desk was right under the window. To the right stood my bed; to the left was a large bookshelf standing against the wall, with books and robot models on it. A small clothes horse stood in the corner between the bookshelf and the open door, with some of my clothes hanging on it.

"'So many robots!' the boys exclaimed in chorus.

"'This is not the right time for studying robots. Search the room closely but keep everything in order. I'll fetch the tape.'

"So saying, Dad left.

"The five boys, like five bloodhounds, sniffed around my room. Ant studied the bed but found no space under it; Fatty fiddled with the books on the bookshelf; Stupid, scratching his head, tapped the wall for hidden cavities; Catty stared at the clothes horse, frowning; Cracker stared fixedly at the robots on the bookshelf, his face twitching.

"'How's it going?' A few minutes later Dad returned with two pairs of scissors and two rolls of tapes. The boys shook their heads.

"'No gifts or secret doors in the room. Agreed?' asked Dad.

"'But...' Ant wiped the dust from his pants, 'the only window in this room is not locked. Santa Claus – if there is a Santa Claus – could get in through the window.'

"'Perfectly true.' Dad walked toward the window. 'I'll lock it from the inside later, and we'll seal the window frame with tape, so that no one can open the window from the outside. Clear the desk, Meng-Hsing.'

"'Sure.'

"After I did so, Dad climbed up and squatted gingerly on the desk. He opened the double window: the aluminum window and the screen.

"'See? This is a normal window, and there are no suspicious devices planted inside or outside....' He leaned out, but failed to keep his balance – Dad fell out of the window!

"'Dad!' I shouted.

"I climbed onto the desk quickly. The others crowded behind me.

"'I'm all right.' Dad stood up, wiping the dust from his clothes. 'Fortunately, your room is on the ground floor. Sorry for scaring you guys.'

"Relieved, I jumped down from the desk. Dad climbed in through the window with our help. He closed it firmly and pointed to the tape and scissors he had brought in earlier.

"'I'll leave the task of sealing the window to you, so as to avoid any question of cheating on my part. Remember to lock the window first. Go.'

"Catty climbed onto the desk and locked the window. Others confirmed that the window was indeed locked. Then, Fatty and Ant pulled the tape straight for Cracker and Stupid to cut with scissors. Catty and I stuck the tape along the window frame. Ten minutes later, the task was done.

"'Good job,' said Dad. 'Next we need to seal the door from the outside. Let's get out.'

"We walked out of the room. Dad pressed the button on the knob down and closed the door behind him.

"'Try the knob and see if the door is locked.'

"Ant and Fatty tried turning the knob in turn but failed. Dad produced the bunch of keys he showed us earlier and picked one out. He turned the key in the knob and pushed the door open.

"'This is to let you know this key is the right one.'

"Dad locked the door again and said, 'Try the knob again.'

"This time Cracker and Catty tried it in turn. The knob wouldn't turn at all. Fatty pushed the two boys aside and said, 'Let me try it.' He stepped back, took a deep breath, dashed forward, and hit the door with full force. He bounced back violently.

"'Watch out!' Dad held out his hands and caught the rebounding Fatty.

"Fatty rubbed his elbow and steadied himself. 'I swear nobody can force this door open without using a key.'

"'Then seal the doorframe with tapes. I'll find you a stool for the work.'

"It was soon done. My room was now perfectly sealed like a gift package, which even a bug couldn't have entered. Could Santa Claus enter this hermetically sealed room without difficulty? Not until I had sealed the room with my own hands did I truly realise the impossibility.

"'You can have my head if anyone can still sneak into this room,' smiled Fatty. He seemed pretty satisfied with his own work.

"'Well done!' said Dad. 'Now go take pillows and quilts. We'll sleep in the corridor tonight.'

"We followed Dad upstairs and carried pillows, mattresses, and quilts downstairs. Since it was cold at night, we put extra quilts above the mattresses to make our temporary beds warmer. The corridor had been carefully cleaned in advance, so there was no problem with making a bed on the ground. We – six kids – lay in three rows right in front of my room, with two persons in each row. Dad lay down at the end of the corridor, right beside the first two kids.

"The keys were already stuck under Ant's pillow.

"'Sweet dreams.' Dad turned off the light in the corridor. Darkness fell.

"I could hear the cry of insects outside, and the whispers of Ant and the others. Five minutes later, Fatty began to snore, and everyone else followed his example.

"My eyes remained opened in the dark. Catty lay on my left-hand side; Cracker and Fatty were almost on top of me. Were it not for the quilt, I'd have been killed by the smell of Fatty's feet.

"I tried to shift my attention to something more beautiful. What happened tonight was like a fantasy. Having dinner with these disbelievers, searching for hidden doors and gifts, sealing the room – it was so interesting and exciting. I had never had this kind of experience. Dad had made this Christmas so different and unique....

"I held out my right hand and touched the door, feeling the wooden texture with my fingers. Would we find gifts in my room tomorrow morning?

"Of course we would! Santa Claus got into the locked house magically every year. But this time the lock was harder to break than ever....

"My vision began to blur. I saw snow, Santa Claus, and his reindeer flying in the sky, and bags of gifts on the sleigh....

"The jingle of bells, and a red silhouette in the sky.

"I found myself standing in the snow, listening to the bells, the snowflakes surrounding me like white music notations. It was so beautiful.

"Suddenly, there was a strange shift of consciousness. I opened my eyes.

"I saw darkness, but the jingle of bells continued. Wait, wasn't this the song 'Jingle Bells'?

"Others seemed to be awoken by the music, too, and sat up. I put my ear against the door. The music was coming from inside the room.

"'How is it there's music?' asked Ant, rubbing his eyes.

"'I don't know. It's from my room.'

"'Santa Claus?' shouted Cracker.

"'You can all hear the music.' Dad stood up, his body towering in the dark. 'It's time we went in.'

"'Now?' I asked in surprise.

"'You all want to see Santa Claus, don't you? Remove the tape.' He turned on the light in the corridor.

"Everyone jumped out of their quilts and did as directed.

"Soon the tape was all removed. We crowded in front of the door, excited. Dad stood behind us and said, 'Open the door.'

"Ant picked out the correct key and tried to insert it in the keyhole, but only succeeded on the third attempt, due to his trembling hand.

"'Hurry up!' shouted Fatty, sniffing.

"As soon as the door was open, Fatty pushed Ant aside and edged into the room. There was darkness inside.

"'The light switch is to your right,' prompted Dad.

"The music continued as Fatty groped for the switch. All of a sudden the room was flooded with light. I squinted and tried to see what was happening in the room.

"I heard someone taking a deep breath, someone screaming, but most of them were shouting.

"At that magic moment, I couldn't believe my own eyes, which I rubbed again and again. The scene before us would be forever burned in my memory, along with the jingle of bells.

"In the center of the room stood a small Christmas tree; a dozen gifts in beautiful wrapping paper surrounded it. A music box stood on the desk; inside it was a small scenic model of Santa Claus in his sleigh, being pulled by reindeer in the snow. An air of magic permeated the room.

"For a moment there was only silence. Dad's voice broke the ice: 'What are you waiting for? Go open your gifts!'

"We rushed to the pile of presents and removed the wrapping with wild excitement. Joyful shouts came one after another.

"'Wow! It's Gundam!'

"'Mado King!'

"As all of us held the robots gleefully in our arms, a louder sound of jingling bells could suddenly be heard from outdoors. I could tell it was not from the music box. It was a jingle of real bells!

"Everyone looked up and out of the window. My heart beat so fast it almost jumped out of my chest!

"Through the sealed window, far away in the darkness, something moved in the sky. It was only visible for a brief moment but it remains engraved in my memory forever.

"I saw the silhouette of Santa Claus on the sleigh pulled by reindeer, bags of gifts hanging down from the back. The team flew across the sky and disappeared into the silent night.

"After the moment of wonder, I heard Ant murmuring to himself, his tone trembling but determined.

"'Santa Claus really does exist after all!'"

3.

Ko looked at Ruoping for comment.

"What happened after that?" asked Ruoping, eyes blinking.

"Nothing significant. We entered the room at four o'clock in the morning and then engaged in a robot war. Dad let them take a gift home. After this event, nobody ever made fun of Santa Claus."

"I see," replied Ruoping in a thoughtful tone. "The music box in your room…was it also a gift from Santa Claus?"

"Yes. I swear I never saw it in the house before that night."

"Did you notice anything unusual with the tape before removing it?"

"Nothing unusual with the tape used to seal the door and the window."

"What about the window lock?"

"It was locked from the inside." Ko gazed at some point in space. "As you see, my room at that time was a hermetically sealed space, watched by seven people. It was impossible for anyone to have delivered the gifts, music box, and Christmas tree into the room without our noticing."

"It's also hard to explain what you saw through the window."

"Yes. The flying Santa Claus and his reindeer…I shall never forget the scene." Ko closed his eyes and sank into the sofa. There was a short silence before he resumed. "The whole event is a paradox. My intuition says that my father had been playing the role of Santa Claus, but the miracle that night shows the opposite."

"Are you sure that your father didn't leave the corridor that night during your sleep?"

"I'm not one hundred percent sure, but he slept at the far end of the corridor. He would have needed to step over us if he wanted to leave. It's a narrow corridor."

"I see."

"Even if he could have moved without disturbing us, it was still not possible for him to have got through the door without anyone noticing!"

"Indeed. Are you sure the gifts were not hidden in the room in the first place?"

"No hiding place. I'm pretty sure."

"No secret doors in the room?"

"No." Ko shook his head.

"Then that was a real miracle."

"Yes, but I don't care whether Santa Claus is real or not. What I really want to know is whether my father could have been responsible and how. Can you help me? I've brought some money to pay for my request. It's not a large sum, but – "

"Wait." Ruoping stopped him. "You don't need to pay anything for this."

Ko was surprised. "Why not? I'm taking your time and time is money."

"Because," replied Ruoping seriously, "love is invaluable."

Ruoping contemplated the mountains far away through the window of Ko's car.

The amateur detective had suggested paying a visit to Ko's place, in the suburbs of Hualien City – ten minutes' drive from Ruoping's university – even though sixteen years had passed. On the way, Ko mentioned that he had been running a studio of robot models and was also an illustrator for a video game magazine. He seemed financially secure.

It was a two-story house, standing against majestic mountain scenery. Ko opened the front door and led Ruoping first into a small living room and then into a corridor, where he stopped before a door on the left-hand side. The wooden door looked old and uninteresting.

The interior of the room was almost the same as Ko had described before, except that the clothes horse in the corner had been replaced by a wardrobe. Ruoping also noticed that there were not as many robot models on the bookshelf as he had expected.

"I have a studio," Ko explained. "Most of my models are displayed there. I keep some of my favorite ones here."

Ruoping walked over to the window and inspected it, first opening the aluminum window itself and then the screen. He could see part of the yard outside. The balmy countryside air drifted into the room. He closed and locked the window and examined the window frame. There were no seams at all along the frame for any thread to pass through.

"Unless Santa Claus broke the window," murmured Ruoping, "he couldn't have got in through here."

"But the window is intact," replied Ko.

Ruoping turned to the door. The knob was a common cylinder lock: Once the button on the knob was pressed down, the knob became locked and couldn't be rotated.

While Ruoping was thinking, Ko received a call on his mobile phone. His face brightened and he excused himself. Ruoping looked around the room and tried to reconstruct in his mind what had happened there sixteen years ago. Six curious and excited kids, under the guidance of a father, came to verify a seemingly impossible event: a plethora of gifts appearing out of thin air in a perfectly locked room. He tried to put himself in the place of one of the kids. Something deep in his mind began to stir....

"Sorry for keeping you waiting."

As Ko came back into the room, Ruoping froze on the spot, gazing at him.

"Was your father standing where you are now when you kids came in and started unwrapping the gifts?" he asked.

"Yes." Ko seemed baffled. "What about it?"

Ruoping took a deep breath and responded in a calm voice.

"I think I know part of the answer. Can we meet here again at 11 o'clock tomorrow night?"

"All right. I'm having dinner with her tomorrow but I'll be back before 10."

"Good. Before I call it a day, I have one or two more questions. In the final year of your elementary school life, did your father have any close friends or relatives except Yen-Min?"

Ko paused before answering the question. "I have an uncle who lived in the city center. My father was on particularly good terms with him and he was a great support for me after Dad passed away."

"Did you see your uncle on that magical night?"

"No."

"Can you give me his address and phone number?"

It was late at night in Ruoping's office. The light from the desk lamp created a small glow in the room. He had just completed an internet search on Ko's business. His studio was well-known in robot-modeling circles and attracted connoisseurs from all over Taiwan, and his column on robot design in the video game magazine was also popular. He had been trained at an art university and possessed excellent drawing skills.

Ruoping closed his eyes and leaned backwards in the chair. He crossed his arms across his chest, running through the whole case in his mind. He had a theory, but didn't have any evidence to test it. He expected to close the case tomorrow night.

Turning off the lamp, he continued his thoughts in the dark.

4.

Ruoping and Ko met again as agreed, in the latter's living room. At Ruoping's suggestion, they went to Ko's room. It looked the same as yesterday, with the window closed and the quilt in disorder. Ruoping began:

"Let me summarize the case so far. There were seven characters in this dramatic event: you, your father and five of your classmates. After dinner, your father urged all of you to engage in a thorough search for hidden gifts and apertures in this room, and you found none. Then, again following your father's suggestion, you locked the window from the inside and sealed the window frame with adhesive tape. Then you left the room, locked the door and sealed the doorframe with tape for the second time. Finally, all of you made a bed on the floor and slept in front of your room.

"At four o'clock in the morning, the melody 'Jingle Bells' awoke you from sleep. Under your father's guidance you removed the tape on the door, unlocked it, and entered the room. About twenty beautifully packed gifts were stacked up around a Christmas tree; there was a music box on the desk, from which the music was coming. Right at that moment, you heard the tinkle of bells outside and saw through the window Santa Claus and his reindeer flying across the sky. This is what happened that night. Anything wrong with my summary?"

"No. That's exactly what happened." Ko stroked his chin.

"Good. So the problems we need to solve are: How were the gifts and other things delivered into the locked room? And what was it that you saw in the sky? Before I get to the answers, I want to make some points clear at the outset." Ruoping paused, then announced in all seriousness: "I never deny that Santa Claus is real, because I can't disprove his existence. Therefore, when I first considered this event I didn't exclude the possibility that the person behind all this could indeed have been Santa Claus.

"However, since it is difficult to verify his existence, I approached the case in a more pragmatic way: I assumed your father did play the role of Santa Claus and, by some trick, he performed the miracle that night. If I can find evidence to support this theory, then the case is solved. This kind of reasoning is generally called inductive logic."

Ko stared at Ruoping, amazed at the philosophical clarity shown by this young associate professor of philosophy. He seemed a different person when solving a case.

"Since our basic premise is that it was your father, not Santa Claus, who performed the stunt, we can exclude any use of magical power. Without magic powers, how did someone deliver the gifts into the locked room without anyone noticing? First of all, what we can be sure of is that the gifts must have been smuggled into the room after your thorough search, because there is no place in the room to conceal them. Secondly, they must have been delivered through either the window or the door, since there are no other openings in the room. Therefore, regarding the route into the room, we have just two options. Is that agreed?"

"Agreed."

"Let's consider the door first. The door was triply locked by the cylinder lock, the tape, and seven people watching the door. It's simply impossible to penetrate this triple barrier without anyone noticing, because anyone attempting to do so would need to perform eight moves in total without disturbing your sleep.

"First, he would need to carry with him over twenty gifts, a music box, and a Christmas tree while moving in a narrow and crowded corridor. Second, he would need to take the bunch of keys from under Ant's pillow. Third, he would need to pick out the right key using some lighting device. Fourth, he would need to unlock the door. Fifth, he would need to remove the tape. Sixth, he would need to shut the door firmly upon leaving. This is because, to lock a door with a cylinder lock from the outside, one needs to press down the button on the knob and then shut the door hard. Eighth, he would need to put the bunch of keys back under Ant's pillow.

"It's fair to assume that our transporter might succeed in some of the moves without arousing you. But it's inconceivable that he could have succeeded in all of them."

"Well..."

"The most powerful reason why the transporter didn't deliver the gifts through the door is this. When you heard the melody of 'Jingle Bells,' did everyone wake up right away?"

"Of course," said Ko, bewildered.

"Is it possible that all of you could have woken up after the music had been continuing for a while?"

"Impossible. I was actually awoken by the music."

"Then we can reasonably assume that all of you woke up soon after the music box was started. In this case, the transporter would have needed to complete the last three moves I mentioned as the music was being played."

"I think I see what you mean." Ko took a deep breath.

"The last three moves have to be done after the transporter started the music box. If all of you woke up soon after the music began, he wouldn't have had enough time to make the last moves.

"Now we have a temporary conclusion: The transporter must have delivered the gifts through the window."

"Window? I can't see how, either!"

Ruoping shifted his gaze to the window. "Let's work it out step by step. The window had to be opened before the gifts could be delivered, and it could be opened either from the outside or inside. Could it be opened from the outside? I examined the window frame yesterday and found no seam or crack for any rope trick to work. It is reasonable to exclude this possibility. Such being the case, the window must be opened from the inside."

"I don't understand."

"If the window was opened from the inside, the transporter must have been in the room from the very beginning."

"It couldn't be! We searched the room from the ground up! No gifts concealed in the room, not to mention a human being!"

"A gift can't move around, but a human being can. You did search the room thoroughly once and found nothing, but did you search again before leaving the room?"

"Again? Why?"

"As I said, a human can move around. If someone sneaked into the room shortly after your search, he could then have succeeded in staying in the room."

Ko frowned deeply. "How did he do that without our noticing? And where did he hide? There is no hiding place in this room!"

"There is one."

Ko kept frowning and surveyed the room. He scratched his chin and said, "I give up."

"You'll see."

Ruoping walked to the door and opened it.

"Ah!" exclaimed Ko. "I've got it!"

"A common blind spot," smiled Ruoping. He pulled the door inward until it formed an angle of 45 degrees with the wall. "I remember the door was open when you did the search, and it was your father who opened the door. He did so for the transporter to sneak in. And don't forget there used to be a clothes horse beside the door, which could serve as part of the cover."

"Who was this transporter? It couldn't have been Dad...."

"Let's call him Accomplice A. I'll get to his identity later."

"But how did...Accomplice A get into the room without our noticing? If he'd just walked in we would have known."

"That's right. Actually he got in when all of you were looking at the opposite direction to the door. Do you remember that particular moment?"

"Let me think...yes! It was Dad! He fell out of the window!"

"That's right. This accident was crucial to the whole trick. That was also why he suggested sealing the window with tape. That way he could fake the accident and create a distraction for Accomplice A to sneak in."

"But how did he get out of the room?"

"I'll get to that. Your father was the last to leave the room, so as to make sure none of you would detect the person hiding behind the door. After you left, Accomplice A waited till after midnight – three o'clock, I think. First, he quietly removed the tape around the window frame. Next, he unlocked the window and opened it. At the same time, Accomplice B outside passed the gifts, music box, and the Christmas tree through the window."

"Accomplice B?" stared Ko.

"That's right. Your father needed another helper to do the trick outside. After everything was smuggled into the room, Accomplice A locked and sealed the window again. He set the Christmas tree and stacked the gifts around it. After that, he placed and started the music box on the desk. Finally he took cover beside the door once more. When the door was opened, he was again covered by it."

"How did he leave the room?"

"In the same way he sneaked in. He left when you were all distracted and looking in the opposite direction – at the flying Santa Claus and his reindeer! To avoid any risks, your father stood by the door at that moment to cover Accomplice A's escape.

"There are two reasons for producing the stunning scene in the sky. First, to create the moment of distraction as said. Second, to reinforce the existence of Santa Claus."

"But how was it done? That seems to be the most baffling part of the event."

"That is actually the simplest part. Have you ever seen the animations or movies of Batman? When the police wanted to contact Batman, they would use a special spotlight that had a symbol of a bat attached to it. The police use this spotlight to project the bat emblem on the sky at night. The same device was used in the Christmas event. Do an internet search and you'll find instructions for making such a spotlight.

"When you and your friends were busy unwrapping the gifts, Accomplice B outside shook the bell in his hand to attract your attention. As you all looked at the window, he turned on the spotlight that had attached to it the silhouette of Santa Claus flying the sleigh pulled by reindeer, and projected it to the sky. The projection must have been rehearsed in advance to achieve the best effect. That's why there must have been an Accomplice B, because that last task could only be done by someone outside the room. The special effect, though simple, was enough to convince kids of your age." Ruoping stopped, looking at Ko.

Ko, once the kid of that age, seemed too surprised to say anything. Lips twitching, he began in a low voice: "Then who were the accomplices?"

"That's pretty easy to guess. Accomplice A must be very close to your father, given that your father allowed him to stay and hide in your house. The most likely suspect is your uncle. As for Accomplice B, I think it was Yen-Min, the young helper in your father's restaurant. It suited him to play the role of midnight transporter."

"Ruoping, your theory explains everything. But do you have any evidence so that I can accept the solution with my whole heart?"

"Here you are." Ruoping produced a yellowing envelope and gave it to Ko.

"What's this?"

"Your father entrusted this to your uncle. I paid a visit to him and he gave it to me. You may want to open it and read the letter now. It's still sealed."

There was neat handwriting on the envelope: "To my son, Meng-Hsing."

Ko opened the envelope and drew out a yellow piece of paper with trembling hands.

Dear Son,

Your reading this letter means you will soon have your own family.

I know my health condition. I won't be able to live long enough to see your family, so I write down these future words for you and entrust this letter to your uncle, who will forward it to you when he knows you have met the love of your life. This is the right time for you to know the truth, because you are mature enough to face responsibilities and difficulties in life.

Childhood is an innocent existence. If an adult no longer has a child's heart, they won't be able to lead their life in a good and honest way, and the world will see more cruelty, calculation, and sin.

That is why I took such pains to create a happy childhood for you. You needn't be excellent in schoolwork, but you must be a kind-hearted person, full of dreams. Yes, dreams.

Kids are full of dreams. They are wonderful storytellers from birth. Their dreams come from an innocent heart, which can hardly be found in the cruel world of grown-ups. This innocence is the purest form of human emotions.

Many parents kill their children's dreams without knowing so. They introduce the realistic picture of life to their children when these little minds are still not ready for it. Children need dreams because they live on dreams, without which they will not find happiness in life.

It's true that life is not always easy, and someday they will know. But they can face up to the frustrations of life only when their souls feed on dreams and imaginings. Not only because their mentality is properly developed, but because the power of dreams will support them forever and ever. They will never give up the hope of seeing light, even in the darkest night.

This is why I entered your world of robots. I bought you robots; we watched robot cartoons together; I encouraged you to make robot drawings; we even discussed the aesthetics of robots. And both of us believed that these robots have souls and minds, that they are real.

My happiest time in life was your childhood, in which you shared the stories of robots with me. I was moved by your smile, and hoped that you could face the world with the same smile as you grew up.

To keep your imagination alive, I introduced the story of Santa Claus, who delivers gifts in snow and is indeed the embodiment of dreams.

I can expect that, after I leave, you'll gradually figure out the identity of the Santa Claus in your childhood.

Every Christmas night, carrying the gift, I moved softly and quietly into your room. I felt warmth upon seeing you deep in sleep. If this tiny gift in my hands could create more beautiful imaginings for you, I'd be gratified. I always stood by your bed after placing the gift on the desk, holding myself back from touching your cheeks, and instead imagining the joy you would show on seeing the gift.

However, the story of Santa Claus was challenged. One day you rushed over in tears to me and told me about the disbelievers in your class. They thought I was your Santa Claus.

They were perfectly right, and I felt an urge to tell you the truth at that moment. But on second thought, I changed my mind. I decided to draw on the very power of dream and imagination, and invite you all to witness its magic yourselves.

Time was limited but I finally came up with the details, most of which were worked out when I was at work. It was worth it. I talked to your uncle and Yen-Min, both of whom I trust very much. I believe they can keep this secret for their whole lives. They were happy to help me on this.

Your uncle will tell you how the magic was done that night if you ask him. It's not my intention to explain it here.

A person of imagination treats their life with more sincerity. This is my lifelong belief. Without my company, you can still surmount any obstacles in life with the support of dreams developed in your childhood.

I've never asked you to do anything for me before, but now there is one thing I'd like you to keep in mind.

Create dreams for your children, and encourage them to do the same. It's a pity your mom left us so early; otherwise she would have been happy to play the role of Santa Claudia. Now you are not alone. You and your wife can do better than I.

This letter is my final Christmas gift to you. It is the wisdom I obtained in my limited life.

Merry Christmas, my son.

Forever,
Dad.

Holding the letter, Ko's hands trembled. Tears were brimming in his eyes.

"Thank you, Dad..."

In the yellowing photo on the desk, the father looked at his son with an eternal loving smile.

Ruoping turned and walked to the window. The bells of some distant church sounded in the dark. It was Christmas.

He looked at the curtain of the night.

Far away in the extending darkness, he seemed to see Santa Claus and his reindeer flying across the sky.

Finland
Seven Brothers (extract)
by Aleksis Kivi

Aleksis Kivi is considered by some to be the Mark Twain of Finland. His book, *Seven Brothers*, published in 1870, was the first novel of significance published in the Finnish language. Up until that time the literary landscape in Finland had been dominated by Swedish writers.

Seven Brothers tells the tale of hard-working and hard-drinking rural Finns, who struggle with one another, the land, and their culture, to eventually become successful, literate men.

This short two-page excerpt from *Seven Brothers* stands on its own as one of the earliest "footprints in the snow" mysteries.

Finally the master opened his mouth and asked his companions: “Men, I want to ask you something; explain this to me. Five days ago, when I was crossing the smooth rise of Koivisto meadow over a fresh, light snow on the ground, like the thin cotton blanket we have now, I saw some marks that my brains can't figure out. Damn it! Night and day my mind has been threshing out the matter, this way and that, along a thousand byways. But listen. I saw some tracks in the field, a man's tracks, which I followed slowly.

“But suddenly the tracks ended, and fox tracks began, clear fox tracks, which continued up the rise and down into the woods. There hadn't been a one, not a single one, up to that point. Where had the man disappeared? He had gone neither left nor right, forward nor back – no, he had stepped straight up into the sky and the fox had stepped down from it to continue his tracks in the snow. Or had the man carried the fox in his arms, and there where his trail ended, mounted the bushy tail and ridden through the grove to the village road? Such tricks are impossible, but I can't think of anything more probable to figure the thing out. What do you think, men? Are there still wizards in our parish? Did the man change himself into a fox through the power of the devil?” So he spoke, and the people were greatly amazed, nor could any of them solve the puzzle, but all concluded that wizards had been at work on Koivisto Hill.

But Lauri's heart could not rest; after eating he set out for Koivisto meadow. Arriving at its smooth slope, he saw that the same phenomenon had been repeated: the change from man to fox tracks in the fresh snow. He flew into a rage and said angrily: “Is the devil himself frisking around here?” He screamed the words through gritted teeth and kicked at a mound of manure that showed under the snow.

Bright metal flashed forth from it, particles of manure and chopped straw flew high in the air, and the stinging jaws of a fierce fox trap clamped the man's ankle in a crushing grip. Lauri's eyes flew open wide and he bent down quickly to loosen the stubborn device from his smarting, swelling ankle.

Shouting curses, he flung the trap far away on the ground. Now he had discovered what trap had been set in his field, but he still did not understand the strange transformation of the tracks in the snow. Angrily he started off for home, limping badly and gritting his teeth when he stepped on the foot caught by the trap. Soon recognizing that he needed support in walking, he began looking for a stick in the grove near the village road. He saw two birch poles in a thicket and when he pulled them out, he discovered that they were a pair of stilts, with a very natural-looking fox paw whittled at the base of either one.

Then his face brightened up and everything became clear to him. Now he knew that the fox trapper, in order to hide all cause for suspicion from the fox's eyes had always approached his traps on this type of stilts when he checked them. With this trick, he left a fox's and not a man's tracks behind him, which the clever Reynard of the hills would certainly have avoided. So the matter was clear to Lauri, and he moved off with a lighter heart, although his shin was aching and as stiff as a cane.

Real Life Impossibility: France
Murder on the Metro

May 16, 1937. At 6:27 p.m. train 282 leaves the Porte Charenton underground station, the terminus of the line. One minute later, it arrives at the next station, Porte Dorée. It's rush hour: a number of passengers make a dash for the second-class carriages. As the train doors close, six of them go into the first-class carriage, which in French underground trains is always sandwiched between two second-class carriages. Some come through one connecting door, some through the other; all were planning to cheat the system. The first-class carriage is empty save for a lone occupant, a young blonde woman wearing a green dress and seated on the side away from the platform. The woman has a knife planted up to the hilt in her neck, just below the right ear. The jugular vein and the carotid artery have both been severed and she is bleeding profusely.

One of the new arrivals is a military doctor. He reaches her just as she is about to keel over. Someone alerts the train driver who stops the train and calls the police. The doctor lowers the woman onto the bench seat. She is still breathing, but he knows there is nothing to be done. In the general confusion, he disappears before the police arrive. Without thinking, the first officer to reach the body pulls the knife out, thus not only aggravating the hemorrhage but also compromising the fingerprints. The unknown woman dies a few minutes later in transit to the Saint-Antoine hospital. (The next day, the military doctor turns up unexpectedly at the local police station to explain that he had a pressing engagement and, given that he could have done nothing to help, had left the scene.)

The police detain the 150 passengers for half an hour and then release them without taking down their names and addresses. Was the murderer one of them?

And even if he was, how had he done it? The riddle of the Porte Dorée murder remains one of the most baffling in the archives of the French police: a real-life locked-room problem worthy of John Dickson Carr himself.

Every hypothesis put forward by the police met an insurmountable obstacle:

Had the killer struck before the train left the terminus? If that were the case, it would be highly unlikely that nobody had seen him: The train was filling up and anyone could have come into the carriage, either through the platform door or through the connecting door as they made their way to the front of the train.

Had the killer stayed in the first-class carriage and then escaped during the brief journey between stations? He would have had time to act and it seemed that the victim was looking the other way when she was attacked, but there was a huge risk she would scream. And how did he escape? He couldn't have jumped onto the tracks, and if he had tried to use one of the connecting doors, he would have been spotted in the crowded train. Likewise, if he had tried to stand between carriages while the train was in motion, he would also have been seen.

Had the killer stayed in the first-class carriage until after the train reached Porte Dorée? The danger of being seen in the crowded train applied. He could not have known how many people would board at the next stop. And, in any case, the testimony of the six passengers who entered the first-class carriage ruled that possibility out.

There was one possible solution, one solution of which any avid reader of locked-room fiction would have been proud: The young woman, whose name was Laetitia Toureaux, had not yet been stabbed when the train arrived at Porte Dorée, and the first on the scene – the military doctor – had administered the fatal blow. This seductive hypothesis has several flaws: How could he have known that Laetitia would be there (unless it was a random killing)? How could he have known she would be alone? And how could he have known he would be the first to get to her? In any case, the other passengers were unanimous: They had all seen the knife planted in the young woman's throat.

Portugal
Lying Dead and Turning Cold
by Afonso Carreiro

Alfonso Carreiro spent many years as a pharmacist in Lisbon, Portugal, writing stories in his spare time.

This atmospheric story, originally entitled “Jaz morto e arrefece”, first appeared in 1952, in a Portuguese magazine called *O Gato Preto* (*The Black Cat*). It has a hint of Ellery Queen, one of the author’s favorite writers. This is its first appearance in English.

Sr. Carreiro was located after a great deal of detective work and was delighted to give his permision. He is now retired and living in Sintra, Portugal.

My uncle settled his ample physique in the chair, uncrossed his legs, and placed his feet firmly on the thick fluffy carpet. He scratched his bushy moustache, protruding in mock menace from a puffy face not unlike a good medieval friar's, cleared his throat, and started:

"Once you leave Barradas da Serra by the road heading to Barrancas you will find, some ten miles from Curtozendo, a dirt road going through spindly pines and boulders ravaged by the hardness of winter. The track through the woods is long and rough. Far away, high in the hills, nestled against the rocky sterile slopes, hides the grey and desolate village of Pedregorda, a frozen handful of back-to-back houses seemingly drowned in snow.

"Guardian's Hall, where Silvestre lives, is a large mountain house, almost a manor. It stands apart and slightly above the village, on a bare and desolate plateau.

"Let me tell you from the start that I don't believe in ghosts or otherworldly beings more than anybody else, but there are times when one can't keep one's imagination from being possessed by such thoughts.

"We had gathered in Silvestre's house. The atmosphere was heavy. The sullenly smouldering fire, the insidious smell of oil from the lamps, the locked windows: all contributed to a general feeling of unease. Moreover, we were all worried, in our various ways, because of Tiago. His presence smothered the whole house in a dark mantle.

"Everybody seemed to be expecting him with the anxiety of the hunter waiting for the beast to pounce."

My uncle fell silent and looked at a vague point in the semi-obscurity in which we were immersed.

The narrative promised to be interesting. I made myself more comfortable and drew a cigarette.

He started, as from a grievous memory and I could sense the dread in his clear eyes. He seemed to be gathering his thoughts.

"Tiago," he said, "was a drunkard of the worst kind, a zestful profligate who took his excesses to the most extraordinary extremes. In the village, he messed with all the women, even the married ones, and committed a series of robberies that would never have stopped, had it not been for the death threats that started to hang around his head. The doctor of the village, a certain Dr. Fonseca, and João Pedrosa – both acquaintances of Silvestre who were there that night at Guardian's Hall – were among the angriest. The former, because

Tiago had soiled his wife's honour. The latter, I learned later, because he had taken his girl and eloped with her to Lisbon.

"Both scandals had been enormous. Silvestre had expelled his son from home and he had vanished from sight like an outcast. He went back to his bohemian life in Lisbon, leaving behind him the suppressed despair of his father and the upraised fists of the husbands. He took with him the money that certain ashamed wives, fearing for the disclosure of their secrets, felt constrained to give him. Yes, he stooped as low as that. Not only did he get money from women, he extorted it under pretexts that amounted to shameless blackmail."

He stopped. With a slow movement, he drew a red striped handkerchief from his trouser pocket and blew his nose. Then, self-consciously, he continued in his deep, unhurried voice:

"That evening, it had been reported that Tiago had returned. For what, one did not know. To ask for money, perhaps. Or worse, to steal.

"When your aunt Ana and I arrived at the Hall the night was already dark. While we were on our way, it started to snow heavily. Ana insisted several times we should go back, but I refused stubbornly and we carried on through the snow, stamping our feet vigorously and moving our arms about to prevent the stinging cold of the open night from entering our blood. From time to time, a hidden piece of rock would force us to squelch around it with aching feet.

"Finally, exhausted and shivering with cold, we arrived at Guardian's Hall.

"It was Dr. Fonseca's wife, Matilde, who opened the door. We laid our hats on top of the enormous chest in the vestibule as we went in.

"The house has two floors. On the ground floor, on either side of a long corridor leading from the vestibule are a serving pantry and a kitchen with one of those enormous fireplaces usually found in mountain houses, in which the flames, burning between two bricks, lick metal vessels hanging from strong hooks. Also on the ground floor, at the end of the corridor, is a very large dining room, also used as a living room. There are shuttered windows in the west wall and a beautiful hearth in the south wall. A long and wide table, equipped with a frame to support a brazier in the bottom, dominates the room. The bedrooms are on the upper floor.

"When we entered the dining room we found everybody assembled. There was old Silvestre, sitting in a large chair made of entwined twig, sheltered from the cold by the thickness of an Alentejan cape, as well as João Pedrosa, Dr. Fonseca, and Dona Alice, Silvestre's wife.

"After the usual greetings we all sat, except Pedrosa, around the hearth. I remember distinctly the air of tragedy everyone bore, as if a breath of disgrace had blown upon them. One felt the presence of the absent Tiago but, as I understood at once, everybody avoided talking about him.

"Only the doctor looked happy. His face, haloed by a half-light, reflected an irritating smile, which contrasted with the concerned look of the others. He held a walking stick which he waved in the air from time to time.

"Your aunt, always so talkative, was not very lively. During our walk to the Hall, we had met a wretched gypsy, in distressing half-nakedness, the bones of her scrawny chest seeming to stick out of dark skin only partially covered by a dirty shawl that reached her ankles. That encounter had impressed her very much. It was as if she had divined the part the old woman was to play in the strange events that would take place that evening.

"Obviously the image of the old woman hadn't left her mind because, suddenly, unable to restrain herself, she said:

"'I'm so scared! Each time I remember a gypsy woman we met on our way – '

"João Pedrosa looked at us sharply. From this unexpected reaction, I gathered that the incident was in some way important to him.

"Dona Alice and Matilde stopped their sewing and crocheting and stared curiously at Ana.

"'A gipsy woman?' asked Matilde. 'What gypsy woman?'

"'The one we met on our way,' your aunt explained. 'She must be a witch. She looked miserable. What eyes, Holy God!' She stopped to make a grimace of suppressed terror and disgust. 'She wouldn't stop babbling unintelligible words. Oh, I'm sure she was drunk.'

"Old Silvestre took the pipe from his mouth and blew a puff of smoke. His eyes were fixed on the fire that crackled in the hearth and he seemed to ignore what was going on around him.

"Matilde laid down the needles in her lap.

"'Indeed?' she asked, incredulously.

"Your aunt nodded and then, waving her hand, exclaimed, as if unburdening herself:

"'I was really afraid, girls!'

"Dr. Fonseca leaned forward and said: 'It must have been Cidália.'

"'Cidália?' I asked.

"'Yes,' he replied. 'People tell fantastic things about her.'

"Pedrosa's lean and tall figure moved by the fire. From my position, I could see the furrows in his forehead and his fixed stare, as if attracted by a distant point.

"'*This lad does not look right,*' I thought. '*Something is eating at him inside.*' He was puffing brief clouds of smoke from the cigarette tightly pressed between his lips.

"Dr. Fonseca interjected in a toneless voice: 'The village people say she's a witch and call the house she lives in the House of the Owl.'

"'Oh, shut up, shut up,' screamed João Pedrosa, pressing his forehead with one hand. 'It's terrible! Don't talk about that woman anymore.'

"Dona Alice came to the rescue: 'Let's change the subject, doctor.' Then, turning to Ana, she said in a very low voice: 'João has been very nervous since the girl left him. He spends the days wandering through the hills or lying on boulders staring at the sky. He's been having nervous distractions lately. He thinks someone is trying to kill him and associates this with the old woman you were talking about. He says he hears the cry of the owl.'

"At this, my wife showed interest. Old Silvestre stirred in his chair. Outside, the distant sound of a wolf howling pierced through the gale. Dr. Fonseca continued:

"'Don't you know the story, Dona Ana?' he asked. One could see that the doctor was anticipating the pleasure of martyring Pedrosa. 'Don't you?'

"We all looked at the boy, fearing for another nervous outburst. Dona Alice tried to protest, but the doctor, indifferent to it all, started to tell his tale.

"'Some fifty years ago, a fellow from Lisbon had the idea of building a house near here, in a place which, by a curious coincidence, was at that time known as the Old Woman's Boulder. Nobody knew the man, but even back then several Lisbon people had already discovered the highlands and had the idea of building cottages here to spend a couple of months a year and practice winter sports, so nobody thought it strange. The land was acquired, plans were made and the house was built and furnished. So far, so good. However, one day the man came to live in the house. That very day, at dusk, he was seen leaving the house and climbing a small elevation, which is still there at the crest of the estate, in a place where the hillside is almost plumb, made of granitic rock, some two hundred and fifty meters deep. There he was seen standing upright, facing south, with his arms crossed, until the night came and darkness surrounded him.' The doctor was quiet for a few moments and in the ensuing silence, we listened to the outer window frames squeaking on their hinges. Then he resumed monotonously, in his bitter and cynical tone: 'That night a hoarse cry, a death cry that today is said to come out of that house, was heard for the first time in the hills – the cry of the owl.

"'The next day, the charwoman knocked on the door and nobody answered. It had to be forced open. The man was not there, and he hadn't even slept there either.'

"'Did he fall from the precipice?' Ana asked.

"The doctor sat by his wife, near the window.

"'No,' he answered, striking the walking stick on the floor. He seemed to enjoy the anticipation in our eyes. 'Here the strange part of the story begins. They searched for his body down in the ravine. It was necessary to go there with ropes, since the place is deep and sloped. The search lasted days, but it was in vain. The body was never found.'

"Dr. Fonseca looked around. He gave a suppressed chuckle. It was clear he was enjoying the story immensely.

"'The devil!' I interrupted. 'The man simply went back, took the train to Lisbon and never returned.'

"The doctor's face swelled with satisfaction. He chuckled again, in a low tone. Then he said:

"'It had snowed the previous day. When the man went to the boulder, he left footprints behind him. They stayed there. It didn't snow again and the snow was left absolutely intact, except for those marks. The man did not go back or fall into the precipice. And so – '

"He paused, and that unfinished '*and so*' made the story more horrible. *And so...* and each of us thought of nameless things.

"'After that, the house was left uninhabited. Neither heirs nor lawyers came to visit, and nobody else has so far shown the slightest interest in it. It turned to ruins without ever sheltering anybody. Black holes appeared in the roof. Hard winters and the stones thrown by the village kids shattered the windowpanes. The ground became overgrown with briars and weeds. They say whoever passes by it at night can hear a hoarse, husky cry that seems to rent the darkness. The local people call it the cry of the owl, since owls have nestled in the abandoned house. Some say the man from Lisbon is still in the house to prevent any human being from setting foot there. One day, some poor devil from the village bet he could spend the night there. From a distance, he was seen entering through the wide-open door and disappearing in the dark. The people swear that the shrill and piercing cry of the owl was heard throughout the village that night. The man was never seen again. He disappeared without leaving a trace in the white mantle of snow that covered the fields around the house. Now Cidália lives there.'

"He let the two last sentences fall like stones, in the simultaneously indifferent and wicked tone that was distinctively his.

"'That's why people now say she has a deal with the devil,' said Dona Alice in an unsteady voice, lifting her eyes from her crochet and looking at Pedrosa.

"Standing against the wall, Pedrosa seemed to be feeling unwell. His hands were shaking visibly. Parallel creases were clear in his forehead.

"'Is anything wrong, João?' Dona Alice asked, eyeing him with anxiety.

"The boy seemed to make an effort. 'I suppose I haven't been feeling very well. Every night I dream a horrible dreams in which she appears.' He took his hands from his pockets and started twisting one against the other nervously.

"'You mean Cidália?'

"'Yes. Cidália and the cry of the owl.'

"Dona Alice stood up and placed a hand on his shoulder.

"'The cry of the owl, son? But what do you dream about?' she asked tenderly.

"He stood silent as if he found it difficult to speak.

"'I dream about an atrocious death, lying in the snow,' he said after some time. 'I am attacked by a strange being I suppose to be Cidália. I feel my throat being clutched by what seems to be claws, red claws dripping blood that I never manage to escape from.'

"Dona Alice swept a lock of red hair back from his forehead.

"The doctor threw him a look that was as curious as it was mocking.

"Pedrosa went on: 'Invariably I scream, and my scream becomes the cry of the owl.'

"'Poor boy!' Dr. Fonseca's wife said.

"'They're only dreams, son,' Dona Alice said, trying to cheer him up. 'Don't pay any importance to them.' She put a hand on his shoulder.

"'I seem stuck to the ground,' the young man went on in the same tone, 'as if I were made of lead. As much as I try to release myself, I cannot do it. My body starts to meld with the snow. Through my heavy eyelids, I see nothing but infinite whiteness, bare and desolate. But the most terrible thing of all is that the ground around me remains unmarked, just as always happens in the stories they tell.'

"He dropped his head. His last words were uttered in despair.

"Dona Alice raised her shoulders and dropped them again in a gesture of discouragement.

"'Let it go. Stop thinking about it.' She withdrew her hand from his shoulder and took him by the arm. 'Come and sit by me.'

"The doctor laughed a smooth and bitter laugh.

"His wife eyed him reproachfully. 'You shouldn't laugh,' she observed.

"Dr. Fonseca looked amused. He stood up and sat in an armchair on the opposite side of the table.

"Outside, the wind blew with increased strength. In the silence that ensued, we listened to it howling and moaning like a deadly wounded animal in a slow and dreadful struggle. A stronger flurry forced the window open with a crash and the cold air whirled inside the room, putting the lights out. It was like a whip to our nerves, already frayed by the stories. I had the clear sensation that it was not a gust of wind that had entered, but some unnameable being.

"In the hearth, tongues of fire threw dancing shadows on the rough walls. I remembered that bit from Virginia Woolf – do you recall? The one from 'The Mark on the Wall': '*...that old fancy of the crimson flag flapping from the castle tower came into my mind, and I thought of the cavalcade of red knights riding up the side of the black rock.*' Terrified, we were all staring at the fire, where from time to time a log crackled, throwing around showers of red sparks.

"When Dona Alice lit the lamps again, the yellow glow revealed our ashen faces. It was then that I became aware that the doctor was gone.

"The fact went unnoticed by the others and everybody continued to behave as before, but I was puzzled.

"Then, all of a sudden, events started to move fast.

"A measured sound was distinctly heard: Knock! Knock! Knock!

"Three hollow blows. We turned around, scared. I felt as anxious as a child locked inside a dark room.

"'Didn't you hear someone knocking at the door?' Dona Alice asked. 'What a night! Goodness gracious! I don't know what's wrong with me, the slightest noise alarms me.'

"'Did someone indeed knock?' I asked, trying to appear calm.

"We looked at each other. Silvestre's face showed a rocklike impenetrability. The eyes of the others were alarmed question marks. 'Has Tiago come back? Is it he knocking at the door?' I thought.

"'Did someone mention a noise?' old Silvestre asked.

"It was the doctor's wife who answered. 'I thought I heard three knocks at the door. But I don't know for sure. I'm so nervous – I won't drink coffee at dinner again.'

"'Oh, it must have been me,' the old man said.

"'You, what? Was it you who knocked?'

"Silvestre showed his pipe.

"'I was emptying my pipe.' After a pause, he went on. 'That must have been it. Then again, perhaps someone did knock. Go take a look, João.'

"Silence descended again upon the room, interrupted only by the firewood crackling in the hearth and the howling of the wind and the wolves. Pedrosa went to the door of the room, which gave access to the corridor, and opened it slowly. He seemed fearful, as if he was scared of seeing what was on the other side. Finally, he opened it, showing a mouth of darkness.

"'Who's there?' he asked in a shrill and unsteady voice. He turned to us, hesitantly. 'It seems someone is there after all. I think I hear steps outside.' Then, aloud and into the dark: 'Is anybody out there?'

"Silvestre stirred in the chair. 'If it is Tiago, I'll break his bones. I don't even want to see him sniffing at the threshold.' His voice was hard and its intonation was rife with menace.

"Dona Alice started to cry. Your aunt was beside her and comforted her. She said something in her ear that I wasn't able to hear. After that, Dona Alice raised her head.

"'Silvestre is so upset....' She was speaking in such a low voice that probably only your aunt and I heard her. 'Ever since he knew Tiago was back he doesn't look like the same person. Oh, I fear something bad will happen....'

"Old Silvestre, standing, seemed to be indifferent to everything. Only what lay beyond the dark interested him. His gaze was fixed on the door opening.

"Pedrosa's voice was heard again. 'Who's there? Who is it?'

"From the dark came a faraway murmur like water running in a mine. 'Oh, it's you,' said Pedrosa.

"'Who's that?' asked old Silvestre brusquely.

"The other came back inside. He was pale and his hands were shaking increasingly. 'Dr. Fonseca,' he explained. His look was full of dread.

"'The doctor? What did he go out for in this weather?' said Silvestre. 'I didn't notice it. When did he leave?' We stared at each other.

"'After the blast of wind that entered,' I clarified. 'He left without saying anything.'

"In the dull half-light the figure of the doctor appeared. There, in the darkness, he looked like a vulture, with his thick black cloak reaching down to his ankles.

"A shuffling of chairs was heard in the room and Dona Alice gave a sigh of relief. Everybody took deep breaths.

"'Damn it, doctor, you almost scared me!' old Silvestre exclaimed. The creases on his face relaxed, and he pulled up the armchair and sat down again.

"'Come on, old friend,' said the doctor. 'I merely went out to exercise my legs.' Then, in an ironic tone: 'Next time I'll ask for permission.' He looked calm and mocking.

"'I don't know how you could have gone out, doctor,' Dona Alice exclaimed. 'In this gale, with the cold and the snow – " Her body shuddered and, with nervous hands, she wrapped the shawl more tightly about herself. 'I wouldn't go out for anything in this world, not in this cold.'

"João Pedrosa rose. 'Do you want me to bring you a blanket?'

"Silvestre's wife looked at him thankfully. 'If you would be so kind...,' she whispered.

"Pedrosa headed towards the door again. Wrapped in the overcoat, his lank form seemed to be reeling and his enormous hands moved around as if they were dancing.

"It was then that we heard a protracted howl, which took on fantastic proportions in our overexcited imagination.

"'The cry of the owl,' Dona Alice whispered, terrified.

"I saw Pedrosa stagger by the door. On hearing the cry, he shuddered as if he had woken up in distress. He turned his face to us and in his demented eyes there was a strange glimmer. Then he raised his hands to his head, clutched his temples, and spoke in a whimpering and fearful murmur.

"'I can't. I can't take it any longer. I'm scared.'

"We looked at each other.

"Dr. Fonseca grabbed his walking stick and waved it in the air.

"'Scared?' His voice sounded frightening in the electrified atmosphere. It was high-pitched, almost joyful and taunting.

"Pedrosa trembled and seemed to have made a decision. He bridged the distance to the door and was swallowed by the darkness. The thumping of his feet could be heard in the corridor. I don't know why, but I felt something strange was about to happen. Thump, thump, thump: the footsteps echoed again. Each one pounded our hearts like a closed fist. Thump, thump, thump. Clear, dull, heavy. The doctor's wife put her hands to her mouth and bit her lip. Silvestre's stonelike profile was motionless. Thump, thump, thump. A vast silence. The young man stopped in the vestibule. The doctor was not smiling. Silvestre's twig chair creaked lightly.

"At that moment, a muffled cry like the one of a wounded animal resounded in the corridor. Everyone jumped in his skin. A bang, a creaking of hinges, a muted exclamation were heard. Beyond the darkness, at the end of the corridor, was a formless shadow strangely illuminated by a fantastic and, at the time, inexplicable light.

"'Did you hear?' Pedrosa shouted from the vestibule, as if blaming us. 'Did you hear? The cry of the owl.' He seemed to have gone mad. 'Listen,' he cried hoarsely.

"From the outside came the mournful wailing of the wind and the wolves. *'And of something else,'* I thought subconsciously.

"Then Pedrosa disappeared from sight. We were left standing thunderstruck like statues. One of the ladies' crochet needles clinked on the floor. From the corridor came a blast of cold air that reached our bloodless faces. I don't know how long we stood like that. Then the doctor quietly exclaimed, as if he were cursing: 'Fool. He went out into the snow.'

"I ran to the windows past the table and the chairs that obstructed the way. I pulled back one of the wooden shutters and flung open a window. A freezing wind hit my face. It had stopped snowing a while ago. Over the pines in the valley shone a baleful yellow moon. Some hundred feet away from the house, on the snow-covered plateau, the black and thin silhouette of the boy stood alone, its overcoat battered by the wind. At his feet lay a dark and long shape that I could not identify from that distance. Was it just an impression or did I really see a figure passing far away and disappearing up the hillside? The whole scene emanated an appearance of unreality. Suddenly I saw Pedrosa deflate like an emptying balloon and fall on the snow. I heard Dr. Fonseca calling me from the door. I shut the window, headed to the corridor, and joined the doctor.

"Without a word we ran through the snow towards the two fallen figures. João's footprints went in a straight line, deep in the smooth surface of the snow. I noticed it as I ran, feeling the overcoat flaps hitting my calves at every step. In moments like that, certain meaningless details seem to be engraved in our memories with an extraordinary and acute clarity. I remember when we were halfway there, a mechanical pencil dropped from my upper jacket pocket into one of my footprints and then glided to one of the parallel, deeper Pedrosa's footprints. The doctor was walking on the other side of the prints, some ten feet away. All this took seconds.

"João Pedrosa was alive. He had merely fainted. Beside him, lying on his back in the snow, was a wide-eyed man. I heard the doctor mutter some words in a low voice and kneel by the stranger. He held his hand and tried to raise it to feel his pulse. He couldn't. The body was already freezing and stiff. In one of his hands he held an unlighted cigarette, crumpled between his fingers. On the snow was an open cigarette case, from which some loose cigarettes had scattered. Mechanically, I looked at all of this and in my mind a stupefying certainty grew. Around the two bodies there were no footprints. Pedrosa's ended beneath his feet. The doctor's and mine ended by ours. Around us, the snow was intact. At the same time, a thought that had occurred on seeing the bloodless face of the dead man hammered in my brain. It is Tiago.

"We took the two bodies inside the house. The women stayed in the upper floor with Tiago's body and the doctor and I reanimated Pedrosa. This part of the evening is like a nightmare to me. I remember, while I was shakily helping the doctor to carry the body into the house, while I climbed the stairs supporting his feet, while I returned outside to bring inside João Pedrosa, while I dragged him through the snow, having recalled the verse from *His Mother's Boy* by Fernando Pessoa: *'In the deserted plain / That a warm breeze heats / Drilled through by bullets / Two, from side to side / He lies dead and is turning cold / From his pocket fell / The brief cigarette case / His mother gave him. It is intact / And fine, the cigarette case. / It is he that is of no use / With outstretched arms / White, blond and bloodless / He stares, with a look languid / And blind, at the lost skies.'* At that point, I almost did not know which one was this *mother's boy*—Fernando Pessoa's, or the body we had found freezing outside."

My uncle rubbed his hands on the arms of the chair. "*Drilled through by bullets / Two, from side to side,*" I murmured. "What had he died of?"

Uncle turned around listlessly and made a gesture that clearly meant: patience.

"Wait. I have told you the story. Now we will proceed in sequence. I will finish giving you the facts...."

"When I saw that there were no footprints around the boy, I had an immediate sensation of fantastic unreality. Do you remember the Chesterton tale in which a wizard flies without leaving footprints in the snow? That was precisely what first came to my mind.

"Tiago had arrived; he had stopped; the snow had covered his freezing feet and he stood isolated like a dark island in the middle of the intact whiteness of the snow. The unfortunate man did not have the courage to enter his father's house, in which he was like a stranger, but he did not have the courage to leave, either. I closed my eyes and I saw him, distant, still and dramatically alone, far from the house, under a sky as dark as black velvet. I saw him draw the humble cigarette case and take a cigarette out. Then, someone had strangled him. His youthful throat kept the already purple marks of the fingers that had harvested his life."

Instinctively, I opened my hands and held myself with impatience. My uncle continued as if he had not noticed.

"When we brought him inside he was frozen. The doctor estimated that he had been dead for more than half an hour. With a lot of scholarly explanations about rigor mortis and the influence a temperature such as that outside could have had on the speed of its setting in, he stated categorically: for more than half hour."

I abandoned an idea that had been percolating in the recesses of my brain.

"Pay attention from now on," my uncle advised. I leaned forward. "Sharpen those ears." I did. "It is then settled: We found the body lying on the snow surrounded by no other footprints apart from our own. The boy was frozen and had been dead for some time. Let us see if we can find an explanation for the lack of footprints of whoever strangled him.

"It had stopped snowing about an hour before. At least we were sure of one thing: The unfortunate Tiago had been there (dead or alive) for more than an hour. Only in that case would the snow have covered the marks of his feet. However, there was another fact that fixed the time of death: the body lying on his back, staring with a languid and blind look at the lost skies, had not caught any snow. It had not snowed on the chest of that black overcoat, on the threadbare scarf, on the open glazed eyes. When the boy had fallen dead, the snow had already stopped *completely.* There could have been no doubt about that."

Slowly I started to grasp the monstrous impossibility of the problem.

"It was eleven o'clock. In short: The boy had died in front of the house between ten (when it had stopped snowing) and ten-thirty (the latest possible time of dead judging from *rigor mortis*). During that time, the snow remained intact. The boy himself must have stood still. Yet, someone went to him, strangled him, and left without leaving the slightest mark on the virgin snow. This is the problem reduced to its simplest expression."

My uncle opened his hands and squeezed them, as if symbolically laying the problem in front of me. He reclined in the armchair, satisfied.

However, I was not. "Wait, wait," I said in earnest. "A lot is missing. What did the young man who fainted say when he regained consciousness?"

"You mean João Pedrosa. Nothing that can help you. We poured sugar-cane rum through his clenched teeth, we took him near the fire and we laid him down. Later, Dr. Fonseca admitted that he had been seriously worried about his condition. The boy was burning with fever: The doctor said he barely escaped brain damage. The excitement and the shock had been too much for him. When he was able to speak he told us that on hearing the cry outside (he meant that owl's cry) he had opened the door. He had seen the shape lying there and had run frantically towards it. When he got there, he saw it was

Tiago. He did not remember anything else. Oh, wait! He seemed to recall seeing something dark crossing the empty air, from one side of the plateau to the other. However, that was probably part of his half-delirious condition – or so we thought. Later we saw we were mistaken."

"About what?" I cut in excitedly, and feeling it must an important clue.

"About assuming the dark thing the boy said had crossed the plateau was a delusion."

"You mean it wasn't?"

"No," said my uncle.

The story of Cidália and the man from Lisbon who had disappeared came to my mind. Was there a connection between all that?

"Was it – was it that Cidália woman?" I suggested fearfully.

"Wait, lad. It is no use to keep on asking if *it was this* or *it was that.* Moreover, more important than to know *who* committed the murder is to know *how* the murder was committed."

However, I saw no way in which it could have been done. "Was the body found at a great distance from the house?" I asked.

"About one hundred feet."

"Are there no trees, signposts, or other similar things in that plateau?"

"Absolutely nothing. Except for the house and the chestnut tree behind it, it is smooth as the palm of my hand," he said, and extended it, large and sturdy.

A new suspicion occurred to me. "Could it be possible that the footprints were already there and that one of you (Uncle, Pedrosa, or Dr. Fonseca) stepped in them and obliterated them while running towards the body?"

"No," my uncle said. "Let me disabuse you straight away about my footprints and Dr. Fonseca's. About Pedrosa's, I hadn't any doubts when I saw them from the window and afterwards, while I was running, I saw very well the intact snow in front of us. I examined them later and there was no doubt: not only were they freshly made, but also it was impossible that the boy had stepped *precisely* on previous hypothetical marks while running. Anyway, if there were any previous footprints coming from the house, they should be present in both directions, and if there had been any coming from the outside, Pedrosa and we could not have stepped on them.

"I don't know about that," I murmured, with a little doubt still gnawing inside me. "There must have been something about your footprints.... What exactly – "

My uncle straightened his head. "One thing I can guarantee you: Pedrosa, Fonseca, and I ran over a smooth surface of snow. This clears that possibility – which, in a way, would render the solution less elegant."

"*Which solution?*" I sighed. "Does the story end here? Or did something else happen that night?"

"Nothing whatsoever with relevance to the case."

"Opportunity, I see none," I whispered. "Motive – who would have a motive to kill Tiago?"

Uncle was impatient. "As usual, almost everybody had one. That is not the way to go, lad."

"Everybody?"

"Yes, my lad, everybody. The dead man had stolen the girl from one of them and seduced the wife of the other. It would be natural if he had demanded money from the latter woman as a payment for not exhibiting some compromising letters. How should I know! Even his father was capable of having thrown himself at the boy in a fit of stupid family pride. Perhaps even Cidália herself. As you can see, motive does not help."

No, in fact it did not. I reviewed the problem again. From ten to ten-thirty. The intact snow. Strangled. The others inside the house. Wait a moment. I had forgotten this one something.

"Didn't Dr. Fonseca go out for a while?" I asked. "Was it before or after it snowed?"

"After."

"And his footprints – "

"Went out from the main door, around the house by the other side, came back from there and entered through the same door. None were in the direction of the body. I, too, thought about them, my lad. But that's the way they were."

"Then the doctor should have seen Tiago – or his body – at that time. Why didn't he give the alarm?"

"He said he didn't even look in that direction."

At this point, the reader is in possession of all the elements needed for a clear solution of the problem. All the data and evidence have been honestly presented. In the manner of Ellery Queen, I issue a challenge to the reader. What is the only possible solution?

I scratched my head. I felt there must be in all of that some trace of truth, some tip that, if pulled, would bring the entire thread with it. I said as much to my uncle.

"Exactly, lad," he agreed. "That was exactly what I felt that night. Do you know how it is when you look for some object in a table full of stuff, and you don't see it, as if you were blind for it, even if it is right in front of you? That's just what happened. Then, at a certain moment, it was as if something clicked inside me and I saw the miraculous and utterly coherent clarity of it all."

"Clarity?" said I, incredulous.

"It was as clear as water from a fountain," my uncle replied, cheerily.

"It can't be. Or else you told the case badly, uncle."

He seemed outraged. "Badly, my foot. All the facts were rigorously told. It was the inferences, lad, the little inferences, that were badly drawn. The doctor – "

"It was he!" I cried.

This time my uncle was seriously irritated. "Curse and damnation!" he exclaimed angrily. "Stop asking stupid questions. And solve it by yourself, if you can."

Humbled, reverent, I ventured: "You were saying, uncle: the doctor...?"

After a brief period of muttering and finger-drumming on the table, my uncle condescended to reply.

"The doctor, when stating the latest possible hour of the death, led me up the garden path – "

"Then that hour was not correct?" I interrupted. "I mean: Could the *rigor mortis* have set in faster?" I, too, knocked with my hand on the arm of the chair. "In that case it was as I initially thought. When Pedrosa reached Tiago, he was still alive. The boy was freezing from catching so much cold and Dr. Fonseca was mistaken about the time." I stopped in triumph.

My uncle caught his breath and seemed about to utter a word that, without any doubt, could not be printed here. He made a grimace of suffering and let out a long resigned sigh.

"No," he said. "It's nothing like that. Do you believe it is possible to strangle someone like that, in a few seconds? And do you believe a doctor wouldn't notice he had just died? My God, what kind of a mind do you have?"

From that moment on, I decided to keep quiet. My uncle, basking in the blissful triumph of having shut me up, spoke in a grave, didactic manner:

"There's another thing you need to learn, my lad: The more contorted a case like this appears, the easier it is to solve. Some ruffian knifes a woman in a dark street late at night and runs away; that is difficult. Just try to prove he did it.

"But when it comes to these problems of apparent impossibility, one just has to spot the nail and hit it right on the head. I racked my brains wondering how the killer managed not to leave any footprints. Once the pure and simple truth dawned, I had solved the problem.

"Don't open your eyes wide like that. I gave you a lot of data. Yes! Data. Do you remember the fantastic light that illuminated Pedrosa in the vestibule and which, after all, came from the descending full moon? Didn't I tell you that dark thing was not Pedrosa's delusion, *et cetera?* Exactly. What do you make of it, Afonso? What are your brains for? And the footprints, son, the footprints? *The footprints!*

"Of course the murderer left footprints. They were there, quite clear, for whoever wanted to see them – in fact, they were even deeper than they would normally be. This is why my mechanical pencil, which fell inside one of my footprints, slid inside another, even deeper mark, which by chance was next to it. The person who left that mark had a build similar to mine and was much less heavy. Therefore, normally, his footprints would not be as deep as mine. Doesn't it look weird to you now?"

"Pedrosa!" I shouted, seeing the problem at last.

"Pedrosa, of course. Pedrosa was burdened when he left the house. How could he not leave deeper footprints if he carried a corpse in his arms? When he got there, he dropped him on the ground. There. So simple! Had we not seen him in the middle of the snow with Tiago at his feet and the straight line of footprints leading right to him?

"The immense and monumental fault in the logic had been the assumption that the body was already outside from the start, when, in fact, it had been brought out from the inside. Once this was understood, everything was simple. Little by little, all the pieces fell into place until the picture was complete.

"The doctor's calculation was correct, but he was wrong. He considered the outside temperature, but the body had been cooling inside the house. Therefore, Tiago must have been dead for a longer time in order for his body to have reached its current temperature. It was completely irrelevant to know the time the snow had ceased to fall: If there was not any snow on the corpse it was because it had been kept under a roof. Tiago had gone into the house, probably a couple of hours before we arrived. He had the bad luck of running first into Pedrosa, who was already there. I don't know what words passed between them, but it is not hard to guess. You know what had happened with Pedrosa's fiancée. Under the ashes, the fire may still burn. It is possible there was no criminal intent between them. However, both were of the overexcitable type. I imagine them in the vestibule, facing each other, ferociously arguing in whispering half-voices. You know Paiva de Andrada's words: *They went from words to squabble, from squabble to shouts, from shouts to threats, and from threats to killing each other.* If the rock hits the stone it cracks, and the stronger one in this case was Pedrosa. A squeeze of those enormous hands terminated the already shaky life of the other. Perhaps everything was quite fast. Afterwards, Pedrosa only thought about hiding the object of his evil deed. Just as a child would have done. He opened the chest in the vestibule (I mentioned it!) and placed Tiago's body inside.

"I don't know if the idea of the small drama in the snow came to him from our talk about supernatural facts or if it was improvised. There is no doubt it was a stroke of genius. However, the excitement of the night, the hypertension caused by those moments with us in the living room, the pressure to behave naturally despite the tension he was feeling, all was too much for him. When he saw his act completed, he was not able to endure it any longer and passed out. This only added verisimilitude to the tragedy.

"Yes, because nobody could have feigned such fainting or the fever he had. What the devilish boy did was to take advantage of it to pull that pseudo-delirious nonsense on us.

"That's why I told you that the dark thing crossing the plateau was not a delusion of his. It was a lie, a bald lie, and trouts and lies are as good as they are big.

"The most dangerous part for him was when he ran through the snow holding the corpse. If he were seen during that course, he was lost. However, he counted on the time we would take to follow him along the corridor or to go across the cluttered room. And he counted well, in either case. Above all, he was extraordinarily helped by the surprise factor. However, in order to be certain of having enough time, he had to prepare himself first: before he screamed in the vestibule, he had already withdrawn the corpse from the chest and even opened the outside door. This is why we saw him lit by the moonlight even before he shouted about having heard that owl's cry. Didn't you notice that his later account contradicted this? And that the bang we heard was nothing but the lid of the chest falling? He was nervous, his arms were busy holding the corpse and he could not sustain it.

"Having thrown the open cigarette case on the ground and stuck a cigarette between the corpse's fingers was also a stroke of genius. Maybe it was not indispensable. But it was so easy!"

I understood that his story had ended. And since I know very well there is nothing he detests more than to be asked questions once he deems an account finished, I swallowed a question that was about to slip from my tongue. Inevitably, one is curious of what became of the protagonists. However, for my uncle the only thing of interest is the "little problem," as he calls it.

And so I kept quiet.

Canada
The "Impossible" Impossible Crime
by Edward D. Hoch

The American Edward D. Hoch lived his entire life in Rochester, New York, just across Lake Ontario from Canada, where this story is set.

Hoch specialized in the detective short story and for over thirty years published one in every issue of *Ellery Queen's Mystery Magazine*, while also writing hundreds of other stories. It's impossible to maintain the highest standards of quality while keeping to such a schedule, but throughout Hoch remained dedicated to fair-play plotting and was surely the all-time master of planting clues in plain sight to be overlooked by the reader. Critics doubtful of Hoch's literary abilities should read "The Most Dangerous Man" or "The Oblong Room," two stories demonstrating the range of a very fine writer indeed.

"The 'Impossible' Impossible Crime" features a grimmer and appropriately colder atmosphere than most Hoch stories.

I'm no detective. But when you are living all alone with one other man, 200 miles from the nearest settlement, and one day that only other man is murdered – well, that's enough to make a detective out of anybody.

His name was Charles Fuller, and my name is Henry Bowfort.

Charlie was a full professor at Boston University when I met him, teaching an advanced course in geology while he worked on a volume concerning the effects of permafrost on mineral deposits. I was an assistant in his department, and we became friends at once. Perhaps our friendship was helped along by the fact that I was newly married to a very beautiful blonde named Grace who caught his eye from the very beginning.

Charlie's own wife divorced him some ten years earlier, and he was at the stage of his life when any sort of charming feminine companionship aroused his basic maleness.

Fuller was in his early forties at the time, a good ten years older than Grace and me, and he often talked about the project closest to his heart.

“Before I'm too old for it,” he said, “I want to spend a year above the permafrost line.”

And one day he announced that he would be spending his sabbatical at a research post in northern Canada, near the western shore of Hudson Bay.

“I've been given a grant for eight months' study,” he said, “It's a great opportunity. I'll never have another like it.”

“You're going up there alone?” Grace asked.

“Actually, I expect your husband to accompany me.”

I must have looked a bit startled. “Eight months in the wilds of nowhere with nothing but snow?”

And Charlie Fuller smiled.

“Nothing but snow. How about it, Grace? Could you give him up for eight months?”

“If he wants to,” she answered loyally. She had never tried to stand in the way of anything I'd wanted to do.

We talked about it for a long time that night, but I already knew I was hooked. I was on my way to northern Canada with Charlie Fuller.

The cabin – when we reached it by plane and boat and snowmobile – was a surprisingly comfortable place, well stocked with enough provisions for a year's stay. We had two-way radio contact with the outside world, plus necessary medical supplies and a bookcase full of reading material, all provided by the foundation that was financing the permafrost study.

The cabin consisted of three large rooms – a laboratory for our study, a combination living room/kitchen, and a bedroom with a bath in one corner. We'd brought our own clothes, and Fuller had brought a rifle, too, to discourage animals.

The daily routine with Charlie Fuller was great fun at first. He was surely a dedicated man, and one of the most intelligent I'd ever known. We rose early in the morning, had breakfast together, and then went off in search of ore samples. And best of all in those early days, there was the constant radio communication with Grace. Her almost nightly messages brought a touch of Boston to the Northwest Territory.

But after a time Grace’s messages thinned to one or two a week, and
finally to one every other week. Fuller and I began to get on each other's nerves, and often in the mornings I was awakened by the sound of rifle fire as he stood outside the cabin door taking random shots at the occasional owl or ground squirrel that wandered near. We still had the snowmobile, but it was 200 miles to the nearest settlement at Caribou, making a trip into town out of the question.

Once, during the evening meal, Fuller said:

“Bet you miss her, don't you, Hank?”

“Grace? Sure I miss her. It's been a long time.”

“Think she's sitting home nights waiting for us – for you?” I put down my fork.

“What's that supposed to mean, Charlie?”

“Nothing – nothing at all.”

But the rest of the evening passed under a cloud. By this time we had been up there nearly five months, and it was just too long.

It was fantastic, it was unreasonable, but there began to develop between us a sort of rivalry for my wife. An unspoken rivalry, to be sure, a rivalry for a woman nearly 2,000 miles away – but still a rivalry.

“What do you think she's doing now, Hank?” or “I wish Grace were here tonight. Warm the place up a bit. Right, Hank?”

Finally one evening in January, when a heavy snow had made us stay in the cabin for two long days and nights, the rivalry came to a head. Charlie Fuller was seated at the wooden table we used for meals and paperwork, and I was in my usual chair facing one of the windows.

"We're losing a lot of heat out in this place," I said. "Look at those icicles."

"I'll go out later and knock them down," he said.

I could tell he was in a bad mood and suspected he'd been drinking from our supply of Scotch.

"We might make the best of each other," I said. "We're stuck here for another few months together."

"Worried, Hank? Anxious to be back in bed with Grace?"

"Let's cut out the cracks about Grace, huh? I'm getting sick of you, Charlie."

"And I'm sick of you, sick of this place!"

"Then let's go back."

"In this storm?"

"We've got the snowmobile."

"No. This is one project I can't walk out on."

"Why not? Is it worth this torture day after day?"

"You don't understand. I didn't start out life being a geologist. My field was biology, and I had great plans for being a research scientist at some major pharmaceutical house. They pay very well, you know."

"What happened?"

"The damnedest thing, Hank. I couldn't work with animals. I couldn't experiment on them, kill them. I don't think I could ever kill a living thing."

"What about the animals and birds you shoot at?"

"That's just the point, Hank. I never hit them! I try to, but I purposely miss! That's why I went into geology. That was the only field in which I wouldn't make a fool of myself."

"You couldn't make a fool of yourself, Charlie. Even if we went back today, the university would still welcome you. You'd still have your professorship."

"I've got to succeed at something, Hank. Don't you understand? It's too late for another failure – too late in life to start over again!"

He didn't mention Grace the rest of that day, but I had the sensation that he hadn't just been talking about his work. His first marriage had been a failure, too. Was he trying to tell me he had to succeed with Grace?

I slept poorly that night – first because Charlie had decided to walk around the cabin at midnight knocking icicles from the roof, and then because the wind had changed direction and howled in the chimney. I got up once after Charlie was in bed, to look outside, but the windows were frosted over by the wind-driven snow, and I could see nothing.

Toward morning I drifted into an uneasy sleep, broken now and then by the bird sounds which told me that the storm had ended. I heard Charlie preparing breakfast, though I paid little attention, trying to get a bit more sleep.

Then, sometime later, I sprang awake, knowing I had heard it. A shot! Could Charlie be outside again, firing at the animals? I waited for some other sound, but nothing reached my ears except the perking of the coffee pot on the gas stove. Finally I got out of bed and went into the other room.

Charlie Fuller was seated in my chair at the table, staring at the wall.

A tiny stream of blood was running down his forehead and into one eye. He was dead.

It took me some moments to comprehend the fact of his death, and even after I had located the bullet wound just above his hairline, I still could not accept the reality of it. My first thought had been suicide, but then I saw this was impossible. The bullet had obviously killed him instantly, and there was no gun anywhere in sight – in fact, Fuller's rifle was missing from its usual place in the corner near the door.

But if not suicide, what?

There was no other explanation. Somehow he had killed himself. I switched on the radio and sent a message to that effect, telling them I'd bring in the body by snowmobile as soon as I could.

Then, as I was starting to pack my things, I remembered the coffee.

Do men about to commit suicide start making breakfast? Do they put a pot of coffee on the stove?

And then I had to face it. Charlie Fuller had not killed himself. It seemed impossible – but there it was. I sat down opposite the body, then got up to cover it with a blanket, and then sat down again.

What were all the possibilities? Suicide, accident, murder – as simple as that. Not suicide. Not accident. He certainly hadn't been cleaning his gun at the time.

That left only one possibility.

Murder.

I walked over and crouched behind his chair, trying to see what he must have been seeing in that final moment.

And then I saw it. Directly opposite, in the center of a frosted window, there was a tiny hole. I hadn't noticed it before – the frost had effectively camouflaged the hole. A few cracks ran from it, but the snow had somehow kept the window from shattering completely. The bullet had come from outside – the mystery was solved!

But as soon as I put on my coat and went outdoors, I realized that a greater mystery had taken its place. Though the drifting snow had left a narrow walkway under the roof of the cabin, drifts higher than my head surrounded us on all sides. No one could have approached the cabin through that snow without leaving a visible trail.

I made my way to the window and saw the butt of Fuller's rifle protruding from the snow. I pulled it out and stared at it, wondering what it could tell me. It had been recently fired, it was the murder weapon, but there was nothing more it could say.

I took it back into the cabin and sat down.... Just the two of us, no one else, and somebody had murdered Charlie Fuller.

As the day passed into noon, I knew I would have to be moving soon.

But could I go back under the circumstances? Charlie Fuller was dead, and I had to discover how it had happened.

Pacing the cabin, I knew that the answer must lurk here somewhere, within the walls of our temporary home. I went back in my mind over our conversations about Grace. He had loved her, he had wanted her – of that much I was certain. Could he have committed suicide in such a manner that I would be accused of his murder?

No, there were two things against that theory – it wouldn't get him Grace, and it wouldn't get me convicted of the crime. Because even now I could change the scene any way I wanted, invent any story I liked. The police would never even make the trip to the cabin to check my story. I had already called it suicide in my radio report, but I could change it to accident. And there was no one to call it murder.

No one but myself.

I went outside again and started sifting through the snow where I'd found the rifle. But there was nothing – a few bits of icicle, but nothing more. Here and there Fuller's footprints remained undrifted, from his icicle-breaking expedition, but I could identify no other prints. If someone had stood at that window to kill Charlie Fuller...

But no one could have! The snow and crystallized frost had made the window completely opaque. Even if an invisible murderer had dropped from the sky, and somehow got Charlie's rifle out of the cabin, he could not have fired at Charlie through that window because he could not have seen him through it!

So I went back inside to the rifle, emptied it, and tried the trigger. It had been adjusted to a hair trigger – the slightest pressure of my finger was enough to click the hammer on the empty chamber.

Suddenly I felt that I almost had an answer. I stood staring at the blanket-covered figure in the chair, then went outside and looked through the bullet hole at it again. Lined up perfectly, even through an opaque window.

And then I knew who had murdered Charlie Fuller.

I was staring at his body in the chair, but it was my chair! Twenty minutes later, and I would have been sitting in that very chair, eating breakfast. Charlie would have called me when the coffee was ready, and I would have come out to sit in that chair as I did every morning.

And Charlie Fuller would have killed me.

It took me five minutes of sorting through the bits of icicle in the snow under the window to find the one that was something more. It was ice, but ice encased in a tiny heat-sealed plastic pouch. We used pouches of all sizes in the lab for the rock specimens we collected. This one had served a different purpose.

Charlie had driven one of the icicles into the snow and balanced the rifle on top of it, probably freezing it to the icicle with a few drops of water. Then he had wiped away a tiny speck of frost on the window to line the gun barrel with the chair in which I would be sitting. He'd fixed the rifle with a hair trigger, and then jammed the tiny plastic pouch of water between the front of the trigger and the guard.

When the water in the pouch froze, the ice expanded against the trigger, and the rifle fired through the window at the chair. The recoil had thrown the rifle free of its icicle support, and the frozen pouch of water had dropped into the snow like a simple piece of ice.

And what had gone wrong? Charlie Fuller must have timed the freezing of the water with a filled pouch, but he probably hadn't timed it in subzero cold with a wind blowing. The water had simply frozen sooner than he'd planned – while he was sitting in my chair for a moment, adjusting it to the precise position facing the window.

But why had he gone to all that trouble to kill me, when we were alone? I thought about that all the way back to Caribou in the snowmobile. He'd probably feared that it would be like the animals he'd told me about, that at the final moment he wouldn't have been able to squeeze the trigger.

Perhaps in the night he'd even stood over my bed with his rifle, unable to go through with it. This way had made it impersonal, like a lab experiment to be set up and observed.

So Charlie Fuller had murdered himself. But for the authorities, and for Grace, I decided to stick to the suicide story. I didn't think they'd bother too much about things like the absence of powder burns. Under the circumstances, they were stuck with my story, and I wanted to keep it simple. As I said in the beginning, I'm no detective.

Real Life Impossibility: France
Hanged Too High

Nestor Bresson owned a farm in Hauts-de-Bonnecourt near Dijon in the late 1930s, and one day he was found hanged from a beam in the farm workshop under circumstances that appeared very suspicious to the local gendarmes. The body was hanging several feet above the floor, but there was no chair or stool under it that would have enabled him to reach the beam on his own. There was a ladder in the room, but it was leaning against one of the walls and completely out of reach of the hanged man.

The police suspected Bresson had been murdered by his nearest neighbour, a drunkard who had sworn to get even with Bresson after a number of violent disputes over the theft of materials, damage to fences, and spoiling of crops. There was no proof, however, so the case was shelved.

Nestor had taken over the farm from his late father, Oscar, who was convinced that the property was cursed: Strange noises could be heard at any time of the day or night, tiles fell off the roof by themselves, his cat had been found with both eyes gouged out, and he believed himself to be pursued in the fields by flocks of crows. Nestor initially refused to give credence to the rumours about a curse on the other property. However, after a few months, he was forced to concede that bad luck or malevolent actions continued to dog his father's estate: disastrous crop failures, cattle dead without apparent reason, farm equipment continually breaking down. As a result of the bad luck and the endless arguments with his neighbour, his wife left him, which caused him to have a nervous breakdown. Then, to cap it all, he was found to have tuberculosis, at a point in time when it was virtually untreatable.

The recently retired chief of police noted all of Nestor's troubles and formulated a theory, which he shared with a friend, a writer and journalist:

"He decided to end it all and frame his neighbour. It was winter, and cold enough to freeze the balls off a brass monkey. He brought in snow in a wheelbarrow, packed it into a mound in his workshop, and returned the wheelbarrow outside. He lit the stove and climbed up the mound until the rope he had prepared fit snugly around his neck, and waited there until the stove started to melt the snow and he was left hanging there. There was no need of a ladder or a stool or anyone to assist him. The snow melted and then the water evaporated. That's how it happened."

Noting the evident incredulity of his friend, the old man reassured him:

"I went over to the farm myself later, after I heard about it. I found the wheelbarrow outside: There was snow still stuck to the bottom and sides with a few tufts of grass. And in the stove there were a few cinders that were still slightly warm. Believe me."

Even though the explanation seems convincing, the case is still classified as unsolved to this day. The story was retold in fictitious form, however, in a novel by Roch de Santa-Maria, *Pendu Trop Court* (1942), and in a film by André Cayatte, *Le Dessous des Cartes* (1948).

Egypt
The Locked Tomb Mystery
by Elizabeth Peters

Dr. Barbara Mertz was an acclaimed Egyptology expert who also found great success writing perennially best-selling mysteries using the pseudonym Elizabeth Peters. Her Amelia Peabody mysteries, starting with the classic *Crocodile on the Sandbank*, inspired generations of women hungry for tales of independent, intelligent, and attractive female protagonists. She founded the Malice Domestic mystery convention held in the Washington, D.C. area each year. She was the recipient of Edgar, Anthony, and Agatha awards and was made a Grand Master by the Mystery Writers of America in 1998. She also wrote supernatural romances as Barbara Michaels.

"The Locked Tomb Mystery" is a baffling story set in one of the most inaccessible rooms ever.

Senebtisi's funeral was the talk of southern Thebes. Of course, it could not compare with the burials of Great Ones and Pharaohs, whose Houses of Eternity were furnished with gold and fine linen and precious gems, but ours was not a quarter where nobles lived; our people were craftsmen and small merchants, able to afford a chamber-tomb and a coffin and a few spells to ward off the perils of the Western Road – no more than that. We had never seen anything like the burial of the old woman who had been our neighbour for so many years.

The night after the funeral the customers of Nehi's tavern could talk of nothing else. I remember that evening well. For one thing, I had just won my first appointment as a temple scribe. I was looking forward to boasting a little, and perhaps paying for a round of beer, if my friends displayed proper appreciation of my good fortune. Three of the others were already at the tavern when I arrived, my linen shawl wrapped tight around me. The weather was cold even for winter, with a cruel, dry wind driving sand into every crevice of the body.

"Close the door quickly," said Senu, the carpenter. "What weather! I wonder if the Western journey will be like this – cold enough to freeze a man's bones."

This prompted a ribald comment from Rennefer, the weaver, concerning the effects of freezing on certain of Senebtisi's vital organs. "Not that anyone would notice the difference," he added. "There was never any warmth in the old hag. What sort of mother would take all her possessions to the next world and leave her only son penniless?"

"Is it true, then?" I asked, signalling Nehi to fetch the beer. "I have heard stories – "

"All true," said the potter, Baenre. "It is a pity you could not attend the burial, Wadjsen; it was magnificent!"

"You went?" I inquired. "That was good of you, since she ordered none of her funerary equipment from you."

Baenre is a scanty little man with thin hair and sharp bones. It is said that he is a domestic tyrant, and that his wife cowers when he comes roaring home from the tavern, but when he is with us, his voice is almost a whisper. "My rough kitchenware would not be good enough to hold the wine and fine oil she took to the tomb. Wadjsen, you should have seen the boxes and jars and baskets – dozens of them. They say she had a gold mask, like the ones worn by great nobles, and that all her ornaments were of solid gold."

"It is true," said Rennefer. "I know a man who knows one of the servants of Bakenmut, the goldsmith who made the ornaments."

"How is her son taking it?" I asked. I knew Minmose slightly; a shy, serious man, he followed his father's trade of stone carving. His mother had lived with him all his life, greedily scooping up his profits, though she had money of her own, inherited from her parents.

"Why, as you would expect," said Senu, shrugging. "Have you ever heard him speak harshly to anyone, much less his mother? She was an old she-goat who treated him like a boy who has not cut off the side lock, but with him it was always, 'Yes, honoured mother,' and 'As you say, honoured mother.' She would not even allow him to take a wife."

"How will he live?"

"Oh, he has the shop and the business, such as it is. He is a hard worker; he will survive."

In the following months I heard occasional news of Minmose. Gossip said he must be doing well, for he had taken to spending his leisure time at a local house of prostitution – a pleasure he never had dared enjoy while his mother lived. Nefertiry, the loveliest and most expensive of the girls, was the object of his desire, and Rennefer remarked that the maiden must have a kind heart, for she could command higher prices than Minmose was able to pay. However, as time passed, I forgot Minmose and Senebtisi, and her rich burial. It was not until almost a year later that the matter was recalled to my attention.

The rumours began in the marketplace, at the end of the time of inundation, when the floodwater lay on the fields and the farmers were idle. They enjoy this time, but the police of the city do not; for idleness leads to crime, and one of the most popular crimes is tomb robbing. This goes on all the time in a small way, but when the Pharaoh is strong and stern, and the laws are strictly enforced, it is a very risky trade. A man stands to lose more than a hand or an ear if he is caught. He also risks damnation after he has entered his own tomb; but some men simply do not have proper respect for the gods.

The king, Nebmaatre (may he live forever!), was then in his prime, so there had been no tomb robbing for some time – or at least none had been detected. But, the rumours said, three men of west Thebes had been caught trying to sell ornaments such as are buried with the dead. The rumours turned out to be correct, for once. The men were questioned on the soles of their feet and confessed to the robbing of several tombs.

Naturally all those who had kin buried on the west bank – which included most of us – were alarmed by this news, and half the nervous matrons in our neighborhood went rushing across the river to make sure the family tombs were safe. I was not surprised to hear that that dutiful son Minmose had also felt obliged to make sure his mother had not been disturbed.

However, I was surprised at the news that greeted me when I paid my next visit to Nehi's tavern. The moment I entered, the others began to talk at once, each eager to be the first to tell the shocking facts.

"Robbed?" I repeated when I had sorted out the babble of voices. "Do you speak truly?"

"I do not know why you should doubt it," said Rennefer. "The richness of her burial was the talk of the city, was it not? Just what the tomb robbers like! They made a clean sweep of all the gold, and ripped the poor old hag's mummy to shreds."

At that point we were joined by another of the habitués, Merusir. He is a pompous, fat man who considers himself superior to the rest of us because he is Fifth Prophet of Amon. We put up with his patronizing ways because sometimes he knows court gossip. On that particular evening it was apparent that he was bursting with excitement. He listened with a supercilious sneer while we told him the sensational news. "I know, I know," he drawled. "I heard it much earlier – and with it, the other news which is known only to those in the confidence of the Palace."

He paused, ostensibly to empty his cup. Of course, we reacted as he had hoped we would, begging him to share the secret. Finally he condescended to inform us.

"Why, the amazing thing is not the robbery itself, but how it was done. The tomb entrance was untouched, the seals of the necropolis were unbroken. The tomb itself is entirely rock-cut, and there was not the slightest break in the walls or floor or ceiling. Yet when Minmose entered the burial chamber, he found the coffin open, the mummy mutilated, and the gold ornaments gone."

We stared at him, open-mouthed.

"It is a most remarkable story," I said.

"Call me a liar if you like," said Merusir, who knows the language of polite insult as well as I do. "There was a witness – two, if you count Minmose himself. The sem-priest Wennefer was with him."

This silenced the critics. Wennefer was known to us all. There was not a man in southern Thebes with a higher reputation. Even Senebtisi had been fond of him, and she was not fond of many people. He had officiated at her funeral.

Pleased at the effect of his announcement, Merusir went on in his most pompous manner. “The king himself has taken an interest in the matter. He has called on Amenhotep Sa Hapu to investigate.”

“Amenhotep?” I exclaimed. “But I know him well.”

“You do?” Merusir's plump cheeks sagged like bladders punctured by a sharp knife.

Now, at that time Amenhotep's name was not in the mouth of everyone, though he had taken the first steps on that astonishing career that was to make him the intimate friend of Pharaoh. When I first met him, he had been a poor, insignificant priest at a local shrine. I had been sent to fetch him to the house where my master lay dead of a stab wound, presumably murdered. Amenhotep’s fame had begun with that matter, for he had discovered the truth and saved an innocent man from execution. Since then, he had handled several other cases, with equal success.

My exclamation had taken the wind out of Merusir’s sails. He had hoped to impress us by telling us something we did not know. Instead it was I who enlightened the others about Amenhotep's triumphs. But when I finished, Rennefer shook his head.

“If this wise man is all you say, Wadjsen, it will be like inviting a lion to rid the house of mice. He will find there is a simple explanation. No doubt the thieves entered the burial chamber from above or from one side, tunneling through the rock. Minmose and Wennefer were too shocked to observe the hole in the wall, that is all.”

We argued the matter for some time, growing more and more heated as the level in the jar dropped. It was a foolish argument, for none of us knew the facts, and to argue without knowledge is like trying to weave without thread.

This truth did not occur to me until the cool night breeze had cleared my head, when I was halfway home. I decided to pay Amenhotep a visit. The next time I went to the tavern, I would be the one to tell the latest news, and Merusir would be nothing!

Most of the honest householders had retired, but there were lamps burning in the street of the prostitutes, and in a few taverns. There was a light, as well, in one window of the house where Amenhotep lodged. Like the owl he resembled, with his beaky nose and large, close-set eyes, he preferred to work at night.

The window was on the ground floor, so I knocked on the wooden shutter, which of course was shut to keep out night demons. After a few moments, and the familiar nose appeared, I spoke my name and Amenhotep went to open the door.

"Wadjsen! It has been a long time," he exclaimed. "Should I ask what brings you here, or shall I display my talents as a seer and tell you?"

"I suppose it requires no great talent," I replied. "The matter of Senebtisi's tomb is already the talk of the district."

"So I had assumed." He gestured me to sit down and hospitably indicated the wine jar that stood in the corner. I shook my head.

"I have already taken too much beer, at the tavern. I am sorry to disturb you so late – "

"I am always happy to see you, Wadjsen." His big dark eyes reflected the light of the lamp, so that they seemed to hold stars in their depths. "I have missed my assistant, who helped me to the truth in my first inquiry."

"I was of little help to you then," I said with a smile. "And in this case I am even more ignorant. The thing is a great mystery, known only to the gods."

"No, no!" He clapped his hands together, as was his habit when annoyed with the stupidity of his hearer. "There is no mystery. I know who robbed the tomb of Senebtisi. The only difficulty is to prove how it was done."

At Amenhotep's suggestion I spent the night at his house so that I could accompany him when he set out next morning to find the proof he needed. I required little urging, for I was afire with curiosity. Though I pressed him, he would say no more, merely remarking piously, "'A man may fall to ruin because of his tongue; if a passing remark is hasty and it is repeated, thou wilt make enemies.'"

I could hardly dispute the wisdom of this adage, but the gleam in Amenhotep's bulging black eyes made me suspect he took a malicious pleasure in my bewilderment.

After our morning bread and beer we went to the temple of Khonsu, where the sem-priest Wennefer worked in the records office. He was copying accounts from pottery ostraca onto a papyrus that was stretched across his lap. All scribes develop bowed shoulders from bending over their writing; Wennefer was folded almost double, his face scant inches from the surface of the papyrus. When Amenhotep cleared his throat, the old man started, smearing the ink. He waved our apologies aside and cleaned the papyrus with a wad of lint.

"No harm was meant, no harm is done," he said in his breathy, chirping voice. "I have heard of you, Amenhotep Sa Hapu; it is an honour to meet you."

"I, too, have looked forward to meeting you, Wennefer. Alas that the occasion should be such a sad one."

Wennefer's smile faded. "Ah, the matter of Senebtisi's tomb. What a tragedy! At least the poor woman can now have a proper reburial. If Minmose had not insisted on opening the tomb, her ba would have gone hungry and thirsty through eternity."

"Then the tomb entrance really was sealed and undisturbed?" I asked sceptically.

"I examined it myself," Wennefer said. "Minmose had asked me to meet him after the day's work, and we arrived at the tomb as the sun was setting, but the light was still good. I conducted the funeral service for Senebtisi, you know. I had seen the doorway blocked and mortared and with my own hands had helped to press the seals of the necropolis onto the wet plaster. All was as I had left it that day a year ago."

"Yet Minmose insisted on opening the tomb?" Amenhotep asked.

"Why, we agreed it should be done," the old man said mildly. "As you know, robbers sometimes tunnel in from above or from one side, leaving the entrance undisturbed. Minmose had brought tools. He did most of the work himself, for these old hands of mine are better with a pen than a chisel. When the doorway was clear, Minmose lit a lamp and we entered. We were crossing the hall beyond the entrance corridor when Minmose let out a shriek. 'My mother, my mother,' he cried – oh, it was pitiful to hear! Then I saw it too. The thing – the thing on the floor..."

"You speak of the mummy, I presume," said Amenhotep. "The thieves had dragged it from the coffin out into the hall?"

"Where they despoiled it," Wennefer whispered. "The august body was ripped open from throat to groin, through the shroud and the wrappings and the flesh."

"Curious," Amenhotep muttered, as if to himself. "Tell me, Wennefer, what is the plan of the tomb?"

Wennefer rubbed his brush on the ink cake and began to draw on the back surface of one of the ostraca.

"It is a fine tomb, Amenhotep, entirely rock-cut. Beyond the entrance is a flight of stairs and a short corridor, thus leading to a hall broader than it is long, with two pillars. Beyond that, another short corridor, then the burial chamber. The august mummy lay here." And he inked in a neat circle at the beginning of the second corridor.

"Ha," said Amenhotep, studying the plan. "Yes, yes, I see. Go on, Wennefer. What did you do next?"

"I did nothing," the old man said simply. "Minmose's hand shook so violently that he dropped the lamp. Darkness closed in. I felt the presence of the demons who had defiled the dead. My tongue clove to the roof of my mouth and – "

"Dreadful," Amenhotep said. "But you were not far from the tomb entrance; you could find your way out?"

"Yes, yes, it was only a dozen paces, and by Amun, my friend, the sunset light has never appeared so sweet! I went at once to fetch the necropolis guards. When we returned to the tomb, Minmose had rekindled his lamp – "

"I thought you said the lamp was broken."

"Dropped, but fortunately not broken. Minmose had opened one of the jars of oil – Senebtisi had many such in the tomb, all of the finest quality – and had refilled the lamp. He had replaced the mummy in its coffin and was kneeling by it praying. Never was there so pious a son!"

"So then, I suppose, the guards searched the tomb."

"We all searched," Wennefer said. "The tomb chamber was in a dreadful state; boxes and baskets had been broken open and the contents strewn about. Every object of precious metal had been stolen, including the amulets on the body."

"What about the oil, the linen, and the other valuables?" Amenhotep asked.

"The oil and the wine were in large jars, impossible to move easily. About the other things I cannot say; everything was in such confusion – and I do not know what was there to begin with. Even Minmose was not certain; his mother had filled and sealed most of the boxes herself. But I know what was taken from the mummy, for I saw the golden amulets and ornaments placed on it when it was wrapped by the embalmers. I do not like to speak evil of anyone, but you know, Amenhotep, that the embalmers – "

"Yes," Amenhotep agreed with a sour face. "I myself watched the wrapping of my father; there is no other way to make certain the ornaments will go on the mummy instead of into the coffers of the embalmers. Minmose did not perform this service for his mother?"

"Of course he did. He asked me to share in the watch, and I was glad to agree. He is the most pious – "

"So I have heard," said Amenhotep. "Tell me again, Wennefer, of the condition of the mummy. You examined it?"

"It was my duty. Oh, Amenhotep, it was a sad sight! The shroud was still tied firmly around the body; the thieves had cut straight through it and through the bandages beneath, baring the body. The arm bones were broken, so roughly had the thieves dragged the heavy gold bracelets from them."

"And the mask?" I asked. "It was said that she had a mask of solid gold."

"It, too, was missing."

"Horrible," Amenhotep said. "Wennefer, we have kept you from your work long enough. Only one more question: How do you think the thieves entered the tomb?"

The old man's eyes fell. "Through me," he whispered.

I gave Amenhotep a startled look. He shook his head warningly.

"It was not your fault," he said, touching Wennefer's bowed shoulder.

"It was. I did my best, but I must have omitted some vital part of the ritual. How else could demons enter the tomb?"

"Oh, I see." Amenhotep stroked his chin. "Demons."

"It could have been nothing else. The seals on the door were intact, the mortar untouched. There was no break of the smallest size in the stone of the walls or ceiling or floor."

"But – " I began.

"And there is this. When the doorway was clear and the light entered, the dust lay undisturbed on the floor. The only marks on it were the strokes of the broom with which Minmose, according to custom, had swept the floor as he left the tomb after the funeral service."

"Amun preserve us," I exclaimed, feeling a chill run through me.

Amenhotep's eyes moved from Wennefer to me, then back to Wennefer. "That is conclusive," he murmured.

"Yes," Wennefer said with a groan. "And I am to blame – I, a priest who failed at his task."

"No," said Amenhotep. "You did not fail. Be of good cheer, my friend. There is another explanation."

Wennefer shook his head despondently. "Minmose said the same, but he was only being kind. Poor man! He was so overcome, he could scarcely walk. The guards had to take him by the arms to lead him from the tomb. I carried his tools. It was the least – "

"The tools," Amenhotep interrupted. "They were in a bag or a sack?"

"Why, no. He had only a chisel and a mallet. I carried them in my hand as he had done."

Amenhotep thanked him again, and we took our leave. As we crossed the courtyard I waited for him to speak, but he remained silent, and after a while I could contain myself no longer.

"Do you still believe you know who robbed the tomb?"

"Yes, yes, it is obvious."

"And it was not demons?"

Amenhotep blinked at me like an owl blinded by sunlight.

"Demons are a last resort."

He had the smug look of a man who thinks he has said something clever, but his remark smacked of heresy to me, and I looked at him doubtfully.

"Come, come," he snapped. "Senebtisi was a selfish, greedy old woman, and if there is justice in the next world, as our faith decrees, her path through the Underworld will not be easy. But why would diabolical powers play tricks with her mummy when they could torment her spirit? Demons have no need of gold."

"Well, but – "

"Your wits used not to be so dull. What do you think happened?"

"If it was not demons – "

"It was not."

"Then someone must have broken in."

"Very clever," said Amenhotep, grinning.

"I mean that there must be an opening, in the walls or the floor, that Wennefer failed to see."

"Wennefer, perhaps. The necropolis guards, no. The chambers of the tomb were cut out of solid rock. It would be impossible to disguise a break in such a surface, even if tomb robbers took the trouble to fill it in – which they never have been known to do."

"Then the thieves entered through the doorway and closed it again. A dishonest craftsman could make a copy of the necropolis seal...."

"Good." Amenhotep clapped me on the shoulder. "Now you are beginning to think. It is an ingenious idea, but it is wrong. Tomb robbers work in haste, for fear of the necropolis guards. They would not linger to replace stones and mortar and seals."

"Then I do not know how it was done."

"Ah, Wadjsen, you are dense! There is only one person who could have robbed the tomb."

"I thought of that," I said stiffly, hurt by his raillery. "Minmose was the last to leave the tomb and the first to re-enter it. He had good reason to desire the gold his mother should have left to him. But, Amenhotep, he could not have robbed the mummy on either occasion; there was not time. You know the funeral ritual as well as I. When the priests and mourners leave the tomb, they leave together. If Minmose had lingered in the burial chamber, even for a few minutes, his delay would have been noted and remarked upon."

"That is quite true," said Amenhotep.

"Also," I went on, "the gold was heavy as well as bulky. Minmose could not have carried it away without someone noticing."

"Again you speak truly."

"Then unless Wennefer the priest is conspiring with Minmose – "

"That good, simple man? I am surprised at you, Wadjsen. Wennefer is as honest as the Lady of Truth herself."

"Demons – "

Amenhotep interrupted with the hoarse hooting sound that passed for a laugh with him. "Stop babbling of demons. There is one man besides myself who knows how Senebtisi's tomb was violated. Let us go and see him."

He quickened his pace, his sandals slapping in the dust. I followed, trying to think. His taunts were like weights that pulled my mind to its farthest limits. I began to get an inkling of truth, but I could not make sense of it. I said nothing, not even when we turned into the lane south of the temple that led to the house of Minmose.

There was no servant at the door. Minmose himself answered our summons. I greeted him and introduced Amenhotep.

Minmose lifted his hands in surprise. "You honour my house, Amenhotep. Enter and be seated."

Amenhotep shook his head. "I will not stay, Minmose. I came only to tell you who desecrated your mother's tomb."

"What?" Minmose gaped at him. "Already you know? But how? It is a great mystery, beyond – "

"You did it, Minmose."

Minmose turned a shade paler. But that was not out of the way; even the innocent might blanch at such an accusation.

"You are mad," he said. "Forgive me, you are my guest, but – "

"There is no other possible explanation," Amenhotep said. "You stole the gold when you entered the tomb two days ago."

"But, Amenhotep," I exclaimed. "Wennefer was with him, and Wennefer saw the mummy already robbed when – "

"Wennefer did not see the mummy," Amenhotep said, "The tomb was dark; the only light was that of a small lamp, which Minmose promptly dropped. Wennefer has poor sight. Did you not observe how he bent over his writing? He caught only a glimpse of a white shape, the size of a wrapped mummy, before the light went out. When next Wennefer saw the mummy, it was in the coffin, and his view of it then coloured his confused memory of the first supposed sighting of it. Few people are good observers. They see what they expect to see."

"Then what did he see?" I demanded. Minmose might not have been there. Amenhotep avoided looking at him.

"A piece of linen in the rough shape of a human form, arranged on the floor by the last person who left the tomb. It would have taken him only a moment to do this before he snatched up the broom and swept himself out."

"So the tomb was sealed and closed," I exclaimed. "For almost a year he waited – "

"Until the next outbreak of tomb robbing. Minmose could assume this would happen sooner or later; it always does. He thought he was being clever by asking Wennefer to accompany him – a witness of irreproachable character who could testify that the tomb entrance was untouched. In fact, he was too careful to avoid being compromised; that would have made me doubt him, even if the logic of the facts had not pointed directly at him. Asking that same virtuous man to share his supervision of the mummy wrapping, lest he be suspected of connivance with the embalmers; feigning weakness so that the necropolis guards would have to support him, and thus be in a position to swear he could not have concealed the gold on his person. Only a guilty man would be so anxious to appear innocent. Yet there was reason for his precautions. Sometime in the near future, when that loving son Minmose discovers a store of gold hidden in the house, overlooked by his mother – the old do forget sometimes – then, since men have evil minds, it might be necessary for Minmose to prove beyond a shadow of a doubt that he could not have laid hands on his mother's burial equipment."

Minmose remained dumb, his eyes fixed on the ground. It was I who responded as he should have, questioning and objecting.

"But how did he remove the gold? The guards and Wennefer searched the tomb, so it was not hidden there, and there was not time for him to bury it outside."

"No, but there was ample time for him to do what had to be done in the burial chamber after Wennefer had tottered off to fetch the guards. He overturned boxes and baskets, opened the coffin, ripped through the mummy wrappings with his chisel, and took the gold. It would not take long, especially for one who knew exactly where each ornament had been placed."

Minmose's haggard face was as good as an admission of guilt. He did not look up or speak, even when Amenhotep put a hand on his shoulder.

"I pity you, Minmose," Amenhotep said gravely. "After years of devotion and self-denial, to see yourself deprived of your inheritance. And there was Nefertiry. You had been visiting her in secret, even before your mother died, had you not? Oh, Minmose, you should have remembered the words of the sage: 'Do not go in to a woman who is a stranger; it is a great crime, worthy of death.' She has brought you to your death, Minmose. You knew she would turn from you if your mother left you nothing."

Minmose's face was grey. "Will you denounce me, then? They will beat me to make me confess."

"Any man will confess when he is beaten," said Amenhotep, with a curl of his lip. "No, Minmose, I will not denounce you. The court of the vizier demands facts, not theories, and you have covered your tracks very neatly. But you will not escape justice. Nefertiry will consume your gold as the desert sands drink water, and then she will cast you off, and all the while Anubis, the Guide of the Dead, and Osiris, the Divine Judge, will be waiting for you. They will eat your heart, Minmose, and your spirit will hunger and thirst through all eternity. I think your punishment has already begun. Do you dream, Minmose? Did you see your mother's face last night, wrinkled and withered, her sunken eyes accusing you, as it looked when you tore the gold mask from it?"

A long shudder ran through Minmose's body. Even his hair seemed to shiver and rise. Amenhotep gestured to me. We went away, leaving Minmose staring after us with a face like death.

After we had gone a short distance, I said, "There is one more thing to tell, Amenhotep."

"There is much to tell." Amenhotep sighed deeply. "Of a good man turned evil; of two women who, in their different ways, drove him to crime; of the narrow line that separates the virtuous man from the sinner..."

"I do not speak of that. I do not wish to think of that. It makes me feel strange.... The gold, Amenhotep – how did Minmose bear away the gold from his mother's burial?"

"He put it in the oil jar," said Amenhotep. "The one he opened to get fresh fuel for his lamp. Who would wonder if, in his agitation, he spilled a quantity of oil on the floor? He has certainly removed it by now. He has had ample opportunity, running back and forth with objects to be repaired or replaced."

"And the piece of linen he had put down to look like the mummy?"

"As you well know," Amenhotep replied, "the amount of linen used to wrap a mummy is prodigious. He could have crumpled that piece and thrown it in among the torn wrappings. But I think he did something else. It was a cool evening, in winter, and Minmose would have worn a linen mantle. He took the cloth out in the same way he had brought it in. Who would notice an extra fold of linen over a man's shoulders?

"I knew immediately that Minmose must be the guilty party, because he was the only one who had the opportunity, but I did not see how he had managed it until Wennefer showed me where the supposed mummy lay. There was no reason for a thief to drag it so far from the coffin and the burial chamber, but Minmose could not afford to have Wennefer catch even a glimpse of that room, which was then undisturbed. I realized then that what the old man had seen was not the mummy at all, but a substitute."

"Then Minmose will go unpunished."

"I said he would be punished. I spoke truly." Again Amenhotep sighed.

"You will not denounce him to Pharaoh?"

"I will tell my lord the truth. But he will not choose to act. There will be no need."

He said no more. But six weeks later Minmose's body was found floating in the river. He had taken to drinking heavily, and people said he drowned by accident. But I knew it was otherwise. Anubis and Osiris had eaten his heart, just as Amenhotep had said.

United States
Deadfall
by Samuel W. Taylor

Samuel Taylor was a prolific novelist, scriptwriter ("The Absent-Minded Professor") and historian, but this is his only impossible-crime short story.

But what a story! After its initial 1958 appearance in *Adventure* magazine, it was chosen for inclusion in Robert Adey and Hidetoshi Mori's *18 Locked Room Puzzles* (Shinjusha, 1996) and Robert Adey and Roland Lacourbe's *20 défis à l'impossible* (l'Atalante, 2002).

To cap it all, it was selected as one of twenty-seven masterpieces (eighteen if you exclude the nine by Ed Hoch) in *1001 Chambres Closes (1001 Locked Rooms)* edited by Roland Lacourbe, et al. (Semper Aenigma, 1997).

A footprints-in-the-snow mystery with two men trapped in a remote cabin. Is one of them a murderer, or is there someone or something else with them in the woods?

SEPTEMBER 28

It snowed last night. That means we're here for the winter. This morning was bright and cold. When I got up and looked out of the little cabin window, everything was sparkling white. The conifers and brush of the mountain slopes were heavy with snow, and I estimated, from the white mound atop the chopping block, that the fall had been about eight inches.

Vince was awake, whittling. He'd had little else to do for the past week, since he got caught in the deadfall and broke his leg. I'd left the lantern on the box beside his bunk when I went to bed, and I don't know how long he'd stayed awake, whittling and brooding, but the pile of shavings on the floor beside the bunk spoke for itself. He'd feel responsible for the fix we were in. But accidents certainly could happen, couldn't they?

I got dressed and began making a fire.

"Look, Jim."

I turned from the stove. Vince was sitting up, displaying a stout stick of scrub oak, which he'd robbed from the bunk. At one end of the stick he'd fitted a short crosspiece to form a crude crutch.

"With this, I can manage, Jim. We'll get out of here, or give it a good try."

"Oh, sure," I said sarcastically, "easy as pie." It had taken us six hours of hiking over the roughest kind of country to get here, from the end of the road where we'd left the car. Fat chance he'd have with a crutch.

I could have gone out myself and got help, except that I didn't have the remotest idea where the car was. It was new country to me. It had been the middle of the night when we left the car and started hiking. Up and down steep slopes, picking a way along ledges, fighting through brush, wading along stream beds, scrambling over boulders –

I'd just followed Vince, with cold venom in my heart, as he kept saying, "Just a little farther," hour after hour, mile after mile, with a bounce in his step and a song in his voice, while I staggered along behind. I paid no attention to direction or landmarks. Sometimes the moon was in the north, sometimes in the south – a new place in the sky every time I looked up. I don't pretend to be the outdoor type. That's Vince's department.

After he broke his leg, I tried to find the car, to get out and get help. But I almost got lost. I was lucky to find my way back to the cabin.

Nobody knew where we were, not even Kay. We'd made plans for camping on the Pitt River, then changed our minds en route and came up here to the Trinity wilderness. Vince knew a place, he'd said, where nobody ever went. He was right – for good reason. The only people who used this cabin were cattlemen, during the fall roundup, when they brought their stock out of the mountains.

I got the kindling started, and was poking wood on it when there was a thump behind me. Vince was off the bunk with that homemade crutch. "See, Jim? Nothing to it. If I'm careful – " He gasped, as the game foot struck the leg of the table, twisting the broken leg. I think he would have toppled over if I hadn't grabbed him. He moaned softly, the sweat beading on his forehead, while I helped him back onto the bunk. He lay there breathing heavily.

"Oh, damn," he breathed. "If I could only do something. This is the first time in my life, Jim, when I've been helpless. I've never had to lean on anybody else."

I turned away, not wanting what I felt to be seen on my face. Maybe the experience would humble Vince a little, I thought. Maybe after this he'd realize there were others in the world, that he wasn't as self-sufficient as he supposed, and that what he wanted wasn't his for the taking.

"I put the coffee pot on, then went out for some wood. But I didn't go far, just one step out the door, and then I froze.

There were footsteps upon the new snow. Human footsteps. Someone had walked from the little cabin porch across the snow to the river. In the bright morning light I could see every step to where the tracks ended at the bank of the stream, some fifty yards away.

There were no prints coming onto the porch, just the single set of tracks leaving, as if someone had been inside and had walked out and into the river.

This, of course, was impossible.

But what gave these footprints an eerie and a creepy touch of fantasy was the fact that they were small, in fact tiny, and feminine – made by the high-heeled slippers of a woman.

Such prints, out here in the wilderness area, appearing on the new snow, coming from nowhere and vanishing into the river. Such is the stuff of nightmares. Such are the hallucinations of the insane.

And it was this experience that caused me to begin this journal. There should be a record, of everything that happens, so that Kay will know. This journal will tell her, if I do not survive.

OCTOBER 22

For the past three days I have been hunting. I am clumsy at it, a novice. But a man does what he has to. I will get meat or we will die. And today I got a deer. A doe, true enough, but this isn't the formalized hunt of sportsmen; this is survival. When we arrived at the cabin there was a little sugar, salt, flour, and coffee, left there by the cattlemen, which supplemented what we carried in on our backs. But it wasn't much, and we hadn't carried in much. That's what we'd live on until spring, now.

I cleaned the deer and brought it in, and when I came into view of the cabin I saw more tracks. The tracks were in the form of a large circle with a cross within it, as if children had been playing the game of fox and geese in the snow. I stopped at the rear of the cabin to examine the tracks, and found two distinct sets of footprints intermingled. One were footprints that would be made by the shoes of a child about six, the other by a child two or three years older.

The tracks came from the beaten path I had made to the woodpile. I didn't attempt to follow them further. With the first prints, the high-heeled tracks leading from the porch to the river, I had gone downstream along the bank several miles, waded across at a ford, then had gone upstream several miles past the cabin, forded again, and come back to where I started, checking to see if the footprints emerged from the stream. They hadn't.

Since then, upon three occasions, there have been new footprints. One time it was the prints of a man's shoe, another time a smaller, flat print, as of a woman's overshoe, and the third time the prints of the two children playing fox and geese.

I hung the deer on a pole Vince had fixed between two trees for the buck he'd shot the day of our arrival, and went inside.

"Nice going, Jim," Vince said. He was on the bunk whittling a bishop. For the past two days he'd been carving a set of chessmen. He nodded at the window. "Saw you toting it in. A beauty. I knew you could do it if you had to."

I picked up a rook from the box beside the bunk. "Say, you're doing a nice job."

"Great," he said sourly. "Too bad there's no yarn to crochet."

I don't know of anybody in the world who would find it harder to be tied to a bunk day after day. Vince's idea of a perfect Sunday was to shoot thirty-six holes of golf, play four sets of tennis, swim for an hour, and then have a good workout in the gym. He was a rather small man, but all muscle. Stripped, he looked like a contestant for Mr. America.

But what can you do with a muscle except exercise it? At school, yes, athletic hero and idol of the campus – and, quite a champ with the girls.

He was good enough to get a bid from the pros, in football. He made the squad with the Chicago Bears, but he was just too small for that league, and was released in mid-season. When he got home he called up his number one girlfriend – to whom he hadn't said goodbye, nor so much as dropped a postcard while he was away – to find Kay married to me.

In a way, I have been deeply grateful to Vince. Except for him, I never would have gotten Kay, or my chance with the company. I was always fat, and clumsy. As a kid, I admired Vince tremendously.

He could chin himself with one hand, do stunts on the bar, walk on his hands, climb a rope, do a somersault from the diving board, hang by his heels – everything I wanted to do, and couldn't.

He was captain of the baseball team, and I used to take his paper route for him so he could practice. In return, he let me shag balls, take care of the equipment, sit with the team during games. One afternoon when I went for the papers, the man in charge asked me if I wanted the route. I told him it was Vince's. He said it was mine, that Vince was through. When I saw Vince later, he said he didn't want it any more.

And that, curiously enough, seemed to be the pattern as we grew up. I was never as good as Vince at anything, nor as smart, and I took the things he didn't want. Of course, as the star athlete in school, he could have his pick of part-time jobs. He pulled me along with him, and that's how I got started with the company. He was offered a good opening upon graduation, but turned it down to play pro football, and it dropped into my lap.

With Kay, it was in a sense the same. She had eyes for nobody else but Vince. So he kept her from getting interested in anybody else, and when he broke her heart, I was there.

From this point on, Vince seemed to stand still. At the time when most of us were getting underway with our life's work, getting married, getting homes, and getting babies, Vince was chasing around with the young crowd, and flexing those muscles, keeping himself fit. Fit for what?

Vince didn't marry. Didn't have to, he'd tell you with a sly wink. He had a number of good openings, but let them slip away. What he required of a job was that it allow him time to keep those muscles in tone; he had to have his golf, he had to attend sporting events, he had to have his fishing and hunting trips. At twenty that's okay, but at thirty-six it was a bit pathetic. Vince just never had grown up. He was still a college boy at heart.

For the past year he'd been with the company as a commission salesman. (I got him the job, and, as a matter of fact, was his boss.) And during the year I'd thought that perhaps Vince was growing up, at last. He'd been chasing the dolls less, and dropping around oftener for an evening with us. He was wild about my kids, Tom and Carla. He thought Kay was just about the best wife a man ever had. He liked the house, he liked the furniture, he liked the gardens, he liked the dog. "Jim," he told me so often, "You've got it made." And occasionally I caught an unguarded look, as when we would be gathered at the TV and I'd glance sidewise and see Vince watching us instead of the program.

This camping trip was, of course, his idea. And from the beginning, on that first night when he practically killed me off on the hike with full pack from the end of the road to the cabin, it was obvious that Vince was showing me how much better a man he was than I. Well, OK, I'd never doubted it. Vince always was a better man, and he could still leave me far behind in the race of life, if he got down to it. He had a tremendous drive, when he wanted something. He had supreme confidence that what he wanted – what he really wanted – he could get.

Here in the mountains Vince had, of course, every advantage. He'd been camping out year after year. I hadn't tried it since Boy Scout days. We ate fish the first day. I managed to catch one while Vince got fourteen. Next day we went hunting. I followed a deer trail while Vince circled the ridge. I saw a deer, all right, but I was shaking too bad to pull the trigger. Vince got a nice buck. I helped him carry it in and hang it on a pole between trees behind the cabin.

Next morning there were tracks below. Vince said a wolverine had been after the meat, and the only way to catch those devils was with a dead fall. He set out with an axe, while I did KP.

We were supposed to go out after my buck in the afternoon, but Vince didn't come back for lunch. In the late afternoon I started out looking for him, following the deer trail, and I found him there pinned by a log, caught by his own deadfall.

I got him in and set the leg myself, splinting it with stakes from the cabin. I'd never done that before, but it had to be done, and, I thought, it would be temporary. But I spent all next day looking for the car, and most of the night trying to find my way back. We were there until he was able to walk. And when it began to snow, it meant we were there for the winter.

If I haven't said much in this journal about the footprints in the snow, it is not because I have accepted so incredible a phenomenon casually. I simply do not know what to write about them here.

A thing is. The evidence is there. There is no sane explanation. Why dwell upon the insane ones?

Vince has, by his attitude, caused me to restrict all mention of the footprints to the bare facts. Since the first ones, those of a woman's high-heeled slippers, he has talked endlessly on the subject. He has driven me out of the cabin by his incessant talk of the footprints.

Now, tonight, as I write this, he keeps telling me to be sure to put in about Tom and Carla's footprints playing fox and geese out behind the cabin. That's who it is, making the prints, my family – in spirit, of course. First it was Kay, waiting at the cabin door on the night of the first snowfall, wanting to help. She has been up once since, this time wearing overshoes. And the kids now were up playing fox and geese. Back home they're worried, Vince says. When they're asleep their spirits come up here. The man's footprints, he says, must belong to some dear friend. Or perhaps they are my own, joining my family in spirit.

Rubbish, of course.

"Are you putting in about Kay and the kids being here?" he has just asked, as I write this.

"Yes, of course."

But one thing I can't understand. Where is the dog?

NOVEMBER 2

To whom it may concern:

I, Vince Crawford, am making this entry in Jim's journal. He is a mad man. Utterly insane. I have been lying helpless in this cabin, dependent upon the whims of a psychopath. Footprints upon the snow – high-heeled slippers, prints of a woman wearing overshoes, a man's footprints, footprints of two children playing fox and geese – utter hallucination, the whole business, and, for one in my position, something to make the flesh creep.

I have been here. I have seen that snow. I have seen him point to an unbroken expanse and claim it contained mysterious footprints that started and ended nowhere. What could I do under the circumstance?

In the presence of insanity, me with a broken leg, all I could do was humor Jim.

"Yes, sure, Jim," I agreed. "I see the footprints." Yes, of course. I had to agree with his every delusion, including his belief that Kay and the kids, together with a man, are haunting the place in spirit form, invisible but leaving footprints.

His hallucination regarding the footprints of the man is the key to the whole thing. That man, to his insane mind, is myself. Jim went off the handle because of me. All his life, Jim has been playing second fiddle to me. All he ever got was what I didn't want – even his wife. Yes, he married Kay, but she loves me. She always has, and always will.

It is an appalling thing to discover that your best friend hates you. It was only upon reading this journal that I realized the friendship went only one way. His amazing rationalization regarding his "success" and my "failure" is a case in point. Jim a success? Well, through keeping his dumb nose to the grindstone Jim has advanced to a pretty good position with the company. He has a nice house (which he'll own in twenty-one years), a beautiful wife, lovely kids. But all this is on the surface. All Jim has are things he can take hold of. Jim is a grind. All he can do is work. He doesn't know how to enjoy life. He has no time to make friends. His entire life is centered around home and family, and he knows it has no foundation. He has Kay's body, but not her love. If she leaves him, she'll take the kids with her. Then what's he got?

Success?

Like all clods, Jim has been envious of a man who could enjoy life. I have time for play. I have time for love. I don't have to cling to a job. I can find work anywhere. I don't have to get married, because I can find girls anywhere. The clods wish they could do the same. Because they can't, they cover their envy by denouncing me. And, because they fear me, they hate me. Jim does, as I have found out.

Of late, I have been thinking of getting married and settling down. Not because I have to, but because I want to. A man's tastes change. Maybe it would be more fun chasing the dollar than chasing dolls. Maybe it would be worthwhile having what they call success, if the right woman shared it with you.

The woman, of course, would be Kay.

I have had many women, but she is the only one I would want for my wife. I could take her away from Jim any time I said the word. I have hesitated only because I felt sorry for him. She's the only girl he's ever had in his life. I didn't want to do it to him. I was reluctant because of friendship. A strange word, now that he has tried to kill me.

I should have realized, when Jim said he'd like to go on a camping trip with me, that something was up. Jim is strictly a motel man when he travels. He hasn't been camping since he was a Boy Scout.

He's a clumsy clown, an awkward oaf. But cunning. The day I got my buck, he was building a deadfall on the deer trail. It was cleverly constructed, so that animals would pass under it, while a man, pushing away the branch that was its trigger, would be crushed. Thank God I have good reflexes. My sudden leap saved me from being killed, although I did get a broken leg. Lying there, thinking back, I saw it all plainly, how his resentment over being inferior had festered, and his fear that I would take Kay from him had become an insane hatred.

The next day Jim left me helpless in the cabin, and deserted me. He just left me to die, while he went for "help." The help never would have arrived, because Jim would have put on his tenderfoot act, and wouldn't have been able to find the road, let alone the cabin. All that saved my life was the fact that Jim was such a greenhorn. He couldn't find the car. He had to let me live, to take him out of the mountains.

I think his mind snapped under the enormity of his act. But I didn't realize he was crazy until he began claiming there were footprints of his family upon the unbroken surface of the snow.

It has stormed for several days. Jim thought he heard a plane overhead as the storm was brewing up, and this morning when it broke cold and clear, with a foot of new snow, he was out early, tramping the word "HELP" in the snow. Then about an hour ago I heard the plane. It circled overhead and dropped a bundle in a red parachute.

Now as I write I can see the bundle with the parachute beside it, lying where it fell. But I can't see Jim. He hasn't gone to the bundle. He has left it lying there, while he does more important things before help arrives. What he is doing, I don't know, for my view is restricted to the tiny window and what I can see from it. But whatever it is, I know its purpose. Now he needs me no longer. He came up here with the intent to murder me. He will concoct some other "accident" to befall me before we are rescued.

That's why I am writing in this journal. As I write, my cocked rifle is beside me on the bunk. When help arrives, only one of us will be alive.

LATER, SAME DATE

This is Jim Roundy again; I began this journal, and this entry will finish it.

From the evidence herein, I am insane, with hallucinations of footprints upon the unbroken snow. If I claim that Vince brought me here to kill me, that he got caught in his own deadfall he was preparing on the deer trail for me, it is merely his word against mine.

The burden of proof is upon me.

When the plane came over, I knew a rescue would follow, so I kept out of sight of the cabin window. I didn't want to be shot. I made my way carefully to the cabin from the blind side, and began whittling upon the crutch Vince had made. I had taken his crutch out with me this morning, for the purpose. His whittling had not been idle. Now, as I crouched outside in the snow, carefully slicing thin shavings of the oak, neither was mine.

When I heard the engine of the approaching helicopter, I was ready, with the crutch reduced to a pile of dry shavings sitting against the cabin shakes. I touched a match to it. The shavings were like tinder, the old shakes caught fire.

As the helicopter hovered overhead and came down in the snow before the cabin, the fire spread along the wall and engulfed the front porch. I knew Vince couldn't get out the little rear window.

The pilot climbed out of the helicopter.

"Hey, is anybody in there?"

In answer to his question, the door banged open. Then Vince came running out. He came running not on his feet, but on his hands, his broken leg safely in the air. And to protect his hands from the fire he held a little block in each of them.

What happened to the various blocks of wood he had carved into the shape of human footprints, I don't know, but as he ran out of the cabin on his hands, the blocks he held left, upon the fallen snow, footprints – of a dog.

Real Life Impossibility: United States
The Murder of Isidor Fink

On March 9, 1929, Patrolman Albert Kattenborn was called to investigate unusual noises reported coming from the laundry business of Isidor Fink, a Polish immigrant working at 4 East 132nd Street in New York City.

Kattenborn tried to look into the laundry from outside, but found that the two windows were both painted over in grey. They also had iron bars set into the sills. The laundry had two doors, both locked securely from the inside. So Kattenborn hoisted a young boy up to the transom over the front door and had him break the transom window. The boy then climbed inside and opened the lock from the inside. The lock was one of the more secure available.

Fink's body was found approximately 30 feet from the front door with three bullet wounds: two in the chest and one in the wrist. There was no gun found in the laundry. The back door, which separated the laundry from the first-floor apartment of a Mrs. Locklan Smith, was locked, bolted, and nailed up.

Money was found in the room, so robbery was ruled out as a motive, and no murderer was ever charged. The police searched for a hidden way into the laundry, but came up empty.

Ben Hecht ("The Mystery of the Fabulous Laundryman," 1932) and William March ("The Bird House," 1954) both proposed solutions to the mystery in their short stories, but the police never came up with one. The case is still unsolved.

Japan
The Lure of the Green Door
Rintarō Norizuki

Norizuki-san is the president of the Honkaku Mystery Writers Club of Japan, the counterpart to the U.K.'s Detection Club.

He made his debut in 1988 with the novel *Mippei Kyoshitsu* (*The Locked Classroom*; not available in English) and has written eight novels featuring his namesake Rintaro Norizuki. He received the 2005 Honkaku Mystery Award (category: fiction) for his novel *Namakubi ni Kiite Miro* (*The Gorgon's Look*; not available in English).

"The Lure of the Green Door' (1991) was published in *EQMM* in November 2014, and was the second of his stories to have been published in English. "An Urban Legend Puzzle" (2001; published in *Ellery Queen's Mystery Magazine* in January 2004) was the first, and it was also later included in the anthologies *Passport to Crime* (2007) and *The Mammoth Book of International Crime* (2009).

"The Lure of the Green Door" is an outstanding bibliophile's mystery with a brand-new locked-room solution.

The Lure of the Green Door

1

“Do you have plans for tomorrow?” Sawada Honami asked from the other side of the counter of the reference corner.

“I have a meeting with an editor at *Shōsetsu Nova*. Probably to ask me to write a short story.”

“Ah, too bad. Just when I wanted to ask you out on a date.”

Those were the words that came out of her mouth, but she didn’t look particularly disappointed. She looked at the other side of the counter with a serious face. The location: the second floor of the municipal library. Honami was the librarian of the public reading room.

Norizuki Rintarō did his utmost to pretend he was not interested.

“Hmm. I can cancel it, that is, if you really want me to go.”

Honami chuckled.

“That is a coincidence. I was just thinking of inviting you – if the great author Norizuki really wanted to go.”

The great author Norizuki? Those words hit him hard. He was totally being toyed with. It is at a time like this that a man has to maintain his dauntless attitude – “I am not that far gone that I will do anything you say, you know.”

Rintarō swallowed the words “I really want to go,” which almost came out of his mouth. Luckily, a man, probably a university student, came to the counter at that moment and returned some back issues of magazines that were available for viewing inside the library. Honami checked the volume numbers, stood up, and went down to the archives. When she came back, Honami said: “I wear contact lenses in my free time.”

Rintarō glared at Honami. “That’s not fair.”

“Oh, I was just talking to myself.”

Ostentatiously, she pushed the frame of her glasses up. A hopeless fight, Rintarō thought.

Honami rested her elbows on the counter and pulled the telephone towards her.

“What’s the telephone number of the editor’s department at *Shōsetsu Nova*?” She wasn’t going to take no for an answer. In his mind, Rintarō clicked his tongue and then told her the number. When the line was connected, she started to speak politely like she was somebody else.

"Hello, am I speaking with the editor's department at *Shōsetsu Nova*? I am Norizuki Rintarō's secretary, Sawada. Regarding the appointment for tomorrow, I am sorry we have to cancel because some urgent business has arisen. Business? Well, don't tell this to anyone, but an unprecedented locked-room murder has occurred and Mr. Norizuki's assistance is requested...."

Rintarō hurried to steal the receiver from Honami.

"This is Norizuki speaking. That wasn't true just now. There is no unprecedented locked-room murder, so please do not worry. But I can't meet you tomorrow. Something urgent. Yes, urgent. No, it is not to rest up from playing around. I really have to attend to this – no, I am not refusing your request for a manuscript. I will write, I will write – with pleasure. *Shōsetsu Nova* is a wonderful magazine. Yes, yes. What? An impossible crime? An unprecedented locked-room murder? Ha ha, no, no problem. Leave it up to me. Page count and the deadline...? Understood. Yes, I know. What? A beautiful secretary? No, that is a misunderstanding. Just a little joke. Please don't come up with strange rumours...."

Emphasizing that, he put down the phone. Honami was laughing as if she had nothing to do with it.

"Do you always talk with your editors in such a flattering tone?"

"You're the one to talk. I was pretty desperate with you having said those weird things. 'An unprecedented locked-room murder' – please don't use those words again so lightly. Because of that, I am now saddled with a difficult assignment."

"But a really urgent business, that has to be something of that caliber, right."

Rintarō sighed. He had given up without even noticing. But he already knew this would happen in the end.

"I know, I know. Life, the universe, and everything, you are always completely and a priori right. I am in love with even just the H of Honami."

"If you had just said that right away."

As Rintarō shrugged his shoulders rather exaggeratedly, his thoughts went to the request he had just accepted from *Shōsetsu Nova*. An unprecedented locked-room murder? That may sound simple, but... If this is what happens just to get one date with her, then I'll be a master of the impossible crime by the time I finally get the girl.

Maybe not too bad a deal.

The next day, Rintarō headed joyously to the place they were going to meet. Honami was already there. He called out to her, but she reacted furiously.

"I had a look at *Shōsetsu Nova*, but it's a magazine with nude gravure shots of adult video actresses on the cover! If you write for such a magazine, then your female readers will turn away from you, you know. Of course, assuming you have female readers."

"That's not a nude gravure," Rintarō said assuredly.

"Lies. If that's not a nude, what is it?"

"A calendar."

Honami puffed her cheeks.

"You have an unbelievable male chauvinistic heart. With such ideas, I wouldn't be surprised if you'll end up as a sacrifice for feminist fighters."

Let's write this down for later. This is like a conversation of a novel by Robert B. Parker. Rintarō then turned to his counterattack.

"Allow me to say something as someone with an unbelievable male chauvinistic heart. You lied to me. You said you wear contact lenses in your free time, didn't you?"

"That's not a lie," Honami said, calm and collected.

"Too bad. Today's work."

"Work…?"

Now that she mentioned it, her wear was rather neat and not meant for a day of fun.

"To keep it short, there was a proposal to donate a private collection to our library some time ago, but some trouble arose afterwards and we're having difficulties with the other party now. And per orders of the library director, I have been dealt the role of doing the negotiations. I finally got an appointment to negotiate directly with the other party and we are going to visit the home of the books' owner right now. As overtime work, of course. So I don't deserve being called a liar. But the appointment is for two o'clock at Kichijōji, so we have to leave now. I'll tell you the details on the way. You did bring your car, right?"

In short, he was to be her driver. No, maybe even less than that. Who is going to pay his overwork time?

Murmuring, Rintarō grabbed the steering wheel. Honami showed some whimsical ardor and started to read the titles of the music tapes on the passenger's seat.

"These are all old songs. Don't you have newer tapes?" she asked.

Rintarō finally chuckled and switched on the player with "Chelsea Girl" and "Like a Day Dream." When the intro to "Chelsea Girl" came out the car speakers, Honami's eyes went wide open.

"What's this?"

"The new sound from Oxford."

"This isn't a demo tape?"

"A star of hope for '90s rock."

With powerful guitar-play that relied on youth as their background music, they went north on the Kanpachidōri drive. And life is what you make of it. Is having a drive with a girl, even if only as a driver, not more fun than a meeting with a magazine editor? Even Murakami Ryū said that. Or did he?

Honami stuck her elbows out.

"Can I turn down the volume? I still have to tell you the details."

"Ah, that's right. Sure, go ahead."

Honami mercilessly switched the sound off. She looked as if this was all she could bear.

"To be honest, the next one is one of Ride's hit songs," Rintarō said to save Ride's honor. "Oh," Honami said, uninterested.

"The person who said he wanted to donate his books is called Sugata Kuniaki – the youngest son of a wealthy family. He's like a fantasy literature maniac turned adult. He had been collecting rare and valuable books, mostly related to occultism and mysticism, since he was young. After university he worked at a bank for a while, but his interest only developed further – he even participated in a fanzine – and he suddenly resigned his job. He was from a wealthy family anyway and probably not very suited for business. Ever since, he has been working as the president of his own fanzine, translating some minor works under the name Kurouri Arashita, and living his life surrounded by the books he loves.

"Kurouri Arashita. A play on Aleister Crowley, known as the greatest ceremonial magician of this century."

"Our library director became acquaintances with Mr. Sugata at some kind of party. Our director is a well-known person at the weirdest places. Thinking Mr. Sugata was an interesting person, we invited him several times for a lecture for one of our library's 'foreign literature seminar'-esque projects. Mr. Sugata was very happy to have been recognized for his expertise it seems and promised to donate his complete collection to us if he were to pass away. He didn't just say it, he really made a provision for us in his will.

Rintarō squinted.

"So that Mr. Sugata died recently?"

Honami nodded mysteriously.

"At the end of last year, he was found hanging in the study of his house."

"So, suicide?"

"Yes. I heard this later, but it seemed like he had manic-depressive tendencies and he had been going to the hospital and taking medicine for that. It may be one of the reasons for him to have quit his job at the bank. He didn't leave any note, but it was probably an impulsive suicide, as he suffered from life."

"That's really sad to hear."

"He didn't have any children, and his wife was his only family. His widow, however, is kind of a suspicious woman and does not agree to giving us the books under all sorts of pretexts. Setting aside the legality of the will and all, we as the library can't just ignore the wife and forcibly take the books, because they were gifts to us from a deceased person out of his good will. We are prepared to listen to what she has to say, but that woman is so vague and just running away from the negotiations, so we can't even talk the matter out."

"For someone all keen on feminism, the way you said 'that woman' sounds rather harsh."

"Don't jump on everything I say."

"Yeah, yeah. And, why doesn't she want to give up the books?"

"We're having troubles, because we don't even know why. Maybe some private collector or bookseller has been trying to buy the books, offering a small fortune. Because it is supposed to be a collection any fan would desire. If that is right, then the wife should just say so to us, then we'll figure something out together, but we really don't know what she is thinking, and even the director is having difficulties with her. And that's why I'll be acting as a proxy today to find out what her real intentions are."

"I see."

Rintarō's interests were aroused. It wasn't just what Honami said, but there seemed something fishy about all this. Tapping his fingers on the steering wheel, he asked: "Was it really a suicide? Was there no doubts of homicide at all?" Honami moved her fingers like a metronome and clicked her tongue.

"That was a rather predictable question."

"My bad, my bad. Comes with the occupation."

"Well, then I'll answer in a predictable way. When the body was discovered, the door was bolted from the inside and they had to break down the door to open it from the hallway. Simply said, the room where Mr. Sugata was hanged was really a locked room and nobody could have entered or left the room."

Rintarō's eyes lit up.

"So, what you said yesterday on the phone, that wasn't just gibberish."

"Precisely. But too bad, I don't think there is a novel-like ending to this case. Locked-room murders only exist in fiction."

Rintarō vehemently shook his head.

"No, no, it's too early to say that. Most importantly, it is very strange for someone who pretended to be the magician Crowley to commit suicide."

"Maybe so."

"It simply is so."

"But isn't that a rather imprudent thing to say?"

"That is a different matter."

Honami looked doubtful and muttered while thinking: "I don't think it was murder, but now that you mention it, there was a strange episode surrounding Mr. Sugata's suicide."

"What?"

"Do you know 'The Door in the Wall'?"

Honami suddenly asked this strange question.

"Yeah, a story by Wells with a green door that leads to a different world. Why?"

"The green door, it's in Mr. Sugata's study."

2

"The Door in the Wall" is a fantasy story by English sci-fi writer H.G. Wells, famous for works like *The Time Machine* and *The War of the Worlds*. The story's protagonist is the young and successful politician Wallace. One night, he confesses the following story to the narrator, with whom he had been friends since their student years.

When he was five, Wallace was playing outside on his own, and he went through a green door in a white wall. What he found on the other side was a different world, a magical country. Marble flowers, frolicking panthers, a beautiful woman, a sublime palace – he spent his time playing wonderful games there. Finally a woman with a faraway look showed him a mysterious book describing his life up until then in detail. As he was reading this book with his own memories, he returned to the city of London, to gray everyday life. When he was nine, as he was playing, he came across the green door again. But because he had told his secret to his friends, the door disappeared. The third time he saw the door was when he was seventeen. He saw the door several times after that, but he never took a look inside. Having found success in his life, he had lost his yearning for the world on the other side of the door.

After that, he continued his life working hard and he didn't see the door again. But lately, as he was nearing his fortieth birthday and staring to feel disillusioned with his life, the door had started to appear again. Forgetting vulgar things like fame and economic interests, he walked around the town impatiently searching for the door.

The narrator doesn't believe his story. But some time later, he finds a news article reporting the death of Wallace. He had fallen to his death in a fenced-off pit at a construction site. One of the workers had forgotten to lock up the door to the pit.

Had Wallace seen some kind of hallucination? At the end, the narrator asks the reader the following question. Did the door betray him? We think that this world is fair and normal. The pit was fenced off. From our point of view, Wallace went from a safe world to the darkness, to danger, to death. But did he think so too?

"Mr. Sugata loved that story," Honami said.

"He probably identified himself with the protagonist, leaving the real world to enter a fantasy world. He loved the story that much that he made his own green door in his study."

Rintarō looked doubtful.

"How? Did he ask the devil to make him a magic door?"

"Of course not. He might have been a specialist on the occult, but of course even he couldn't make a door to a different world. Mr. Sugata's house is an old Western mansion, and there were originally two oak doors in his study, but the hinges of one door were rusted or something like that and wouldn't move at all. And so Mr. Sugata painted that door green. That was his green door. There was another door to enter and leave the room, so he had no troubles there and they say the door hadn't been opened for ten years already. But it seems that in the end, the door understood that its master had died."

"So that's it. I was thinking about some kind of dimensional gap or supernatural phenomena."

"Too bad. Anyway, when he was still alive, it seems Mr. Sugata had said to his friends that 'when I die, the green door will open again.'"

"And that locked door really opened?"

As if to dodge the question, Honami shrugged her shoulders.

"It didn't really open, so he was wrong. The door that was busted open when they found the body was the other door, and if the green door could have been opened, then the study wouldn't have been a locked room. The police have examined it and they concluded that it was suicide, so it is probably so."

"I see."

Generally, occult maniacs love things like prophecies and looking into the future, but they are never right. This prophecy of Sugata Kuniaki was one of those examples too. Like Honami said, it was nothing more than a strange episode.

"But we may have to take a look at his study and the green door just to be sure. Can you play along with me in front of the wife?"

"Sure. But I really don't think it's a locked-room murder. It's not my fault if you end up making a fool of yourself."

"Warning duly noted."

A collection of occult books and a locked door with a story. It smelled slightly of crime, but he couldn't be sure. There was a big chance it was just nothing, but he also had to consider his own dignity in front of Honami. A great detective capable of solving the impossible, or just a driver. Go for broke.

The mansion stood north of Kichijōji Station, in the middle of a residential area near the border with Suginami Ward. "Western mansion" sounded fancy, but it was a decrepit wooden building with two floors, looking like one of those private hospitals.

"I had heard the rumors, but this is the first time I've seen it. Like it has trouble just keeping upright."

"As the dwelling of an occultism specialist, it seems ideal though."

"If this was my home, I would faint. Hello, is there someone home?" Honami said and the door slowly slid open, making a sound like a frog croaking. There stood a woman dressed in dark indigo Japanese traditional clothing.

"Are you from the library?" she asked.

Honami nodded.

"We talked over the telephone the other day. I'm the librarian Sawada."

"Ah, yes, Miss Sawada. I'm Sugita's wife."

The infamous widow. She was thirty-seven, thirty-eight, and good looking. Long-slitted eyes, a slender nose, and shining lips. The white skin of her neck had something erotic to it.

"And your companion…?"

Her captivating look was turned to Rintarō and his heart started to pound fast.

"My name is Norizuki."

"You don't look like someone from the library. Are you a lawyer or something like that?"

"No, I am just an innocent bystander. Ever since I went to Mr. Sugita's seminar last year, I have been a devotee of him and I really wanted to visit his home. I really begged Miss Sawada here to allow me to come today. If it is no trouble, I would like to see his study. It would make me so happy."

It was just a lie he made up together with Honami, but the widow didn't seem to doubt it.

"I see. No, it's no trouble at all. Please, come inside."

The two were guided to the guest room. When the widow left to prepare some tea, Honami punched him on the shoulder as if she had been holding it in for a long time.

"That was really pathetic. Looking at that woman with that lecherous look!"

"I didn't!"

"I know, I know. All men are weak to that kind of physically beautiful woman."

"Is this what they commonly call 'jealousy'?"

"Too bad. It was just a warning before you fall flat on your face."

"I now understand why the director sent you to do the negotiations with the widow."

Then the topic of this conversation came back into the room, so the two stopped talking. As she was lining up some fancy porcelain teaware on the table, the widow said: "Sorry you had to come all this way. I have a rather weak body and going outside tires me greatly, making me very sleepy."

"Have you been alone since your husband's death?" Rintarō asked.

The widow sat down on the seat opposite to him and said: "A dispatch housekeeper comes here every other day, but I've been alone for the rest. For a widow, this house is too big. If only we had children..."

Honami suddenly coughed, interrupting her silly complaints.

"Mrs. Sugata." It was a sudden, harsh tone.

"This is rather abrupt, but let's begin our business. The reason we came today is naturally to talk over your husband's donation. I will ask you bluntly, why are you refusing to hand over the books?"

"Refusing is such a harsh word...."

"Until now we have made several attempts, but you are just giving us vague replies, so this is the only conclusion we can make. We are not criticizing you, but we would like to know why. If something has come up, please tell us. If you have a good reason, we will also be reasonable about that."

The widow hesitated for a while, but after a short while, as if to show she had made up her mind, sat upright and placed her hands on her knees. She slowly opened her mouth: "I apologize for causing you trouble. I thought that if I would tell you, you wouldn't believe me anyway, so I kept silent about it, but actually, he appeared...."

"He?"

"My husband..."

The two looked at each other, surprised.

Honami asked carefully: "Do you mean...your husband's ghost?"

"Yes," the widow nodded as she averted her eyes, "it was a night about two days after the seven-day period of mourning. In the middle of the night it felt like my hairs stood up and when I opened my eyes, my husband was sitting near my pillow. I think they call it sleep paralysis, but I couldn't move my body nor say anything. And when I looked into his eyes, he said: 'Hey, Yoshiko (that's my name), when I think about how my books are going to be given away, I just can't find spiritual rest. 'Cause those books I collected, they are my life, you know. It would be more fitting if they were to stay here and rot away together with the house. I was too hasty when I wrote that will. I hadn't thought it through. I'm sorry, but I want you to protect my books and hand them to nobody while you are still here. This is the only regret of my life.' He asked me the same thing over and over again and when the sun came up, he simply disappeared. As proof that it wasn't just a dream, I found, the next morning when I opened my eyes, my husband's bookplate placed near my pillow. There was no sign of that the evening before, of course. That's when I understood that my husband's ghost really did come. I won't repeat it all, but he came again several times after that, saying the same thing. I don't think you will believe me, but I made up my mind at that time. So the reason I have been so reluctant in giving up the books is because I was following my late husband's wishes. The reason I have kept quiet about this until now is because I thought that even if I told you this honestly, you wouldn't believe it. Even while I am telling you this, I understand that this is not a convincing story. Having come to this, I know that this is rather selfish, but could you, following my husband's ghost's wishes, maybe forget the whole donation?"

Having finished her story, the widow looked to Honami with determination. It was a desperate attempt, but she had really tried her best on the story. Honami looked bewildered, not sure how to react. If she just called her a liar, it would lead to an endless discussion. It didn't seem like the widow would listen to reason. Honami would have trouble convincing her. Whatever it would be, Rintarō had no intention of being witness to a fruitless argument.

"As an outsider, I think it would be better for me to leave. Could I maybe take a look at Mr. Sugata's books?"

"Yes, go ahead."

The widow surprisingly easily allowed Rintarō to go.

"The library is on the second floor. Go up the stairs and then the door straight ahead. It's not locked, so feel free to look around."

"Mr. Sugata's ghost does not haunt the place?" Rintarō said jokingly, but the widow said calmly: "It's all right if you are just looking."

"Well then, as you are so kind..."

As Rintarō stood up, he felt Honami's eyes piercing him. As if looking at a soldier fleeing from the front lines. He answered her look with a wink.

This is a joint operation, you understand. Your mission is to keep the widow here while I am investigating the study. I am counting on you.

He intended to communicate that, but he wasn't sure whether she understood it. He had some trouble shutting the badly fitted door, but Rintarō finally fled out of the room.

When he went up the turning stairs, every step made a squeaking sound. It was like the house had grown old and become senile. If he set one or two ghosts free in such a house, he doubted they would complain to him. He counted the steps of the stairway. Precisely thirteen. Someone had been attentive while designing the house.

The library ran from the eastern wing to the middle of the house, taking about one third of the surface of the second floor. Opening the door, he was met with the particular damp, stuffy smell of old books. This wasn't just a library, this was an archive. Bookcases that could be moved along rails were lined up neatly and were all stuffed with books. Even a rough estimate wouldn't be a figure lower than 8,000 books.

Struck with awe, Rintarō stared at the precious collection Sugata Kuniaki had left behind. Before he knew it, he had let out a deep sigh. This wasn't something you could find anywhere. Rintarō fought for a while with the temptation, and having killed the bookworm inside him, he returned to his duty as a detective and started his businesslike and illiterate investigation.

3

When he went down to the guest room, the women had stopped talking and were drinking their tea. It was like a short rest time after a fierce fight, but the tense atmosphere was almost painfully clear.

"That was long," Honami said as if criticizing his long absence. If he wasn't careful, she might vent all her anger on him. Don't do anything to anger the gods. Rintarō pretended to have been distracted by all the books on the second floor and said: "Very impressive, Mrs. Sugata, that was like a mountain of treasures. It feels like I had to be pulled away before I was able to leave the room. Even in one hour, I still hadn't seen everything. Books that are too important to bury away."

"It was my husband's pride," the widow said carefully.

"That's why it would be better if more people could – " Honami said, but Rintarō interrupted her.

"Especially Mishima's *Evil Spirit* was surprising. I had heard the rumors, but I had never thought it would actually exist."

Honami's look became serious at once.

"Mishima's *Evil Spirit*? What do you mean?"

"A detective novel Mishima Yukio wrote somewhere in Shōwa 40 (1965), under the pen name Hirai Koutarō. A continuation of the half-finished story of Edogawa Rampo. According to the real mystery maniacs, it is rumored to be the ultimate anti-mystery novel, but because nobody has ever seen the real thing, people have doubts whether it really exists. There is a privately published version of *Evil Spirit* here."

Honami was not sure whether to believe him, and simply said: "That seems amazing."

"It is amazing! Right, Mrs. Sugata?"

He turned to the silent widow, but she was looking at him as if he was speaking Chinese. Rintarō dropped the subject and went on: "By the way, Mrs. Sugata, I want to ask you another thing. They say that in your husband's study, there is a door painted green. And that Mr. Sugata had said before he died that 'when I die, the green door will open again.' That is really interesting. For future reference, I would like to take a look at the real thing."

For a moment, the widow looked at him very suspiciously. She quickly hid the look and said nonchalantly: "Of course. But that was a form of amusement for my husband, so you will probably just be disappointed when you see it. Miss Sawada, would you also like to take a look?"

"Yes, please. For future reference," Honami said, smiling like a Buddha.

The late Mr. Sugata's study was in the corner of the east wing of the first floor. It was located precisely under the library on the second floor that Rintarō had just investigated. The widow pushed open the old oak door. Rintarō noticed that the hinges on the door were new. Even though it was noon, the room was dark and the air was stuffy. Even after the widow had switched on the lights, it seemed like there was more shadow than light, making Rintarō think of a cave.

"Sorry for the mess. After my husband died, I didn't feel like cleaning up the room, and it has been like this for three months."

It was indeed messy. There was a sturdy writing desk and a space heater under the lights, and surrounding that a jumble of piled books and vinyl records. The records were of baroque and religious music. On a stained couch, the impression of a man was still visible. It told Rintarō the custom of the former owner of this room. The north and south walls weren't visible, blocked by slanting bookshelves. The placing of the books was random and things like magazines and dictionaries stuck out. It looked like everything of importance was just placed where it could be reached. It felt like the workroom of a writer and was the complete opposite of the neat comprehensiveness of the second-floor library.

Rintarō looked at the ceiling. The library on the second floor was a heaven made of books, while the study on the first floor was like a symbol of the imperfect life of man. That was probably an allegory thought up by the occultist.

"There is a window to lighten up the place at the back, but my husband nailed it shut and placed a bookcase in front of it, so no light enters the room. He said dark was better," the widow explained. Honami found a bronze candleholder beneath a pile of books.

"There are traces of wax here. Did he really use this?"

"Yes. He read by the light of a candle. I told him countless times to stop it, as I was afraid of fire, but even until recently the room occasionally smelled of candles. That man was really strange at times."

Rintarō went to the green door. There was no bookcase only at the back of the room, at the eastern wall. Turning back, he saw that it was right across the door leading into the doorway. He turned his gaze back to the green door. It might have been brilliant green when it was first painted. But now the color had faded and had turned moss green. Maybe that is why the door didn't match his own image that he made after hearing the story. If the protagonist of Wells's story had seen this door, he would have been disappointed. Even the props at a high school play would have looked better.

"Can I touch it?" he asked the widow. No problem, she said, and Rintarō grabbed the doorknob. The nob seemed a bit rusty, but would turn if you added a little power. He grabbed it strongly and pulled the door.

It didn't move.

"Doesn't it open outward?" Honami said from behind his back. Rintarō nodded and pushed this time. But it didn't move an inch.

When he rammed his shoulders against the door with all his might, he fell back.

Honami moved forward.

"And?"

"It is made to open outward. But it doesn't budge at all."

"I'll help."

With the help of Honami, he tried again, but even with the weight of two persons, nothing changed. Because the bookcases were almost falling because of the shock of their body slam, they had to stop their attempts to force open the door.

"It won't open no matter what," the widow said, seemingly trying to hide her smile.

"When my husband committed suicide, the police said they had to examine the room and five police officers pushed and pulled the door and made a big fuss about it, but the door didn't move at all. If we force it open, the whole mansion might collapse. You often see that in those old comedy movies, right?"

"I see."

Rintarō wiped off the sweat on his forehead.

"But why doesn't it open? Has it been like this since this house was built?"

The widow slanted her head.

"Maybe. I don't know about the past, but it was already like this when we married. Maybe my husband nailed the door shut in a way that is not visible. My husband had a childish side...."

"But what about your husband's prophecy? Didn't anything change about the door after his suicide?"

The widow shook her head.

"Nothing at all. I don't think my husband said that seriously. He probably said it as a wish of some sort."

Rintarō turned back to look at the green door.

"What's on the other side of the door?"

"The garden. There is a little porch, so it was designed so you could leave the room and go into the garden directly. But because the door won't open, it's quite useless."

"Is this door the same color on the other side?"

"No, the other side is still in its original color."

Rintarō rubbed his forehead again and turned away from the green door and went to the writing desk. And then he asked the widow with a serious tone: "Your husband died in this study, right?"

"Yes. He had tied his belt to the hanging light here and hanged himself from it."

"I heard that when he was found, the door was bolted from the inside."

"Yes."

"Could you tell me more about it?"

"You are asking me police-like questions," she said a bit hesitantly. "It was at the end of last year, on the twenty-second. My husband had always been a late riser, but he didn't wake up even in the afternoon, so I went to check up on him. He would often be up all night and fall asleep in the study. But the door was bolted, so I couldn't get inside. I called out for him several times, but he didn't react, so I started to worry. The housekeeper wasn't in that day and I wasn't able to break down the door on my own, so I quickly called for an ambulance through the emergency number."

"An ambulance?"

"Yes. I wouldn't call it a woman's intuition, but I had a bad feeling about it. My husband had been diagnosed as manic-depressive and he attempted to commit suicide before. He even made a will, even though he was still so young. I thought of the worst possible scenario. And if it turned out to be nothing, then it would just be a funny story for later. But my bad feeling was correct...."

The widow started to cry and stopped her words. Too bad it looked like she was acting. Rintarō continued his questions.

"So it was the ambulance crew that forced the door open?"

"Yes. I was just looking confused at them from behind, but because the door's bolt was too strong, they had to break the hinges. When they opened the door, I saw the bare feet of my husband hanging in the air. I became unwell and left the place immediately."

Rintarō placed his fingers on his jaw. If what the widow said is correct, then she wouldn't have any opportunities to destroy any evidence after the discovery of the victim. This was a difficult problem.

"To come back to the topic of the prophecy, did your husband say literally, 'the green door will open'?"

"What do you mean?"

"He didn't say, for example, the green back door?"

The widow looked troubled.

"No, he didn't say that. But what if he had said the green back door?"

"It was just a thought I had." Rintarō started his explanation: "Colloquially, they call American dollar bills greenbacks there. Because dollar bills are green. And that door is at the back of the house, right? So it's a back door. American dollars, greenbacks. And Mr. Sugata was so proficient in English that he could work as a translator. The green door might have been a play on the green dollar. So Mr. Sugata might have hidden money there and intended to leave it to you. Couldn't his prophecy be a message to lead you there?"

The widow laughed at Rintarō's ideas.

"I don't think he has hidden some treasure. Even if he had such money, he would have used it for his books. Your idea is interesting, but not realistic at all."

"Indeed. Who would even say green back door?"

Even Honami protested against the idea. Rintarō grabbed his head and said: "That's why I said that it was just a thought...." At that moment, the standing clock in the hall rang four o'clock. Time for the detective who forced himself inside to leave.

"Ah, is it this late already? I have to leave. You have been very kind."

"Wait, but I still have business – " Honami started, but Rintarō interrupted her.

"But you have time for a next meeting, right? We have to hurry, or else we won't make it. So Mrs. Sugata, let's leave it at this for today."

"Well, come back anytime."

Rintarō said his goodbyes and pulled away the furious Honami with him, rushing out of the Sugata mansion.

"Why did we have to leave so suddenly?" Honami asked after they entered the car. "We didn't make an appointment for a next meeting. We came to get a clear answer from Mrs. Sugata, but we haven't got anything. How do I explain this to the director?"

"I'll explain to him. With that ghost story, any attempt at negotiation would have been useless. She has no intention of handing over the books at all."

"But I wanted to hear the reason for that at least."

"She won't tell you."

Honami tilted her head. As Rintarō started the car, she sighed heavily.

"Maybe you're right. Even when you were away, we didn't go anywhere with our discussion. I had the feeling it was all over when she came up with that ghost story. Who is going to believe such a story!? It's clear that it was just a way to buy time. There's probably someone who wants to buy the books."

"No, I don't think so," Rintarō said calmly.

"Why?"

"If there was a buyer, someone would have gone over the books after Mr. Sugata's death in order to make an estimate of the value. But as far as I could see, there were no signs of anybody having entered the library for a while now. Judging from the amount of dust accumulated, I was the first to have entered there after the case.

"You were kinda taking your time there," Honami said, as if she just remembered.

"Yes. So I think it's safe to say there is no other buyer. There is also the possibility that, well, it has to do with what we just discussed in the study, but somewhere among the books there might be something important that the wife doesn't want to lose, but she doesn't know where it is exactly, so she can't find it. So, she might just be refusing to hand over the books to buy herself some time. But this seems a bit improbable, because she wouldn't have let me, someone she had never seen before, go into the library alone, with the risk of me running away with a treasure."

"That's true."

"Furthermore, looking at how we left just now, I could have easily stolen one or two rare books and she wouldn't have noticed anything. In other words, she has no interest in the value of the books themselves. Not only that, but I don't think she has any knowledge of her husband's collection at all."

"What do you mean?"

"I talked about Mishima Yukio right? That was just a made-up story."

Honami looked angrily at Rintarō and said: "I thought it was! I hadn't heard anything about that at all. But that was a rather overblown lie, don't you think?"

"That was just the beauty of it. I wanted to see how she would react. I'm betting she doesn't know anything about Mishima and Rampo. Such a person wouldn't be interested in the collection at all. She has to have some sort of dark reason for not handing over the books."

Honami nodded strongly.

"So, that greenback story just now was also to see how she would react?"

"It was more like a smokescreen to disguise my real intentions. I had been asking her all kinds of things about when her husband died. That's also why we had to leave so fast. It would be bad if she started to have doubts about us now."

"What do mean 'doubts'?"

"I am sure she has killed her husband and made it seem like suicide. The reason she doesn't want to hand over the books is probably because they are somehow connected to her crime," Rintarō said with no pretense at all. Rather than surprised, Honami looked indecisive.

"Her motive for killing Mr. Sugata?"

"That's what we have to investigate now."

"But the room was a perfectly locked room. Even if she was a murderer, how did she escape from a locked room after the crime? It's for certain that the green door doesn't open, and I don't think she could have used some trick on the bolt as the emergency crew broke the hinges open."

"No, I think calling the emergency number was actually done on purpose. She called an ambulance to have a third party witness to the locked room. Becoming unwell and not entering the study was also an act to show that she had no chance to destroy any evidence. It was just one part of her perfect crime."

Honami suddenly tilted her head.

"I see, but there is no evidence to prove that. There is no entrance to the room except for the door to the hallway. The window has been nailed shut and there is no chimney or air vent or anything like that there. Or is it time for your favorite trick, the secret passage?"

"Hey, don't say such things! That's a forbidden trick!"

"But there is no other way around it. Locked-room murders like you read about in novels don't lie around every corner you know. I am not trying to defend her, but the police consider her innocent of any crime and I don't think she has been lying about that either. Just admit it was just a suicide. It's just physically impossible to escape from that room."

"Physically impossible...."

As Rintarō repeated those words, Honami shrugged. She stared at Rintarō as if he had gone mad and asked in hesitation: "Don't tell me you read some book in that library and got some strange idea in your head?"

"Strange idea?"

Honami said almost boastfully: "You know, like the green door is the entrance to a parallel world and the criminal fled there, or there is a dimensional gap in that room because of some gravitational force."

Rintarō laughed and winked at her."

"You are very close actually."

4

That night, Rintarō returned home and had a long talk about the mysterious death of Sugata Kuniaki with his widower father, who worked at the homicide department of the Metropolitan Police Department. Police inspector Norizuki showed great interest in the case and made a plan to help his son. The following day, Rintarō and his father visited the Musashino police station to exchange information with the detective in charge of the case. At first, the people at the Musashino police station weren't cooperative, but after a long talk, Rintarō's ardor and the police inspector's persuasion paid off and it was decided a temporary investigation headquarters would be set up that same day inside the station.

"She is quite an accomplished liar."

Three days later, Rintarō visited the reference corner of the library to report to Honami.

"I got the cooperation of the Musashino station after we split up and had Mrs. Sugata's close relations investigated. We found quite a bit. Firstly, a child."

Honami rested her head on her arms.

"Child? But they don't have any children."

"That was a lie. When we investigated the files, we found out that they have a girl who is almost seven years old. It is really their child, but she isn't living with her parents. After her birth, a congenital disorder was diagnosed and they put her in some kind of institution. They only pay the medical bills and never visit her, just leaving her be. Mrs. Sugata has never done anything motherlike for her."

"That poor child."

"Not only that, she even lied to the neighbors, saying that her child died at birth. She might just have been keeping up appearances, but it's really a horrible story."

"Precisely. But how is that related to Mr. Sugata's death?"

"Let me explain this all in order. She is a failure not just as a mother, but also as a wife. She had betrayed her husband and is having an affair with a man called Fujimoto Shinji, a young director of a transport company in Nerima Ward. He is not married. She is two years older and they have been having an affair for about three years."

Honami guessed what was coming.

"He found out about their affair."

"Yes. Mr. Sugata probably found out about his wife's affair a bit before the murder. He of course had a big row with her. From about mid-December on, they had fights every day. I think Mr. Sugata told her around that time that he was going to divorce her. She probably decided to kill him then."

"Why do you think so?"

Rintarō answered in a grave tone.

"It's the old story, money. You said that Mr. Sugata was the youngest child of a wealthy family, right? When I looked into that, I found out that he was one of the bourgeoisie. His father, more than 70 years old, is the major stockholder of a nationwide hotel chain and his personal capital is at least five billion yen. Because he was a bit strange, Mr. Sugata wasn't usually treated as one of the family, but he was sure to inherit a great fortune."

"So the wife has had her eyes on Mr. Sugata's father's fortune from the start?"

"Probably. She was waiting for her father-in-law to kick the bucket and for everything to fall in her husband's pocket. But something unexpected happened. Mr. Sugata found out about her affair so he decided to divorce. If they had divorced before her father-in-law died, then she could say goodbye to the blessings of that fortune. And she would also have to pay compensation money because her love affair was the reason for the divorce. So to save her future fortune, she decided to kill off her husband. And here is where their daughter's handicap becomes important. Under stipulations of the Civil Code, article 887, clause 2, regarding inheritance by representation, the right to inherit goes to the daughter. And because her daughter is incapable to manage such a fortune, her mother would receive the supervising authority. That was Mrs. Sugata's plan. But I think that behind her back, her lover Fujimoto was the one pulling the strings."

Rintarō stopped his words and a cloud came over Honami's expression and she sighed heavily.

"This is a really disheartening story."

"Precisely. But regarding this motive, you can consider it confirmed. The final problem is the problem of the locked study."

"Is what she told us the other day true?"

"Yes. I have talked with every man on the emergency crew that was there when they discovered the body, and there was not a single lie in her story. The door to the hallway was locked completely. And she didn't enter the room either."

"And the details of the police examination?"

"The same. After the suicide was reported, they investigated the whole room, but they concluded there was no other exit except for the door to the hallway. The windows were really nailed shut and they actually tried to break open the green door with five men, but it didn't budge at all. And there were no signs of the door having ever been forced open. And of course there was no secret passage."

Honami, still leaning on her cheek, shook her head.

"As I see it, this seems rather hopeless."

"Too early to say that. Ah, before I forget, let's talk about the autopsy report. The estimated time of death was the day before the body was found, around 9 p.m. Going by the evidence of a cable (the belt) having been used to hang him, it was concluded to be suicide by hanging and that was all in the report. The doctor in charge probably assumed from the start that it was suicide and overlooked any evidence pointing at murder. When I asked for confirmation with the doctor, he hesitantly admitted that his autopsy might have been insufficient. It happens often with these kinds of cases."

"Wait a minute. How could the wife have hanged the body of a man from the ceiling? That would be quite heavy."

"I haven't said that she did it by herself. I'm sure her lover helped her. In fact, Fujimoto has no real alibi for the night Mr. Sugata died. He said he was drinking with young people from his transport company until morning, but that doesn't count as an alibi. He's the director, and everyone under him would say anything he would tell them to say."

Honami thought for a while. She then looked up and pushed up the frame of her glasses.

"That really so?"

"What?"

Rintarō became a bit red.

"But there is something else that bothers me. The widow has been planning to rebuild the house in Kichijōji. It was going to start during the long holiday in May. She said it was because the house had become decrepit and hard to live in, but it is to destroy the crime scene, to destroy every bit of evidence before anyone would look back at the crime and solve the mystery of the locked room. The fact that she is planning such a reconstruction is proof that she is guilty."

"But that is hardly convincing evidence. As long as you don't solve the locked room, you can't prove her to be a murderer."

Rintarō laughed.

"That's true. I came to visit you because of that actually. I have to ask your director something."

"The director?"

"I need the cooperation of this library."

Two days after that conversation, in the afternoon, with police inspector Norizuki sitting beside him in the passenger's seat, Rintarō headed for the Sugata house in Kichijōji. The wind felt cold on his skin, but it was a clear blue day. On the road in front of the house stood a transport-company truck, and men wearing orange work uniforms were carrying boxes of books into the truck. It was the truck Honami's library had hired to get the books.

"An amazing amount of books," the police inspector said. Rintarō got hold of one of the workers and asked how the operation was going.

"We have cleared about eighty percent. We are a bit behind schedule, but we'll be finished in another thirty minutes."

Rintarō smiled. Everything was going as planned. As the two moved toward the building, they heard a shouting woman. At the entrance, Honami and the widow were having a row. Or rather, the widow was just yelling one-sidedly, while Honami wasn't really making any effort to actually listen to her.

"Don't think that you can do this without any consequences! I'll report you to the police for housebreaking!"

"Please calm down a bit."

Police inspector Norizuki stepped in. The widow stopped talking, surprised and hesitating at this unknown person's intrusion. Norizuki ignored her expression, and while showing his police notebook walked toward her.

"I am Norizuki of the Metropolian Police Department."

The widow's expression turned blue in an instant. When she saw Rintarō standing next to the police inspector, her eyes squinted to become as sharp as knives.

"You are all in this together."

Rintarō didn't even smile and said: "I've solved the mystery of Mr. Sugata's prophecy. I've come here to confirm my thoughts, so could you lead us to the study again. No, it won't take long. We'll just take a look from the garden."

The widow stood still, staring at Rintarō's face. Everybody was silent for a while. Finally the widow nodded, sighed, and dropped her shoulders. Her expression however was sharp. As if she was prepared for the worst, she walked steadily through the house, toward the eastern wing of the building. The other three followed her.

At the mansion's eastern wing was, as the widow had said before, a small porch. Without taking his shoes off, Rintarō stepped on the steps of the decrepit porch. The widow had stopped in front of the steps and didn't say anything, looking down. Rintarō stood in front of the door. Because it had stood there in the outside air for many years, it had turned black. He placed his hand at the doorknob, and pulled softly. While it did feel like it was stuck a bit at the beginning, the green door opened unexpectedly easy.

Rintarō turned around. Inspector Norizuki nodded and said to the widow: "We have questions regarding the death of your late husband. Would you please come with us?" The widow nodded without saying a word.

The next day. The library's reference corner.

"Mrs. Sugata confessed," Rintarō said.

"Her motive and method were precisely like I thought. The arrest warrant for the accomplice Fujimoto will be out today."

Honami stopped her work and sat back in her chair.

"So she was refusing to give us the books because she didn't want someone to find out the trick behind the locked room, right?"

"Yeah. The main point of this case doesn't lie in the value of the books, but in the weight of the books. When you notice that, then the mystery of the green door is easy. Because of the build of the house and because it had gone decrepit, the weight of the books in the second-floor library was focused on the door facing the garden one floor below. The green door couldn't be opened because of that pressure. You shouldn't underestimate the weight of books. It's not strange that five adult men couldn't move the door even an inch."

Honami listened carefully to his words and reacted: "Now that you mention it, I once heard a story about a university teacher who used one room in his apartment as a library and the weight of the books cracked the concrete floor. It's a miracle nothing happened when Mr. Sugata's body was hanging from the ceiling. And Mr. Sugata already knew this?"

"Of course. That's why he left a prophecy saying 'When I die, the green door will open again.' If his collection was to be donated to the library, then the pressure on the door would disappear and it would be possible to open the green door again. Just like how I opened it yesterday. Mr. Sugata was someone with a very playful heart. It would have been interesting to talk with him."

Rintarō leaned back on his chair, and crossed his arms. That was his only regret.

"It's ironic that his playful heart is what gave his wife the idea for the locked-room murder. And how was the crime committed?" Honami asked.

"She got help from her lover. Fujimoto runs a transport company. He had ordered his employees to move the books in and out of the library in the middle of the night. After killing Mr. Sugita and making it seem like suicide, they worked together to move the books from the second floor to the first. That way, he was able to open the green door, so he bolted the door to the hallway, and left through the green door. Then he closed the door, and they moved the books back to the second floor. The employees who were there are professionals at moving and did their work fast and efficiently. That day I investigated the library, I hadn't seen any irregularities among the books, so they must have been working very carefully. Anyway, quite some people were involved with this crime. Just keeping everyone's mouths shut alone must have been difficult. Which means that to Fujimoto, the fortune of the Sugitas must have been very tempting. According to the widow's confession, they had promised to give them half of the fortune for their part in the crime."

Honami placed her elbows on the counter and thought for a while. Then she suddenly opened her mouth, confusing Rintarō.

"That first day when we went to Kichijōji, you said something strange. What did you mean?"

"Strange?"

"You know, you were hinting at some kind of occult phenomena or something. Was that just a joke?"

"No, it was then that I found out the truth behind the locked room. I wasn't really thinking of something occult. But your comment is quite interesting. Don't you remember what you said?"

Honami tried to remember, but shook her head.

"Not the details."

Rintarō laughed.

"You mentioned a dimensional gap because of some gravitational force. And that's when you happened to hit at the secret of the green door."

Honami wasn't looking particularly happy. Maybe that's to be expected from an intelligent woman.

"And another question. You had already solved the case, but why did you need to use our library's name and move the books out of the house? I had to suffer quite a bit, being yelled at by that woman."

Rintarō shrugged.

"I'm sorry for that. But like you said, I hadn't anything to prove my deductions. So I couldn't get a search warrant either. So to get Mrs. Sugata to confess, we had to solve the mystery of the locked room in front of her, making her understand the game was over. So that's why I resorted to that."

"Well, I'll forgive you for that this time."

"I'm grateful."

Rintarō looked calmly at his wristwatch.

"I'm sorry, but I have to go now. Anyway, I just came to tell you she confessed. Now I have to quickly start on the manuscript for *Shōsetsu Nova*."

"The unprecedented locked-room trick, it's going to be that?"

Rintarō nodded and stood up.

"Yep. I have to thank you for that. Because I accompanied you with your work, I came up with the idea for my story. I'm still not satisfied with the contact lenses thing, but that's something I'll look forward to the next time."

"I see. The next time, we'll just go out privately, without any work," Honami said laughing. "Because I've had enough of murder."

Italy
The Barese Mystery
by Pietro De Palma

Pietro De Palma was born in Bari, Italy – the setting for this story – in 1963, and is married with a fourteen-year-old son. By the age of 18, he was hooked on the locked-room mystery. He considers Carr the greatest mystery writer for both "narration and quality of the deductions."

De Palma's blogs, Death Can Read, generally about mystery fiction, and Vanished Into Thin Air, focussing on impossible crimes, are both extremely informative and entertainingly opinionated, although readers should be warned that De Palma reveals solutions.

In "The Barese Mystery" he has created an ingenious, simple, and eminently practical variation on the locked room mystery that calls to mind other Locked Room Afficionado's short stories like "The 51st Sealed Room" by Robert Arthur and "The Man Who Read John Dickson Carr" by William Brittain.

The narrator and detective is a locked room enthusiast of the first order, hoping to read a lost manuscript by C. Daly King. But that's not all: the victim is a wealthy man, able to populate a private library with rare locked-room specimens by Orr, MacDonald, Wynne, and Ellery Queen.

I was passing through the old town of Bari one morning in September 1972. The air was crisp, even with the sun rising, illuminating the hidden arches and open spaces of the streets. The night before, it had rained, even poured, and the roads were wet; here and there streams ran down along the sidewalks where they formed puddles which the sun was trying to dry. The rain exposed the ingenuity that had enabled people of previous centuries to escape when the city was besieged; it made the giant black stones of the checkerboard road blacker, intensifying the contrast with the white stones. At night, under attack, with soldiers storming the streets trying to steal, kill, or rape, people used to escape the city by carefully travelling on the black stones only, whilst remaining almost invisible.

I should introduce myself: my name is Piero Alteri. I'm the scion of an ancient family, once lofty but no longer so. When I was young, I lived life to the full: roaming up and down Italy, usually with my large circle of friends, seeking Romanesque churches, crypts, castles, dusty libraries, and galleries full of art. When alone, I spent my time playing the piano, or reading history books or mystery novels.

My passion has always been detective fiction. I have an extensive collection, but the kind I prefer are those featuring impossible crimes or locked rooms. I had always dreamt about solving a real case, and on that September day I got my chance.

I was walking carefully, so as not to step on any loose stone that might splash water on my trousers and soil them, when I arrived at my palace, which faces the sea next door to the Basilica of St. Nicholas. Maria, my housekeeper, told me that a friend of mine, Vice Quaestor Gregorio Longhi, was on the phone. I'd last seen him a month ago, when he'd shown me a collection of Attic vases, cups, and bronze swords that an operation of the state police had unearthed in a private home – true archaeological finds which would have been smuggled abroad if they had not intervened in time.

"Hello Gregorio? How are you? To what do I owe the pleasure?"

"What are you doing today?"

"I'd been planning to stay at home."

"You told me once that you'd visited Count Rambaldi. Well...now he's dead."

"Good grief! What happened?"

"They found him the day before yesterday and the circumstances were…strange," he said slowly. "Listen…can you come over here? I'm going to seal the rooms, but I'd like to show you something first."

This was unusual. Although Gregorio was always happy to discuss his work – something I enjoyed immensely – he'd never invited me to a murder scene. He was forever pointing out that what I read in books was nothing like the reality the police faced every day. Ingenious crimes with convoluted solutions only occurred in the kind of books I liked to read: in real life, if they found someone dead, it was usually because they'd been robbed, were a victim of a mob reprisal, or were a hooker killed after being raped.

An hour and a half later I was there. The house showed no signs of what must have been a hive of activity earlier. But Gregorio was there, in his signature brown velvet jacket, green moss pullover on a light brown dirty shirt, brown corduroy pants, and tan boots. He had an ordinary-enough face, I suppose, with a military moustache the same colour as his black hair, but he had extraordinarily deep eyes which seemed to reflect the fifty years he'd spent in the police, clashing with students in city squares or investigating terrorists in those dark years of political assassinations and massacres.

Smoking a cigarette on the terrace with him was Inspector Giraldi: about thirty, blond, hairless as a young boy, and dressed in jeans and black leather jacket.

"What's that smell?" I asked.

"The stink of cadaver," replied Gregorio. "Your Count had been dead for five days when they found him."

"Good grief! Didn't anyone notice? He had a housekeeper, a cook, and a butler, all of whom lived in."

"Can you give us their names?"

"The housekeeper...Elisa Pedrini, I think. The butler…Giovanni. The cook was an Argentine named Juan. Also, the count was seeing a woman. The neighbours may have more details."

"Ah. That explains why we found two toothbrushes, combs, women's creams, and a pink bathrobe! And also…other things."

"Like what?"

"The kind of stuff you find in sex shops in Milan."

"Well, that's not particularly unusual."

"So you didn't know this woman?"

"No. Once, when the count had sold me a rare thirties mystery by Virgil Markham, he'd casually invited me to a threesome. But I declined."

"Do you happen to know where I could find her, Piero?"

"The count told me once that she lived near the port."

"She didn't live with him?"

"Only the cook, the butler, and the housekeeper, as I told you. They have rooms on the second floor. But listen, Gregorio, why did you call me here? You could have asked me these questions over the phone."

He hesitated. "OK. Come with me."

We went into the count's study. There were two windows, both wide open, and a cool breeze was blowing. I buttoned my jacket.

The room was a mess. Books lay scattered all around and in the middle there was a mahogany table littered with papers. A large bloodstain had spread on a huge Persian carpet which covered almost the entire floor. There were paintings on the walls: a Cascella, two De Chirico, a De Nittis. In one armchair a photo album lay gutted, and two other chairs had been overturned.

Gregorio gestured. "The count was lying here on the carpet. It seems he shot himself." He emphasized the "seems." "Did he keep any valuables here?"

"Only books, I think. Some valuable, very valuable. Novels, first editions. He collected rare mysteries, which is how I knew him. Six months ago he told me he'd managed to get hold of the manuscript of C. Daly King's seventh novel."

"Who's that?"

"A great author of the '30s and '40s who published six novels. It was said he'd written a seventh which had never been published. The first editions of his novels have gone for staggering sums in the collector's market."

"And where did he keep it?"

I'd never actually seen the manuscript, but I knew where the count would have kept it. I walked over to a wall mirror with light sconces on either side. I turned one of the sconces clockwise. There was a click and the mirror moved, revealing an opening in the wall. Inside was a shelf, on which were placed a manuscript with a cover, some old movie reels, and several highly personal photographs. In one of them, a woman was naked in an obscene pose; in another she was lying topless beside an SS officer.

I went to pick up the manuscript, but Gregorio stopped me. "That's evidence."

This was frustrating. I wanted nothing more than to read that King story. Instead, I thought about what Gregorio had said earlier. "Why did you say it seems that he committed suicide? You're not sure?"

"It's a strange thing. The count was ambidextrous, although few people knew. Generally he used his right hand, but at the shooting range he used his left. And the hole in his temple is on the right side, not the left. Why? He had a bump on his head consistent with falling after being shot. But that doesn't rule out murder made to look like suicide. The lump could have been the result of a stroke before his death, which stunned him. But the door was locked from the inside, which is why I called you. You read a lot of those books. Perhaps you might have an idea.

"It has a modern snap lock." He demonstrated. "You see? The knob turns to the right to open the door and to the left to close it, and a vertical lever turns to the left to bar the door. In addition we have this burglar-proof lock with two bars entering holes in the ceiling and floor and one in the left wall. It seems that when the count closed the door, he really didn't want to be disturbed." He sniggered. "By the way, that big armchair hides a folding bed, inside which we found an assortment of sadomasochism objects."

"Ever the pervert!" I exclaimed. "But if the door was closed, and assuming he didn't commit suicide, how did the murderer get in? Were the windows open when he was found?"

"The one over the balcony was open, but at the same time closed. The other one – "

"What?"

"The other one was open. But it looks out over a sheer vertical wall with no handholds. The one overlooking the balcony was locked, but the window was open."

"Sorry, I'm not following. Was it closed or open?"

"The window itself was open, but there's an armoured shutter that can be closed."

"Ah, now I'm beginning to understand. It can be raised and lowered?"

"Yes."

"Heavy?"

"Really heavy."

"Could a man raise it?"

"Impossible, except with a hoist. But in that case there would have been some marks on the floor, and there weren't any. It's as clean as a whistle."

"Can I see how the shutter works?"

"Of course. I'll lower it."

He pressed a button which started a motor, and an iron shutter descended slowly from a slit in the ceiling above the window. He waited until it was completely lowered. "Now let's try to lift it by hand."

Gregorio, the inspector, and I tried to lift it together. My foot slipped a couple of times, but even when we all had a firm footing, we couldn't lift the shutter by any significant amount.

It seemed clear to me. "So he committed suicide."

"So it would appear. But if it were that easy I wouldn't have called you. It still looks like a fake suicide to me."

"But if you can't show how anyone got out..."

"That's why you're here."

"What's in it for me?"

"How about an expensive seafood dinner?"

"Not enough."

"Well then, suppose I let you read the King manuscript?"

"Done!"

At that moment the phone rang and Gregorio answered. A woman had been stopped at the Bari centre – the count's housekeeper. They had brought her to the police station. Her name was Elisa Pedrini; she hadn't heard from the count for several days and had been at a friend's house.

Gregorio put the phone down. "I have to go. You can look around – we've already checked for fingerprints – but don't touch anything."

"Whose prints did they find?"

"The count's, the housekeeper's, the cook's, and the butler's. They're all suspects, and we don't think it could have been an outsider."

"Why not?"

"The main door is opened by pressing a button hidden behind the umbrella stand. Only those who live in the house would know how to open it."

Gregorio left, leaving the inspector outside, and I began to examine the room.

It was quite large, I would say six metres by four. The floor was covered in books scattered everywhere. Some were damaged and torn. Someone had treated them roughly, not respecting their merit and value. Among others I noticed two books by Maspléde, books by Lacourbe, Adey, dozens of issues of *Ellery Queen's Mystery Magazine*. A lot of first editions: Orr, Philip MacDonald, Rupert

Penny, Anthony Wynne, Ellery Queen, Michael Innes...along with encyclopaedias and essay collections. Under the armchair I could see the corner of a jacket: It was Hake Talbot's first novel.

In that book – *The Hangman's Handyman* – there was also a decomposing corpse and a locked room, just as in this case. I noticed a stain on the inside front flap of the cover and smelled it: grease or oil.

I realised immediately that the count would never have let this happen to one of his books. That settled it: it was definitely murder.

The more I looked at the window and the door the more I became convinced that there had been a murderer in the room who had somehow escaped. But how? I called Inspector Giraldi.

"When you got in, were the lights on or off?"

"Off."

I thought about it. If someone had found a way to escape from the window, surely it must have occurred late at night, when no one would have witnessed anything. Across the street sat an apartment building.

"Have you questioned the neighbours?"

He nodded. "Nobody saw anyone doing anything suspicious. One neighbour walking by across the street heard a loud noise on one of the nights, like the sound of breaking pots. He looked over and thought he saw someone on the balcony, kneeling before the closed shutter. He called out, but the person waved in a way which seemed familiar. So he returned home without raising the alarm."

Why was he kneeling? Because he was entering, or because he was leaving? Supposing he had been leaving, wouldn't he have to bend down and then stand up?

Why the disorder? Was the killer looking for something? Not all of the books had been disturbed, as if the murderer, having found what he sought, didn't need to disrupt the rest. I examined each of the books on the floor, and one caught my attention: It was a collection of short stories by Melville Davisson Post, and there were several photos spilling out from between the pages. They were of an obscene nature.

I had an idea....

I examined every book in the study. And two hours later I understood how the murderer had got out of the room: clever, no doubt about it! Clear determination and cunning – not anger – had been the cause of all the disorder!

But the murderer had made a mistake. I called my friend.

"Search the homes of the suspects. Look for something that's dirty – dirty with grease."

"Grease?"

"Yes, I know how it was done, and that's the only evidence that will point to the murderer."

They found it. In Elisa Pedrini's home. On a pair of pants. She confessed. The count had been blackmailing her for a long time. She had tried to break with her past: She had been a whore and had worked in a Milan brothel in the '40s. But he had found photos she thought no longer existed and had induced her to work for him. He had forced her to do things she no longer wanted to do. So one day, when she thought the count was out, she had begun to look for the photos, but he returned unexpectedly and discovered her. She managed to shoot him and leave the room, setting the stage for suicide. She'd already considered killing him as a last resort, and had a plan ready.

"So how did you work it all out?" asked Gregorio, as we were about to be seated in a fine restaurant by the sea, where I was looking forward to my meal.

"The books were the first clue. I found one with a spot of grease on the inside cover, and another in which a portfolio of compromising photos had been hidden, and then I began to systematically check them all. At one point I detected the same odour, strong, very strong. I was holding a thick book containing old American magazines with stories by Joseph Commings: on the dark brown cover, the smell was very clear. I went over to the window and examined the sill where the shutter came down. In some spots there was a little grease and along the guide rails there was quite a lot. I remembered the Count had once told me that the shutter kept jamming, so he had greased it generously so it would travel smoothly along the tracks. But how did the grease get on the covers of books which would normally be on a shelf?

"Two of the books smelled of grease and one was stained. What could it mean? Then I remembered my foot slipping when we tried to lift the shutter. Grease again?

"What if the shutter had been blocked from fully descending by two stacks of large books? The fugitive could have crawled out under the shutter and then, once on the other side, maybe sitting on the ground, he could have kicked the two stacks of books, scattering them on the floor and instantly freeing the shutter to close after him."

"Ingenious! But why did you think the murderer managed to get grease on himself?"

"Because I found a spot of grease on the balcony floor near the shutter. And I imagined that, crawling under it on all fours, one could easily have touched the grease without noticing. Strangely, much of the shutter was greasy but the only part that was clean was the bottom of the last slat, the lowest. It should normally have been the greasiest, what with the grease dripping down, but instead it was clean. And I also found, after inspecting the two volumes that smelled like grease, some deep indentations in the covers the same thickness as the shutter.

"The iron gate, pressing down, had marked them."

"Indeed."

Gregorio summoned the waiter. "Luigi, what have you in the way of raw fish?"

"Scampi on ice and baby octopus, fresh. Ecco!"

We splashed on some lemon juice and I asked the question I'd been dying to ask.

"Gregorio! The manuscript? Can I see it now?"

He had obviously been waiting for the moment and brought it out with a flourish. "Here you go."

It took me only one look to see that the pages were not made of '40s paper: They were modern. The count had been cheated. And I would never read the missing manuscript by C. Daly King.

"Gregorio, hand me those sea urchins."

At least I would have a good meal.

Real Life Impossibility: United Kingdom
The Murder of King Edward II

The end of Edward II's reign was precipitous. His wife, Isabella of France, led an invasion against him in 1326, his government fell apart, and he fled to Wales. Captured there by Henry of Lancaster, he was imprisoned in Kenilworth Castle. Although there were multiple rescue attempts, one of which succeeded, Edward was recaptured and died in custody on September 21, 1327.

Although it was generally reported that Edward was murdered by suffocation or strangulation, Thomas More and Ralph Holinshed reported a more grotesque method. By their account, the killers wanted to avoid the appearance of murder and ensure his death was attributed to natural causes, in which they succeeded.

They are alleged to have inserted an ivory hunting horn into Edward's posterior, and then inserted a red-hot poker through the tip of the horn, burning his insides and causing death. The thick sides of the horn would have prevented any post-mortem investigation from detecting the murder method.

The story may not be true, and it's been suggested that Edward's rumoured homosexuality may have inspired a fabrication.

Germany
The Witch Doctor's Revenge
by Jochen Füseler

Jochen Füseler was born in Schönaich, near Stuttgart, Germany, in 1957, and still lives there, working as an SAP computer scientist at Litreca AG.

He acquired the locked room habit at a young age after reading *The Clue of the New Pin* by Edgar Wallace. He remembers listening to a radio documentary about "an American author who had written about two seemingly unexplainable murders in snowy London." He didn't remember the title or author but never forgot the description.

Some years later, he read Carr's *Dark of the Moon* and *Papa La-Bas*, and was unimpressed.

Finally in 1983 he learned from Julian Symons's *Bloody Murder* (*Mortal Consequences)* that Carr's pre-war work was much better, and got his hands on an English-language copy of *The Three Coffins* (*The Hollow Man)*. From then on his interest in locked rooms, and his ability to read English, developed rapidly.

Herr Füseler's writing career began when he and a friend each decided to try to write a film script. Although his script was rejected, he continued writing and this fine story is the result. He is also completing an impossible crime novel, *Circus Air (Zirkusluft).*

He picked up the phone.

"Hello?"

"Hi, it's me," said an excited voice. "Do you know what day it is?"

He smiled.

"June 22, 1966."

The voice became a little more excited.

"I know it's June 22. Do you know what that means?"

His smile became broader.

"I'm sure you'll tell me."

The voice became insistent.

"Twelve years, and fifty-one weeks. Eh?"

He thought long and hard.

"I give up," he said at last.

"In exactly seven days, he will return!"

"Who will?"

"HE!" The voice on the other end of the line cracked. "HE will return!"

He laughed a short, humourless laugh.

"Oh my – do you really still think of...?"

"Of course I do," the voice screamed. "One week left, and the thirteen years are over.

"Don't you remember what he said? 'First, you will feel the same pain I do, then the two of you will vanish off the face of the Earth as if you had never existed. Thirteen years from now. Exactly thirteen years!"

"Don't be silly," he replied. "I bet nothing's going to happen."

"You bet!" the voice cried. "And who will pay the bet if you lose?"

He thought again.

"Okay," he replied, at last. "I don't believe in – but maybe you are right."

There came a sigh of relief from the other end of the line.

"Okay," he said again. "If you want to, we might take some precautions. First of all – you leave your apartment and move to a hotel room. Next, you – "

"Good morning, Fräulein." The tall, slightly overweight man took off his coat and hat and hung them on the office coatrack. "It's the coldest and wettest summer I ever saw."

The secretary, a young and rather attractive woman with blue eyes and swept-up hair, agreed, fluttering her eyelashes. "Good morning, boss. It certainly is."

"Anything special this morning?"

She shook her head. "Not yet. No spectacular murder cases in sight, again."

He had just sat down when the secretary's phone rang.

"Hello, police station Boeblingen – yes – yes, Hauptwacht – yes – of course – no – just a sec – "

Shaking her head, she held the receiver towards the sergeant. "I think you should take it. He sounds completely confused. Something about a witch doctor..."

He went over to her desk.

"Hauptwachtmeister Faust here," he said. "Yes, I see. You have – what? You're sober, aren't you? Okay. Where are you?" He wrote something on a notepad. "Good. Don't do anything. Just sit in the hotel lobby and wait. Maybe help yourself to a schnapps."

He put the notepad in his desk and headed to the door to collect his still-wet coat and hat. As he left, he called over his shoulder to his secretary: "The fellow thinks his friend's been murdered by an African witch doctor who was hanged thirteen years ago."

"Sounds interesting," she replied. "Shall I call the asylum?"

"Not yet, Fräulein Kaechele. First I have to check if he's right or not."

Sitting in his police car, Faust decided to take the route running through the villages Schoenaich and Holzgerlingen. That might not have been the shortest but probably the quickest and, by no means, the most beautiful one.

Driving through Schoenbuch forest, he spontaneously decided to stop and take some deep breaths of the fresh air of the rainy beeches before heading on to his destination, Waldenhausen.

The hotel there was easy to find as it was the only one in that small village.

Waldenhausen was a small village in the Black Forest, less than an hour's drive from Boeblingen. There was only one hotel in the village and only one man in the lobby. The sergeant introduced himself:

"Hauptwachtmeister Faust."

The other man, a slender, forty-something man with blonde hair and a worried facial expression, stood up and took the offered hand.

"Manfred Baumann," he replied, obviously nervous. "Shall we go upstairs?"

"Not yet," the sergeant replied. "First, I need some information."

"But my friend is upstairs – in danger of his life."

"I like to know what's going on before I burst into a room," insisted the sergeant.

He offered the man a cigarette.

Manfred Baumann took a deep puff and began:

"When we were young, my friend Karl Jakob and I were modern adventurers. You may have seen our names in the newspapers at the time...?"

Faust shook his head.

"Doesn't ring a bell."

"Okay. Karl and I were making expeditions all over the world – South America, Australia, and, alas, Africa as well. It was in the jungle of Central Africa that we discovered a tribe hitherto unknown. In the beginning the natives were frightened and even suspicious of us, as they'd never seen a white person before. Eventually, though, we managed to win their confidence. Then, one day, the chief's daughter developed a violent headache and fell into some kind of a coma. All the attempts of the tribe's witch doctor failed to wake her, so in desperation, Karl, who always carried aspirin with him wherever he went, gave her some. Miraculously, she awoke shortly thereafter and made a complete recovery. To cut a long story short, the chief rewarded Karl and myself with the tribe's biggest honors but sentenced the witch doctor to death. It was intended that he should suffer the same pains as the chief's daughter had before him. So they hung him by his feet from a high tree, head down, until the blood pressure made the veins in his head explode.

"Before that happened, however, he put a curse on the both of us. Exactly thirteen years later, Karl would die in exactly the same way he was about to, and the two of us would then vanish into thin air and never be seen again. We tried everything to save the poor devil, but pitted against the whole tribe we had no chance. We returned home after that and I quickly forgot about the curse. But Karl didn't. He called me last week, as the thirteen years were nearly up, and I recommended he move to a hotel and hide if he was so frightened. And early this morning, I received an emergency call from him. He screamed out, 'He's coming – my God, Manfred, help me – ' and all of a sudden, there was silence. I rushed out here as fast as I could and knocked on his door, but he didn't answer. That's when I decided to call you. I ask you again: Come upstairs with me – maybe it's not yet too late!"

"Okay, calm down," said Faust. "If he's not answering your knocks, maybe he's not in the room at all. Have you tried looking through the keyhole?"

"No, I never thought of that. Let's go up and look now."

They ran upstairs and Baumann, who was leading the way, stopped in front of the door to room number 17. He knocked loudly – no response. Faust tried turning the doorknob, to no avail.

"Locked," he declared, before bending down to look through the keyhole. Baumann followed suit.

"The key's on the inside," said Faust. "We'll have to try pushing it in, and if that doesn't work we're going to have to break the door down."

Baumann smiled weakly and produced a pair of tweezers out of his jacket pocket.

"I always carry these, ever since I fell onto a cactus during one of our South American expeditions," he explained. "I couldn't sit down for a week afterwards."

He inserted the tweezers into the keyhole and, after a few twists and turns, the key fell to the floor inside the room. "Voila," he said triumphantly as he bent down to look through the empty keyhole.

"My God!" he exclaimed. "Here, take a look for yourself."

Faust bent down. "What do you see?" asked Baumann.

Faust swallowed hard. "I can see a window to my left," he said in a sepulchral voice. "And in the centre of the room there's a man hanging upside down from the ceiling. His mouth and eyes are wide open and his left arm is stretched out. We'll have to break down the door."

He pulled a handkerchief from his pocket and mopped the perspiration from his brow.

"If I may make a suggestion," said Baumann, "the desk clerk has a skeleton key which will fit all the rooms. I'll call her up."

Two minutes later, a young woman in a hotel uniform appeared and unlocked the door. Before she could step inside, Faust thanked her and sent her away. He turned the knob and pushed, but the door didn't move.

"It's blocked," he said, stating the obvious. "Let's both try to push it open together."

After several attempts the door opened suddenly with an enormous crash, followed immediately by a thud. They stumbled into the room. There, hanging down from the ceiling lamp hook, was a rope with a noose just wide enough to hold two human feet.

The noose was empty.

They looked around. There was no one else, living or dead, in the room.

Faust looked at the floor. There was a cheap plastic key fob with a metallic ring, just the kind you pull the key head through, and obviously the reason for the blocking of the door. "I advised Karl to keep the windows closed, the door locked and blocked with a wedge."

"That's a great way to keep a ghost out of a room," observed Faust drily.

He looked around.

The big crash had apparently been caused by a small pedestal table which had been pushed against the door and had tipped over when the door had been flung open. The floor was littered with objects which had obviously been on the table when they broke in: a broken bottle of table water, the pieces of a drinking glass, some books and a sheet of paper lying in the spilled water, three framed photographs, a pen – and the room key.

The bed was still freshly made and had obviously not been used. Two chairs had been neatly placed around a larger table in the middle of the room, on which sat a second drinking glass and a telephone, its receiver hanging down over the edge of the table.

Faust picked up the phone and held it to his ear. There was a busy signal. He replaced the receiver and went back to the door to pick up the wet sheet of paper. With difficulty he read out what had been written:

"Dear Manfred and everyone,

Today is the day we find out if the witch doctor's curse shall strike.

Manfred, you didn't want to believe in it, but I did. I hope you're right.

But if you're wrong, I hereby declare that all my fortune shall be divided between the three people I love the most in this world, my loving wife, my daughter, and you Manfred, my best friend.

If the curse does strike I hope the witch doctor will be satisfied with my sacrifice and will spare Manfred.

In all love,

Karl"

"What do you make of it?" he asked Baumann, who had gone deathly pale.

"W-What can I say? I d-didn't believe in the curse, but I was w-wrong."

Faust picked up the drenched books and the three photographs and placed them on the large table along with the letter. He spoke over his shoulder to Baumann:

"The books are all from the public library. Goethe – complete works, vol. I; Karl May, 'Across the desert'; the Donald Duck anthology. A man of varied tastes, it seems."

He looked at the photographs: "That's his wife, I assume. Quite a beauty. And that must be their little daughter. And I assume that's Karl with his right arm up as if he's greeting someone. He's quite handsome himself, wouldn't you say?"

Faust turned to look at Manfred Baumann…and froze.

There was only a white wall.

Manfred Baumann had vanished.

Hauptwachtmeister Faust threw the photos down on the table and ran out of the room into the corridor. He looked left and right but there was no one there. Frantically, he rushed down the staircase to the desk clerk and asked her if she'd seen the man who had been with him in the lobby. She had been at the desk ever since he'd dismissed her and had seen no one.

He went back upstairs to Karl Jakob's room. Seemingly at a loss, he looked around the room once more. He picked up the key, the pen, and some pieces of broken glass. The pen was a beautiful old-fashioned silver fountain pen, surely rather expensive. The glass came partly from the bottle of water and partly from what looked like a brandy snifter. As he tried to arrange the framed photos on the table, one of them fell over; he had inadvertently tried to stand it upside down.

Faust sat down on one of the chairs and thought about how he should explain the events of the rainy morning to his chief. As he thought and his eyes roamed the room he suddenly sat up and dialled a familiar number.

"Fräulein Kaechele? Fine. Would you please be so kind to come over to the address you find on my desk? It's a hotel, yes. Tell Roswitha to take the hotline for an hour. And, please, bring with you a bottle of Asbach Uralt and two brandy snifters. I'll explain when I see you."

Half an hour later Elfriede Kaechele, carrying a bag, knocked apprehensively on the door. "Is that you, Fräulein Kaechele? Come in, there are no bodies in here – at least no dead ones."

Hesitantly, his secretary stepped inside and looked startled at the sight of the noose.

"Don't be afraid," said Faust. "The vengeful ghost has left the building! Did you remember to bring the brandy and glasses?" He opened her bag and placed the contents on the large table.

Next, he gave her a short report about his morning adventure. "Do you believe the ghost story about the witch doctor?" she asked.

"If I did, I'd be working in the wrong office," he replied.

"So what do you make of all this?"

"Before I answer that question I'd like to conduct a small experiment. By the way, do you have a hairpin with you?"

By way of answer, she raised her hand to her hair and her light brown locks tumbled to her shoulders. She held up a black hairpin. "Thank you," he said. "Now would you please go outside and wait a few minutes?"

Elfriede obeyed and he closed the door behind her.

As Elfriede was pacing up and down the corridor she suddenly heard a low metallic noise coming from the keyhole, followed by a "swoosh" and then a low thump.

"Can you hear me?" came Faust's voice from inside the room.

"Loud and clear," she replied.

"Good. Now tell me what you see through the keyhole."

She bent down. "Nothing. The key's in there."

"Correct, in a manner of speaking. Now please use your hairpin to push it inside."

Elfriede did as he asked and immediately heard a metallic sound.

"Congratulations. You pushed the key out at your first attempt!"

Flattered, Elfriede smiled. “I was lucky,” she replied.

“Now bend down again and tell me what you see now.”

Elfriede peeped through the keyhole.

After he heard the dull thud from the corridor, Faust quickly opened the door and knelt beside his prostrate secretary. He propped her up and patted her face until she opened her blue eyes again.

“He's dead,” she murmured. “The curse...”

“I am so sorry, Fräulein Kaechele. I hadn't thought my little experiment would have such an effect on you.”

Before he helped her up he stepped back into the room, moved something aside, and opened the door wide. He led her to one of the chairs and sat her down.

“The man was dead,” she mumbled. “Hanging from the ceiling. What happened to him?”

She looked around the room. The door was still wide open, to the side stood the pedestal table with one of the framed photographs on it, and on the floor lay the silver fountain pen.

“And how did you know how...?”

“Let me answer your last question first, please.

“First of all, I am gifted with far too little imagination to believe in ghosts.

“Next, I don't know too much about African culture, but if – as the honourable Herr Baumann stated – the tribe of that vengeful witch doctor hadn't been discovered before, I wonder how he knew about the Gregorian calendar. Thirteen years, to the day, the curse said, do you remember? And I wonder where he heard about that unlucky number thirteen.

And last, if you believe in ghosts, how can you be so naive as to think barring a room might prevent a disembodied soul from sliding in?”

“Suppose that’s all true,” said Elfriede, “why perform that whole comedy? Was it a practical joke?”

“I'm afraid not,” replied Faust. “There was a reason for it, and I think I know what it is. Something did happen thirteen years ago. But it wasn’t a curse. And it didn’t happen in Africa. It occurred right here in our regional capitol Stuttgart. And it was nothing more or less than a robbery. Now, there’s no reason for you to know anything about the case, but I was involved as a young Polizeihauptwachtmeisteranwaerter.”

"It was a jewel robbery, executed by three masked gangsters. The jeweller was shot dead, and there was a very large reward. Two of the robbers managed to escape but the third one was caught in the act, severely injured by a police bullet, and taken to court. He didn't give his partners away, and as there was no proof that he was the one who had fired the shot that killed the jeweller, he was sentenced to just thirteen years in Stammheim prison. You see? *Thirteen* years. He swore revenge on the two others who hadn't tried to prevent him being caught. And the thirteen years are up tomorrow. I remembered that one of the associates of that third man looked very much like the handsome and allegedly cursed Herr Karl Jakob, who might have had another name back then. Even though he was older I recognized him straight away from the framed photograph over there."

"So why all the business about a curse? Why not just go and live in Bolivia?"

"Well," replied Faust, scratching his head, "I suspect they wanted it officially recorded that they'd vanished without trace from the face of the Earth, so that searching for them would be useless. That way the third man's revenge might never happen."

Elfriede pulled a face. "Okay, so there was no curse and no witch doctor. But you scared me to death with that dead body hanging from the ceiling. How was that possible?"

Faust smiled and took a deep breath. "Before I answer your question, after Baumann vanished I immediately called my colleagues to alert all airports. I'm pretty sure our two adventurers will have been arrested by now."

"By the way," interjected Elfriede, "have they ever been explorers?"

"Never. Baumann's question about the newspapers was just a bluff. And that's why I'd never read anything about them." Faust waved his hand. "And even there had been – "

"Now, come on," moaned Elfriede. "You've kept me on tenterhooks for long enough. How did they do it?"

Faust pointed to the fountain pen.

"That's the key, to start with."

"The key?" repeated Elfriede. "So, the pen was pushed into the keyhole to pretend it was a key and the door wasn't locked at all?"

"It was locked all right," replied Faust. "But not from the inside."

"Aha. And those last words on that sheet of paper were written purely to explain the presence of the fountain pen, I suppose? Now, what about that dead man hanging from the ceiling? Was it the photograph?"

"Of course," answered Faust calmly.

Elfriede picked up the photograph.

"But that can't be. I saw him hanging down, with his left arm extended. On the photo, it's his right arm."

"Well, if you say so." Faust smiled encouragingly. "What might be helping the illusion?"

"A mirror!" she exclaimed, looking around the room.

"Not quite," said Faust. "Look around. The only mirror in here is that large one on the front of the wardrobe, and it's screwed in place. And you would have noticed the picture frame. No, it wasn't a mirror."

"I see," replied Elfriede, thinking furiously. "And, to make matters worse, the photo should be turned upside down." She reached for it. "And if I try to place it upside down it falls over because the stand only allows it to be upright in one position, which shows a man standing on his feet."

"Everything you say is true. By the way - have you ever thought of how the plastic key fob was fixed?"

"With a string?" she suggested. "The same way we did it when we were children to prevent our parents going into our rooms while we were out?"

"Exactly. The fob was placed on the floor right behind the partly open door, with a loop of string threaded through the ring. When the door was closed, a pull on the string would jam the fob under the door to keep it tightly shut. Then you pulled on one end of the string to remove it. By the way, when you were a child how did you get back into the room?"

Elfriede laughed. "Can't you guess? Ha! You thread a second string through the ring all the way across to the window and drape it over the sill. You climb out through the window and shut it on top of the string. To get back in, you yank on the string and it pulls the fob out from under the door."

Faust applauded. "Now, let's get back to Herr Baumann's magic dead-man trick.

There was a bit of preparation needed. First, of course, everything had to be arranged on the small pedestal table. The table itself had to be placed at a distance of a foot or so from the door, slightly to its left, for two reasons: On the one hand, to give Jakob the opportunity of leaving the room through that narrow one-foot gap, and on the other to give the small table the opportunity of tumbling over when we were pushing open the blocked door in order to spill the tools used in the miracle all over the floor. Jakob placed the original hotel room key on the floor before he left, and he locked the door from outside with a duplicate he had made beforehand. Finally, he pushed the silver pen into the keyhole, and the illusion of a key inserted from the inside was perfect.

"Now, getting back to what I said before about your statements concerning the upside-down hanging victim: everything you said is correct. The illusion was created with the aid of that photograph of Jakob. And the picture had to be mirror-inverted. But it also had to be turned upside down, and both are not possible – or are they?"

"Ta-dah!" exclaimed Elfriede. "So, how?"

"Go outside again, please," said Faust, "and have another look through the keyhole."

Elfriede, obviously getting irritated, did what she was told and left the room to bend down and look through the hole once more. She could hear Faust moving the table, this time without trying to avoid any noise.

"Okay," she said. "There's the photo of – what's his name? – Jakob, standing with his feet on the ground and waving to the camera with his right arm outstretched."

"And what about now?" asked Faust.

She shot upright, pushed open the door, and stared into the room: "What on earth...?"

She saw the table. On it, she saw the photograph. And, on the tabletop, between the keyhole and the framed photograph, she saw one of the brandy snifters she had brought with her, filled with clear water. The photograph frame and the snifter were each standing on a book.

She closed the door, got down on her knees in front of the table, and looked at the photo through the water-filled glass.

Karl Jakob was hanging upside down from the ceiling, his left arm outstretched, and the picture frame had become a transparent, thin, bowed, nearly invisible line.

"Well, I'll be...!" she said.

"You see," explained Faust, "when I was looking at the broken glass on the floor, I noticed it was partly from the water bottle, and partly from something like a brandy snifter. Why, I wondered, would anyone drink table water out of a brandy snifter when there is a freshly washed water glass standing on the other table? The answer is: He didn't use it to drink. He used it for his trick.”

Faust pointed to the brandy glass. “It's a matter of light refraction, entrance angle, and distances between keyhole, glass, and picture,” he explained. “If you just have a regular water glass filled with water, looking through shows the object behind mirror-inverted. If, however, the glass has a balloon shape, you see the object behind, in addition, upside down.”

Faust helped Elfriede up, and she asked: “And why the other photos? Of his wife and his child?”

“That’s easy to guess,” said Faust. “Why should someone place a picture of himself in a hotel room? That would look mighty strange! On the other hand, if there were photos of the whole family, who would suspect anything? That's what Baumann thought, anyway.” Faust smiled.

“And the books...”

“Not for reading – just to bring keyhole, glass, and photograph all on the same level.”

“That’s amazing.”

“Well, I do think I played my part of the gullible, non-suspecting, simple-minded Hauptwachtmeister rather well, if I do say so myself.”

“But what about Manfred Baumann? How did he manage to vanish into thin air as well?”

“To be honest,” said Faust frankly, “that was the biggest puzzle of all.” He paused dramatically.

“Do go on,” said Elfriede.

“You remember, I was talking to him after we had burst into the room, and all of a sudden, he was gone – lost, vanished. When I noticed, I ran out of the room into the corridor, looked to the left, looked to the right, and ran down to the desk clerk – nowhere was there the slightest trace of Herr Baumann.”

“The witch doctor's curse, finally?” suggested Elfriede.

“Not really,” replied Faust. “It was actually quite simple. He’d rented the room next to Jakob wearing a disguise of a false beard and sunglasses, which he’d removed in order to meet me. While I was talking to him with my back turned, he slipped silently out of room number seventeen and into room number sixteen. After I returned from checking with the desk clerk and went into Jakob's room to call my colleagues, he put on his disguise again and sauntered down to check out, having previously called for a taxi to the airport."

He laughed and took a deep breath.

"Now one final question," said Elfriede. "What did you need the brandy and the second brandy snifter for?"

"For this reason, my dear," he said.

He took the bottle in one hand, the glasses in the other, and led her over to the large table. They both sat down and he poured out a hefty measure of the brandy into each glass. He looked into her eyes as he handed her a glass.

"By the way," he said. "My first name is Heinrich."

"Heinrich," she whispered, leaning closer to him. "I'm Elfriede."

"I already know that," he whispered back.

Iraq
All the Birds of the Air
by Charles B. Child

Charles B. Child was one of the pen names of the prolific British writer Claude Vernon West, who started his literary career at an early age writing thrilling tales for boys' magazines and went on to become one of the 200 or so (mostly pseudonymous) authors of the Sexton Blake stories. He joined the Royal Air Force as a Flight Lieutenant at the outbreak of World War II and was stationed for most of the time in Baghdad and the Kurdish territories, where he worked with military intelligence.

He developed considerable respect for the mental agility of the locals and, when he settled in Connecticut with his American wife after the war, he created the character of Inspector Chafik J. Chafik, said to be a composite of several of the people he met in Iraq.

As Charles B. Child, he wrote some thirty detective stories featuring the little Inspector for *Collier's* magazine, where they became very popular.

"All the Birds of the Air" appears in the collection *The Sleuth of Baghdad*, published by Crippen and Landru, and is one of three impossible-crime stories therein.

They found Hadji Hussain huddled on a chair in the summer room of his house on the banks of the Tigris. He had a bruise above the forehead and died from a brain hemorrhage shortly after they carried him out.

The room was actually a deep windowless cellar with a single entrance at the foot of an outside flight of steps. An air shaft led to the roof and trapped the river breezes, making the *surdab* a pleasant retreat from the excessive heat.

Inspector Chafik of the Criminal Investigation Department of the Baghdad police appreciated the coolness. Outside, the white light of noon glared on the tiles of the courtyard. The Inspector's shirt stuck to his thin body and disturbed him; he was fastidious about his clothes. Wiping his swarthy face with a handkerchief sprinkled with orange water, he announced, "I consider it unreasonable for people to die on such a hot day."

His assistant, a tall unemotional sergeant, understood why the Inspector was worried about Hussain's death. The Hadji, who was loved and venerated in Baghdad, was head of the courts where ecclesiastical matters such as divorce, questions of Moslem theology, and disputes concerning religious institutions were brought for settlement.

Recently the old man had handed down a decision that concerned a property willed to the Shafiite shrine at Zagros. He had favored the relatives who had brought a complaint of coercion against the shrine. In consequence the Shafiites, a small but fanatic sect, had threatened reprisals, and a police guard had been placed at the Hadji's house.

This affected Sergeant Abdullah personally because the detail had been in his charge, so he began anxiously, "Permit me to report – "

Chafik said, "Later, I have not yet digested the medical report. It is always an unappetizing dish. They tell me the violence of the blow might have killed a younger man. The Hadji was old, frail. If he fell and struck something – "

"Sir, there is nothing to indicate it," said the sergeant. "And what was he doing in the chair?"

"It is possible that after the first impact of the blow he recovered sufficiently to find his feet and stumble to the chair. He may have retained consciousness until the clot formed."

The Inspector had strange dun-colored eyes, flat and expressionless except when he was worried. He looked around trying to visualize what had happened. The room was very simply furnished. There were a cot, a few chairs, straw mats on the tiled floor, a bedside lamp – near the lamp was an open copy of the Koran which had been put down so hurriedly the edges of the pages were folded. A light blanket was flung back from the foot of the bed.

Chafik said, "There is the impression of a head on the pillow; the Hadji was reposed. And the position of the Koran, the blanket, tells us he was rudely disturbed. The interruption occurred shortly after he came to rest, otherwise he would not have been reading. The aged do not have to woo sleep."

He folded his slender hands and glanced at the sergeant, who knew what was expected and immediately began to quote from memorized notes, "Sir, the Hadji entered the *surdab* after the noon prayer. He was escorted by a retainer named Murad, who closed the door behind his master and then proceeded to other duties. Murad is the house watchman."

"Where were you stationed, Abdullah?"

"I was in the courtyard, sir, where I could observe all the people of the house. First, there is Mr. Romani, the deceased's nephew, visiting from Amara – "

"A lawyer, I know of him," Chafik said.

"Then there is Mr. Sadir, a young man who lives here."

"His father died two months ago and was a close friend of the Hadji, who was appointed guardian to the youth. I find it strange," Chafik added, "that an adult should require a guardian, but there are rumors Sadir preferred Cairo to Baghdad. Life there is gay."

"A sinful city," said the sergeant.

"The mole," remarked Chafik, thinking of his own city of the dusty plain, "without doubt calls the lark sinful. But continue."

"Sir, Mr. Sadir and Mr. Romani also retired because of the heat. Their rooms are on the second floor. The servants, too, were in their quarters. Only the watchman Murad remained active. He stood at the main gate within my view." The sergeant cleared his throat, then stood rigidly at attention and said without inflection, "It is now necessary to make a confession – "

"You slept?"

"Because of the heat, I dozed, sir. Briefly, only a few minutes, but I deserve reprimand. When I opened my eyes I saw Murad running toward the *surdab*. I halted him. He said he had heard the door open and thought his master had called out. We both proceeded to the spot. The door was indeed open and we saw the Hadji collapsed on the chair. I sent Murad for Mr. Romani, who came at once. Over protests, he carried his uncle to an upper room."

"It was unwise to move a dying man, but in this case, it probably made little difference. You searched the room after the Hadji was taken out?"

"Diligently. There was nothing that resembled a weapon here."

"And where was Mr. Sadir?"

"In his room, sir. He is a heavy sleeper and had to be roused."

The Inspector looked at the bare walls of the *surdab*. The only break in the smooth brickwork was the air shaft; it resembled a narrow chimney and ended about six feet above the floor in an open vent. Chafik could see a small square of sunlight far above. The twittering of many birds echoed down the shaft and reminded him that the old man had loved birds and given them sanctuary in his garden.

"This place may be cool," the Inspector said, "but I do not find it restful. The birds are noisy."

Sergeant Abdullah interrupted, "Now what a knucklehead I am! I forgot to tell you about the bird."

"A bird?"

"Dead, sir, here in the *surdab*. It lay on the Hadji's lap, in his hand. I have labeled it as an exhibit."

He produced a pathetic bundle of black and white feathers. The bird had a forked tail and rakish wings; there was a chick's down on the breast.

Chafik said, "A swift." He touched the dangling head. "The neck is broken, it has not been dead long. A lazy fledgling that refused to fly until it was pushed from the nest. Possibly it tumbled down the air shaft, a not uncommon occurrence. Or perhaps it fell against the door. The thud might have disturbed the Hadji, made him leave his cot and open the door – "

He stopped and gave Abdullah a sharp look; the sergeant's rare expressions were easy to read and Chafik said with sudden wrath, "So you think somebody was waiting outside the door?"

"Sir, it did enter my mind."

"Was this person invisible that he wasn't seen by the watchman at the gate? Was he foolhardy enough to stand there while you were briefly dozing a few yards away? What fiction have you been reading?"

As he left the room, the Inspector added indignantly, “Must everybody die murdered to please you, Abdullah?”

The house was a relic of old Baghdad. Rooms opened on an inner courtyard tiled with honey-colored brick. An archway led to a terrace that faced the river. There was a garden bright with flowers and shaded by ancient trees, all enclosed within a high wall.

Chafik joined two men who were waiting on the terrace. One was the Hadji's nephew, a middle-aged man with the sallow hungry look of a sufferer from a stomach ailment. Romani, who practiced law in the southern town of Amara, came to Baghdad several times a year to visit his uncle.

His companion was much younger, little more than a youth, and had a downy mustache. He looked bored. The cut of his clothes and the way he wore them gave Chalik a twinge of envy and he hoped that one day he, too, might visit a Cairo tailor.

Reluctantly, he looked away from the dapper Sadir and waited for the older man to speak.

Romani asked, “Have you formed a conclusion?”

“I let facts form their own conclusions.”

The Hadji's nephew nodded approval. “It is a definite fact,” he said in his clear voice, “that my uncle was threatened. The Shafiites are a lawless people.”

“In the past they have not stopped at assassination,” the Inspector said.

“On the other hand,” Romani said, “it is wrong to use the history of yesterday as evidence of violence done today.”

Chafik made a little bow. “How justly you correct me! But I can say what I say about them because you alone took serious view of their threats. Your uncle did not.”

“In point of fact I agreed with him. But I advised him to ask for police protection as a precautionary measure, and when he refused, I took the step myself. Naturally.”

Chafik thought he knew why Romani's law practice was small. The man was cautious. He had a good reputation, always refused doubtful cases, but such legal ethics did not appeal to minds nurtured by the labyrinth of bazaars where business was conducted in Iraq.

The Inspector turned for relief to Sadir. “What did you think of the threats?” asked the young man.

Sadir was polishing his manicured nails. He looked up languidly and said, "I am used to the civilized life in Egypt. I confess I paid little attention to this talk of threats and violence." He mopped his face with a handkerchief. "Such heat!" he complained.

"You miss Cairo?" Chafik asked.

Surprised and pleased that somebody should understand him, Sadir became confidential. "This place destroys me," he said. "There is no beauty here. Life is crude, so lacking in urbanity – "

Romani interrupted, "Do not take our time with your foolish problems, Sadir. I know you wish to return to Cairo. It matters little to me personally, but the legal aspect of your case must be carefully considered. You were made my uncle's ward for two years. But we will discuss this later."

The young man flushed and moved away up the terrace. Romani shook his head and said sternly, "He has no sense of responsibility. Have you any more questions, Inspector?"

"I was going to ask if you entirely rule out the possibility of an intruder."

The Hadji's nephew looked down at the river, at a fisherman who stood in the shallows, his brown arm lifted to throw a weighted casting net. "I rule out nothing," he said finally. "But how could an intruder pass the police guard? Observe, for example, the height of the wall on the river side. The Tigris is at its lowest, there is a drop of thirty feet to where that fisherman stands. The door at the top of the step that leads down to the water is always locked."

Chafik interrupted, "What do you know about Murad, your uncle's watchman?"

"I believe he is able and trustworthy."

"He has a Kurdish name. The Shafiites are a Kurdish sect – "

Romani said, "I close my ears. What you say is slanderous, even defaming, and as a lawyer I advise you to be more cautious."

The Inspector permitted himself the thought that this man probably tested the temperature of his bathwater before he put a toe in it. Venturing another question, he asked, "Did you know your uncle was nursing a dead bird when he was found?"

Romani was startled. "A dead bird? No."

"It may have fallen down the air shaft or against the door. Your uncle loved birds. Something disturbed him in the *surdab*. If it was the bird he would have jumped up to succor it, and then – "

"In his haste he slipped, struck something – "

"Conjecture," Chafik said, smiling at his mild triumph. "But you may be right." He stopped, almost deafened by a shrill outcry from the many birds perched on the roof. "How noisy they are!" the Inspector said.

"I do not share my uncle's affection for birds. He would not allow a single nest to be destroyed." The thin voice trailed and Chafik looked at the man curiously.

Meeting the Inspector's eyes, the lawyer explained, "I had a thought. I reprimanded you for an unjust suspicion; now I find I have one myself."

"Concerning whom?"

"Murad. On previous visits I noted his sober habits. He rarely left my uncle's side. But lately I have seen him in cafés frequented by people of his class. I thought it odd because he is careful with money."

"What do you suggest?"

"I suggest nothing. I merely present facts." The lawyer turned away as a solemn procession began to file through the house gate. "The corpse washers and mourners are here," he said. "Excuse me, Inspector, I have my sad duties."

He went away, carefully choosing the middle of the tiles that flagged the terrace. The Inspector shrugged and turned to Sergeant Abdullah, who stood at his elbow. "You wish to interrogate the watchman, sir?" asked Abdullah.

He indicated Murad, who stood in the background at attention and holding a heavy brassbound staff at his side in the position of a grounded rifle. The man had a soldier's straight carriage. His hair and mustache were grizzled; he was quite old.

Chafik said, "Sometimes discreet inquiries are more fruitful than interrogation. I am told this man has changed his habits and become a frequenter of cafés. You will check this information."

"At once, sir."

When Abdullah left, Chafik completed his inspection of the house. He climbed high steps to the gallery surrounding the upper floor. Here had been the quarters of the harem women, but it was many years since bright eyes had peered through the iron latticework of the windows.

One door was open. The Inspector glanced inside and nodded approval of neatness. This must be Romani's room, he thought.

More steps led to the flat roof which had served as a promenade for the women in the cool of the day. At this hour it was exposed to the glare of the sun and Chafik covered the nape of his neck before venturing out.

He was greeted by a scolding chorus from the gathering of birds and was puzzled by their behavior until he looked up and saw a hawk poised in the sky. They were swifts, a gregarious species that banded together against an enemy, commonly nested in old buildings.

Chafik loitered to watch a pair perched on an air shaft. The cock picked a wisp of straw and offered it to the hen, who chirped plaintively and ruffled its feathers. Such obvious dejection roused the Inspector's sympathy and he said, “The fledgling that fell, was it yours?” He heard himself and was embarrassed because it was an old habit, this talking to himself.

Briefly he looked at the air shaft which rose a few feet above the parapet of the roof. The small vent in the side faced upriver to catch the prevailing summer breeze. Possibly this was the shaft which fed the *surdab*. There were traces of a nest in the vent, and Chafik wondered who had destroyed it. The Hadji would not have sanctioned it, but a servant might have taken unauthorized action.

“Was it your nest?” Chafik asked the unhappy pair, who had made shrill complaint at his approach.

He was again embarrassed by the sound of his voice making foolish conversation with birds. Walking to the far side of the roof, which overlooked the river, he glanced over the parapet. The fisherman he had noticed earlier was still standing motionless in the shallows.

The Inspector watched idly and then called down, “What fortune?”

The man looked up. “Fortune will come if Allah wills,” he answered.

“Do you expect fish to rise in this heat?”

“Who can be certain of the ways of fish and men?” the man said, shrugging. “I know there is a fish. It jumped and roused me when I was sleeping after the prayer. A very big fish, it made a big splash. I will get half a dinar for it in the bazaar.”

“You are patient. It is three hours since the noon prayer.”

The man said stubbornly, “He will rise when the sun goes down.”

“May you be rewarded,” Chafik said.

He went down the steps and passed the ground-floor room where the Hadji lay on the funeral bier, surrounded by chanting mourners. In the garden Chafik found Abdullah, who announced, "Sir, I have made the inquiries you requested. It is true about Murad."

"He frequents cafés?"

"Yes, sir. And I am informed he chooses places that have a Kurdish clientele. The Shafiites are a Kurdish – "

"Yes," said Chafik, twisting the signet ring on the little finger of his left hand. "I trust you made your inquiries discreetly?"

"I am your disciple, sir. I picked one of the lesser servants as a likely informant. When he talked, I arrested him on suspicion of theft so that no gossip of what I asked might reach Murad."

"You are as cautious as Mr. Romani. And now it would be tactful to remove ourselves from this house of mourning," the Inspector said. "My head whirls and I am going home to rest."

Entering his home on the Street of the Scatterer of Blessings, Inspector Chafik removed his jacket, loosened his tie, and announced to Leila, his wife, "I shall forgo food. Food causes a body to perspire. A perspiring body is as unpleasant as a dead one." He dropped into a chair under the ceiling fan.

There was an illusion of coolness; shutters had been closed at an early hour and the tiled floor was sprinkled with water to sweeten the air. The fan, rapidly drying Chafik's dank hair, chilled him, and he said irritably, "Wife, cover my head. You know I am susceptible to colds." He looked at the small boy who waited to greet him and added on a severe note, "A son should help his mother. Remove my shoes, Faisal." The boy squatted on his heels. Then, looking up at the tired man in the chair, he asked, "Was it a very bloody murder? Was his throat cut?"

Chafik forgot the heat. He said, "Such words from such tender lips! But the error is mine; I forgot you had ears."

The ears of the eight-year-old boy who had been a waif in the bazaars of Baghdad and adopted as the son of a childless marriage were small and pointed, and he had enormous eyes. The father tweaked an ear and smiled, then looked at his wife who took Faisal away.

She returned to cover her husband's head with a shawl and when he took her hand and held it to his cheek, she knew he was troubled. "Let me share the burden," she said softly.

"Did I speak? Voice a thought? It is such a disturbing habit, this talking to myself."

“You were silent, but a wife reads her man's thoughts,” said the small dark woman.

Chafik sat up and lighted a cigarette. “Yes, I am troubled,” he admitted, and told her of the death of Hadji Hussain.

Leila exclaimed, “Oh, the poor old man! He was so saintly, so beloved.”

“His death is a reflection upon my department.”

“So it was murder?”

“An accident,” Chafik said shortly.

“Then, my man, there can be no blame!”

“Women and ostriches,” said her husband, “both seek sand piles for their heads when faced by an unwelcome fact. The Hadji died surrounded by men. Therefore I am responsible, accident or not.”

“But it was an accident,” Leila insisted.

He said impatiently, “Yes, yes, an accident. It could not be otherwise since the house was so carefully guarded. I do not believe an enemy entered invisibly, struck him and vanished. But – “ Chafik looked for an ashtray for his cigarette and she hurried to bring one, “the watchman, Murad, changed his habits,” he finished.

“That worries you?” She did not understand, but let him talk to ease his mind.

“Everything would seem to indicate that Hadji Hussain's death was accidental. But the behavior of Murad is not clear. And then there is the dead bird. Did it fall inside or outside the *surdab*? And the open door. Did the Hadji open it? Before or after his fatal fall? I must satisfy myself on these points before I make my report,” Chafik added as he settled back to rest.

Leila left him and presently he was lulled by the swish of the ceiling fan. He slept for perhaps half an hour, restlessly, muttering to himself. Then something disturbed him and he was abruptly wide awake.

A rhythmic tapping came from the hall adjoining the room and a voice timed to it chanted in a whisper, “Wunna two, abbookel my shoe, three, four, shutter door – “

Inspector Chafik rose and drew back the bead curtain from the doorway. His small son was bouncing a hard ball against the floor; the ball was attached to an elastic band looped to Faisal's finger, which made it snap back into his hand.

“Fwife six, piccup six – “

Chafik said, "Macbeth murdered sleep; you murder sleep and the English language. They do not teach you well at school. Say, 'Five, six, pick up sticks.'" The father instructed with the precision that characterized his second tongue. "Six is a numeral. Sticks are instruments of chastisement. I am tempted to use one on you."

He took the ball, looped the elastic over a finger, and idly bounced it. When you can clearly say, 'One, two, buckle my shoe,' you may have this back," he said to Faisal.

Chafik turned away so that he should not see the tears in the boy's eyes; the man who had brought punishment to so many found it hard to punish his own child. "But, my father, already I speak English well," Faisal pleaded for approval. "Today I learned 'Hookilt cockerobbin.'"

"You learned what?"

"Hookilt – "

Chafik put his hands to his ears. "The word is neither Arabic nor English. Surely you mean, 'Who killed – ' and it goes on about a bird. A pity I cannot remember the rhyme exactly, to school you in it. I believe there is something about a sparrow."

The boy interrupted eagerly, "I sedder sparrow wit' my bowen narrow."

"Then," said Chafik, still trying to remember, "there was a fly. And Cock Robin's funeral was quite a social affair. All the birds of the air gathered – "

He stopped and looked blankly at his son and repeated, "All the birds gathered because one died. Yes, they do. Particularly gregarious birds such as swifts and sparrows." He opened his hands in a groping gesture and Faisal's ball fell and dangled unnoticed on its elastic. "I had assumed the hawk had alarmed them," Chafik went on. "A wrong assumption; they gathered to keen the end of the fledgling. And the dead bird in the Hadji's lap, when was it killed, how long before?"

Faisal was bewildered, angry, and tearful. "A bird, Father? Who has murdered a bird?"

"Who has murdered, and how?" Chafik repeated softly. Absently he began pulling up the dangling ball by its elastic, then suddenly let it fall and once more pulled it up, watching with growing excitement.

He announced, "There was a fish. It jumped. And a fisherman, a fisherman with his net."

"A net, Father?" Faisal repeated.

"The threads weave a pattern. But who was Death? Who – "

Chafik ran from the house, hatless, into the sun of late afternoon. He was halfway up the road when the wail of his son's voice penetrated the fog of his thoughts.

"Father, my father, you have forgotten your shoes!"

The Inspector hired a boat at the top of his street and dropped downstream to the river house of Hadji Hussain. He urged the boatman to make speed; he was afraid the fisherman might have gone away.

But the man was still there and looked up reproachfully as the boat floated under the high wall. "You scare my fish," he grumbled.

Chafik said, "It has not risen? Then cast your net. Here is a dinar; let me see your skill. Cast where you saw the splash."

The fisherman whirled the circular net and released it. Opening in midair, skiming the water like a giant bat, it struck the spot where he had seen the splash five hours earlier. Weights carried it down and with a leap the man was on it, feeling with his toes for what he had caught.

"There is something, but not a fish," he said with disappointment.

He ducked under and gathered the net around his prize. Shaking out the sand and gravel, he untangled an object from the mesh and brought it to the boat.

"A stone wrapped in a cloth," he said with disgust. "My fish!"

Chafik silenced him and examined the catch. Double folds of cloth were fashioned into a small stout bag. Inside was a smooth rock or lump of metal; the weight was about three kilos, the Inspector judged. The neck of the bag was strong twine which had been cut short and left a dangling end.

When Chafik looked up he had the face of a hanging judge and he said to the fisherman, "This day you have netted a man's head." Then he ordered his boat to shore.

He was admitted to the Hadji's house by the watchman.

Chafik said, "Oh, man of the hills, why did you change your habits and go to cafés? To places frequented by Shafiites?"

Murad answered directly, "I have eaten my master's salt these many years and went to look for his enemies among those who had threatened him. I would have killed them. Was that not proper?"

The Inspector looked at the man and saw tears in his eyes. He patted Murad's arm and said, "Forgive me, my mind follows tortuous paths. I did not perceive this simple explanation. Go with God, faithful servant."

He ran up the steps to the roof. Swifts were darting to and fro in the golden light of early evening, but the disconsolate pair he had noticed on his previous visit still perched on the *surdab* air shaft.

Chafik said, “Be comforted, you who witnessed this thing. Your evidence is very clear.”

He put the weighted bag by the shaft and went down to the gallery on the second floor. The mourners were still chanting below and there was an odor of incense.

The Inspector entered Romani's room and made a careful search of closets and drawers. His task was simplified by the lawyer's tidiness and he was soon finished. Empty-handed and troubled, Chafik announced in a flat voice, “Of course, one so cautious might have destroyed it.”

He went out and tried several of the other rooms. Left of the steps leading to the roof he found another that was tenanted and when he saw the clothing scattered around, the cluttered drawers, he had censorious thoughts for youth. But he searched methodically and disregarded the impulse to tidy the shambles.

With long, sensitive fingers he probed the confusion in the drawers of the dressing table. Then, from the jumble of odds and ends, he took out a tangled ball of strong cord. He put it in his pocket and continued the search.

There were letters with Cairo postmarks. He skimmed through them unaware that the chanting below had stopped, that the ceremony of preparing the corpse of Hadji Hussain was over. He was still reading, oblivious to his surroundings, when instinct warned him and he looked up.

Sadir stood in the doorway, and behind him was the gaunt figure of Romani. Sadir said petulantly, “What are you doing in my room reading my letters?”

“You will explain, Inspector,” interposed Romani sternly. “I strongly disapprove of this irregular action. As a lawyer – “

“The hyena,” said Chafik, “normally follows in the wake of the lion. I have not yet made the kill.”

“I shall complain – “

“Complainants, some of them, await on the roof. Let us join them.” The Inspector made his little bow.

He escorted the two men from the room and up the steps. Sadir had a dazed look and he stumbled. Romani's thin body was stooped. No one spoke.

When they were on the roof, Chafik said, "The open door of the *surdab* led me astray, but now I know who opened it. The Hadji received a fatal blow, and when he was able, he stumbled to the door for help. But already it was too late, and he collapsed after he opened it."

"An accident," insisted Romani. "My uncle tripped and fell."

"It was murder."

"He was alone in the room."

"Yes," said Chafik. "He was alone, yet he was attacked. I will show you how it was done. But we lack a dead bird, a fledgling. There was one in a nest here." The Inspector pointed to the vent of the air shaft. "Your uncle did not permit nests to be destroyed, but it was necessary to remove this one to clear the shaft. The marks on the stone prove it was done recently. Even more conclusive is the agitation of the birds. Have you noticed how many swifts have gathered, a whole community rallying a bereaved family?"

Romani said, "Come to the point. I know nothing about birds."

Chafik said, "Fortunately I have a son who remembered an English nursery rhyme. But to continue. The nest was destroyed, the neck of the fledgling was twisted, and as bait for the old man who loved birds it was dropped down the shaft."

He looked from one man to the other. The lawyer was tense, his forehead furrowed as though he concentrated on a difficult brief. Sadir's dazed eyes stared and chewed his underlip.

"The Hadji was reading," continued Inspector Chafik. "He was disturbed by the fall of the bird and rose to succor it. He picked it up, wondered what had caused the fatality, and naturally looked up the air shaft. Then this happened."

Chafik produced the weighted bag found in the river and knotted to the neck the ball of twine from Sadir's drawer. He said conversationally, "This is how a man was killed," and dropped the weight down the shaft, retaining the end of the line in one hand.

Nothing in forty feet of smooth brickwork impeded the fall. When the bag struck the floor of the *surdab* the sound echoed back.

"Not a perfect test," Chafik apologized. "It was not so noisy when it struck the Hadji's head. The force of a three-kilo weight falling forty feet can be calculated. It was not necessary to practice marksmanship – the opening is small and the target was large. Even a glancing blow would have been fatal to a frail old man."

He stopped and for the first time looked directly at Sadir. The young man's mouth opened, but no sound came from it.

"And then," the Inspector said pitilessly, "you hauled up your weapon, cut the line short and threw the bag into the river. Did you fear the line would float? But how careless of you to leave it in your room! Otherwise you planned well, took nice advantage of foolish threats made against your victim by quite harmless people. You reasoned that with a police guard around the house the death of a man in a closed room would be considered an accident. And you would have been right if parent birds had not keened the cruel death of a fledgling, if my son had not played with a toy which I found very suggestive. And if there had not been a patient fisherman." Romani shook his head and said in his thin voice, "This case has a weakness. What was the motive for the alleged crime?"

"You yourself told us this wretched young decadent preferred Cairo to Baghdad. Also there are letters from a woman which suggest a powerful motive. Sadir was desperate to get back to her, but the Hadji had been appointed his guardian and controlled his money and his freedom. Young, spoiled, ruthless – I trust you are convinced, Mr. Romani?"

Lulled by the cadence of his own voice, the Inspector was unprepared when the lawyer turned with unexpected speed and caught Sadir by the throat. "You killed my uncle! You killed my uncle!" he screamed as he forced the young man to his knees.

Chafik broke the death grip. "Restrain yourself!" he said sharply, and then smiled as he added, "Such depth of emotion, Mr. Romani! How admirable – and unexpected in one so cautious!"

Real Life Impossibility: United States
Miracle on 42nd Street

A strange experience befell Mr. & Mrs. P. of New York as they returned to their apartment on West 90th Street after a Broadway show.

As they descended into the subway at 42nd Street, they saw a train was already in the station and so hastened down the steps. Mrs. P. managed to get on board before the doors closed, but Mr. P. collided with a passenger coming up the steps and did not. So Mr. P. remained stranded on the platform.

At 96th Street Mrs. P exited and turned south to make her way home, deciding not to wait for Mr. P. As she passed the other station exit, situated between 94th Street and 93rd Street, she was astonished to see her husband in front of her, waiting for the 93rd Street traffic lights to change.

How was this possible? The doors had not opened a second time to allow anyone else to get on; there was but a single subway track, so no train could overtake another; there was no other subway line he could have taken; and a taxi would have been too slow. How was it that her husband was now standing before her?

While Mrs. P.'s train left the station with her in the front car, Mr. P. headed south down the platform, taking about two minutes to reach the far end (under 40th Street). New York subway trains are two blocks long and take about two minutes to enter the station, discharge and load passengers, and depart. It just so happened that the next train arrived almost immediately after the one before, so by the time Mr. P. reached the end of the platform, he was at once able to board the rearmost car.

When Mrs. P. arrived at 96th Street, she was closest to the northern exit. On reaching the street she turned south to go in the direction of her apartment. As she was walking south, she had to wait for two traffic lights. Mr. P.'s train arrived later, but since he was in the rear car he was right by the south exit of the station, and simply walked up the stairs to reach the corner of 93rd Street. O! Miracolo!

Ireland
The Warder of the Door
by L.T. Meade and Robert Eustace

Elizabeth Thomasina Meade Smith (1844–1914), born in County Cork, Ireland, was a successful writer (as L.T. Meade) of children's stories for over twenty years when she started writing mysteries of ingenuity and suspense, both on her own and with a series of male collaborators. In a little under fifty years, she wrote 280 novels, sixty-five mysteries, and dozens of short stories. Multiple locked-room short stories can be found in the collections *A Master of Mysteries* (U.K., Ward, 1898) and *The Sorceress of the Strand* (U.K., Ward, 1903).

Eustace Robert Barton (1854–1943) was an English doctor who successfully collaborated with several mystery writers, including Meade and Dorothy Sayers, as Robert Eustace. He is responsible, along with co-author Edgar Jepson, for the classic impossible-crime story "The Tea Leaf."

Together Meade and Eustace wrote eleven impossible-crime stories, six of which featured John Bell, a professional investigator of ghosts and other supernatural phenomena. "The Warder of the Door" is typical of the Meade stories, a fast-paced, seemingly paranormal thriller with an ingenious and logical solution.

"If you don't believe it, you can read it for yourself," said Allen Clinton, climbing up the steps and searching among the volumes on the top shelf.

I lay back in my chair. The beams from the sinking sun shone through the stained glass of the windows of the old library, and dyed the rows of black leather volumes with bands of red and yellow.

"Here, Bell!"

I took a musty volume from Allen Clinton, which he had unearthed from its resting place.

"It is about the middle of the book," he continued eagerly. "You will see it in big, black, old English letters."

I turned over the pages containing the family tree and other archives of the Clintons till I came to the one I was seeking. It contained the curse which had rested on the family since 1400. Slowly and with difficulty I deciphered the words of this terrible denunciation.

"And in this cell its coffin lieth, the coffin which hath not human shape, for which reason no holy ground receiveth it. Here shall it rest to curse the family of ye Clyntons from generation to generation. And for this reason, as soon as the soul shall pass from the body of each first-born, which is the heir, it shall become the warder of the door by day and by night. Day and night shall his spirit stand by the door, to keep the door closed till the son shall release the spirit of the father from the watch and take his place, till his son in turn shall die. And whoso entereth into the cell shall be the prisoner of the soul that guardeth the door till it shall let him go."

"What a ghastly idea!" I said, glancing up at the young man who was watching me as I read. "But you say this cell has never been found. I should say its existence was a myth, and, of course, the curse on the soul of the first-born to keep the door shut as warder is absurd. Matter does not obey witchcraft."

"The odd part of it is," replied Allen, "that every other detail of the abbey referred to in this record has been identified, but this cell with its horrible contents has never been found."

It certainly was a curious legend, and I allow it made some impression on me. I fancied, too, that somewhere I had heard something similar, but my memory failed to trace it.

I had come down to Clinton Abbey three days before for some pheasant shooting.

It was now Sunday afternoon. The family, with the exception of old Sir Henry, Allen, and myself, were at church. Sir Henry, now nearly eighty years of age and a chronic invalid, had retired to his room for his afternoon sleep. The younger Clinton and I had gone out for a stroll round the grounds, and since we returned our conversation had run upon the family history till it arrived at the legend of the family curse.

Presently, the door of the library was slowly opened, and Sir Henry, in his black velvet coat, which formed such a striking contrast to his snowy white beard and hair, entered the room. I rose from my chair, and, giving him my arm, assisted him to his favourite couch. He sank down into its luxurious depths with a sigh, but as he did so his eyes caught the old volume which I had laid on the table beside it. He started forward, took the book in his hand, and looked across at his son.

"Did you take this book down?" he said sharply.

"Yes, father, I got it out to show it to Bell. He is interested in the history of the abbey, and – "

"Then return it to its place at once," interrupted the old man, his black eyes blazing with sudden passion. "You know how I dislike having my books disarranged, and this one above all. Stay, give it to me."

He struggled up from the couch, and, taking the volume, locked it up in one of the drawers of his writing table, and then sat back again on the sofa. His hands were trembling, as if some sudden fear had taken possession of him.

"Did you say that Phyllis Curzon is coming tomorrow?" asked the old man presently of his son in an irritable voice.

"Yes, Father, of course, don't you remember? Mrs. Curzon and Phyllis are coming to stay for a fortnight – and, by the way," he added, starting to his feet as he spoke, "that reminds me I must go and tell Grace – "

The rest of the sentence was lost in the closing of the door. As soon as we were alone, Sir Henry looked across at me for a few moments without speaking. Then he said:

"I am sorry I was so short just now. I am not myself. I do not know what is the matter with me. I feel all to pieces. I cannot sleep. I do not think my time is very long now, and I am worried about Allen. The fact is, I would give anything to stop this engagement. I wish he would not marry."

"I am sorry to hear you say that, sir," I answered. "I should have thought you would have been anxious to see your son happily married."

"Most men would," was the reply, "but I have my reasons for wishing things otherwise."

"What do you mean?" I could not help asking.

"I cannot explain myself; I wish I could. It would be best for Allen to let the old family die out. There, perhaps I am foolish about it, and of course I cannot really stop the marriage, but I am worried and troubled about many things."

"I wish I could help you, sir," I said impulsively. "If there is anything I can possibly do, you know you have only to ask me."

"Thank you, Bell, I know you would, but I cannot tell you. Some day I may. But there, I am afraid – horribly afraid."

The trembling again seized him, and he put his hands over his eyes as if to shut out some terrible sight.

"Don't repeat a word of what I have told you to Allen or any one else," he said suddenly. "It is possible that some day I may ask you to help me – and remember, Bell, I trust you."

He held out his hand, which I took. In another moment the butler entered with the lamps, and I took advantage of the interruption to make my way to the drawing room.

The next day the Curzons arrived, and a hasty glance showed me that Phyllis was a charming girl. She was tall, slightly built, with a figure both upright and graceful, and a handsome, somewhat proud face. When in perfect repose her expression was somewhat haughty, but the moment she spoke her face became vivacious, kindly, charming to an extraordinary degree; she had a gay laugh, a sweet smile, a sympathetic manner. I was certain she had the kindest of hearts, and was sure that Allen had made an admirable choice.

A few days went by, and at last the evening before the day when I was to return to London arrived. Phyllis's mother had gone to bed a short time before, as she had complained of headache, and Allen suddenly proposed, as the night was a perfect one, that we should go out and enjoy a moonlight stroll.

Phyllis laughed with glee at the suggestion, and ran at once into the hall to take a wrap from one of the pegs.

"Allen," she said to her lover, who was following her, "you and I will go first."

"No, young lady, on this occasion you and I will have that privilege," said Sir Henry. He had also come into the hall, and, to our astonishment, announced his intention of accompanying us in our walk.

Phyllis bestowed upon him a startled glance, then she laid her hand lightly on his arm, nodded back at Allen with a smile, and walked on in front somewhat rapidly. Allen and I followed in the rear.

"Now, what does my father mean by this?" said Allen to me. "He never goes out at night – but he has not been well lately. I sometimes think he grows queerer every day."

"He is very far from well, I am certain," I answered.

We stayed out for about half an hour and returned home by a path which led into the house through a side entrance. Phyllis was waiting for us in the hall.

"Where is my father?" asked Allen, going up to her.

"He is tired and has gone to bed," she answered. "Good night, Allen."

"Won't you come into the drawing room?" he asked in some astonishment.

"No, I am tired."

She nodded to him without touching his hand; her eyes, I could not help noticing, had a queer expression. She ran upstairs.

I saw that Allen was startled by her manner, but as he did not say anything, neither did I.

The next day at breakfast I was told that the Curzons had already left the abbey. Allen was full of astonishment and, I could see, a good deal annoyed. He and I breakfasted alone in the old library. His father was too ill to come downstairs.

An hour later I was on my way back to London. Many things there engaged my immediate attention, and Allen, his engagement, Sir Henry, and the old family curse sank more or less into the background of my mind.

Three months afterwards, on the seventh of January, I saw to my sorrow in the *Times* the announcement of Sir Henry Clinton's death.

From time to time in the interim I had heard from the son, saying that his father was failing fast. He further mentioned that his own wedding was fixed for the twenty-first of the present month. Now, of course, it must be postponed. I felt truly sorry for Allen, and wrote immediately a long letter of condolence.

On the following day I received a wire from him, imploring me to go down to the abbey as soon as possible, saying that he was in great difficulty.

I packed a few things hastily, and arrived at Clinton Abbey at six in the evening. The house was silent and subdued – the funeral was to take place the next day. Clinton came into the hall and gripped me warmly by the hand. I noticed at once how worn and worried he looked.

"This is good of you, Bell," he said. "I cannot tell you how grateful I am to you for coming. You are the one man who can help me, for I know you have had much experience in matters of this sort. Come into the library and I will tell you everything. We shall dine alone this evening, as my mother and the girls are keeping to their own apartments for tonight."

As soon as we were seated, he plunged at once into his story.

"I must give you a sort of prelude to what has just occurred," he began.

"You remember, when you were last here, how abruptly Phyllis and her mother left the abbey?"

I nodded. I remembered well.

"On the morning after you had left us I had a long letter from Phyllis," continued Allen. "In it she told me of an extraordinary request my father had made to her during that moonlight walk – nothing more nor less than an earnest wish that she would herself terminate our engagement.

"She spoke quite frankly, as she always does, assuring me of her unalterable love and devotion, but saying that under the circumstances it was absolutely necessary to have an explanation. Frantic with almost ungovernable rage, I sought my father in his study. I laid Phyllis's letter before him and asked him what it meant. He looked at me with the most unutterable expression of weariness and pathos.

"'Yes, my boy, I did it,' he said. 'Phyllis is quite right. I did ask of her, as earnestly as a very old man could plead, that she would bring the engagement to an end.'

"'But why?' I asked. 'Why?'

"'That I am unable to tell you,' he replied.

"I lost my temper and said some words to him which I now regret. He made no sort of reply. When I had done speaking he said slowly, 'I make all allowance for your emotion, Allen; your feelings are no more than natural.'

"'You have done me a very sore injury,' I retorted. 'What can Phyllis think of this? She will never be the same again. I am going to see her today.'

"He did not utter another word, and I left him. I was absent from home for about a week. It took me nearly that time to induce Phyllis to overlook my father's extraordinary request, and to let matters go on exactly as they had done before.

"After fixing our engagement, if possible, more firmly than ever, and also arranging the date of our wedding, I returned home. When I did so I told my father what I had done.

"'As you will,' he replied, and then he sank into great gloom. From that moment, although I watched him day and night, and did everything that love and tenderness could suggest, he never seemed to rally. He scarcely spoke, and remained, whenever we were together, bowed in deep and painful reverie. A week ago he took to his bed."

Here Allen paused.

"I now come to events up to date," he said. "Of course, as you may suppose, I was with my father to the last. A few hours before he passed away he called me to his bedside, and to my astonishment began once more talking about my engagement. He implored me with the utmost earnestness even now at the eleventh hour to break it off. It was not too late, he said, and added further that nothing would give him ease in dying but the knowledge that I would promise him to remain single. Of course I tried to humour him. He took my hand, looked me in the eyes with an expression which I shall never forget, and said:

"'Allen, make me a solemn promise that you will never marry.'

"This I naturally had to refuse, and then he told me that, expecting my obstinacy, he had written me a letter which I should find in his safe, but I was not to open it till after his death. I found it this morning. Bell, it is the most extraordinary communication, and either it is entirely a figment of his imagination, for his brain powers were failing very much at the last, or else it is the most awful thing I ever heard of. Here is the letter; read it for yourself."

I took the paper from his hand and read the following matter in shaky, almost illegible writing:

"My dear boy, when you read this I shall have passed away. For the last six months my life has been a living death. The horror began in the following way. You know what a deep interest I have always taken in the family history of our house. I have spent the latter years of my life in verifying each detail, and my intention was, had health been given me, to publish a great deal of it in a suitable volume.

"On the special night to which I am about to allude, I sat up late in my study reading the book which I saw you show to Bell a short time ago. In particular, I was much attracted by the terrible curse which the old abbot in the fourteenth century had bestowed upon the family. I read the awful words again and again.

"I knew that all the other details in the volume had been verified, but that the vault with the coffin had never yet been found. Presently I grew drowsy, and I suppose I must have fallen asleep. In my sleep I had a dream; I thought that someone came into the room, touched me on the shoulder, and said, 'Come.' I looked up; a tall figure beckoned to me. The voice and the figure belonged to my late father. In my dream I rose immediately, although I did not know why I went nor where I was going. The figure went on in front, it entered the hall. I took one of the candles from the table and the key of the chapel, unbolted the door and went out. Still the voice kept saying, 'Come, come,' and the figure of my father walked in front of me. I went across the quadrangle, unlocked the chapel door, and entered.

"A death-like silence was around me. I crossed the nave to the north aisle; the figure still went in front of me. It entered the great pew which is said to be haunted, and walked straight up to the effigy of the old abbot who had pronounced the curse. This, as you know, is built into the opposite wall. Bending forward, the figure pressed the eyes of the old monk, and immediately a stone started out of its place, revealing a staircase behind. I was about to hurry forward, when I must have knocked against something. I felt a sensation of pain, and suddenly awoke. What was my amazement to find that I had acted on my dream, had crossed the quadrangle, and was in the chapel, in fact was standing in the old pew! Of course there was no figure of any sort visible, but the moonlight shed a cold radiance over all the place. I felt very much startled and impressed, but was just about to return to the house in some wonder at the curious vision which I had experienced, when, raising my startled eyes, I saw that part of it at least was real. The old monk seemed to grin at me from his marble effigy, and beside him was a blank open space. I hurried to it and saw a narrow flight of stairs. I cannot explain what my emotions were, but my keenest feeling at that moment was a strong and horrible curiosity. Holding the candle in my hand, I went down the steps. They terminated at the beginning of a long passage. This I quickly traversed, and at last found myself beside an iron door. It was not locked, but hasped, and was very hard to open; in fact, it required nearly all my strength. At last I pulled it open towards me, and there in a small cell lay the coffin, as the words of the curse said. I gazed at it in horror. I did not dare to enter. It was a wedge-shaped coffin studded with great nails. But as I looked my blood froze within me, for slowly, very slowly, as if pushed by some unseen hand, the great heavy door began to close, quicker and quicker, until with a crash that echoed and re-echoed through the empty vault, it shut.

"Terror-stricken, I rushed from the vault and reached my room once more.

"Now I know that this great curse is true, that my father's spirit is there to guard the door and close it, for I saw it with my own eyes, and while you read this know that I am there. I charge you, therefore, not to marry – bring no child into the world to perpetuate this terrible curse. Let the family die out if you have the courage. It is much, I know, to ask, but whether you do or not, come to me there, and if by sign or word I can communicate with you I will do so, but hold the secret safe. Meet me there before my body is laid to rest, when body and soul are still not far from each other. Farewell. Your loving father,
Henry Clinton."

I read this strange letter over carefully twice, and laid it down. For a moment I hardly knew what to say. It was certainly the most uncanny thing I had ever come across.

"What do you think of it?" asked Allen at last.

"Well, of course there are only two possible solutions," I answered. "One is that your father not only dreamt the beginning of this story – which, remember, he allows himself – but the whole of it."

"And the other?" asked Allen, seeing that I paused.

"The other," I continued, "I hardly know what to say yet. Of course we will investigate the whole thing, that is our only chance of arriving at a solution. It is absurd to let matters rest as they are. We had better try tonight."

Clinton winced and hesitated.

"Something must be done, of course," he answered. "But the worst of it is Phyllis and her mother are coming here early tomorrow in time for the funeral, and I cannot meet her – no, I cannot, poor girl! – while I feel as I do."

"We will go to the vault tonight," I said.

Clinton rose from his chair and looked at me.

"I don't like this thing at all, Bell," he continued. "I am not by nature in any sense of the word a superstitious man, but I tell you frankly nothing would induce me to go alone into that chapel tonight; if you come with me, that, of course, alters matters. I know the pew my father refers to well; it is beneath the window of St. Sebastian."

Soon afterwards I went to my room and dressed, and Allen and I dined tête-à-tête in the great dining room. The old butler waited on us with funereal solemnity, and I did all I could to lure Clinton's thoughts into a more cheerful and healthier channel.

I cannot say that I was very successful. I further noticed that he scarcely ate anything, and seemed altogether to be in a state of nervous tension painful to witness.

After dinner we went into the smoking room, and at eleven o'clock I proposed that we should make a start.

Clinton braced himself together and we went out. He got the chapel keys, and then going to the stables we borrowed a lantern, and a moment afterwards found ourselves in the sacred edifice. The moon was at her full, and by the pale light which was diffused through the south windows the architecture of the interior could be faintly seen. The Gothic arches that flanked the centre aisle with their quaint pillars, each with a carved figure of one of the saints, were quite visible, and further in the darkness of the chancel the dim outlines of the choir and altar table with its white marble reredos could be just discerned.

We closed the door softly and, Clinton leading the way with the lantern, we walked up the centre aisle paved with the brasses of his dead ancestors. We trod gently on tiptoe as one instinctively does at night.

Turning beneath the little pulpit we reached the north transept, and here Clinton stopped and turned round. He was very white, but his voice was quiet.

“This is the pew,” he whispered. “It has always been called the haunted pew of Sir Hugh Clinton.”

I took the lantern from him and we entered. I crossed the pew immediately and went up to the effigy of the old abbot.

“Let us examine him closely,” I said. I held up the lantern, getting it to shine on each part of the face, the vestments, and the figure. The eyes, although vacant, as in all statuary, seemed to me at that moment to be uncanny and peculiar. Giving Allen the lantern to hold, I placed a finger firmly on each. The next moment I could not refrain from an exclamation; a stone at the side immediately rolled back, revealing the steps which were spoken of by the old man in his narrative.

“It is true! It is true!” cried Clinton excitedly.

“It certainly looks like it,” I remarked. “But never mind, we have the chance now of investigating this matter thoroughly.”

“Are you going down?” asked Clinton.

“Certainly I am,” I replied. “Let us go together.”

Immediately afterwards we crept through the opening and began to descend. There was only just room to do so in single file, and I went first with the lantern. In another moment we were in the long passage, and soon we were confronted by a door in an arched stone framework. Up till now Clinton had shown little sign of alarm, but here, at the trysting place to which his father's soul had summoned him, he seemed suddenly to lose his nerve. He leant against the wall and for a moment I thought he would have fallen. I held up the lantern and examined the door and walls carefully. Then approaching I lifted the iron latch of the heavy door. It was very hard to move, but at last by seizing the edge I dragged it open to its full against the wall of the passage.

Having done so I peered inside, holding the lantern above my head. As I did so I heard Clinton cry out:

“Look, look,” he said, and turning I saw that the great door had swung back against me, almost shutting me within the cell.

Telling Clinton to hold it back by force, I stepped inside and saw at my feet the ghastly coffin. The legend then so far was true. I bent down and examined the queer, misshapen thing with great care. Its shape was that of an enormous wedge, and it was apparently made of some dark old wood, and was bound with iron at the corners. Having looked at it all round, I went out and, flinging back the door which Clinton had been holding open, stood aside to watch. Slowly, very slowly, as we both stood in the passage – slowly, as if pushed by some invisible hand, the door commenced to swing round, and, increasing in velocity, shut with a noisy clang.

Seizing it once again, I dragged it open and, while Clinton held it in that position, made a careful examination. Up to the present I saw nothing to be much alarmed about. There were fifty ways in which a door might shut of its own accord. There might be a hidden spring or tilted hinges; draught, of course, was out of the question. I looked at the hinges, they were of iron and set in the solid masonry. Nor could I discover any spring or hidden contrivance, as when the door was wide open there was an interval of several inches between it and the wall. We tried it again and again with the same result, and at last, as it was closing, I seized it to prevent it.

I now experienced a very odd sensation; I certainly felt as if I were resisting an unseen person who was pressing hard against the door at the other side. Directly it was released it continued its course. I allow I was quite unable to understand the mystery. Suddenly an idea struck me.

"What does the legend say?" I asked, turning to Clinton. "'That the soul is to guard the door, to close it upon the coffin?'"

"Those are the words," answered Allen, speaking with some difficulty.

"Now if that is true," I continued, "and we take the coffin out, the spirit won't shut the door; if it does shut it, it disproves the whole thing at once, and shows it to be merely a clever mechanical contrivance. Come, Clinton, help me to get the coffin out."

"I dare not, Bell," he whispered hoarsely. "I daren't go inside."

"Nonsense, man," I said, feeling now a little annoyed at the whole thing. "Here, put the lantern down and hold the door back." I stepped in and, getting behind the coffin, put out all my strength and shoved it into the passage.

"Now, then," I cried, "I'll bet you fifty pounds to five the door will shut just the same." I dragged the coffin clear of the door and told him to let go. Clinton had scarcely done so before, stepping back, he clutched my arm.

"Look," he whispered, "do you see that it will not shut now? My father is waiting for the coffin to be put back. This is awful!"

I gazed at the door in horror; it was perfectly true, it remained wide open, and quite still. I sprang forward, seized it, and now endeavoured to close it. It was as if someone was trying to hold it open; it required considerable force to stir it, and it was only with difficulty I could move it at all. At last I managed to shut it, but the moment I let go it swung back open of its own accord and struck against the wall, where it remained just as before. In the dead silence that followed I could hear Clinton breathing quickly behind me, and I knew he was holding himself for all he was worth.

At that moment there suddenly came over me a sensation which I had once experienced before, and which I was twice destined to experience again.

It is impossible to describe it, but it seized me, laying siege to my brain till I felt like a child in its power. It was as if I were slowly drowning in the great ocean of silence that enveloped us. Time itself seemed to have disappeared. At my feet lay the misshapen thing, and the lantern behind it cast a fantastic shadow of its distorted outline on the cell wall before me.

"Speak, say something," I cried to Clinton. The sharp sound of my voice broke the spell. I felt myself again, and smiled at the trick my nerves had played on me. I bent down and once more laid my hands on the coffin, but before I had time to push it back into its place Clinton had gone up the passage like a man who is flying to escape a hurled javelin.

Exerting all my force to prevent the door from swinging back by keeping my leg against it, I had just got the coffin into the cell and was going out, when I heard a shrill cry, and Clinton came tearing back down the passage.

"I can't get out! The stone has sunk into its place! We are locked in!" he screamed, and, wild with fear, he plunged headlong into the cell, upsetting me in his career before I could check him. I sprang back to the door as it was closing. I was too late. Before I could reach it, it had shut with a loud clang in obedience to the infernal witchcraft.

"You have done it now," I cried angrily. "Do you see? Why, man, we are buried alive in this ghastly hole!"

The lantern I had placed just inside the door, and by its dim light, as I looked at him, I saw the terror of a madman creep into Clinton's eyes.

"Buried alive!" he shouted, with a peal of hysterical laughter. "Yes, and, Bell, it's your doing; you are a devil in human shape!" With a wild paroxysm of fury he flung himself upon me. There was the ferocity of a wild beast in his spring. He upset the lantern and left us in total darkness.

The struggle was short. We might be buried alive, but I was not going to die by his hand, and seizing him by the throat I pinned him against the wall.

"Keep quiet," I shouted. "It is your thundering stupidity that has caused all this. Stay where you are until I strike a match."

I luckily had some vestas in the little silver box which I always carry on my watch chain, and striking one I relit the lantern. Clinton's paroxysm was over, and sinking to the floor he lay there shivering and cowering.

It was a terrible situation, and I knew that our only hope was for me to keep my presence of mind. With a great effort I forced myself to think calmly over what could be done. To shout for help would have been but a useless waste of breath.

Suddenly an idea struck me. "Have you got your father's letter?" I cried eagerly.

"I have," he answered. "It is in my pocket."

My last ray of hope vanished. Our only chance was that if he had left it at the house someone might discover the letter and come to our rescue by its instructions. It had been a faint hope, and it disappeared almost as quickly as it had come to me. Without it no one would ever find the way to the vault that had remained a secret for ages. I was determined, however, not to die without a struggle for freedom. Taking the lantern, I examined every nook and cranny of the cell for some other exit. It was a fruitless search. No sign of any way out could I find, and we had absolutely no means to unfasten the door from the inner side.

Taking a few short steps, I flung myself again and again at the heavy door. It never budged an inch, and, bruised and sweating at every pore, I sat down on the coffin and tried to collect all my faculties.

Clinton was silent, and seemed utterly stunned. He sat still, gazing with a vacant stare at the door.

The time dragged heavily, and there was nothing to do but to wait for a horrible death from starvation. It was more than likely, too, that Clinton would go mad; already his nerves were strained to the utmost.

Altogether I had never found myself in a worse plight.

It seemed like an eternity that we sat there, neither of us speaking a word. Over and over again I repeated to myself the words of the terrible curse: "And whoso entereth into the cell shall be the prisoner of the soul that guardeth the door till it shall let him go." When would the shapeless form that was inside the coffin let us go? Doubtless when our bones were dry.

I looked at my watch. It was half-past eleven o'clock. Surely we had been more than ten minutes in this awful place! We had left the house at eleven, and I knew that must have been many hours ago. I glanced at the second hand. The watch had stopped.

"What is the time, Clinton?" I asked. "My watch has stopped."

"What does it matter?" he murmured. "What is time to us now? The sooner we die the better."

He pulled out his watch as he spoke, and held it to the lantern.

"Twenty-five minutes past eleven," he murmured dreamily.

"Good heavens!" I cried, starting up. "Has your watch stopped, too?"

Then, like the leap of a lightning flash, an idea struck me.

"I have got it, I have got it! My God! I believe I have got it!" I cried, seizing him by the arm.

"Got what?" he replied, staring wildly at me.

"Why, the secret – the curse – the door. Don't you see?"

I pulled out the large knife I always carry by a chain and swivel in my trouser pocket, and telling Clinton to hold the lantern, opened the little blade-saw and attacked the coffin with it.

"I believe the secret of our deliverance lies in this," I panted, working away furiously.

In ten minutes I had sawn half through the wooden edge, then, handing my tool to Clinton, I told him to continue the work while I rested. After a few minutes I took the knife again, and at last, after nearly half an hour had gone by, succeeded in making a small hole in the lid.

Inserting my two fingers, I felt some rough, uneven masses. I was now fearfully excited. Tearing at the opening like a madman, I enlarged it and extracted what looked like a large piece of coal. I knew in an instant what it was. It was magnetic iron ore. Holding it down to my knife, the blade flew to it.

"Here is the mystery of the soul," I cried. "Now we can use it to open the door."

I had known a great conjurer once, who had deceived and puzzled his audience with a box trick on similar lines: the man opening the box from the inside by drawing down the lock with a magnet. Would this do the same? I felt that our lives hung on the next moment. Taking the mass, I pressed it against the door just opposite the hasp, and slid it up against the wood. My heart leapt as I heard the hasp fly up outside, and with a push the door opened.

"We are saved," I shouted. "We are saved by a miracle!"

"Bell, you are a genius," gasped poor Clinton. "But now, how about the stone at the end of the passage?"

"We will soon see about that," I cried, taking the lantern. "Half the danger is over, at any rate, and the worst half, too."

We rushed along the passage and up the stair until we reached the top.

"Why, Clinton," I cried, holding up the lantern, "the place was not shut at all."

Nor was it. In his terror he had imagined it.

"I could not see in the dark, and I was nearly dead with fright," he said. "Oh, Bell, let us get out of this as quickly as we can!"

We crushed through the aperture and once more stood in the chapel. I then pushed the stone back into its place.

Dawn was just breaking when we escaped from the chapel. We hastened across to the house. In the hall the clock pointed to five.

"Well, we have had an awful time," I said, as we stood in the hall together, "but at least, Clinton, the end was worth the ghastly terror. I have knocked the bottom out of your family legend forever."

"I don't even now quite understand," he said.

"Don't you? But it is so easy. That coffin never contained a body at all, but was filled, as you perceive, with fragments of magnetic iron ore. For what diabolical purposes the cell was intended, it is, of course, impossible to say, but that it must have been meant as a human trap there is little doubt. The inventor certainly exercised no small ingenuity when he devised his diabolical plot, for it was obvious that the door, which was made of iron, would swing towards the coffin wherever it happened to be placed. Thus the door would shut if the coffin were inside the cell, and would remain open if the coffin were brought out. A cleverer method for simulating a spiritual agency it would be hard to find. Of course, the monk must have known well that magnetic iron ore never loses its quality and would ensure the deception remaining potent for ages."

"But how did you discover by means of our watches?" asked Clinton.

"Anyone who understands magnetism can reply to that," I said. "It is a well-known fact that a strong magnet plays havoc with watches. The fact of both our watches going wrong first gave me a clue to the mystery."

Later in the day the whole of this strange affair was explained to Miss Curzon, and not long afterwards the passage and entrance to the chapel were bricked up.

It is needless to add that six months later the pair were married, and, I believe, are as happy as they deserve.

Japan
The Locked House of Pythagoras
by Soji Shimada

Soji Shimada is one of the top contemporary writers specialising in impossible crimes and locked rooms, along with Paul Halter. Both authors appeared on the May 21, 2012 Radio 4 programme Miles Jupp in a Locked Room, which attracted 500,000 listeners.

On January 29, 2014, Shimada's *The Tokyo Zodiac Murders* was listed in second place (just behind John Dickson Carr's *The Hollow Man*) in Adrian McGinty's Top 10 Locked Room Mysteries. The novel, published in 1981, was credited with sparking a Japanese renewal of interest in novels featuring the classic Golden Age puzzle plot, known in Japan as *honkaku* ("authentic" or "orthodox''). Prior to his arrival on the scene, Japanese detective fiction was dominated – as is western detective fiction to this day – by the *shakaiha*, or social school, which focused on motive and police procedure rather than the classic detective fiction of the 1930s.

Shimada worked tirelessly with "detective clubs" formed in Japanese universities and with selected Tokyo publishers to create a cadre of young writers such as Yukito Ayatsuji, whose *The Decagon House Murders* was a phenomenal success, to the point that *honkaku* novels now dominate Japanese mystery fiction and mangas (graphic novels intended principally for young readers).

As Ayatsuji himself says, through one of his characters: "To me, detective fiction is a kind of intellectual game: a logical game that avoids readers' emotional feelings about detectives or authors.... The point is to take pleasure in the world of reasoning. But intellectual prerequisites must be completely met."

Two of Shimada's short stories have already appeared in *Ellery Queen's Mystery Magazine* – "The Executive Who Lost His Mind" in August 2015 and "The Locked House of Pythagoras," which appears here, in August 2013."Pythagoras" is remarkably complex for a short story and, as with all his work, highly ingenious.

It had rained heavily all day. Because she had been assigned to clean-up duty, Eriko and a friend were still in the classroom after school, removing posters and students' projects tacked to the walls.

A tall, skinny boy stood awkwardly by the entrance to the classroom.

"Are you throwing that away?" he asked Eriko.

He pointed to a large, torn poster in vellum paper taped to the rear wall. The homeroom teacher had asked that it be taken down.

"Yes," Eriko replied. The boy seemed a couple of years younger than she was.

"Oh...then can I have it?" asked the boy, meekly. Eriko helped him bandage the tear and roll up the large vellum paper into a scroll.

"Thanks," said the boy. When Eriko asked him what he needed the paper for, he blushed a little and told her that he was going to fold it into a helmet.

"A helmet?" repeated Eriko, taken by surprise but handing him the paper. The skinny boy said nothing more, however, and walked out of the room.

Eriko's classmate, who had overheard them talking, told her that the boy's last name was Tsuchida and he was the son of the famous artist who had been on the selection committee for the Mayor's Award, given to the winner of an art competition involving works nominated by Yokohama's elementary and middle schools. Eriko's friend Kiyoshi Mitarai had previously been one of the nominees in the contest, although he wasn't a particularly talented painter.

Eriko was surprised to hear of the boy's identity, because she knew that the Mayor's Award had recently been cancelled due to a tragic event involving the boy's father, the famous painter Tomitaro Tsuchida.

At first, the Awards Committee had declined to give the reason for the cancellation, but it quickly transpired that Tsuchida had been murdered, along with his mistress Kyoko Amagi, during the time he was judging the submissions in his house in Uguisuoka.

It was not just the murders that caused the cancellation of the Mayor's Award, for replacement judges could have been found. There was another reason: The paintings, which had been found alongside the bodies of the murdered couple, were said to have been "tainted," but no further explanation had been given. Naturally, that aroused the parents' curiosity, particularly when it was learned that none of their children's paintings had escaped damage and therefore none would be returned.

So when Eriko realized that she had been talking to the son of the late artist, she was surprised at the boy's nonchalant attitude, given the recent loss of his father. She had lost her own father at a young age, and while she couldn't exactly recall how she behaved following his death, she knew for certain she wasn't as relaxed about it as the helmet boy had been. His shy grin remained engraved in her memory.

Eriko knew Kiyoshi liked crime mysteries, so she gleaned what she could of the Tsuchida case from conversations she overheard between her mother and the customers at their family-owned bar.

Tomitaro Tsuchida had been a good-looking man in his fifties, constantly involved in scandals with female models, pupils, and admirers. But it was his relationship with Kyoko Amagi, an accountant at the Yokohama city board of education, which remained the strongest. He paid for her apartment in Honmoku, where she lived away from her legal husband Keikichi Agami, a racehorse trainer. Before he rose to national prominence Tsuchida had lived with his wife Haruko and their son Yasuo – the helmet boy – in a tiny house across the river from the studio where he was found, but he had long since abandoned them.

It had been a month since the murders, but no progress was being made in its resolution. According to Eriko's mother, the Tsuchida murders were anything but ordinary, and the police were up against a brick wall for two main reasons.

First, the couple were murdered in a house that was completely locked from the inside. All the doors and windows were secured and none showed any evidence of tampering.

Second, the murders took place just after a heavy rainstorm, when the grounds surrounding the property were still wet. Yet the only sets of footprints found circled the house but did not enter or leave. One of the sets belonged to the estranged husband, Keikichi Amagi; despite the fact that his footprints didn't lead into the house, the police arrested him anyway. Although the police did not yet know it, the problems involving the locked building and the footprints in the mud were the least of their worries. An even greater mystery concerning the Tsuchida house was about to surface. Locked rooms and footprints in the mud were only the beginning.

Eriko and Kiyoshi attended The Wadayama School, located at the foot of the "Amerika zaka" ("America Slope"), so named because of the U.S. army base nearby. Every morning, Eriko waited for her friend near the entrance to the base, and the two of them then headed down the slope towards the school.

As they walked to school the day after her encounter with Tsuchida's son, Eriko told Kiyoshi about his strange request for the vellum paper to fold into a helmet, and also the latest information she had collected from her mother about the Tsuchida murders: its peculiar locked-room situation and the perplexing case of the footprints around the house.

"A helmet?" asked Kiyoshi, ignoring the news about the locked room and the footprints.

"Huh? Oh, yeah, he said he was going to make one," she replied.

"Hmm."

"Kiyoshi, is that something important?" Eriko was a bit surprised.

"Hey, wait up kids!"

A voice called out from behind them. It was Mr. Sakata, the homeroom teacher, who had been the Wadayama School representative on the Mayor's Awards committee. Mr. Sakata wore glasses and had a jocular demeanor. Never boastful and very friendly, he was popular among the students.

"Mr. Sakata, you chose the works of the awards finalists, right?" Kiyoshi asked.

"Well, I chose the ones from our school. Goodness, that must've been early May."

"There were a lot of finalists, weren't there?" Kiyoshi continued.

"That's right. Each school was given a quota."

"How many in total?"

"Seventy from all the elementary schools in Yokohama, and seventy from the middle schools. It was a nice round number, so I remember it very well," said Sakata.

"So one hundred forty total?" asked the boy.

"Yes, but this year they cut it back to one hundred and thirty-something."

"Do you know why they did that?"

"I don't know. They wanted to increase the number of elementary school submissions and reduce those from the middle schools. The committee proposed ninety and fifty respectively, but Mr. Tsuchida suggested eighty-eight and forty-eight. Since he was doing the final judging, the committee went along with his request."

"Strange, one thirty-six isn't a very round number, is it?"

"Apparently, by taking out four pictures, Mr. Tsuchida was able to make the process a lot easier somehow. It was a mystery how he could judge all those pictures inside his own house, which wasn't all that big, instead of using the school gymnasium. I guess he wanted privacy."

"I bet if we could work out why he took out four pictures, we could solve the whole mystery: the footprints, the locked room, and all the rest of it," Kiyoshi said, as they entered the school.

When Eriko came into Kiyoshi's classroom after classes were over, she found him leaning over his desk measuring the dimensions of a piece of drawing paper. Then he pulled out a magnifying glass from his pocket and began to look hard at its surface.

"Kiyoshi-kun, what are you doing?" she whispered. Without looking up, he said, "Examining a picture."

"A picture of what?"

"This piece received an honorable mention at last year's awards," he said, nonchalantly.

"What are you doing? What are you looking at? You know that's the back of the picture, don't you?" she asked him.

"Yeah."

"So that picture wasn't returned to its owner?" This time there was no reply. "You're not going to look at the front? Isn't the picture important? What's on the back? Kiyoshi-kun, why do you need a magnifying glass for that?"

"I'm pretty much finished. It's exactly what I thought," he said.

"What is?"

"The numbers. Three hundred sixty-four and five hundred fifteen. Now let's put this back in its place...." Kiyoshi lifted the back cover of the frame and put the picture back on the glass. He hung the picture back on the wall.

"Were you able to solve something?" asked Eriko.

"Yup, I've solved what Mr. Sakata was talking about this morning, about how Mr. Tsuchida was able to select one finalist out of one hundred and thirty-six pictures."

"You're so smart, Kiyoshi! So have you solved the murders?"

"I've only got the general idea. I still need to go to the site. If only I could get inside the house – that's going to be difficult. But let's go anyway."

"What, where?"

"To Mr. Tsuchida's house. Where is it, exactly?"

"My mother told me it's in the fourth block of Uguisuoka, by the river in the Honmoku district. A really weird-looking house with three two-story blocks arranged around a triangle, right next to a tall steel tower. But why are we going? We're only kids, we can't go to a real-life murder site!"

"We've got no choice. The police officers need me."

"Really? They can't solve it?"

"This case is too difficult. They don't even know how Mr. Tsuchida managed to select the finalists from inside his house! That's why they don't know who the murderer is, even after a month on the case. They're all confused and don't know what to do. That's why I've got to go."

The two left school and went up the hill towards the Honmoku district. They walked past trees with branches dripping rain and fields of tall weeds, and came to a narrow, winding road through green farmland. Eventually they could see a tall silver tower on elevated ground.

"That must be Mr. Tsuchida's house. Let's get closer," Kiyoshi said. Eriko shivered, partially because of the cold, but also from fear. It was the site of a double murder, after all.

"See, a river. Mr. Tsuchida's son – the boy you met yesterday – lives in one of those little houses on the opposite bank. His name's Yasuo, and he lives with his mom, Haruko. They don't have a telephone in their house," he continued.

"They're not living with his father?"

"No, they're living apart. The dad was living in the big house in front of us."

"Kiyoshi-kun, how do you know so much about this?"

"I asked the teachers. Adults follow this kind of stuff," Kiyoshi said, smirking.

Although it had been a month since the murders, there was still police tape at the entrance to the house. There was one uniformed police officer holding an umbrella and one detective wearing a raincoat over his hat. The moment he saw the men, Kiyoshi called out to them.

"Hello officer, did Mr. Amagi explain how he killed Mr. Tsuchida?" The man stopped and looked back at Kiyoshi curiously. Eriko nervously awaited his reaction. The detective was fifty or so years old, old enough to be their father. He was skinny and had protruding buckteeth.

"What do you want?" he demanded.

"Can we have some information about the room where Mr. Tsuchida was murdered? What were his surroundings like?" Kiyoshi asked.

The detective gave a condescending sneer, as the two had anticipated.

"Who do you kids think you are? Go back home," he said and began to walk away.

"Hold on, Mr. Amagi hasn't told you how he did it, right?"

"He doesn't need to, we already know."

"Then how?" Kiyoshi asked, and the detective scoffed.

"Why do I have to tell you kids? Get lost."

"You want to know, right? I know you're having trouble finding the killer. I can help you, and I can tell you how he did it."

The bucktoothed man, reacting to such a bold declaration from a mere boy, burst into loud laughter.

"Hey kiddo, you best stop your jokes right there, or I'll really get angry. I told you we've already got the killer."

"I hope so."

"What did you say?!" With a frightening glare he began to walk towards them. Eriko shrank away as far as possible.

"Look here, brat. You'd better watch what you say, huh? This is a real-life murder, not a detective game." His gaze was serious and menacing, but Kiyoshi didn't flinch.

"But I'm serious about this. You've got to listen to me, if you want to solve the case!"

"I've told you that we've got the killer!" the man's face grew red with fury.

"But the footprints, they only circle the house, don't they? They don't go in. And every window and door is fastened on the inside, right? How was Mr. Amagi able to kill them?"

"We know all about that, kid. So are you telling me Tsuchida committed suicide?"

"I'm sure there are people who think that."

"Well that's impossible. Tsuchida was stabbed in ten places, and the weapon is nowhere to be found."

Kiyoshi was visibly pleased with this statement. He had been able to extract a valuable piece of information. He continued:

"I know it's not suicide. The pictures, they were dirty, right? How were they dirty?"

"That's confidential info, kiddo. Haven't even told the press about that," he said, starting to walk away.

"Please, you don't need to tell me everything. I already know about most things. I'm doing this for your sake!"

The detective stopped again in his tracks, and with a contemptuous, cold smile on his face, he spat out in the cruelest way possible:

"All right, why don't you tell me how he was killed, huh?" He turned his head back and called out to his fellow police officer. "Hey, you got the dimensions of the room? We'll see if we need them later, but do you have them with you now?"

"Five thousand one hundred and fifty millimeters!" screamed the boy suddenly. The detective froze. The officer in the distance heard, too, and stopped dead in his tracks.

"The two were killed in a square room, each side five meters and fifteen centimeters long."

The detective slowly turned around and faced Kiyoshi. His little eyes were bulging and his jaw had dropped wide open.

"And although there were tatami mats over the floor of the room, you couldn't see them when you went in. Why? Because every space on the floor was filled with the pictures for the Yokohama Mayor's Awards. Am I right?"

The men didn't answer. They heard only the sound of the rain beating down.

The police received a call at 5:43 p.m. on May 25. Suspicions arose from the fact that Kyoko Amagi had not returned home to her apartment on the evening of the twenty-fourth, nor had she attended the educational board meeting in the city hall the following morning. Minetaro Nagaoka, a member of the city council, had tried to phone the Tsuchida residence but there had been no reply. Sensing something was wrong, he had gone to the house and then phoned the police.

The estimated time of death was between 3 p.m. and 5 p.m. on the twenty-fourth. Up until two-thirty in the afternoon of the same day, it had been raining nonstop. The soggy ground would have captured the footprints of anyone who had entered or left the house after that time. No decorative ornaments or stepping stones were to be found around the Tsuchida home; there was nothing but soft, bare earth.

Muraki and Hashimoto of the Honmoku police department, accompanied by two crime scene investigators, arrived on the scene at six-twenty on the evening of the twenty-fifth and immediately placed caution tape around the house.

The investigators shone their flashlights on the sodden soil and identified two separate sets of footprints, as evident from the differences in the depth of the imprints. One set of shoes had left their mark immediately after the rain, and the other set long after it had ceased. The lab investigators made plaster molds of the prints, which were later identified as belonging to Minetaro Nagaoka and Kyoko's estranged husband Keikichi Amagi.

Because every door and window was tightly closed and locked from the inside, the officers had to break the glass door of the front entrance and force their way in. They found themselves in a roughly triangular hallway, widening out towards the rear, with a staircase to their right. They took off their shoes and proceeded up the stairs. They found themselves in a hallway that was a perfect right-angled triangle with the shortest wall directly ahead of them and a longer wall, perpendicular to it, on their left. The doors in both walls were open.

The policemen went into the room to their left. Due to a large skylight, the square room was eerily bright; the moon and stars illuminated an empty easel, a wooden box containing tubes of oil paint, an empty vase, and a tall, decorative set of shelves. When they switched on the light, they could see a pair of sliding windows in front of them and another pair to their left. All the windows were framed by half-drawn dark, floral-printed curtains and locked with half-moon latches. On closer inspection, the curtains were found to be speckled with paint, which suggested the room was Tsuchida's principal studio. Otherwise the room was very clean, with no traces of blood anywhere.

The two detectives proceeded next to the adjacent smaller room. It, too, was square with a skylight and had curtained sliding windows on three sides of the room, all fastened shut with the same half-moon locks. Through the window straight ahead of them they could see a row of beech trees, behind which they could make out the lights from the houses on the other side of the river. There was another view of the river and some flat fields from the window to their right. When they crossed the room and opened the third window, they were startled to see a steel pylon obstructing the view. It stood about three meters away from the window; looking down, they could see the steel fence surrounding it at the base, bedecked with DANGER signs. The room itself was empty except for a couple of watercolors on the walls, an easel, and an empty vase. Tubes of paint, brushes, palettes, and drawing paper were scattered around on shelves fitted to the walls; curiously, all the red tubes of paint looked to have been squeezed dry. The room appeared to have been an ancillary workshop to the main studio and was, if anything, even cleaner; a mop lay under the window.

Muraki and Hashimoto made a brief examination of the remaining two upstairs rooms whose open doors were set on either side of the stairwell. The first appeared to be a bedroom with a couch, a table, and a television set. There was a nude portrait of Kyoko Amagi on one of the walls; she sat vacantly on the same couch that was in the room.

The second appeared to be a storage room with a glass-fronted alcove but no furniture. Each room had several sliding windows, all firmly locked in the same manner as the others. They went downstairs.

At the foot of the stairs, along the longest wall, was a door which was locked. They decided to inspect the other rooms first. Immediately opposite the locked room was an open door leading to a kitchen which, in turn, led out into a garden. The kitchen was empty except for a stack of cleanly washed paint dishes stacked on the stainless steel sink, and appeared to be spotlessly clean. The windows over the sink and the door to the garden had been locked from the inside. Adjacent to the kitchen was a dining room with only one set of windows, firmly locked. The connecting door between the kitchen and dining room was open.

Almost perpendicular to the dining room, and directly beneath the workshop on the floor above, was a suite of bathrooms. The men's room, women's room, and main washing room were all empty and all had securely locked windows. The two detectives returned to the room with the locked door at the foot of the stairs and one of the investigators broke down the door.

They stopped dead in their tracks at the sight that greeted them.

Tsuchida and Amagi were lying side by side in a sea of red. Almost the entire floor area was colored with a blinding hue of red. At the same time, the two detectives were assaulted by an intense odor which rushed out the moment the doors were broken down.

"What a foul smell, I wish I could open the windows. What is this red...?" said Muraki.

The combination of the smell and the blinding red color made them feel faint, even though they were veterans accustomed to seeing blood. Speechless, they stared at the panorama of red for several moments.

The room itself was the largest in the building and was perfectly square except for a narrow south-facing veranda directly in front of them, which stuck out into an equally narrow garden, and a storage alcove which ran most of the length of the wall to their right and contained zabuton floor cushions, a couple of low tables, a flower vase with a needle point holder, and other paraphernalia for *ikebana* flower arranging. In the corner to their left was a small *tokonoma*, a ceremonial display space whose four corners were lined with bamboo sticks. There were several staggered shelves on its walls, on which were placed small wooden chests. The wall of the *tokonoma* to the policemen's immediate left featured a wooden transom with two small rectangular openings separated by a thin bamboo rod.

As they stared, the reason for the redness began to dawn on them. The floors were lined with red paper. It seemed to be thick paper, and upon close observation it became clear that it was drawing paper. Each paper was colored red and carefully placed on the floor, without gaps and without overlap, just like tiles. The paper reached from wall to wall, except for the *tokonoma*, the storage alcove, and the veranda.

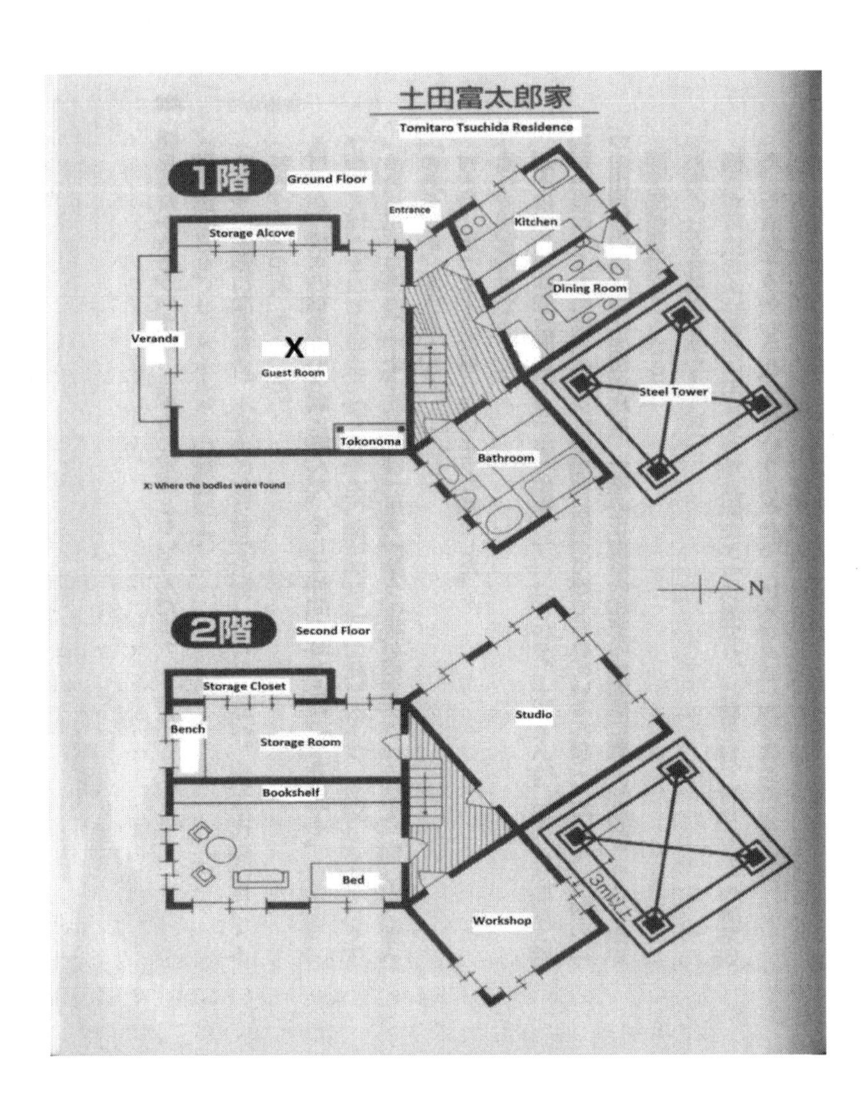
土田富太郎家
Tomitaro Tsuchida Residence
1階
Ground Floor
Entrance
Storage Alcove
Kitchen
Dining Room
Veranda
X
Guest Room
Steel Tower
Tokonoma
Bathroom
X: Where the bodies were found
N
2階
Second Floor
Storage Closet
Studio
Bench
Storage Room
Bookshelf
Bed
3m以上
Workshop

The *tatami* mats which normally covered the floors in a Japanese-style guest room were not visible.

"Muraki-san, I think this may be children's artwork," said his partner, Hashimoto. "I can vaguely see pictures beneath the red. My guess is that they are the finalist pieces for the Mayor's Awards."

"Why are the pictures on the floor?"

"Tsuchida-san was in the process of choosing the winner. The rumors said he always did the selection process in this house by himself instead of an open space like the school gymnasium, for privacy."

"Let's pull out some of this paper and form a path so you can get to the bodies," suggested one of the investigators. He used white gloves to remove ten pictures, which he gently placed in order by the broken door.

After a narrow path had been created, it could be seen that the light-brown *tatami* didn't seem to be tainted at all; no blood had leaked between the papers.

Hashimoto led the way to the bodies and squatted down.

Tsuchida and Amagi were lying close to one another, but no part of their bodies was touching; they were not even holding hands. There was no sign of their clothes having been pulled off or being in disarray. The color of their clothes was almost unidentifiable because their bodies were soaked in blood, now darkened and caked onto the fabric. Tsuchida was holding a paintbrush in his left hand.

"This is awful," said Hashimoto.

"What is?" Muraki said as he crouched by his side. "Ahh," he grunted in understanding: there were simply too many wounds on the two bodies. They had been pierced just about everywhere, and the blood had caused the paper beneath them to harden onto their clothes.

"They've each been stabbed through an artery. Especially Tsuchida, on his chest, underarms, thighs, arms, you name it. At least ten stabs. The woman has slightly less, but she's still stabbed through and through."

"The room was locked on the inside. Tsuchida must have killed Amagi and then himself," said Muraki.

Hashimoto looked at Muraki. "So, what are you saying? Tsuchida first stabs the woman all over her body, then uses his brush and paints all of the artwork with her blood. Then he comes back to the middle of the room without leaving any footprints and commits suicide by stabbing himself ten times?"

Muraki stayed silent.

"Just from seeing these wounds, that's clearly impossible. Tsuchida has slashes all over his body, all extremely deep and each stab potentially fatal. Even if he were able to stab himself with such force, at the very most it would be twice. The same goes if the woman kills Tsuchida first. So this can't be suicide. And where's the knife anyway?"

They looked around. No weapons or other objects were to be seen anywhere in the room. Muraki became pensive. Hashimoto's analysis was difficult to deny.

"And another thing: There's very little trace of the blood that oozed out of the bodies. Most of it has been used to cover the paintings, and yet the blood from two bodies couldn't possibly stretch to the area of this whole floor."

"If it's not suicide, then why was the entrance to this room locked from inside?"

"Well that's obviously a problem. But I can guarantee you that this isn't suicide. Not only is there no weapon, there's no water cup nearby to clean up the spilled blood on the *tatami*, and there are no paint dishes or palettes in sight. To paint the whole room, the brushes would have to be cleaned at least once, and the blood would have to be thinned to spread it all over the 'canvas.' The reason why these supplies are missing is because someone else did it. Whoever it was washed the cups and dishes and put them away."

"What about the locks?" Muraki asked again.

"It's gotta be some kind of trick." Hashimoto kneeled down and investigated another sheet of paper. "Wait a minute, this is only red paint!"

"Some of the red is watercolor paint," said the investigator. "They used both blood and paint to cover everything. It looks as though some pictures are covered with only blood, and some with only paint. You can tell because the gloss is different." He pointed with his gloved hand.

"See, this part – it's got a whiter hue. That's paint, most likely watercolor. That paper there is somewhat darker and browner, so it's blood. If you look closely, you can see a clear distinction."

"What is used more, blood or watercolor?"

"At a glance, I'd say watercolor."

Muraki crossed his arms. Hashimoto asked:

"Why were the paintings laid down side by side, in such orderly fashion? If this were a murder, I'd expect the paper to be everywhere, crinkled and torn at the very least."

"That's true," Muraki agreed.

"But each painting is neatly arranged, without any trace of damage."

"Well either they were arranged after the murder, or put in place before the murder."

"Why'd they do that?"

The two became quiet again.

From a quick scan of the room, there seemed to be no trace of even blood-tainted scratches or marks, much less fingerprints. Also, there was no blood on the white curtains which had been drawn closed. They counted the paper sheets: There were forty-eight pictures in the area surrounding the bodies which were covered in blood and eighty-eight pictures on the periphery which were covered in red water color, for a total of one hundred thirty-six.

"Why forty-eight with blood and eighty-eight with paint? What do these numbers mean?" asked Muraki.

"I don't know."

"And why are they carefully spaced apart? Why's everything so damned organized? Why can't the paper be strewn all over the place?"

"Again, I don't know."

"And why the hell does this room have to be locked from the inside too?!" Muraki often thought out loud by yelling at his partner.

"Really sir, I don't know."

"This is completely incomprehensible. I've never seen anything like this in my life!" Muraki had completely lost it.

The next morning, Muraki and Hashimoto went into the city to visit Kyoko Amagi's apartment in Honmoku. Kyoko had been living there for six months already, kept by Tomitaro Tsuchida.

Kyoko's husband had adamantly refused to accept a divorce. Of course this bothered Tsuchida, but it especially affected Kyoko. After she moved out, Keikichi visited her apartment every night. When Kyoko refused to see him he would eventually retreat back home, but not before throwing rocks at her window and screaming abusive language. Already the neighbors were predicting it would end in murder.

The detectives next visited the racetrack in Negishi, because Keikichi Amagi had listed his profession as trainer. But when they got there, his fellow workers said he had been absent for several months. He had been living alone in the Amagi marital home in Sasashita city.

Muraki and Hashimoto visited the Amagi house the following day. Even though it was early afternoon, Amagi was already inebriated. When asked to accompany them to the police station for further questioning, he vacuously answered that he didn't mind. When they took his shoes and compared them to the plaster molds they had created from the footprints around the Tsuchida residence, they matched perfectly.

The footprints, plus his motive for killing Kyoko, strengthened the case against him and he was arrested the day after the police visit. At this point the Tomitaro Tsuchida murders had already made the headlines nationwide. Amagi was put in a detention center and subjected to intense interrogation for twenty-three days.

He initially denied killing his estranged wife, but eventually, after many days of violent accusations by the police, coupled with lack of sleep, he finally gave in and admitted to the double murder. He obediently signed the written statement affirming his crime. Thus the Honmoku police station was able to accomplish a speedy arrest.

However, while Keikichi admitted to the murders, he gave no explanation about the footprints, the locked rooms, or the blood on the paintings. When given the details of the red paper laid out on the first floor, he expressed astonishment. The investigators were in a quandary: They had reached the conclusion that Amagi was the killer, but they could not come up with a valid explanation for the execution of his crime. This meant that they were unable to accuse Amagi in court. That being so, they would need to release him from custody. The prosecutors would need an opening statement, but this would be impossible to construct, considering they had no explanation. The Honmoku police would become the laughingstock of the nation. Muraki and Hashimoto were truly stuck.

Kiyoshi Mitarai visited Muraki and Hashimoto in the rain again just when they were at a complete dead end and desperate for any help they could get. If someone could save them from a lifetime of shame, they were willing to swallow their pride and even accept the advice of amateurs. With the exception of children.

"Kid, how did you know the dimensions of that room?" Muraki demanded of Kiyoshi, piercing him with a threatening glare.

"It was deduction. You just needed to think a little."

"He knew the dimensions of the room. Five meters fifteen centimeters square."

This time it wasn't Muraki, but the other detective, who had just walked out of the house. He was a younger man and bigger-boned, with large eyes.

"Let me look around the house and I'll tell you how it was done."

"You're just a kid. We don't need any help from you," said Muraki.

Hashimoto held up his hand as if to quiet him.

"There's a lot of blood inside the house, kid. Are you all right with that?" he asked Kiyoshi.

"I'm fine. You can't solve murder mysteries if you're afraid of blood."

"Okay. Tell me how you knew that the dimensions were five meters fifteen centimeters," Hashimoto asked as a test.

"Five hundred fifteen times ten. You can do it in your head."

Hashimoto's gaze suddenly turned serious. Muraki, too, stared.

"What's five hundred fifteen?"

"The centimeter length of a B3 sheet of drawing paper. The Mayor's Award submissions were all on B3-size paper."

"And?"

"Mr. Tsuchida brought all of the finalists' pictures into his house, laid them on the floor of the guest room, and walked on top of them to decide the winner." The two were completely flabbergasted.

"What the – " They hadn't thought of that.

"Now that I – so that's why they were on the floor!" said Muraki.

"Tell us more, how many of those B3-size sheets were there?" Hashimoto pulled out his notebook. The boy continued:

"On a square floor, you would have to lay down one hundred forty such rectangular sheets of paper to fill it up. So, it would be fourteen rows of ten sheets per row. That would just about fill a room five meters fifteen centimeters square."

"But there weren't one hundred forty. There were only – "

"One hundred thirty-six. Four were missing." Kiyoshi interrupted.

Hashimoto paused, nodded, and turned to the boy.

"You're exactly right. Four were missing. Why was this?"

"I don't know, I can't just deduce this, I have to go see the place. That's why I'm here."

Hashimoto nodded twice.

"All right, come with me."

The guest room looked hardly different from how it did a month ago. Not knowing what to do with such an unprecedented crime scene, they had left it the way it was. Kiyoshi was in luck, for the police had been planning to clean it all up that night.

Kiyoshi put his umbrella in the stand by the door. There was an old, battered black one already there.

"What's this?" he asked.

"It's been there since we broke in. Probably Mr. Tsuchida's."

"Was it wet when you found it?"

"It was."

Kiyoshi stepped into the hallway and looked around. The rooms were getting dark, so Hashimoto turned on the light.

Muraki said, "I'll show you the upper floor in a minute. The hallway's not quite the same."

"It's a right-angled triangle, isn't it?" said the boy. Muraki gave a grunt.

Hashimoto went in and turned on the light in the guest room. Even fearless Kiyoshi paused for a minute, absorbing the disturbing sight before him. The bodies had been carried away, but the sheets of red paper had all been left the way they were.

Kiyoshi stepped past Muraki, took one of the sheets and examined the back of it with his magnifying glass. "There's not much blood there, on the *tatami*," he said, pointing to the center of the room. "Tell me, was there any paint?"

"There was." Hashimoto replied. His tone was dead serious.

"And the paint was…watercolor."

"That's…right. Forty-eight were blood, eighty-eight were paint."

"Just what I thought!" said Kiyoshi. "That's why there are four missing."

"So, have you figured it out?"

"Yup, just a bit more to go."

"How? You figured out the locked-room part too?"

"Locked room?"

"Ha, so you don't even know about that? A locked room is when these doors are locked from the inside – "

"Oh, I figured that out at the very beginning!" Kiyoshi cut him off, waving his hand. "That's how I was able to solve it."

"So it's Amagi?"

"So it's not Amagi."

"It's not?"

"Of course not, how can he kill two people if he never stepped inside the house?"

After a slight pause, Hashimoto said, "Good point..."

"They shouldn't have made this a locked room. Then I might not have been able to solve it. The killer must have panicked, after committing the murder. Can I go upstairs now?" Kiyoshi asked coolly.

"First tell me the dimensions of the second floor! Prove to me that you've used your brains for this."

"The dimensions for what?"

"The…well, how about the triangular hallway?"

"Approximately three meters nine centimeters, four meters twelve centimeters, five meters fifteen centimeters."

Muraki looked desperately towards Hashimoto. "Is that right?"

Hashimoto took out his notebook, flipped through the pages, and slowly nodded.

"Exactly right."

Muraki gritted his teeth.

They went upstairs and entered the larger of the square-shaped rooms. It was relatively bright, because it was still light outside. Kiyoshi saw some patterns moving along the wall, and realized they were caused by water slithering down the skylight. The rain was coming down hard again. He looked around the room and said, "This must be the room Tsuchida used to do his watercolor paintings. The wallpaper is vinyl coated, and there's an easel, oil painting kit, flower vase – are they exactly where they were when you first came in?"

"Yes."

Kiyoshi went to one of the windows. "Aluminum sash sliding windows with half-moon latches," he announced.

"All you can see is fields and forests," said Hashimoto. "It's like that from every window. You can see some houses, too, but they're a long way away."

The three stayed a little while longer, staring at the landscape through the rainy haze.

"Okay, next room." The boy led the way to the smaller room and the two detectives followed suit.

Kiyoshi walked first to the window to their left and stared at the wet, silver tower.

"This tower's pretty far from the window isn't it?"

"Yes, about ten feet."

"There's a steel frame on the tower here just at eye level. And what's that small roof down there?"

They looked down. A rectangular tin roof could be seen adjacent to the tower.

"That's a storage shack. Mr. Tsuchida just renovated the house, and they've stored some of the extra construction supplies in that shack, like wooden planks and plywood."

"What's this mop?"

"It was on the floor."

"On the floor where?"

"Just there, at the foot of the wall," said Hashimoto.

"So the handle was facing towards the latch. What can you see out of the other windows?" Kiyoshi walked over to the window opposite the door.

"Ah, the stream. And the trees along it. They're in leaf but you can see the houses behind through the branches. Is that a kitchen window? Oh look, there are people. You can easily see what's going on from here."

"Hey, enough of that, did you figure it out?"

"Yup, completely solved." Kiyoshi's face was glowing. The detectives didn't say a word. They were waiting for him to speak.

"Thank you, both of you, now I'm completely satisfied. I've got to go now, Eriko must be scared out there alone." He began to walk briskly out of the room. The detectives followed him.

"You don't need to see the other rooms?" Muraki said, curious.

"Nope. I'm in a hurry."

"Come on boy, can you please tell us what you know before you go?" Hashimoto said. "We made a promise earlier didn't we?"

"What's going to happen to Mr. Amagi?" asked Kiyoshi.

"He's scheduled to go to court," answered Hashimoto. "And then jail. Then he'll be put to death. He's charged with double murder."

"Without proof?"

"He's confessed," Hashimoto said.

"He confessed? He said he killed them?"

"He did." The three arrived at the front door. Eriko beamed with relief, seeing that Kiyoshi was back. He silently put on his shoes. Then he stood at the entrance without saying a word.

"Can you tell us what you discovered?" Hashimoto asked. The boy didn't answer. He pulled out his umbrella from the rack.

"You really want to know?"

"Yes," nodded Hashimoto.

"What about you?" he turned to Muraki, who said nothing and kept a smug face. Kiyoshi turned his back on them again.

"Wait, just wait. You don't want to help Amagi?" Hashimoto asked. "You said it wasn't him, right? He's going to die, you know!"

The boy stopped. He turned his head to the side, silently.

"If you really want to know, come at noon to the front gates of Wadayama School. And bring this umbrella." He pointed at the worn, black umbrella left limply in the rack.

"This? To your school? Why?"

"I'll show you the killer. I've solved it, but I have no proof. I can confirm it using this umbrella."

"Really?"

"Yes, but I need the umbrella. Please bring it. If you don't, I can't tell you anything. All right, I'll let you two decide whether you want to visit tomorrow. Thank you for your time today, and for showing me the house. Let's go, Eriko."

The two walked outside, the rain beating down upon them. They left the detectives standing by the entrance, speechless.

The next day the clouds hung heavily in the sky above, but there was no rain. The two detectives were standing by the sycamore trees near the front gates of Wadayama School, looking bored and detached. One of them held a large black umbrella. It was five minutes to noon.

Kiyoshi, who had been sitting on a bench near the water fountain, stood up and walked over to the detectives. Eriko followed.

"Here's the boy genius!" Hashimoto exclaimed. Muraki was silent.

"Let's go," said Kiyoshi. "Follow me."

He walked into the school. They took off their shoes in the entrance hallway and Kiyoshi led them to one of the classrooms.

"Eriko, which one is Yasuo?"

"That's him!" she said and pointed to a tall, skinny student buttoning the pocket on his white long-sleeved shirt.

"Can I have the umbrella now? Okay, I'll be right back."

The detectives stood near the lockers, and Eriko hid behind a column. Kiyoshi walked up to Yasuo and showed him the umbrella. After a brief conversation, the boy took it. Kiyoshi came back, and the boy went away with the umbrella in hand.

"He took it," he said. "He shouldn't have, but he did. All right, now it's confirmed. Let's go everyone, let's get out of here." They headed back to the school gates.

"So tell us," said Hashimoto. "Is he the suspect? That boy?"

"No. He was the accomplice."

"With the killing?"

"No, with the cleanup. He was summoned."

"By who?"

"The killer, of course."

"Who is that?"

"Hold on a second," said Kiyoshi, and became lost in deep thought.

"In any case, Amagi isn't the suspect, right?" Hashimoto asked.

"Definitely not, let him go now, the longer you wait the more complaints you'll get."

"That's only when we find the real suspect." Muraki said. "Who was that kid, anyway?"

"Yasuo Tsuchida. Mr. Tsuchida's son."

"Ah, he's the one living away from Tsuchida. He's the kid who doesn't have a phone in his house."

"All right, if you want to know everything, pick me up by car at 7 p.m. tonight. We'll go together to the site and I'll explain everything there."

"What about me?" asked Eriko.

"You stay at home. I'll explain everything tomorrow."

"There's no fear of the suspect escaping?" Muraki asked sternly.

"No."

"Can't you just tell us now?" asked Hashimoto.

"I have to do it there," Kiyoshi insisted.

"Let's go now, then. We're busy people you know, we can't waste time. I know you kids might have homework or something – "

"I don't care about homework. I just can't confirm anything unless it's dark," Kiyoshi said.

"You just did with the umbrella, didn't you? Isn't that enough? How much longer do we have to wait?"

"Just a few more hours! I've worked out the situation, but it's only a theory. The umbrella's not enough proof. Please, I'm about to accuse a grown adult for murder. Don't you want to confirm that everything I say is right?"

After a pause, Hashimoto said, "All right." He seemed resigned.

Even Muraki seemed convinced.

At 7 p.m. that night, the two detectives collected Kiyoshi as planned. He sat in the back seat with a spray bottle on his lap.

"What is that?" asked Hashimoto.

"I'm using this to prove whether my theory is correct," Kiyoshi said rather excitedly.

"I sure hope you're not going to set the house on fire," Muraki grumbled.

The caution tape still surrounded the house. The detectives walked over it, while Kiyoshi ducked underneath. The driver remained in the car. When the engine was shut off, the entire place was dead silent. A crescent moon glowed in the sky.

Muraki had the keys to the house. When he turned it, the glass door made a deafening crack, throwing them off guard. Even the smallest sound was like a gunshot in the quiet of the house.

Muraki turned on the switch to the entrance. Hashimoto and Kiyoshi followed him inside.

"I want to go upstairs first," said the boy and led the way up to the smaller studio. He flipped on the switch, then sprayed the walls, shelves, windows, curtains, floors, door, doorknob, easel, and vase with his bottle. He sprayed the entire room without missing a spot.

"Hey…hey! What are you doing?" Muraki asked.

"It's not gasoline, don't worry! Just let me do this first and I'll explain everything."

They went to the room next door, then the triangular hallway and down the stairs into the guest room, finishing up in the kitchen.

"All right, finished!" said Kiyoshi. "Now I'm going to show you two something cool. Let's go back upstairs."

He led the way again, back to the door of the smaller room, which he opened slowly.

"Wow!" The detectives exclaimed. It did not look like the room that they had just been in.

"What is this?" Hashimoto asked.

"It's like phosphorus glowing," observed Muraki.

A bluish-purple glow was being emitted from all around the room.

It was as though blue, moonlit water droplets had fallen from the skylight. The light created a pattern all along the room as if the walls were doused with rainwater, which dripped along the window frame and formed pools near the shelves. The most striking part was the floor, where there were several puddles forming designs like geometric art. The easel and vase remained dark.

"What is this?" Hashimoto asked, entranced.

"These are traces of blood," said Kiyoshi.

"Blood? What do you mean?"

"This is a reaction called chemiluminescence. When certain types of chemicals are mixed, they form a chemical reaction in the form of light. The chemical I sprayed over the rooms was a liquid called luminol. It glows when it comes into contact with acids like ferricyanide in blood." The two detectives were speechless at the beauty of the scene.

"The splashes of blood are like fireflies!" Muraki exclaimed.

"Luminol's not widespread in Japan yet. But very soon it will be used by the police too," said Kiyoshi.

"So you're saying there was all this blood in the room?" Muraki asked.

"Right. It was wiped clean after the blood got all over the place. This was possible because the wallpaper was vinyl. Though we couldn't see it then, we can now, using luminol."

"So there was a bloodbath in this very room?" Muraki asked.

"Probably an artery. Or the jugular vein," said Hashimoto.

"But everything was wiped clean…so what does that mean?"

"The two were murdered here," explained Kiyoshi.

"Then what about the guest room?" Muraki wanted to know.

"It wasn't there, it seems," said Hashimoto.

They walked into the triangular hallway. Kiyoshi turned off the lights.

"See?" They needed no explanation. When the lights turned off, the floor was suddenly aglow with fireflies again. There seemed to be an army of them, leading out of the room they were just in outside, and down the stairs.

"So the bodies and paper were dragged outside and down to the guest room. They went back and forth so many times, forming a path." The detectives sighed.

"Look here, you can just about make out footprints."

"You're right!" a pair of bare feet glowed through the blood trail. They led to the staircase. Hashimoto compared the mark to his own foot.

"It's small! Is this a woman's?"

"It might be Kyoko's," said Muraki.

"Where did you get this chemical, boy?" Hashimoto asked.

"I live on a university campus. I borrowed some from the lab – after I asked for permission, of course."

Hashimoto whispered into Muraki's ear. "This is like a science lecture," he said.

Kiyoshi opened to the door to the second, larger room. This room remained completely dark. Not a single drop of blood could be seen there. Compared to this room, the neighboring room was like a city full of neon lights.

"So the two were not killed in this one but in the smaller room, and the bodies were carried down the stairs and into the Japanese guest room?" Hashimoto asked, and the boy nodded.

The three went downstairs to the guest room and turned the lights off. Compared to the city glow upstairs, it was much like an aerial view of a quiet town in the countryside. None of the walls, doors, curtains, or panels was glowing. The pool of blood in the middle remained dark and black because Kiyoshi hadn't sprayed that area, for obvious reasons.

"Not very dark. So this must mean not much blood had flowed here."

"Just the blood that spilled after the trip downstairs."

"Right, that's why it's only on the mats. The walls were untouched."

"Wait, I still don't understand," said Muraki. "So the murderers dragged the slaughtered bodies down here into this room. Then they placed them on the paper and colored them with the remaining blood, is that what happened?"

"I suppose so," said Hashimoto. "Is it, boy?"

"Actually, no," Kiyoshi shook his head. "Let's go upstairs again."

He walked back inside the luminescent room. "See the floor? See these lines, sort of like the grids of a checkerboard? Do you know what that is?"

"No," said Hashimoto. Muraki was silent but he didn't know either.

"It's the blood that seeped between the drawing paper!"

"Oh, wow, I see!" Hashimoto exclaimed.

"So the artwork was originally here too?" Muraki asked.

"That's right. The thin lines indicate that the blood dripped between the paper. The puddles indicate that the paper became disarranged and the blood seeped onto the floor. The killer and the victims must have had a wrestling match here."

"Hmm, but didn't Tsuchida always judge the artwork in the guest room downstairs? I thought that was what you told us."

"This year was different. He decided to do the judging in this room and the one next door."

"In two rooms?"

"To separate the elementary and middle school divisions."

"I'm completely blown away. So, what exactly happened on the day of the murder?" Hashimoto asked.

"First, Mr. Tsuchida sorted out all finalists from the middle school division and placed them here on the floor. He did the same thing with the elementary school division in the next room, which is larger. But he was killed in this room."

"On top of the artwork?"

"That's right. That's why there was blood all over it, and it splashed on the walls.

"There was so much blood they were able to paint all the pictures here with it. But, there was a reason why the killers didn't want to leave the bodies here."

"Killers? Plural?"

"Yes. I think so. Yasuo Tsuchida isn't the killer for sure. But legally he would also be accused. So yes, plural."

"Why isn't he an absolute suspect?"

"I'll explain that later. In any case, the killers didn't want to leave the bodies here. So, they dragged them downstairs."

"Why didn't they want to leave them here?"

"Because of that," he said and went over to the window opposite the door. "See those lights?"

The detectives followed the direction the boy was pointing.

"That house? What's that?"

"Yasuo's house. His mom lives there too."

"Ah, Tomitaro Tsuchida's former residence."

"Yes. His mom stood here, opened the window, and summoned her son after she'd killed Tsuchida and Amagi."

"What? By yelling?"

"Yup, the neighbors are too far away to hear."

"Why didn't she just call?"

"They don't have a phone," said Hashimoto.

"Oh, right."

"The two of them are very poor. So then, Yasuo came over to this window by climbing up the tower." Kiyoshi moved over to the window opening on to the tower.

"That's about ten feet away, you can't jump."

"Exactly, so he went to the storage room at the base of the tower. And he brought back several wooden boards that were over ten feet long, stood on the frame there, and handed one end of each of them to his mom. He then set them across between the window and the tower and walked into the room."

"Why did Haruko kill Tomitaro?"

"I don't know. You'll have to find that out. There was probably an argument that he wasn't giving them enough money. Anyway, they realized that leaving the bodies here wasn't a good idea. First of all, this is the only window in the entire house that looks out over their house, and this room also has the only window that faces the tower. If the bodies were left here, there was a chance that they would be accused immediately."

"True. We detectives would have quickly deduced that," Muraki asserted, modestly.

"And so they moved the paper and bodies to the first floor guest room."

"Yes."

"Can you really do that? You said the room next door was also filled with artwork from the elementary school division, right?"

"Right."

"So they combined the two sets of artwork, and laid them down in the guest room? How did they know they could do that? It would be a pain to deal with if they had some extra artwork. Or worse, if they had too little, it might reveal the fact that they were moved from the room upstairs," Hashimoto said. The boy shook his head.

"No, that wouldn't have happened. That's where the Pythagorean Theorem comes in."

"What's that?"

"You should have learned this in middle school. With any right-angled triangle, the area of the square whose side is the hypotenuse is equal to the sum of the areas of the squares of the other two sides."

"Huh?" Muraki said, so Hashimoto took out his notebook and drew a picture. He drew a right triangle, and three squares that bordered the edges of the triangle.

"Like this?"

"Yes," Kiyoshi said.

"The sum of the squares of the two smaller sides is equal to the square of the large one."

"Is that possible with a triangle of any size?"

"If it's a right triangle, definitely."

"This is very interesting," said Hashimoto.

"It's a very old theorem developed by the ancient Greeks. A mathematician named Pythagoras discovered this," Kiyoshi said.

"Amazing."

"This house is built using the Pythagorean concept. The sum of the areas of the two studios upstairs is equal to the area of the guest room downstairs."

"Oh! I get it!" Hashimoto exclaimed.

"Hmm, I see, that's how it was done," Muraki also affirmed, though it was unclear whether he fully understood.

"Yasuo knew that, because of the right-angled triangle, if the artworks fit into the two rooms upstairs, they would fit into the room downstairs. That was true. But there were only one hundred thirty-six pictures this year, by design, so they didn't fill the room. In fact there were four pictures short. I knew that, if Tsuchida had judged the pictures in the guest room, he would have used all the space and there would have been one hundred and forty as there were last year. That's why I knew the guest room wasn't where the pictures were judged this year, and so it couldn't have been the crime scene."

"Wow...you're truly amazing, kid," said Hashimoto, genuinely impressed.

"When I came here yesterday, you told me that forty-eight pictures had been covered in blood and eighty-eight had been covered in paint.

As soon as I saw the rooms upstairs I realized that they must have been killed in the smaller room – the workshop. Then, because they didn't want anyone to figure that out, they covered all the pictures that were in the larger studio with paint mixed to match the color of the blood."

The two detectives said absolutely nothing. Hashimoto was silent from admiration, Muraki from incomprehension.

"So I knew that there had to be some determining factor that made it necessary for the murderers to go through all this trouble. That's when I saw Yasuo's house through one of the windows and the steel tower through the other."

"After Haruko and Yasuo carried all the painted bodies and pictures downstairs, they carefully cleaned the entire house, wiping away every speck of blood, every fingerprint. They wore gloves so they wouldn't leave their fingerprints behind and washed all the rags and gloves in the kitchen. You saw the sink glowing."

"What about the keys?" asked Hashimoto.

"When they were cleaning up, they probably locked every door from the inside and drew the curtains so no one could see inside. Then no one would come in when they were cleaning up."

"Ah, I see. The mother must have washed the dishes and brushes then."

"Hey wait, how can you say she was responsible for all of this?" Muraki said.

"I think we've proved that already, sir," Hashimoto said. "First, Haruko Tsuchida's home and the tower could be seen from the window in the smaller studio, and secondly she knew, as his wife, the detailed dimensions of this house enabling her to carry out this plan. Do we need further evidence? Her case is much more credible than Keikichi's, to say the least. All that is left to do is gather more detail, do a quick search of the house for the knives, rags – "

"The umbrella," said Kiyoshi.

"Umbrella?"

"The black one you brought today. Yasuo and his mother shared that umbrella. The day it rained, Haruko used this umbrella to come here. Then after she killed the two and called her son over to do the cleaning, they forgot to take it. They went out the window down the tower anyway, and it was no longer raining. It was the one defect in the entire plan."

"Oh!" Hashimoto exclaimed. "So then you gave Yasuo the umbrella – "

"It was their only umbrella. The next time it rained, Yasuo constructed a huge hat with vellum paper, and used that to go home."

"Why?"

"They couldn't afford to buy another umbrella, since they're a fatherless family. Earlier today I asked him if the umbrella was his. He asked where I found it, and I told him it was near the path on Uguisuoka. He seemed a bit confused, but he took it. That's when I knew my theory was correct. He shouldn't have taken it. But I guess he took it from me because I was older than him, and he really needed another umbrella."

"I see..." Hashimoto began to feel pity.

"That's also when I realized he wasn't the killer. Yasuo was just an accomplice. If he were the killer, he would never, ever have taken the umbrella from me."

"So they are poor," Hashimoto said to himself.

"That's probably the reason behind this mystery too. You should investigate that."

"Hey, why didn't he just come back to the house to get the umbrella? He used planks to get to the second floor, right? Why didn't he just come back up to retrieve it?" Muraki seemed in a perpetual state of bewilderment.

"He had locked the window from the inside when he left, so he couldn't get back in."

"How did he do it?"

"He used this mop." Kiyoshi picked up the mop that had been found on the floor the day before.

"I'll show you. He held the mop upright with one hand while he lifted the lever on the half-moon lock on the inside window with the other. Then he slid the outside window to within inches of the closed position and quickly pulled his hand away from the mop and shut the outside window. When the mop fell, it struck the lever of the half-moon latch. You only need to give it a gentle tap for the window to be secured."

"Does that really work?"

"He kept picking up the mop until he succeeded. It probably took a dozen tries. Then he went back down the tower, returned the wooden boards to the storage shed, and went back across the river to his home."

"All right then, how was the guest room locked from the inside?"

"Oh, that's the easiest one! He climbed up the shelves of the tokonoma, and squeezed through the transom. He's a very skinny kid, remember, and his mom stood in the hallway and helped him down."

"I suppose young boys have plenty of practice climbing about."

"That's right. Can we go now? I'm going to be late," said Kiyoshi. "I don't want to get into trouble at home."

Permissions and Acknowledgments

All the stories are copyright in the name of the individual authors or their estates. Every effort has been made to trace the holders of copyright. In the event of any inadvertent transgression of copyright, the editors would like to hear from the author or their representatives. Contact us at pugmire1@ yahoo.com.

Foreword by Otto Penzler

"Jacob's Ladder" by Paul Halter. English language version originally published in *Ellery Queen's Mystery Magazine*, February 2014. Original title "L' Échelle de Jacob." Translated by John Pugmire. Reprinted by permission of the author.

"Cyanide in the Sun" by Christianna Brand. Originally published in *The Daily Sketch* in August 1958. Reprinted by permission of A.M. Heath Literary Agency.

"Windfall" by Ulf Durling. English language version originally published in *Ellery Queen's Mystery Magazine*, November 2016. Original title "Fallfrukt" 2014. Translated by Bertil Falk. Reprinted by permission of the author.

"The Case of the Horizontal Trajectory" by Joseph Škvorecký. From *The Mournful Demeanour of Lieutenant Boruvka* by Josef Škvorecký (Faber & Faber, 1988). Copyright © 1966 Josef Škvorecký. With permission of the author.

"The Twelve Figures of the World" by Jorge Luis Borges and Adolfo Bioy Casares. English language version originally published in 1981. Original title "Las doce figuras del mundo." Translation and permission to reprint by Donald Yates.

"The Martian Crown Jewels" by Poul Anderson. Copyright 1956 by Davis Publications. First published in *Ellery Queen's Mystery Magazine*, February 1958. Published by permission of The Trigonier Trust c/o The Lotts Agency, Ltd.

“Leaving No Evidence’ by Dudley Hoys. Originally published in *The Passing Show* 1938. Every effort has been made to trace the copyright holder, without success.

“The Venom of the Tarantula” by Saradindu Bandyopadhyay. English language version originally published in *Picture Imperfect*, Penguin Books India 1999. Originally published as “Makorshar Rosh” 1933. Translated by Sreejata Guha. Reprinted by permission of Penguin Books India and Prabir Chakravarti.

“Seven Brothers (extract)” by Aleksis Kivi. English language version originally published in 2005. Translation and permission to reprint by Richard Impola.

“Lying Dead and Turning Cold” by Afonso Carreiro. English language version original to this anthology. Translated by Henrique Valle. Originally published as “Jaz Morto e Arrefece” January 1952. Reprinted by permission of the author.

“The ‘Impossible’ Impossible Crime” by Edward D. Hoch. Originally published in *Ellery Queen’s Mystery Magazine*, April 1968. Reprinted by permission of Sterling & Byrne Literary Agency.

“The Locked Tomb Mystery” by Elizabeth Peters. © by Elizabeth Peters. Originally published in *Sisters in Crime*, 1989. Reprinted by permission of Dominick Abel Literary Agency.

“Deadfall” by Samuel W. Taylor. Originally published in *Adventure* March 1958. Every effort has been made to trace the copyright holder, without success.

“The Lure of the Green Door” by Rintarou Norizuki. English language version originally published in *Ellery Queen’s Mystery Magazine*, November 2014. Original title “Midori no Tobira wa Kiken”. Translated by Ho-Ling Wong. Reprinted by permission of the author.

“The Barese Mystery” by Pietro de Palma. Original to this anthology.

Printed by permission of the author.

"The Witch Doctor's Revenge" by Jochen Fueseler. Original to this anthology. Printed by permission of the author.

"All the Birds of the Air" by Charles B. Child. Originally published in *Collier's*, June 1950. Reprinted in *The Sleuth of Baghdad*, Crippen & Landru 2002. Reprinted by permission of David Higham Literary Agency.

"The Locked House of Pythagoras" by Soji Shimada . English language version originally published in *Ellery Queen's Mystery Magazine*, August 2013. Original title "P. no Misshitsu". Translated by Yuko Shimada. Reprinted by permission of the author.

Printed in Great Britain
by Amazon